TWIN SECRETS

BY
JULES BENNETT

First Published in Great Britain 2017
By Mills & Boon, an imprint of HarperCollins*Publishers*
1 London Bridge Street, London, SE1 9GF

ISBN: 978-0-263-92813-6

51-0317

Our policy is to use papers that are natural, renewable and recyclable products and made from wood grown in sustainable forests. The logging and manufacturing processes conform to the legal environmental regulations of the country of origin.

Printed and bound in Spain
by CPI, Barcelona

National bestselling author **Jules Bennett** has penned over forty contemporary romance novels. She lives in the Midwest with her high-school-sweetheart husband and their two kids. Jules can often be found on Twitter chatting with readers, and you can also connect with her via her website, www.julesbennett.com.

This goes to Stacy Boyd, who said she loves cowboys and baby stories…so I delivered an entire series of both! Thanks for the ideas!

One

How the hell could her father have gambled away all of his savings? As in, every last penny to his name. His reckless way of living finally caught up with him…with them. He'd lost major things before: his car, his retirement funds, all of her mother's jewelry—save for the one piece Annabelle had hidden away. But he'd gone too far this time.

As if Annabelle Carter didn't have enough on her plate. She'd come home to Stone River, Texas, to start over. She'd brought her sweet twins, six-month-old Emily and Lucy, and planned to offer them a new life and begin building her dream…a vision of her late mother's.

But, no. Now Annabelle was driving to the ranch next door to do damage control. As she turned onto the long drive, flanked by a pristine white fence, she pulled in a breath. The arched, metal sign over the entrance was a good indicator of the amount of money these people had. The stone columns suspending the sign were nothing short of remarkable. The beauty started from the street and she could only imagine what she was about to see at the end of this drive.

Pebblebrook Ranch was one place she'd never ventured into. It was owned by the hoity-toity Elliott family, and they didn't necessarily run in the same circles. The five–thousand-acre spread boasted several massive homes. Just one of their mansions was worth more than Annabelle's entire farm.

And that was when they'd actually had livestock. Her father, however, had gambled animals away, too. She'd been gone two years, living in Houston, and in that time he'd completely lost everything.

Rage ripped through her. What would he have done had she not come back home to nurse her own wounds? A fresh wave of anger surged through Annabelle as she remembered her sister and fiancé's betrayal. And the crippling effects of her sister's recent death. So much pain, Annabelle wasn't sure how to log it all inside her heart.

Now she had to deal with Colt Elliott on top of everything else. She'd never met the man, but she knew of the Elliott brothers. Sexy ladies' men, all much older than her. If she recalled correctly, Colt was a twin. Were the twins the youngest of the siblings?

None of that mattered. What mattered was that her father had borrowed money to pay off the farm loan before it could go into foreclosure, without informing her. Of all people to go to, her father had gone to Colt Elliott. Not that there were many people who could've helped, but Neil Carter could have come to Annabelle first. She didn't have that chunk of cash, but she would've gone through hell before borrowing from the Elliotts.

Now her father owed Colt instead of the bank. Perfect. Just perfect. The loan had been so close to being paid off, but her father just couldn't hang on any longer. He'd gone through all the money he'd put aside. Thankfully, Annabelle had set aside money for her sister's funeral expenses, or her father would've gone through that, as well.

According to her father, he and Colt had come to an agreement that he had to pay off the debt within three months. The bimonthly payments couldn't be a day late or a penny short or the farm would permanently belong to Colt.

Fine. Annabelle had no problem taking over her dad's end of the bargain. She refused to lose the only thing she had left. Her childhood home would not go to the family whose hobby was probably sitting around counting their wad of cash.

Annabelle's father claimed Colt was helping, but she didn't believe that for a second. People like the Elliotts didn't just do things out of the kindness of their hearts. In terms of wealth and influence, they were a giant leap above all other people in this town. With their mansions on the sprawling estate, the billions of dollars that passed through the farm from all their livestock…the rest of the businesses in the area didn't even compare. They were Stone River's answer to a cattle monopoly…if that was a thing. Random people didn't just go to Pebblebrook. It was like some sacred ground that mere peons didn't dare trespass on.

Well, too bad because she wanted to know what Colt's agenda truly was. She suspected he wanted her land for himself and she was going to have no part of that. She had her own dreams: marriage, siblings for her twins, opening her bed-and-breakfast. She'd already lost so much—she wasn't about to lose her home or her future.

Annabelle approached the sprawling three-story log and stone home. Sturdy wooden porches stretched across the first and second floors and two balconies extended from double glass doors off the third floor. Probably bedrooms. She imagined Colt on a balcony overlooking his massive estate, as if he were a king overlooking his kingdom. Annabelle swallowed. She couldn't even fathom the money these people had.

When a horse came from around the side of the two-story stable, Annabelle immediately forgot about the house. And it wasn't even the striking black stallion that had her attention.

Hellllo, Shirtless Stable Boy.

She may be nursing a shattered heart but she wasn't dead, and this hottie with excellent, tanned muscle tone was a perfect temporary distraction. How much work did it take to get ripped like that? Ranching certainly produced some fine—

Annabelle jerked as her car hit something and came to an abrupt stop. Gripping the wheel, eyes squeezed shut, she had no clue what had just happened, but she'd been distracted and obviously ran into…*oh, please don't be a person or an animal.*

Opening one eye at a time, she saw nothing but the barn and grassy fields…and the shattered post where the fence had been. Mercy, she'd been so caught up in the hunk on horseback, she'd run into the fence. Way to make an entrance.

As if she needed another problem in her life.

Mortified and shaken up, Annabelle shut off her car, thankful the babies weren't in the backseat. Her door jerked open, startling a squeal out of her.

"Are you all right, ma'am?"

That perfect Southern drawl combined with the bare chest she now stared at was enough to render her speechless. But even that couldn't override the reason she came. Just because she'd wrecked her sporty car, her only material possession worth any money, didn't mean she could deviate from her plan. What was one more setback at this point?

"I'm fine," she stated, trembling more from the sight of the sexy stranger than the actual accident.

Annabelle swung her legs out and came to stand, but the cowboy didn't back up. With one hand on her open car door and the other on the hood, he had her trapped. On any other day, she would've welcomed this stranger getting in her space and making her forget her cheating fiancé, but today there was no time for lustful thoughts. She shivered again as his eyes swept over her.

"Sorry about the fence," she stated, shoving her hair away from her face. "I'll pay to have it repaired."

With the savings that were supposed to go toward realizing my mother's dream.

"The sun was in my eyes," she went on. No way was she about to admit she'd been staring at his perfect…riding form.

"Don't worry about the fence."

Now he stepped back, but just enough for her to take in his well-worn cowboy boots, fitted jeans over a narrow waist…that glistening chest and his tipped cowboy hat. Black, of course.

"What brings you to Pebblebrook?" he asked, propping his hands on his hips.

Annabelle pulled in a breath. "I'm here to see Mr. Elliott. My name is Annabelle Carter and I live next door. Well, I used to a few years ago, but I'm back now."

Despite the chiseled jaw and the heavy-lidded gaze, the man's mouth tipped into a slight grin. "Well, ma'am, Mr. Elliott is busy right now. Is there something I can help you with? A glass of sweet tea? You look like you could use a break."

Sharing a sweet tea, or anything else with this hunky stranger, was tempting, but not on her agenda.

Annabelle blew out a breath. Mr. Elliott was busy. Of course. Probably at the bank purchasing more properties to add to his collection. A man like Colt didn't work outside in the heat tending to his own animals and land. That would be too far beneath him.

"You work here?" she asked, crossing her arms.

His mouth twitched again. “Yes, ma’am.”

“Then give your boss a message.” She may not be able to talk to the man himself, but she would leave her mark—and she didn’t mean the broken fence. “I’d like to talk to him about my ranch next door and the agreement he made with my father. Please tell Mr. Elliott, when he’s done getting his manicure or finished stealing puppies from children, he will be dealing with me from now on. I’ll be waiting at my house for his visit.”

Because she certainly wouldn’t be showing her face here again.

The stable hand simply tapped the brim of his black hat and tipped his head. “I’ll be sure to let him know.”

His eyes raked over her once more, sending shivers through her despite the Texas heat. “Are you sure you don’t want something to drink? Have a seat on the porch. You look like you could use a break.”

Oh, she could use a break. Like a monthlong vacation somewhere exotic with a fruity umbrella drink full of alcohol and unlimited refills. But she’d just settle for a break from all the pain life kept dishing out.

“No, I don’t have the time.” Not to mention, she couldn’t stay in his presence too much longer. It was difficult keeping her eyes off that broad chest sprinkled with dark hair and the tattoo on his right bicep.

“Is there anything else I should pass on?” he asked.

Since she was in a mood, she nodded. “I’m not a pushover like my father. Make sure you tell him he has twenty-four hours to contact me.”

The “or else” hung in the air, but she had no idea what her “or else” threat would be so she left it at that. She hoped she sounded badass, but it was kind of hard with her bright red car mounting the fence.

The cowboy stepped toward the front of her vehicle,

assessing the damage. She didn't even want to know how this would affect her insurance. *One crisis at a time.*

"Your little car has quite a bit of damage, ma'am."

With a flick of his fingertip, he adjusted his hat, bringing that cobalt blue gaze up to hers. The striking color of his eyes only added to his appeal. Did all the stable hands at this ranch have the qualifications to do calendars? Because she wouldn't mind buying one of those.

"I'm pretty sure this would fit in the bed of my truck," he muttered around a grin. "Should I haul it next door for you?"

Annabelle ignored his snarky jab. It was only because of his sex appeal that she let the question slide. Besides, she wasn't here to impress people or make friends.

"I can drive. Thank you."

She turned to get back into her car. As she started it up again, the cowboy closed her door, then leaned inside the window. "I'll be sure Mr. Elliott gets in touch with you today."

Annabelle nodded and shifted into gear. He stepped back, giving her one last glimpse of the fine body she didn't have time to fully appreciate.

Disappointed that she hadn't gotten face time with Colt Elliott, Annabelle headed back down the drive and prepared the speech she'd deliver when she did see him. She was done letting life—and men—rob her of her dreams.

He watched her tiny red car until it disappeared at the end of the drive. Annabelle Carter was one fired-up woman. The vibrant red hair and flashing green eyes had him more intrigued than he should be.

When he'd come around the side of the barn to put Lightning away after his morning ride, he'd caught a glimpse of the car just before it missed the turn in the drive and slammed into the fence.

"Colt?"

He turned to see Josh, one of his best stable hands, heading his way.

"Everything all right?" he asked. At nearly forty, Josh was probably Colt's hardest worker.

Colt nodded toward the fence. "This is top priority. Tell Ryan to assist you. I'll put Lightning in her stall."

Colt almost wished he hadn't fired a worker last week, but the guy had it coming and Colt didn't put up with lazy. He worked too damn hard. Just because his bank account had more zeroes than this town had ever seen, didn't mean he wasn't a hands-on type of guy—in business and in pleasure.

Josh nodded. "Is the lady okay?"

Speaking of hands-on...

Was she? Colt thought of the way she'd demanded to see "Mr. Elliott." He nearly lost it when she mentioned a manicure and puppy stealing. She truly didn't have a high opinion of him, but that was fine. He'd seen the sexual interest when he'd gotten close. She was pretty damn sexy herself.

But Colt hadn't been ready to tell her who he was until he knew what she wanted. Being mistaken for a worker was just one of the advantages of loving the ranch life. He may be the owner, well, he and his three brothers, but Colt was by far the most active. He took pride in what he had. There was no question of authority around here and his staff respected him. He wouldn't have it any other way.

Keeping in control of every situation is what led him to the success he had today. So, letting Annabelle believe he was just a ranch hand had definitely worked to his advantage. Now he had time to plot, to think of exactly how he wanted to play this situation out.

She said she was back in town, and he hadn't missed the way she'd looked at his chest. Maybe a little flirting, even a little seduction, would be in order.

Colt mounted Lightning and trotted back to the stable while Josh went to get supplies to fix the broken fence. Annabelle may be more financially savvy than her old man, but that wouldn't change the outcome.

The documents Neil Carter had signed without taking the time to read were completely legal and binding.

Colt had been wanting to get that land for years. The Carter's five-hundred-acre farm wasn't vast in comparison to his, but he and his brothers had shared a vision of owning it. Their main goal was to turn the property into an adjoining dude ranch. The Carter home was perfect for additional housing for guests.

Colt's father had always been a dreamer, not a doer. He'd discussed owning a dude ranch, having people come to stay on their property and learn the ways of their life, but he'd never gotten beyond the talking stage. Dementia had stolen Grant Elliott's mind, leaving Colt to carry on and bring his father's legacy to life.

From the time Colt was a young boy, he'd itched to see this property grow, to see people from all over flock in and see what they'd created. He refused to let anything stand in the way of his goal, even the sassy, beautiful Ms. Carter.

After putting the saddle and blanket away, he grabbed the brush to groom the dust from Lightning. While stroking the stallion, an epiphany struck him. Colt was a smarter businessman than Neil, clearly. Hell, Colt knew Neil had no idea what he'd agreed to when he'd accepted the money to pay off the loan—the man had been too desperate. But Colt would give Annabelle a chance to pay that debt. There were six installments left. Three months was all that stood between him and everything he'd ever wanted.

Suddenly being one stable hand short wasn't such a hardship. Perhaps Annabelle would be interested in a little work to help pay off the debt. She no doubt wanted to discuss the arrangement. She'd controlled her anger with him, thinking she'd just been talking to a stable hand, but there had been fury in those deep green eyes. Well, he'd use that fury to his advantage and make her an offer she couldn't refuse.

Colt patted the side of the stallion and finished brushing him as his brilliant plan took shape. He had no intention of ever handing that land over again. It finally belonged to him, but her father had to learn a lesson. He owed more than just this debt, but Annabelle didn't need to know that.

Having such a beautiful woman on his property sure would perk things up around here. She had drive and determination. He couldn't help but admire her spirit.

Colt whistled as he headed back toward the main house. His limp from the accident wasn't even bothering him today. Sometimes it ached, but right now, he had his mind on other things…like the sexy redhead he needed to properly introduce himself to.

He made his way to his third-floor master suite to get ready for a very important meeting. He owned the land, now he wanted to own the woman. And Colt Elliott always got what he wanted.

Two

Infuriating man.

Annabelle found herself on Colt Elliott's property for the second time today. She'd wanted to have the meeting in her house, where she could have some level of control. But when Colt's assistant or minion, or whatever, had called, he'd made it clear that Colt would meet with her, and only her, at precisely 7:00 p.m. at Pebblebrook. Otherwise, the meeting was off.

Damn infuriating man. She'd never met him and she already despised the air he breathed.

Whatever. She just wanted this to be over with. The sooner she could get Colt to agree to her terms, the better. Hopefully he'd see that this new arrangement would be beneficial to both of them. No matter what he threw at her, Annabelle wasn't leaving until she had something to cling to, some hope that she wasn't doomed to a life of failure when she was only twenty-four years old.

She was a mother to two beautiful twin girls now. Her father was doting all over them at the moment and would have to be her babysitter when she found a job. He was responsible with children, just not money. Besides, she couldn't afford to pay a sitter for one kid, let alone two.

First, she had to get this debt straightened out, and then she'd focus on getting that job. Surely, there was something in town she could do. At this point, she wasn't going to be picky.

Smoothing her hands down her green sundress, she pulled in a deep breath. Her nerves weren't about to abate, so she rang the bell and stepped back…waiting to enter the enemy's lair.

This place was so huge, it was almost intimidating. A wooden bridge arched slightly over a creek that ran in front of the house between the drive and the entrance.

The man literally sat in his castle, complete with moat, waiting on the town peons to enter his kingdom. Oh, how she wished someone would knock him down a peg or two. She had an unhealthy dose of anger stored up with Colt Elliott's name written all over it.

She wasn't even getting into the anger she had toward her father for putting her in this position to begin with. All he'd told her is that Colt had fronted the money and the loan was paid off. Now they owed Colt, not the bank. She made sure her father got that in writing from Colt and Neil had said he did sign a paper and it had been notarized. So, at least her father had been smart enough not to just do things the old-fashioned way with a handshake and a promise. Because Annabelle didn't trust Colt Elliott. Not one iota.

The double doors swung open and an elderly man stood before her. Annabelle thought the Elliott boys' father had passed some years ago, so she wasn't sure who this man was.

"Come in, Ms. Carter. Mr. Elliott is expecting you."

She stepped over the threshold and nearly gasped. If she'd thought the outside was spectacular, the inside was breathtaking.

The entryway allowed her to see all the way up to the

third story. An open walkway on both floors connected each side of the house, allowing anyone upstairs to see the entire foyer.

Annabelle was getting a vibe that Colt liked to look down on people, to belittle them. Well, he may have pushed her father around, but he was about to deal with a whole new game player. She wanted to know precisely why he'd extended his hand of generosity to her family. Nobody did something like this just to play nice.

"I'm Charlie." The older gentleman closed the door and tipped his head down in greeting. "If you'll follow me, I'll take you to Mr. Elliott."

Annabelle continued taking in all the beauty of this home, and tried not to let jealousy take over. The Elliotts existed on a whole other level than her family ever had, especially now that they had nothing. But Annabelle wasn't about to let life run her over. She'd had enough and Colt Elliott was about to get the brunt of her frustrations.

The calming trickle of water drew her attention as she passed by a sunken living area. Who the hell had a waterfall wall in their home? Oh, right. The people who counted their billions as a hobby.

Annabelle forced her frustrations aside and continued on behind Charlie. There was a bigger issue at hand. She wasn't going to spend her time assessing how this family lived so lavishly when everything had been robbed from hers. Everyone created their own destiny; unfortunately, she was the victim of her father's.

No more. Annabelle had a vision for her future and it certainly didn't involve giving up her childhood home. Once she got to the bottom of this ordeal, she could start on rebuilding her life. Because she wasn't just worried about herself anymore, there were two sweet babies to consider.

Charlie led her through a maze and she wondered if

she'd ever find her way out once this meeting was over. Finally, he stopped in front of an oversize arched doorway. He tapped his knuckles on the door before easing it open.

"Sir, Ms. Carter is here."

Nerves gathered heavily in her belly as she smoothed her sundress down one last time. She didn't care what her emotions were, and there were plenty, but she had to keep them hidden. Someone like Colt Elliott would home in on any weakness and use it to his advantage. Clearly, or she wouldn't be here trying to get her house back from the man who'd snatched it from her father during one of his worst moments.

Charlie eased the door open and stepped back with a nod before disappearing back down the labyrinth of hallways.

Shoulders back, ready to battle the enemy, Annabelle stepped into the spacious office complete with a wall of windows overlooking back acreage. The second she shifted her focus to the other end of the room, she stilled. Her heart clenched, breath caught in her throat.

"You," she gritted through her teeth. If it wasn't Shirtless Stable Boy himself.

Colt had been right. She was just as stunning as he remembered. He wondered if he'd still feel the same way once he'd had time to process the events of earlier. But now that Annabelle Carter was in his home, he took another moment to appreciate the entire package.

That vibrant red hair, wide green eyes, simple makeup and a green dress that she probably thought practical…he found it tempting. How long would it take to undo each of those tiny buttons down the front?

"You lied," she accused him, not moving any farther into the room.

Colt rose from behind the antique desk that had belonged to his father, and his father before him. He circled it and came to lean against the front. Crossing his ankles, he rested his hands on either side of his hips and shrugged. He always appreciated a good sparring opponent.

"I didn't lie," he amended. "I told you Mr. Elliott was busy when you asked. And I was. I had just finished exercising my stallion and needed to get him brushed and fed. I wasn't getting a manicure or stealing puppies. I save those fun events for Saturdays."

Her expressive green eyes narrowed as she slowly made her way across the room. Oh, she was going to be so fun. He didn't miss the way she took her time in assessing him, as well. Let her look. If all went as planned, she'd have plenty of opportunities to do more than caress him with her eyes.

"What is it you wanted to see me about?" he asked, ready to hear what she thought she could do to rectify this situation. He had a plan of his own to throw at her.

"I hardly recognize you with your shirt on."

So, Ms. Annabelle had claws. He liked that in a woman, preferably when she clawed at his back, but verbally would do…for now.

Colt couldn't hide his smile. She was definitely going to be more of a joy to deal with than Neil Carter.

"If you're requesting I take it off, I'm happy to oblige."

She crossed her arms over her chest, doing nothing to deter him from appreciating her lush shape. "The only thing you can oblige me with is discussing the terms of this contract you have with my father."

"Not my first choice during a meeting with a beautiful woman." Colt stood straight up, ready to get down to business. Obviously, they would have to get this out of the way first. "The arrangement is simple, as I'm sure he told you. He has six payments left on the property. I paid off his loan and now he owes me. I'm not charging interest like the bank, so the payments are actually cheaper than he was used to. He came to me for help, and—"

"How kind of you," she stated drily.

Colt shrugged with a smile. "I thought so."

Annabelle sucked in a deep breath and dropped her hands to her sides. Stepping forward, she came within a couple feet of Colt, enough for him to see the variation of green in her eyes. Definitely eyes a man could get lost in. Not him, but some other man. Colt only did physical relationships, nothing more.

"You'll be dealing with me from now on."

Oh, he sure as hell hoped so.

"I will take over the payments, but I need you to give me a few weeks to get on my feet. I have no job, since I came back to Stone River sooner than I'd expected," she went on, a flash of sadness flickering in her eyes. "Our savings are…well, that's none of your concern. But I already called a few places this afternoon and I'm sure I'll have a job shortly."

She couldn't be playing any better into his scheme. Before he could present her with his brilliant plan, she held up her hand.

"If you can give me two weeks off initially, I'll make sure you get interest as a sign of good faith." Annabelle's lips thinned. She was furious with her old man, as she should be. "I have plans for my home, so believe me, I don't want to drag this out any longer than necessary."

Colt admired her determination. Hell, he knew all about setting sights on a goal and going straight for it. Hadn't he lived his entire life by such ideals?

The dude ranch dream he shared with his father was just the final piece of his life he needed to click into place.

There had been setbacks along the way. Colt hadn't expected his father to slip into dementia and require around-the-clock care. Colt hadn't planned on breaking his back and shattering his hip bone while rebuilding the barn after a tornado ripped through town last year. His brothers had instantly reminded him there was no need to lift a hammer, they hired their work done.

But Colt loved manual labor. He loved this farm and he wasn't about to let anyone, even his sexy neighbor, stand in the way of him taking it to the next level.

"Here's the deal." He took one step forward, closing the gap between them. Head tilted up, her eyes locked on to his. "You will make the payment on time, as was agreed by your father. One late payment and the land will permanently be mine."

It would be in the end anyway, but if a payment was missed, at least Colt would have his property sooner.

Those green eyes narrowed. "I had no idea about this deal until last night when I returned home. I've been back less than twenty-four hours. I need some time to make job arrangements before the payment is due next week. Surely you're not that coldhearted."

Part of him felt sorry for her, but he was about to extend the proverbial olive branch...whether or not she chose to accept it was on her. Either way, he would be the real winner at the end of the day.

"Not at all." He offered a smile that he knew had brought women to their knees...literally. "I have a position for you right here at Pebblebrook."

Silence settled between them as he waited on her response. They both knew he held the upper hand, but she could make this entire encounter much easier on herself.

The muscles in her jaw clenched as she glared at him. Damn if her sass and grit weren't the sexiest things he'd seen in a long time.

Agreement or not, this woman would be in his bed. Visions of that crimson red hair spread all around his navy sheets flooded his mind. But seduction would have to wait, at least until she wasn't shooting daggers at him.

"I don't even want to know the position you think I'm qualified for."

Colt laughed, realizing he'd felt more alive being the target of her snarky attitude than he had in a long time. "I like you."

"Well, right now, I hate you."

He shrugged. "You're the yin to my yang. Sounds like we're going to get along perfectly in the stables."

"Stables?" she repeated, with a quirk of a brow.

"I'm short a stable hand and you need a job. You can start tomorrow and I'll use your wages toward the payments."

Annabelle pulled in a breath and shook her head. "I can't work long hours. I have another commitment and I need a job that offers some flexibility."

He leaned forward, pleased when her eyes flared. "The way I see it, you don't really have a choice. So, if this other obligation is going to get in the way, I suggest you give it up now."

For a split second Colt was convinced she was going to cry. He didn't like being played and he figured she'd try to get his sympathy by weeping. But when she blinked and glanced away, Colt realized she was simply trying to control herself.

Yeah, Annabelle was quite a strong woman to come here and face her father's problem. Colt despised the man for putting his child in such a position. Everyone had their breaking point and Colt figured she'd dealt with her father's addiction for far too long.

The strength she projected was quite the turn-on. Too bad all this business got in the way of him getting her into his bedroom. Soon, he vowed.

"Whatever this other commitment is, you're going to have to let it go."

She shoved her hair behind her shoulders and turned her attention back to him. "I can't. I will work here, but you have to understand there are times I will have to adjust my schedule. I can give you a few hours at a time."

Colt considered her ultimatum. He wasn't one to give in to demands, but he had to admit, he liked what he saw with his new neighbor. Someone with that much grit would be a fun way to break up his days. Besides, remaining somewhat on her good side would only aid in his seduction plan.

"Fine. I'll pick you up at seven tomorrow morning," he informed her.

Annabelle laughed. "I can drive myself."

"If you hit another section of my fence, I'll have to take the repairs out of your check and you're indebted to me already. The transportation is nonnegotiable."

When she let out an extremely unladylike growl, Colt forced himself not to crack a smile. Not even a little one. He may hang out with cowboys all day and make business deals all other waking hours, but he knew how to treat a woman. His father had instilled manners in him—somewhat—and Colt wasn't about to laugh in her face. But he couldn't resist the fence jab or the scheme to get a few minutes of alone time with her each day.

"Fine," she gritted out between her teeth. "I'll be ready."

When she turned to leave, he couldn't help but take in the fine sway of her skirt and imagine what lay beneath.

"Oh, one more thing." He waited until she stopped, throwing a glance over her shoulder. "Be sure to wear old clothes. We tend to get dirty."

Her eyes flared before narrowing. "Did I mention that I hate you right now?"

"It will pass," he informed her with a smile. "See you first thing in the morning."

Three

"You don't have to do this, honey."

Annabelle pulled in a deep breath and attempted to count backward from ten. She moved off the last step and met her father's worried gaze.

Neil Carter stood next to the front door, his hair messed from more than just sleeping. She hadn't expected her father to be waiting on her so early, but that's the type of man he was. Neil may be a professional gambler, losing pretty much all he'd worked for and all he'd provided, but he loved his family. He'd been the rock when her mother passed while Annabelle and her sister had been in grade school—well, until it all became too much and he turned to gambling. But he hurt, too, and Annabelle knew he was devastated after Trish's death only weeks ago. They both were. But for now, she could only deal with one crisis at a time.

The mourning would have to come later, at least for her...because she had to get over the betrayal first and she truly didn't even know if that was possible.

"I do have to do this, dad." Now was not the time to get into her arrangement with Colt, not when her ride was due any minute. "You left me no choice since we have no other way to pay."

Her father had lost his job at the factory one county over when he couldn't make it to work on time. He'd been embarrassed to tell her, but now that she was back, there was no way to hide anything. She needed to be aware of every ugly truth so she could make things right.

Her father raked a hand down his face and stared up at the ceiling. "I'm sorry, baby girl."

Wasn't he always sorry after the fact? This time, though, she had to put her life on hold and dig them both out of this hell. She didn't know what he would've done had she not come home.

"I can't do this right now, Dad. Between you and Colt, I'm pretty stuck. But we'll get through this."

"I'll talk to him," her father vowed, his gaze seeking her once more. "I can make this work, Belle. I can stop gambling. I'll get another job and help out. I know you and—"

"No." She held up a hand, not ready for him to take this conversation in another direction or make promises he couldn't keep. "We're going to be fine. I'll still do everything I'd planned to, it's just going to be on a different timeline."

As in, years away. The family life, the bed-and-breakfast…those plans would have to wait.

The doorbell rang and Annabelle jerked her attention to the old oak door. Her father turned, but Annabelle stepped forward to cut him off.

"I'll get it." Closing the space between them, she put her hand on her dad's shoulder. "Maybe you shouldn't be in here right now."

"But—"

"No. You and I will talk, but not now and you're not talking to Colt. You've done enough."

Her father cringed, but she refused to feel guilty. This was a mess—a mess he'd gotten them into. Perhaps he needed a dose of reality.

Finally, her father nodded and headed toward the steps. Annabelle waited until he was gone before she pulled in a breath and opened the front door.

Colt stood on her porch with his black hat in hand, as if he were there to ask her on a date. Damn that man. As if his Southern charm and manners would make her not loathe him on sight.

But he was a sight to behold. A black T-shirt stretched across his broad shoulders and those well-worn jeans fit in all the right places. She'd never seen a finer cowboy. If she were to pass Colt on the street, she'd never guess him to be a billionaire rancher who swooped in and stole properties while trying to charm the panties off unsuspecting women. There was no way he didn't have his own agenda with her family's land, and regarding this little matter of him giving her a ride. If that wasn't the worst use of a euphemism, she didn't know what was.

Colt raked his eyes over her and she forced herself not to fidget. Someone like Colt probably had eye candy for every night of the week, one on each arm. No doubt leggy blondes with big hair and big boobs, hanging on his every word. They probably wore booty shorts and cowgirl boots, too.

"I see you dressed for the day."

She'd found her oldest jeans and a simple tank. Any girl from Texas had a great pair of worn boots, so she'd thrown those on and pulled her hair into a ponytail. No makeup, no fuss. She was there to save her home, not get marks for her grooming.

Behind her, Annabelle heard the familiar sounds she'd grown to love over the past few months. Before she could turn or say a word, Colt's gaze widened and she knew exactly what he saw.

Not that she wanted him to have any part of her personal life, but she was pleased to render him speechless for a bit. Maybe Colt Elliott could be shaken and knocked down a peg.

"And who are these pretty girls?" he asked, still keeping his eyes over her shoulder.

Annabelle smiled. "Emily and Lucy. My twins."

Colt was rarely at a loss for words, but seeing Neil hold two mini versions of Annabelle was quite shocking. She hadn't mentioned having a baby—or babies. Now he understood why she needed a flexible work schedule...and he felt like a complete jerk.

Twins were definitely a handful. He should know, considering his mother always said that about him and his brother Beau. Colt wondered how Annabelle thought she could work and manage two infants back at home, but—

No. He wasn't going to get involved. Business and seduction were the only items on his agenda.

But could he still seduce her? Was she taken? There hadn't been a ring on her finger and she'd never said anything about having a husband...not that he'd asked her any such thing.

Annabelle turned, crossed the foyer and kissed each girl on the cheek. Instantly, one of the girls reached for Annabelle, but she shook her head.

"I'll be home soon. I love you both."

As she came back to him, one baby started to fuss, which somehow triggered the other one to start whimpering. Annabelle kept walking until she was out the door. With his hands full of unhappy infants, Neil held on to Colt's gaze, but Colt didn't feel a bit guilty. That man had done some major damage to his family...damage Colt hoped Annabelle never found out about. He'd lost their home and that was bad enough. But there was more and it was certainly not Colt's place to share.

He closed the door behind him, settled his hat back

on his head and turned to Annabelle. She swiped at her cheeks, as if he didn't notice the tear tracks.

Guilt punched him in the chest.

"Where's the truck?" she asked, obviously not wanting to address her emotions.

Fine. He wasn't one to get in touch with his emotions, either. Just another area he realized they may be more alike than he'd care to admit. They both clearly had a love for their family and were determined to get what they wanted.

But only one of them would be the winner in the end… and he never lost.

Colt stepped off the porch, making mental notes to expand its width and put in a stone walkway when the place was officially his. He needed to stay focused on the goal. While this house had good bones and was fine for everyday living, Colt wanted it to be up to the standards of his ranch. If they were going to merge the properties and open it to the public, all homes had to be similar in upgrades.

Colt nodded toward the side of the house. "I didn't bring my car."

Walking ahead of him, Annabelle rounded the house and stopped. "You've got to be kidding me?"

Colt shook his head. "She needed a walk, so we're taking him."

Annabelle stood next to Lightning and glared his way. "I'm not riding with you."

Glancing around, he held his arms out, palms up. "I don't see another horse. Do you have one?"

Her lips thinned. He knew damn well she had no animals. Her father had sold them all.

"I seriously hate you," she murmured.

Yeah, he got that. But Colt also saw how she looked at him. She may hate his actions, but she appreciated him as a man and he was more than fine with that. Keeping things physical would assure that everything stayed simple.

When he stepped forward to help her up, she shot him a stare that could've frozen hell over. He held up his hands to signal that he was backing off.

Hands on her hips, Annabelle stared at the horse as if weighing her options. She had none really.

"I'll just drive," she told him.

"That wasn't part of our deal. Get on the horse."

Her hand went to the reins. "Do you ever ask people nicely?"

"I can be very nice, Annabelle." He stepped closer. His hand covered hers as her eyes widened. "Get on the horse or I'll be forced to assist you like the gentleman my father raised."

She pulled her hand from beneath his and let out a mock laugh, hoisting herself up onto the horse. "I haven't met your brothers, but you are certainly no gentleman."

Colt slid his foot through the stirrup and settled in right behind Annabelle. Her backside was nestled between his thighs and he was starting to question his own motives. He'd wanted this alone time. He'd purposely made this stipulation so he could use these moments to seduce her. The concept of riding the horse developed after the deal had been made.

Colt had no idea he'd lose grip on his power. He never thought she'd be the one seducing him…and she didn't even have a clue.

The last woman he'd let have control over his emotions had left him mentally scarred and jaded. Colt pushed aside thoughts of his ex and reached around Annabelle to grab the reins. Her entire body tensed.

"Relax." He snapped the straps lightly, sending Lightning into motion. "We're just going next door."

Which would take several minutes because of the expansive fields between their properties, and he had every intention of taking the scenic route.

"Why are you heading toward the back of the property?" she asked.

Strands from her ponytail blew in the breeze, tickling the side of his neck. Images of that hair spread all over him assaulted his mind. The floral scent from her shampoo or soap assaulted his senses. She shouldn't smell like heaven, shouldn't have the ability to affect him without saying a word.

"You've only seen this land from your side," he explained. "I'm going to familiarize you with Pebblebrook."

"I thought I was just going to be in the barns cleaning horse sh—"

"Oh, you will," he laughed. She truly despised him, yet there was a fine line between lust and hate. He'd wear her down. "There will be times you'll accompany me in the fields and you need to know the area. With five thousand acres, it's easy to get turned around. But you'll be working directly with me every day."

Her shoulders slumped. The movement was slight, but being this close, he was attuned to every aspect of her.

"And what happens at the end?" Her voice was so low, almost defeated. "You're just going to give the property back and play hero for saving the day?"

"I'm not a hero." Her body rocked back and forth against his as he murmured into her ear. There was no way he was going to answer that question outright. "I do have motives, but we don't have to talk about that right now."

Annabelle jerked around. "I knew you weren't doing any of this out of the kindness of your black heart."

Facing the open fields once again, she asked, "So why this game with my father?"

"I'm not a complete bastard, Annabelle." Though some would say otherwise. "I'm giving your father a chance to redeem himself. I don't think he can, but everyone deserves a second chance."

"You weren't expecting me to come home."

"A minor glitch, but a pleasant surprise," he replied as he neared the fence line separating the two properties.

"This isn't a game, Colt." She glanced back over her shoulder, her deep green eyes piercing his. "You're playing with our lives, my dreams."

His father had dreams as well, and Colt was going to see them through no matter what sultry beauty stood in his way. Business first, seduction second—and nothing else mattered.

"I'm fully aware of the stakes," he informed her. "I have a vision, too."

"To toy with people's lives and count your money?"

He couldn't blame her for being angry. He'd feel the same if he were in her position. But he'd never let himself get into this predicament. His land was his life. From the time he was a toddler with his first set of boots and shiny belt buckle, he knew ranching was the only future he wanted. His brothers all set out in different paths, but Colt wanted to stay right here. And yes, money was a nice byproduct of the lifestyle he loved so much.

All the Elliott boys had grown up with a rather lavish lifestyle. They were all doing what they loved, but they'd also been handed a handsome inheritance when their grandfather passed away. Still, regardless of their last name, they worked hard and played hard.

"You aren't the only one with goals," he stated as he steered Lighting toward his brother's house, settled in the back of the property. "That log home back there is Nolan's."

She may not care about his family, but she was going to be working for him and he took his ranch very seriously. At the end of the day, regardless of the fact he wanted her physically, she would have to do the job he hired her for.

When she remained silent, he kept going. "He's the

oldest. He'll help occasionally, but he's a surgeon so his time is limited."

"He sounds nice."

Colt agreed, even though her comment was a jab at him. "I have another brother, Hayes. He's in the army."

"Wow. Two brothers who give back and help others, then you who steal. We haven't even discussed your movie star brother."

Colt swallowed. "My twin, Beau. He rarely comes home. Ranch life was never for him."

Beau and Colt never saw eye to eye on most things, but they had a special bond. Colt loved Beau, even though he wished he would've stuck around. Apparently fame was more important than family.

"Sounds like they made wiser life decisions."

Colt had developed thick skin over the years. He couldn't be in the ranching industry and not toughen up. But he wasn't about to sit there and have her question his integrity or his purpose.

"My grandfather built the first house on Pebblebrook, the one Hayes lives in when he's home. Then he passed this land down to my father who ended up building the house I live in. We all work hard, Annabelle. We do what we love, we make good money, and that's nothing to be sorry for."

Once again, those green eyes turned to him. "No, you have plenty of other things to be sorry for."

Perhaps he did. Maybe he was no better than her father who'd put her in this position. Colt didn't want to expose his reasons for paying the loan. The fact she knew he had a motive was enough for now. A wise businessman never showed his entire hand from the get-go.

Annabelle hated him, that was definitely no secret. But he wasn't backing down. Not on the land and certainly not on the woman.

Four

Annabelle absolutely loathed being on this horse with Colt. Well, her body enjoyed the ride, but that physical reaction didn't mean a thing. So what if his body fit perfectly against hers? So what if his voice tickled her ear and sent shivers through her? She could handle that. She had bigger issues to deal with than her body's unwanted reaction.

Colt seemed like such a normal guy in some ways. When he discussed his family there was such love, such adoration. The love and adoration she had for her own family had been shattered, broken, and she was left to pick up the shards and attempt to piece them back together.

The twins were the one bright spot in all of this chaos. They were precious, innocent, and Annabelle intended to keep them protected from the worries she faced. They would have a stable family life, maybe not the traditional family she longed for, but what was traditional these days?

Circling back to her more lustful thoughts, Annabelle couldn't ignore the tingle each time his body rocked against hers. That broad, strong chest would brush her back, his muscular forearms aligning with hers. His tanned skin to her pale. They were completely opposite in every way imaginable.

Colt Elliott was a gorgeous man, there was no denying that fact. He was also arrogant, frustrating, and the bane of her existence.

"I'm sorry to hear about your sister." Colt's words broke through her thoughts, and he actually sounded sincere. "I know you don't want to hear it from me, but losing a family member is hard."

Harder when there was betrayal involved.

She didn't want his pity or his kind words. She couldn't afford to accept that there may be a nice bone in his body. "I'm more concerned with my father and how he will handle the loss."

"That's why you came back?"

Annabelle swallowed. "One of the reasons. My fiancé and I had plans, but…"

She was so not getting into this with him. She didn't want to talk about how her entire life had blown up in her face over the past few months. The only bright spots were Emily and Lucy, and everything Annabelle did from here on out was for those sweet angels.

"I didn't realize you were engaged."

Pain pierced her heart, but not necessarily because she thought he'd been the one. Looking back now she realized she wasn't in love with him so much as the idea of being in love. She wanted to be a wife and mother, come back to Stone River and open her bed-and-breakfast.

She'd always wondered about fulfilling her mother's dream, but over the past year, she'd decided to just go for it. Yet now she was stuck in an arrangement with Colt, who, despite massive personality flaws, had more sex appeal than should be legal. Annabelle had to get her life back on track. She couldn't handle this lack of control and uncertainty.

"My fiancé is no longer in the picture."

Even with the bright morning sun beating down on

them, she shivered. The pain, the loss, the trust she'd once had in people she loved was all too much. This topic wasn't bearable.

"How many acres did you say you have?"

"Just over five thousand. There are three homes, mine, Nolan's, and Hayes's, for when he's stateside. We have seven ponds and eight barns."

Pebblebrook was like a city in itself. Annabelle would be lying if she didn't admit that she was jealous. Not that she wanted a large spread like this, she'd be so content with getting her bed-and-breakfast up and running. Still, she was envious that Colt had known exactly what he'd wanted, apparently from the time he was a kid, and had accomplished it all. Granted, the majority had been handed to him, but Colt had stepped up as part of the new generation to lead the ranch to the next level and beyond.

Anger bubbled within her. He had it all and he still wanted more. She wasn't about to go down without a fight. The bed-and-breakfast, her childhood home, was all she had to make something of her life and to secure a stable future for Emily and Lucy. So whatever he had in his head about her land, he could think again.

"Do you plan on taking me back and forth several times a day?" she asked, glancing back at him.

She hated looking over her shoulder because each time she did, she saw that sexy scruff along his jawline and those striking blue eyes. Not to mention the movement pressed her lower half deeper into the V of his thighs. It was like this man was created to drive her out of her ever-loving mind.

And she couldn't forget the fact she'd seen him sans shirt. Like that was an image she'd ever forget. Colt Elliott had embedded himself in her deepest fantasies…not that he would ever know.

"If I'm not around, I will have Ryan or Josh take you. They are my most trusted employees."

"It's a ride home, Colt."

His bright blue eyes zeroed in on hers, then dropped to her lips for the briefest of seconds. "They're both married."

"Just because they're married doesn't mean they're committed," she countered, hating the bitterness in her tone. "And I can take care of myself. I'm working for you, I'm not a little sister you need to watch over."

A corner of his mouth kicked up in a naughty grin that had her toes curling in her boots. "Considering my thoughts, it's best we aren't related in any way."

Annabelle jerked back around, her heart beating double time in her chest. "You aren't going to flirt with me, Colt. I'm here to make sure those payments are made on time and I get to keep my house. So whatever it is you're thinking, keep it to yourself."

"But you'd enjoy every one of my thoughts," he whispered in her ear.

The brush of his lips along her cheek sent tremors racing through her. How could she hate him and be so turned on at the same time? This man stood in the way of her only chance at a stable future.

No, her father had stood in the way, Colt was just an extra hurdle she had to jump. She really didn't want to be one of those bitter, scorned women, but every man in her life had let her down. Why the hell would she expect any different from her new employer?

Besides, he was just trying to throw her off her game. And, damn it, it was working. She had to be sharper from here on out…and he needed to keep his shirt on.

"Let's just stick to business," she suggested as they neared a massive two-story barn.

She forced herself not to gape at the large stone archway that led into the tunnel where the horses were kept.

The wide planked sides were weathered, but in that deliberate, expensive way. A smaller door up top no doubt led to the hayloft.

Annabelle couldn't help but wonder how many women Colt and his sexy, Southern charms had seduced up into that romantic space. She vowed not to be one of them. She wasn't naive. She knew he looked at her with interest, but she and her fiancé hadn't even consummated their relationship, and she sure as hell wasn't going to let Colt Elliott charm her into bed.

"These are the stables for our older horses. We have two mares and three stallions housed here. Ryan tends to oversee this group."

A man in a fitted plaid shirt stepped through the doorway, leading a gorgeous black stallion by the reins.

Colt steered Lightning toward the barn. As they neared, the forty-something man turned toward them.

"Ryan, this is Annabelle Carter," Colt said. "She's going to be working with me for the foreseeable future."

"Ma'am." Ryan nodded with the tip of his hat. "Pleasure to meet you. Colt, the engineer called earlier and needs you to call when you get a chance."

"I'll do it this afternoon," Colt replied.

Every time he spoke, the rumble in his chest vibrated against her back. There was something entirely too intimate about this situation. The way she fit so perfectly between his thighs, the way her body heated that had nothing to do with the sun, the way he looked at her mouth like he wanted to devour her.

And she knew without a doubt he'd methodically planned this mode of transportation and made it nonnegotiable just so he could annoy her further. Added to that, he must be well respected because his employee didn't bat an eye at the sight of the new recruit and the way she'd arrived on the scene.

"Also, Monte from the feed store called and our truckload will arrive around two this afternoon."

"We'll unload it in the barn on the west side. Make sure to tell Josh. We need all hands for that."

Ryan nodded once again and tugged on the reins of his horse. "Nice to meet you, ma'am."

He climbed onto the stallion and headed around the side of the barn.

"He seems nice. It's strange how the two of you get along."

"You're hurting my feelings, Belle."

She cringed. "Don't call me that."

"What do you prefer? Annabelle suits you, but it's a mouthful. Besides, I want my own name for you."

"Ms. Carter would work fine. Or, you don't have to refer to me at all."

That low chuckle sent even more tremors through her, causing her body to respond in ways she did not want where Colt was concerned.

"Oh, come on now, Belle. That's no way to start your first workday."

Fisting her hands on the horn of the smooth saddle, Annabelle forced herself to take calm, deep breaths. "I offered to get a different job, I'd prefer a different job, actually. I just needed some time to start getting a paycheck."

"I can give you time, but then you'd lose your land."

"Isn't that your ultimate goal anyway? To see my father and me fail? I'm not naive, Colt. I figure you want our property for something."

"I don't like to see anyone fail," he corrected as he led them toward the front of the property. "But if I'm going to be in a fight, I want it to be fair so my victory is that much sweeter."

A fight. She had to remember that's exactly what this was with him. She was fighting for her life, her future.

All she'd wanted was to take her meager savings and start minor renovations on her house to bring it up to par for her dream.

But then life had intervened. Her sister and fiancé were taken away, Annabelle found herself an instant mother to twin babies, and her father had ultimately failed her when she'd needed him most.

She wasn't going to fail him, though. He was hurting. He'd lost his daughter, was trapped in his own hell with his addiction, and Annabelle would fight to the death if necessary to keep her family safe. She would make a home for Emily and Lucy, take back her land, and see the B and B come to fruition. Anything less was not an option.

Colt Elliott may have knocked her down a peg, but she was determined to fling him off his podium.

Colt's shoulders burned, his arms strained as he hoisted the last bag of feed onto the pile he and Ryan had created. Josh had been taking loads and dispersing them to other barns.

And Annabelle had been holding her own. Sweat had her little tank clinging to her back. Damp tendrils of hair had escaped her ponytail and were now plastered against her neck. She'd gone home for lunch and had returned just before the shipment had arrived. He'd been busy and asked Ryan to take her and bring her back…using the truck.

But there was no way he was missing an opportunity to deliver her back home. They'd worked hard and he was utterly exhausted. He could only imagine how she felt as someone who wasn't used to this type of work every day.

He had a walk-in shower with three rain heads and jetted sprays waiting on him. Not to mention a bottle of bourbon he'd just acquired from a special selection that had been aging in a barrel for decades. He loved his contacts in Kentucky.

Guilt nipped at his conscience. When Annabelle went home, she had two babies to take care of and he highly doubted she took any downtime for herself.

Annabelle continued stacking boxes from the pallets into the corner of the barn. She didn't once stop to look his way, didn't say a word, and didn't complain. She was already a better employee than the stable hand he'd fired last week…only she wasn't a regular employee. She was there under duress, against everything she wanted.

Part of him wanted to tell her to go, to let her father handle the mess he'd made, but he knew she wouldn't go for that. She was too proud, too loyal to her family. She'd lost her sister and her father had completely let her down. And from her tone when she'd briefly mentioned her fiancé, he'd let her down, too. Colt had to assume the man was the twins' father, but he honestly had no clue…and it wasn't his right to ask.

The more tidbits into her life he discovered and pieced together, the more admiration he had for her. "That's the last of it," Ryan stated.

Colt pulled his hat off, swiped his forehead with his arm and turned to Ryan. "Go ahead and take off. I'll finish up here."

"Want me to give her a lift on my way out?" Ryan asked, nodding toward Annabelle on the other end of the barn.

"I'll take care of her, as well."

Ryan eyed Colt and he knew what was coming.

"Don't say it."

Ryan merely shrugged. "Someone needs to. You're playing with fire."

Oh, he sure as hell hoped so. Was there any other way to play a game of seduction?

"I know what I'm doing."

Ryan's brows lifted. "Do you? Because your father

may have had a vision, but he wouldn't have put someone through this just to gain the land."

Colt jerked his work gloves off and shoved them into his back pocket. "Which is why she'll be with me. I won't let her do more than she's capable of."

"Did you know her hand was bleeding?" Ryan asked.

Colt jerked his attention toward her once again. "What?"

"When I walked by earlier, she was wiping her hand on her pants and I saw blood. She'd torn her work gloves."

Damn stubborn woman wouldn't ask for help no matter what.

"I got her another pair," Ryan went on. "But I have a gut feeling she'd fall over before she came to one of us for help."

That she would. Colt raked a hand over the back of his neck and nodded. "I'll make sure that doesn't happen again."

"That land is going to be yours regardless," Ryan added in a low whisper. "Why don't you just let her go?"

Reasons he couldn't even explain. When she'd shown up yesterday morning and literally busted through his ranch, he hadn't been able to take his eyes off her. He'd always gone after what he wanted—livestock, business deals, employees…women.

Annabelle Carter was a total game changer.

Colt kept his eyes on Annabelle as she stacked her last box. Guilt slammed into him when she pulled off her glove and examined her hand.

Without glancing at Ryan, Colt said, "See you in the morning."

His trusted worker wisely walked away. Colt moved across the cobblestone walkway, closing the distance between him and Annabelle.

"Why didn't you tell me you were hurt?"

She spun around, clearly startled. "I'm fine."

With a hand to her chest, she tipped that defiant chin. Damn if he didn't want to kiss her. That fire in her eyes dared him to come closer, so Colt took a step forward until they were toe to toe. He'd never backed down from a challenge and Annabelle was one fight he was enjoying…except for her injury.

Colt gently curled his fingers around her wrist and pulled her hand out so he could examine it. She had a nasty blister that had been worked too hard.

"I have a first aid kit in the office."

When he met her eyes, he was surprised anger didn't look back at him. If anything, he saw desire. Interesting… and useful. Passion left people weak and he'd definitely home in on that.

Annabelle blinked, as if she realized she'd been caught staring at him. Pulling her hand back, she held it against her chest once again.

"I'll take care of it when I get home. I need to start dinner."

"The hell you say?" He hadn't meant to shout, but was she kidding? "You've worked all day."

Annabelle let out a humorless laugh. "Well, Colt, in the real world people work, make their own meals and tend to their families. We all can't live the life of luxury and sit back, living the dream."

Is that how she saw him? He'd worked his ass off taking over this ranch when his father had fallen ill. He'd poured more blood, sweat and tears into this land than any male in the Elliott family. Being the youngest, he always felt the need to prove himself, especially against his brothers. How the hell could he compete with a surgeon, a war hero and a Hollywood star? He was a damn rancher. A billionaire, but still a man who wore dusty boots, a worn hat that had been his father's, and holey jeans.

"You can take two minutes and let me clean that wound up."

When she stifled a yawn with her good hand, he muttered a curse and stomped off to get the first aid kit. Why did she have to be so stubborn and why did he have to find her even more attractive because of it?

By the time he came back, she'd taken a seat on one of the heavy wooden benches between the stone stalls. Her lids were lower and she seemed to have finally run out of steam. Perfect. Then she wouldn't be able to argue with him.

"You work harder than nearly any man I know," he told her, opening the kit.

"Does that mean I get a raise?" she asked, leaning her head against the wall behind her.

Colt laughed as he placed her hand in his palm. He swiped around the perimeter of the cut with an alcohol pad, careful not to get near the wound. He blew on her hand to dry the moisture. When she trembled, he glanced up to find her eyes on his. That shade of green never failed to kick him in the gut. She could pierce a man with that stare and have him wound in her web so fast, he'd have no idea he was caught until it was too late.

"I know you hate me, but you really shouldn't be fighting your father's battles."

A sad smile crossed her face. "Isn't that what family is all about? When one is weak, others stand up and take the lead. We're all we have left. My mother passed when Trish and I were younger. Now that Trish is gone..."

She shook her head and he wanted to know so much more. When he'd wanted a woman in the past, he'd never asked personal information. Backstory had no place in the bedroom. He had to remember that here because he could so easily let this niggle of guilt guide his emotions.

He had a goal. He had a vision he would see to the end,

to honor his father, to prove to his brothers he wasn't just playing cowboy and to prove to himself he could do it. The dude ranch was only one more business deal away… he just had to get past this fiery vixen to make that vision a reality.

Five

"What the hell, Colt?"

Nolan slammed the office door, jerking Colt's attention from his empty tumbler. He was going to need another round because he'd been waiting on his oldest brother to show up and let him know exactly what his thoughts were on Annabelle.

Gripping the glass, Colt met his brother's angry gaze. "All right, get it out of your system."

"Did you think to ask my opinion—"

"Not once."

Nolan crossed the room and flattened his palms on the glossy desk. "You have Neil Carter's daughter working here for what purpose?"

"He owes me money. She confronted me and said she was taking over the payments."

"So you put her to work like some pack mule?" Nolan shouted. "Do you think Dad would want this?"

Slowly, Colt came to his feet. He refused to sit there and let his brother talk down to him. "Dad left the control of this ranch to me because I understand his vision and I'm the one who's busted my ass my entire life to stay true to it."

"Don't throw that in my face," Nolan countered.

Colt shrugged. "Simply stating a fact. I don't tell you how to do surgeries."

The muscles in Nolan's jaw ticked. Colt wasn't trying to be a jerk, but he wasn't going to be reprimanded or have his decisions second-guessed. He'd done enough doubting of his own actions…something he never did with business.

"You want this dude ranch so damn bad, but you're going about this the wrong way."

Colt grabbed his glass and headed to the bar in the corner. His hip irritated him a bit more today, but that was expected on days he worked harder. It was just one more area where he refused to give in and let life get him down.

"We need that property and Neil was about to lose it to the bank. If I hadn't stepped in, someone else would've. Besides, it's all over now and perfectly legal."

Nolan turned, crossed his arms over his chest and nodded. "I agree that someone else would've gone after that land. It's your actions afterward that I don't understand."

Colt had gone over this in his own head, as well. "At first I wanted Neil to learn a lesson and actually work for something. Then when Annabelle showed up, hell… I couldn't resist."

He didn't look up at his brother, didn't want to see disappointment staring back. Colt had his reasons for his actions and he wasn't going to be deterred by anyone…not even his oldest brother.

"I don't want to see you hurt again," Nolan stated as he crossed the room to stand before the bar. He rested his palms on the etched edge. "Dad would be proud of how smooth this place is running and the growth since he's been in the assisted living facility. You don't have to prove anything at this point."

Colt grunted as he poured two fingers of amber liquid. "I started this for him, but now it's also for me. I want that dude ranch. I want people from all over the world to know Pebblebrook is the greatest ranch, the best getaway money can buy. I want to share all of this work our family has done and if I happen to have a little fun along the way, then so be it."

Colt held out a glass and Nolan shook his head. "I'm on call." He took a seat on the bar stool, lacing his hands together. "This is the first girl you've mentioned at all since Layla."

Colt took a hearty sip. "I'm not looking to settle down. And Layla has nothing to do with now. There's only one thing I'm focused on and that's making the dude ranch happen. Annabelle is working here to pay off the debt. If she misses one payment or can't come up with the entire sum at the end of the time frame, then it's completely mine. But it's mine in the end anyway. They just have to pay off their original debt. Neil paid no attention to the paperwork he signed."

Nolan stared for a minute before shaking his head. "You can handle this how you want, but I'm telling you it's a moral mistake."

With a shrug, Colt finished his glass and recapped the bottle. "I've made mistakes before. And, if Annabelle is a mistake, then she'll be the sexiest one I've ever made."

Layla had been his one and only serious relationship. He should've known it was too good to be true when she'd wanted to marry so soon after they'd started dating. Colt had thought she was interested in him and shared a passion for the farm. She'd shared a passion all right…for his bank account. She didn't care about the land, the animals, his vision. She cared about how she could keep up with the latest trends in clothes, vacations, cars. Colt had been completely blind and eager to give her anything she wanted.

When he'd had an accident and been laid up with broken bones post-surgery, he found out all too quickly just how little she cared about him. She'd told him she needed a break from their lifestyle and then jetted off to his vacation home in Aruba...with another guy. If Colt's cleaning service hadn't told him, the joke would still be on him.

While recovering from surgery, Colt broke off the relationship, kicked Layla and her stud out of his house and sold the place, deciding he didn't like the beach anyway. He needed nothing but his home in Texas. He loved to travel, but what did he need a second home for? His jet and his pilot would take him anywhere he wanted to go.

He was finished with romantic entanglements and refused to get sidetracked by such emotions as love. Hell, he hadn't even been in love with Layla. He'd wanted a family one day and he figured he and Layla were the best match. He still carried that goal of having a wife and children. There was nothing he wanted more than to raise another generation of Elliotts and keep the ranching tradition going. Family and loyalty were everything to him.

He'd let his libido guide him once before, but now he knew exactly what he was feeling. Everything inside him that flared to life around Annabelle was pure lust. He wanted her, he'd have her. End of story.

"Is this necessary?" Annabelle asked.

Colt held tight to the reins, his body aligning perfectly with hers. She hadn't just dreamed of his strength. When she'd woken in the middle of the night after a vivid, detailed dream regarding her new employer, she'd thought her imagination had just gotten the best of her.

But now she knew better. She'd tried to avoid his touch yesterday, but being on horseback with him made that impossible. Maybe it was time Annabelle renegotiated this whole pickup routine.

"It's a perfect day for a ride," he replied.

His low, soft tone was in direct contrast to the chaos

she felt inside. She wanted to continue hating him, and she would, but why did she have to be attracted to him at the same time? It truly made for some mixed up hormones and she couldn't keep eating her weight in doughnuts like she wanted to. Her favorite jeans were already snug as it was.

"I'd be fine to drive myself," she retorted, keeping her eyes on the bright horizon, as opposed to focusing on the proximity of his hands to her inner thighs. "Or Josh or Ryan can take over delivery duties."

"I'm a hands-on employer," he murmured against her ear. "You'll get used to it."

That was the problem. This was day two in her duties and she could honestly say she didn't hate this part. She wanted to hate it. She wanted to stomp her foot like a toddler and declare her independence by not getting on that horse with him.

But she was still a woman. Despite her jaded view on men and their loyalties, and ignoring the fact Colt had her in a tough position, she was a woman with basic desires. And her body felt exactly the way it should when a sexy man entered the scene: tingly, hot, achy.

"You're thinking awfully hard about something," he stated. "You tensed up on me."

"Just counting down the days until we're free of each other and I can go about my life with my house."

"You've still got quite a while. I wouldn't be making those plans just yet."

Annabelle shrugged. "I'm optimistic. I know I won't miss a payment and I have every reason to keep going, even if I want to give up."

She felt her hair shift aside seconds before his fingertips trailed across the back of her neck. Annabelle jerked to glance over her shoulder.

"What are you doing?"

His mouth was only inches from hers and completely

tempting, so she focused back on the fence line dividing the properties. It had to be a sign, a symbol of exactly how different they were and how she needed to compartmentalize their arrangement.

"Your hair tickled my face. Why didn't you put it in a ponytail?"

She held up her wrist. "I have my band here. I didn't get time before you arrived because Emily was sick last night and I was trying to get her sheets washed and put back on the crib so Dad could lay her down for a nap later."

Why had she told him all of that? He had no place in her personal life.

"You could've texted me to give you an extra five minutes."

"That would've made me late. You're not going to win that easily, Colt. Just forget I said anything," she quickly added. "I'm not looking for sympathy or special treatment. After this debt is paid, I'm going to pursue my dream."

"Care to share what that dream is?"

Annabelle bit the inside of her cheek and thought for a half second, but shook her head. "Nope. You've stolen enough from me. I won't give you my hopes, too."

"It's not your secrets I'm after, Anna."

Every part of her stilled. He wanted her, that was obvious. He wasn't even trying to pretend otherwise. But she wasn't about to comment on that.

"Don't call me Anna."

His soft chuckle had his entire body vibrating against hers. "I'm willing to call you anything, but you don't like any name I've chosen."

"Like I said before, maybe it would be best if you didn't address me at all, except for work purposes, and then you can call me Ms. Carter."

Colt pulled back on the reins, bringing Lightning to a stop at the edge of the property line. "And what about now, when we're alone and not working. What should I call you?"

Slowly, Annabelle turned her head slightly, knowing full well he'd eased forward and his face would be right there. And it was. Those lips mocked her, the edge of his hat bumped the top of her head, bright eyes stared back, daring her to answer the question.

"Maybe we shouldn't talk."

The instant his eyes flared, darting to her lips, she realized he took her comment as a challenge. He eased forward, his eyes locked on hers the entire time. Her mind told her to stop, but his eyes mocked her as if he knew she would. So she didn't.

His lips grazed hers and everything in her stilled. The slow caress of that mouth had her closing her eyes and forgetting who they were. For once, she was going to just take this moment of pleasure and ignore all the warning bells inside her head.

Colt eased her mouth open beneath his and Annabelle responded as if it were the most natural thing in the world. She wanted Colt's mouth on hers, she wanted him to…

No. This wasn't right. Annabelle pulled away, instantly feeling a chill from the loss of his touch.

"You can't possibly believe you're going to get anywhere with me," she stated, needing to get control back in her grasp. That kiss had only temporarily caught her off guard. Still, his body rubbed against hers, making her want things she'd never had.

"I tend to get what I want," he whispered. "And from the way you responded, I'd say we want the same thing."

She was out of her league with this one. He was charming, smart and devious. But she was determined not to succumb to his attempt at seduction. And that was exactly what he was doing, no doubt so she would lose focus and hand over her property. Not in this lifetime.

"Then I'd look elsewhere because this will never be yours."

"And you?" he asked, quirking a brow and smiling.

Anna reached around and palmed the side of his face. His jaw muscle ticked beneath her hand as she looked into his eyes.

"You won't get that lucky," she said sweetly, then patted his face before letting go. "Now get me to work."

When he didn't reach for the reins again, she lifted them, lightly tapping Lightning into motion again. Which she instantly discovered to be a mistake.

Colt's hands flattened against the tops of her denim-clad thighs. She refused to tense, refused to even comment on his actions. They'd already crossed a professional boundary, but it wasn't like this was a typical boss-employee relationship. Nothing here was normal. She had no idea how to react, what to say. All she knew was that Colt challenged her minute by minute and she had to stay on her toes and never let her guard down again.

She could still taste him, though, knew exactly how he felt, how gentle he'd been. She'd expected someone like Colt to go in full attack mode when trying to seduce a woman. It was like he knew her situation and catered specifically to her needs...her desires.

Surprisingly, he let her guide them straight to the barn. Annabelle figured his cockiness, as shown by him keeping his hands on her, overrode the need to be in control for now. But she wasn't under the illusion that he was relinquishing his power.

"What's on the agenda today?" she asked as she stopped in front of the barn.

Barn was such a generic, ridiculous term for such a structure. The interior of the barn alone rendered her speechless, she couldn't imagine what the other barns and homes on the property looked like inside.

He slid his hands over hers on the reins. "You and I will be going out and checking the fence lines around the property. I tend to have Josh and Ryan do that, but I'm giving your hands a break after yesterday."

The warmth from his touch, the way he literally enveloped her would be so easy to get caught up in if this were any other type of situation. But he was the main obstacle standing between her and her bed-and-breakfast, and the life she wanted for Emily and Lucy.

Annabelle worried Colt had something up his sleeve… something she wouldn't see coming until it was too late.

"I don't want special treatment. My hand is just fine." Sore, but she'd put some antibiotic ointment and a bandage on it. "Treat me like you would any other stable hand."

Colt grunted. "That's not going to happen."

He eased off the horse, then extended a hand to assist her. "I can get down myself."

As she slid off the side, firm hands gripped her waist. "A gentleman always helps a lady."

Annabelle turned in his arms and placed her hands on his chest. A very firm, solid, muscular chest. She pulled in a deep breath and forced herself to focus.

"If you're trying to seduce me, it won't work." But it could if she didn't keep giving herself mental pep talks. He had to keep those lips to himself, though. "And if you're trying to make this process more difficult, then don't waste your time. I'm not backing down and I'm not quitting. So, tell me where I'm working today and knock off the shenanigans."

He pursed his lips and she knew from that naughty twinkle in his bright eyes that he was holding back a laugh. With a tip of his hat, he took a step back.

"Then that goes both ways."

Shocked, Annabelle held a hand to her chest. "Excuse me?"

"No seducing me. I know, it will be tough to control yourself around me, but try. I'm not just here for my looks."

When he let go and offered a full smile, she smacked his shoulder. "Get out of my way, you arrogant jerk. I will not seduce you. I'm sure a number of women find you charming, but I am certainly not one of them."

Annabelle started to move, but he snaked an arm around her waist. Bringing his lips next to her cheek, he whispered, "You will be."

Before she could reply, he turned and headed into the barn. As if she weren't irritated enough, the man had the gall to start whistling. Annabelle gritted her teeth and fisted her hands at her sides.

Colt Elliott was not going to get under her skin. She would not find that arrogance attractive, nor would she allow herself to feel any more attraction to the sexy cowboy. She'd been burned too many times and if she didn't keep her guard up, she'd find herself hurt more than ever before.

Maybe it was time to give Colt a little dose of his own medicine.

Six

"I think Genesis will be the perfect mare for you to use while you're here."

Annabelle slid her hand down her new friend's velvety nose. Josh had pulled this mare from her stall when Annabelle came in to find Colt and give him a piece of her mind. But he was nowhere to be found. Probably off in some corner plotting on new ways to drive her out of her mind—and off her land—with that killer body of his. If he strutted in there with no shirt, she wasn't so sure she'd be able to resist.

Mercy, when had she gotten so pathetic and weak? An impressive collection of muscles only went so far…and she had too much in her life to get distracted.

"She's beautiful." Annabelle looked into the mare's deep brown eyes. "I miss riding."

When she'd been younger, she and her sister both had horses. Their father would take them riding nearly every day, especially during the time when their mother was ill. But then her mom had passed and soon her dad's gambling began, the debts piled up and the horses were sold. Their lives had crumbled so quickly, there wasn't even time to adjust.

She wanted to hate her father, she truly did. She hated the decisions he'd made, she hated his addiction, but she loved him and she wasn't about to give up.

"I believe you and Colt will be riding the perimeter today," Josh went on. "Looks like your face got a little pink from working outside yesterday."

Instinctively, Annabelle tapped a fingertip to her cheek. "Yeah, a little. I thought I had used enough sunscreen."

"I can get you a hat," Josh told her as he looped the reins around the horn. "We have plenty in the office."

"I've got one right here."

Annabelle turned at the sound of Colt's voice. He came sauntering up the stone walkway, hat in hand. That flutter in her chest had her cursing. How could she be strong when he made her want so much? She'd never been this drawn to a man physically. Even her fiancé hadn't given her that nervous flutter in her stomach.

Why did it have to be the one man she wanted to hate? And why did he have to do little things to make it seem as if he actually had redeeming qualities?

"Ryan is in the steer barn," Colt said to Josh. "There's a calf that isn't looking good. I called the vet, but I'd like if both of you were there. Take the radio with you and keep me informed."

"Sure thing." Josh glanced at Annabelle and nodded. "See you later."

She waited until they were alone before she turned her attention back to Colt. "Do you ever ask anyone politely or do you just enjoy ordering people around?"

"I have a busy schedule and those guys don't need coddling." Colt slapped the hat on her head. "If you have a problem with how I run my ranch, you're free to go at any time."

Annabelle adjusted the hat, narrowing her eyes. "You know I can't."

"Then stop trying to school me on manners. My guys and I get along just fine and run this place quite successfully."

Annabelle's phone vibrated inside her pocket. She pulled it out, glanced at the screen, then looked at Colt. "I have to take this."

She didn't wait for his reply as she swiped her finger over the screen. "Dad, this isn't a great time. Can I call you back in a bit?"

"I think Emily has a fever."

Annabelle pinched the bridge of her nose and willed herself to remain calm. She had no experience with sick babies. She was still getting used to being a guardian, but she would always put them first. Before the farm and before her father's addiction. She adored those babies, hated when she was away from them. They were a balm on her battered heart.

Annabelle could tell by the concern in her father's tone that she had to keep a level head, even if worry flooded her. Between the two of them, they were still figuring out their new normal.

"When I fed her around four this morning she was fine. Did you take her temperature?"

Boots shifted over stone behind her and Annabelle tried to block out the fact that Colt was no doubt clinging to her every word. Again, she didn't want him involved in her personal business any further.

Cooing in the background brought her back to reality. If Emily was getting sick, Annabelle didn't want the girls close together. The last thing anyone needed was two sick infants.

"I can't find a thermometer."

"Go into my room and look in the top nightstand drawer. I have one in there as well as some infant pain reliever. Take her temperature and call me right back."

She disconnected the call and turned back around. Colt's eyes studied her, as if he were waiting on her to open up about the call and her life. Not likely.

Colt took a step forward. "Do you need to go back home?"

"I'm fine." A little worried, but she'd never let him see it and this was none of his concern.

"Take Genesis and go check on Emily."

Before she could answer, her phone vibrated in her hand. "Dad," she quickly answered. "What was it?"

"It's 99.9."

Okay, not terrible. "Give her a dose of that medicine. Just measure it in the dropper. The dosage is on the back for her weight. Is she acting okay? How's Lucy?"

"Lucy is perfectly fine. Emily seems more tired than usual, but she's not cranky."

"That's good," Annabelle muttered. "Just keep me posted. Even if it's to say she's still fine, I want you to text me updates until I get back for lunch."

"All right. And, Belle," he added softly. "I'm sorry. For all of this."

Tears pricked her eyes. He was always sorry, and she truly believed for the moment that he was. Only time would tell if losing everything could really change a man. So far, since she'd been home, she hadn't seen any signs of his habits returning, but that didn't mean anything. He'd always managed to sneak some game, race or sporting event. He'd gamble on the color of the sky if that was an option. Neil Carter never turned down a bet.

"I'll be home in a few hours."

As she slid her phone in her pocket, Colt continued to study her. "Nolan is home this morning. Do you want me to send him over?"

"The doctor?" Annabelle asked. Part of her was touched that he offered, but she didn't want anything from Colt or his family…other than her house back. But, if Emily got worse, she wouldn't turn down at-home care…especially since she couldn't afford a doctor. "Emily will be fine."

Colt stared another minute before reaching up onto Genesis and pulling the reins down. "Then you have work to do."

Annabelle led the mare from the barn before mounting her. Why was Colt being so nice? The hat so her face wouldn't burn, the simple day so her hand wouldn't hurt, the offer to send his brother over to check on Emily…all of that showed there was a kindhearted man inside. But he still made no apologies for planning to take over her land or trying to seduce her.

When Colt came up beside her, she kept her eyes on the horizon. He'd opted to take Phantom out today instead of Lightning. All of his horses were gorgeous animals. Annabelle couldn't pick a favorite. They were all so well mannered, so loving.

Pebblebrook was a beautiful spread, there was no denying that. Colt was obviously passionate about ranching. She was curious about his limp, there had to be a story there, but he'd never mentioned it or acted like it hindered his work. And she couldn't help but wonder why he was still single. Not that she cared, but he was rather blatant with his advances toward her. Which reminded her, she could play that game, too.

"Lead the way, Boss."

He threw her a glance before getting Phantom into gear. Annabelle followed to the side, staying back just enough to appreciate the view—the land and the cowboy.

As he headed toward the fence that ran as far as the eye could see, Annabelle started thinking, remembering. There was a time she'd wondered what the other side of this fence held. She'd wondered about the family who lived here, the house they must love and the number of people who must work here to keep such a place running.

Her family's farm had been minute compared to this one, but she'd loved her animals, her childhood. She couldn't complain about the first ten years of her life.

"You're quiet back there, Belle." Colt cast a glance her way. "Plotting revenge?"

She tapped her heel into Genesis's side to come up even with Colt. "Don't call me that."

"Still waiting on you to give me something you'll answer to that doesn't sound like you're my grade school teacher."

"You'll be waiting awhile," she replied. "And I wasn't plotting revenge, not yet, anyway. I was just thinking about my own farm from when I was little."

"I didn't know you or your sister," Colt stated as he kept Phantom at a steady pace. "Our fathers knew each other, though."

"Really?" Annabelle asked. She shifted her hat to block the morning sun. "I wasn't aware of that. I don't recall Dad ever mentioning yours."

"No. He probably wouldn't have."

Confused, Annabelle slowed her horse, reached out to touch Colt's arm. "What's that supposed to mean?"

He brought Phantom to a stop and shook his head. "Exactly what I said. You were young, so I doubt your father would mention mine. That's all."

Annabelle had a gut feeling he was hiding something. Dread spread through her. Surely their fathers hadn't gambled together. People as successful as the Elliotts didn't get a ranch like this from betting their earnings away. Did her dad owe them, too?

She had to know. "Does my dad owe you all money? Aside from the house?" She glanced down to her tight grip on the reins.

Silence settled between them and Annabelle glanced at Colt from beneath the brim of her hat. He stared out into the pasture, his jaw muscles clenching.

"How much?" she whispered.

"There's no debt other than the house."

But he wouldn't look her in the eyes, so there was something. An old debt, at least a story, and he didn't want to tell her. Was he protecting her?

Damn it. She'd only been with him two days and already he showed her more good sides than bad. But the bad outweighed the good. Didn't it?

"I want to pay you for everything he owes," she went on, needing him to understand. "I'm sure you're not the only person he's indebted to—"

"There's nothing. Let it go."

His stern tone, so final and angry, had her stopping short. Something had happened, but if she wanted to know, she'd have to go to her father and confront him. She almost didn't want to find out the truth.

They rode for another hour, randomly stopping to check the fence. Colt would type notes into his phone and Annabelle tried not to think about how he seemed like such a genuine guy. He worked hard, he obviously didn't want to upset her earlier about her father, but he wasn't sincere. He was a business shark.

As if she could forget.

They approached one of the ponds and Annabelle spotted movement amidst the cattails. She steered Genesis away from Colt and made her way over. She squinted, trying to home in on where she saw something.

"What's up?" Colt trotted beside her. "Wait, I see it."

Annabelle pulled back on her reins, but before she could hop down, Colt was off his horse and carefully moving toward the edge of the pond. He limped slightly, favoring his left side, but she wasn't about to question him.

Colt squatted down, extending his hand and muttering something Annabelle couldn't decipher. She waited, then sucked in a breath when he came to his feet. The sight of Colt cradling the cutest, chocolate-colored puppy had Annabelle climbing off her horse.

"Is this your puppy?" she asked as she approached.

He stroked the top of the puppy's head. "I've never seen this little guy before. But it's not unusual for us to have strays on the farm. People drop them off at the end of our drive all the time. Pisses me off."

"Do you think there are others?" she asked.

Colt shook his head, still staring down to the pup. "I have no idea. I would assume they'd all be together, but we'll ride around this area and see. They could be anywhere. Damn it. I hate when people treat animals like this."

Oh, no. He could not be an animal lover, too. Her emotions were still raw, still so exposed that she couldn't afford to let any more of his kindness seep in.

"Will you keep him?"

Colt met her gaze. "Do you want him?"

She hadn't thought about having a dog, but she'd always had one growing up. Honestly, over the past several years, she'd missed animals. When she'd lived in an apartment in the city, she hadn't been able to have them. She'd worked in a bakery and was gone all hours.

As she stared at the poor pup shaking, her heart went out to him. She totally could relate to being scared of what would happen next.

"I'll take him if you don't want him."

Colt nodded. "Fair enough. If you think you can handle a puppy and babies. Otherwise, I'll keep him."

Annabelle had a feeling the puppy would be the easiest aspect of her life. And having an animal that could grow up with Emily and Lucy would be precious. Plus, it was another way for Annabelle to establish roots in her home—well, it would be her home once it was paid off.

She eyed him, purposely zeroing in on his mouth. "I can handle anything."

When his nostrils flared, Annabelle reached forward in an attempt to get the pup, but Colt twisted his body away. His gaze remained on hers as he cocked his head to the side to avoid bumping their hats.

"You know exactly what happens when you play with fire," he growled.

A tingling swept through her, but she shrugged. "I've been burned before, Colt. I'm immune."

He stepped closer, easing the puppy into her arms and deliberately brushing his forearms along her chest. "You've never dealt with someone like me. You may like it."

Oh, she had no doubt. If that kiss yesterday was any indicator, she knew full well just how much she'd like it. But then she'd have to live with the consequences and she wasn't ready for anything like that. She was a forever kind of girl. If he only knew what she'd gone through with her ex and just how inexperienced she truly was…

"I'm sure I'd disappoint," she stated simply. Not because she doubted herself, but she knew, given their age difference, that he was much more experienced. There was no way she'd be able to live up to his expectations… and someone as sexy and wealthy as Colt definitely would have high expectations for a woman.

The puppy snuggled against her chest and Colt ran a bare fingertip up her arm, smiling when she shivered.

"I'm sure we'd both be thoroughly satisfied."

Why did that sound like a promise and not just a hypothetical situation?

The radio in Colt's saddlebag screeched, breaking the tension. He stared another moment before turning to grab the handset.

Annabelle cradled the dog in one arm and hoisted herself up onto her horse with the other. She listened as Josh assured Colt that the calf was going to be just fine and the vet had done a thorough workup and left antibiotics.

When Annabelle grabbed the reins and started to turn her horse, Colt jerked his gaze to hers.

"I'll be back after lunch," she told him as she trotted away.

Okay, so she was running, just via horseback. But she couldn't get into any more sexually charged talks with that man. Besides the fact that she was probably the only twenty-four-year-old virgin in the world, she would not get swept into Colt Elliott's web of charm, deceit and sex appeal. He was probably just trying to keep her sidetracked and it could very well work. But she had a larger goal in mind than just cashing in her virginity for a night with a sexy cowboy.

She'd dated guys before her fiancé, but never felt a passionate desire to get intimate. Then when Matt came along and they'd gotten engaged, she'd wanted to wait until they were married. He'd been fine with that, telling her he wanted it to be special. That bald-faced lie had made her feel special. If only she'd known he'd found her sister the better option. So here was Annabelle, nearly a quarter of a century old and untouched. That was definitely not something to brag about, so she tended to keep that tidbit of information to herself.

But for a minute, okay maybe more, she wondered what it would be like to be taken by someone so experienced, so powerful.

Annabelle held the pup a little tighter as she rode home on Genesis. She hadn't asked to take the horse, but she couldn't stand the tension simmering between her and Colt another minute.

When he'd touched her just a moment ago, her entire

body had felt the zing…the same type she'd felt when he'd kissed her. What would happen if she gave in to those blatant advances and let him have his way?

If her entire future weren't hanging in the balance, she'd very likely find out.

Seven

"Your basket is ready."

Colt had just stepped into the kitchen to find Winnie, his cook and all-round awesome woman, patting the top of a picnic basket. He'd requested something extra for today and, as always, she'd delivered.

He circled the large granite island and kissed her on the cheek. "You're amazing, Winnie. I'm going to marry you one day."

She swatted him with her towel and laughed. "Get out of my kitchen, boy. It wasn't that long ago I spanked your bottom for stealing cookies before dinner."

Colt shot her a grin as he picked up the basket. "I still swipe your homemade cookies before dinner. I hope you put some in this basket."

"Of course I did."

She grunted as if he'd offended her. But Winnie Miller had been with this family for nearly forty years. Taking care of cowboys broke anyone of having thin skin.

"Mind telling me where you're taking that?" She raised a brow. "Maybe to see some lady friend?"

"Nothing so exciting," he replied as he headed toward the back patio doors.

"You're going to have to settle down and bring some babies in this house eventually," she called to his back. "Too many empty bedrooms."

Considering she had her own suite on the first floor, she knew exactly how many rooms sat empty now. With his father in the nursing home, the absolute best they could find, and his brothers gone, Colt was also aware of how lonely this house was. Winnie only stayed over on occasion, but she mostly went back to her cottage on the edge of town.

Deciding not to take Winnie's bait, Colt headed out the back doors and gripped the basket as he made his way across the concrete drive and stone path leading to the barn. Annabelle should be finishing up brushing the horses and then she'd be heading home for the day. He hadn't pressed her further when she came back after lunch. He knew he'd shaken her up with the sexual innuendos.

Part of him wanted to get a rise out of her, but there was something so sweet about her flirting, he was starting to wonder if he was out of his depth. Maybe she hadn't come up against real men before...men who wanted more from her than a nice, calm romp.

He could do slow. Clearly, by the pace he was setting to get Annabelle's property, he was a patient man when he wanted something.

He stopped short at the entrance to the barn. The sun was starting to set, casting an orange glow through the wide opening on the opposite end of the structure. Annabelle had lost her hat some time back, and her ponytail swayed against her back as she shifted with each brushstroke. Damp tendrils clung to her face. She never failed to shock him with her hard work. She didn't complain, never had a negative word—other than those directed straight at him and his character—and she seemed to care for these animals like they were her own.

But when she'd asked about her father owing money,

Colt had clammed up. The way dread had laced her tone, her facial features, he just hadn't had the heart to come clean.

If it were up to him, she'd never have to know. She was already hurting enough and he was going to take her land. He couldn't deliberately add to her heartbreak.

Colt took a step into the barn, and his boots scuffing against the stone pulled Annabelle's attention toward him. Brush in hand, she gestured toward the basket he carried.

"Bringing a picnic for the horses?" she asked, going back to finish stroking the mare.

"Actually, this is for you."

Annabelle froze, throwing him a side glance. "Nice try, Romeo. I'm not having a picnic with you."

He couldn't help but smile at her immediate rejection. Good to know. Not that he wanted to have dinner with her, he was thinking more along the lines of sheets, showers, and haylofts. Besides, sharing a meal was too intimate.

"I had Winnie make dinner for you and your dad."

He set the basket down on one of the benches between the stalls. Shoving his hands in his pockets, he narrowed the space between them.

"Winnie?" Annabelle asked as she tossed the brush back into the bucket. She turned, crossing her arms over her chest. "Is she part of your harem of women who bow at your every command?"

Colt burst out laughing. He couldn't help himself. Damn if Annabelle Carter wasn't a good time. He could almost be her friend if business and his hormones weren't in the way.

"Winnie is actually my cook, but she'll get a kick out of your guess."

Annabelle eyed the basket, then narrowed her eyes back on him. "Why did she do that? I can make my own dinner."

"You can," he agreed. "But you were exhausted when you left here yesterday and still had to go home and cook.

Then I heard you tell your dad you were up at four this morning to feed Emily and I'm sure you were up with Lucy, as well. No reason I can't make your situation a little easier."

He wasn't sure what reaction he expected her to have, but when she threw her arms in the air and turned to pace, he waited. If nothing else, the woman always kept him on his toes.

"You can't do things like this," she all but shouted as she whirled back around. "I'm trying to hate you, to remind myself that you're the enemy. But part of me wants to believe you're not a monster and when all is said and done, I won't get hurt."

Guilt slid through him, but he couldn't let it hinder his plans. He still had a goal. But damn it. Annabelle touched something in him that he couldn't identify and he had no clue how he could make the outcome less painful for her. There was no happy ending.

Still, she made it impossible not to like her. She made him want to go the extra mile to make her days easier and ignore the inevitable pain he would cause.

Life was so much easier when Colt was only dealing with Neil.

"But you do things like this and I don't know what angle you're working," she went on, her tone lowering as she seemed to be running out of steam. As she spoke, he advanced, step by slow step. "If you're trying to seduce me, I can tell you you're wasting your time. Even if I find you attractive, that doesn't matter. I can't—"

Colt gripped her shoulders, backing her up to the post between the stalls. "You find me attractive?"

Her lids closed as she blew out a breath. "That is all you would take away from what I said."

How could he not? He was going to take this minor victory and run with it. Not that he hadn't already guessed it, but to hear her admit her thoughts had his body tightening.

Colt knew he'd have to take advantage of every moment of her weakness if he wanted to penetrate that wall of defense she'd erected.

He leaned in closer as he flattened his palms on either side of her head. Her flush from the work she'd done, her musky scent, the way her chest rose and fell against his own, it would be so easy to turn this into something more right here and now. They were alone, there was nothing stopping him. And he knew Annabelle was his for the taking.

Colt shifted until his lips grazed across hers like a whisper. "A man could get used to hearing a beautiful woman give him compliments."

"Then maybe you should find a beautiful woman who wants to," she murmured.

He nipped at her bottom lip. "I've found her."

"Colt." Her hands came up to his chest.

The way his name came out on a breathy sigh had his entire body stirring to life. The fight she attempted to put up was weak. There was no conviction in her tone, no pressure from her hands to push him away.

How could he want someone so desperately? He had always been able to control his needs, but not with Annabelle. She challenged him in so many ways, and she was the one woman he really shouldn't want.

Still, seducing her was too sweet, too perfect.

Keeping one hand beside her face, he ran the other over her hip. His thumb slid beneath the hem of her tank. Her smooth skin beneath his touch was everything he'd been dreaming of…and he'd dreamt of her plenty last night.

"I want you."

"No, you want to control me."

"Only in bed."

Her eyes met his. "You're blunt."

"Honest," he corrected, going in to graze her lips once again.

"You have no idea what you're doing," she muttered, as if thinking out loud. "I'm not… Trust me when I say you don't want me."

He cupped her cheek with one hand, his other still at her hip. "Don't put yourself down. I know exactly what I want and I assure you, it's you."

"I'm not putting myself down or fishing for compliments. But you need to know that I'm…"

"What?" he urged.

Now she did push him away. "Not for you."

She picked up the basket, keeping her back to him. Shoulders hunched, she appeared to be defeated. How was that possible? His body was revved up and she seemed as if she'd just lost a battle. They could both win here if she'd just quit fighting the chemistry.

"Just take me home," she whispered. "I can't do this."

When he didn't make a move, she turned to face him, tears swimming in her eyes. "Please."

Whatever internal battle she waged with herself, Colt wanted no part of it. He'd wanted simple, he'd wanted sex. He still did.

Someone like Annabelle would take time to seduce, but he wasn't about to back down. She was needy, aching, just the same as him. He'd felt her heart beat against his chest, felt her arch into him slightly before she pushed him away.

It was only a matter of time before he unleashed that passion.

Annabelle's hands still shook as she unloaded the basket.

Get a grip.

She tried to focus on the amazing food that Colt's cook had prepared. The fact he'd done this for her simply because he'd heard her discuss her hectic home life… Annabelle had no words to describe her emotions.

Of course, maybe she was speechless because her brain was totally fried after that heated encounter in the barn. Yet as hands-on and blatantly sexual as he'd been, he was a total gentleman on the ride home—in his truck. He'd also procured a bag of dog food for the new pup. Confusing, frustrating man. And she'd never wanted anyone more.

"What's all this?"

Her father stood in the doorway, holding Emily and patting her back.

"Dinner. Where is Lucy?"

"She's content chewing a doll head in the Pack 'n Play. I actually just fed her some apricots." He eased Emily into one of two high chairs. "Where on earth did you get all of that food?"

"Colt's cook made extra."

She didn't look up as she busied herself unwrapping everything. No way did she want to see her father's face. She already knew she'd have to answer questions.

"Colt's cook, huh? Sounds like you're getting friendly with him."

Friendly wasn't the correct term. But she truly didn't know what label to give this warped situation. She was caught in between the proverbial rock and a hard place, all the while getting completely turned on by her boss.

Of all the men she could feel a stirring for, why did Colt Elliott have to be the one? She hated her emotions, but the reality was, she felt more of a need, an ache for Colt than she ever did with Matt, and they'd been engaged.

In light of all that had happened, though, Annabelle was relieved she hadn't slept with Matt, that he'd respected her wishes to wait until they were married.

But if the scenario were different and she were engaged to Colt, she couldn't guarantee she'd wait.

"Belle?" Her father waved a hand in front of her face. "What the hell is going on? You bring home this food, you're daydreaming. Is that Elliott boy pressuring you?"

Boy? Not hardly. Colt was all man.

Annabelle circled the long farm-style table and crossed to the high chair. Emily's big green eyes met hers and Annabelle's heart melted. She loved her girls so much. Even though her sister had betrayed her in an unforgivable way, they'd still been family and these twins were all Annabelle had left.

She kissed Emily on her head, smoothing the red curls aside. "He's my temporary boss, Dad. Nothing more."

That wasn't a lie, not for lack of trying on Colt's part, but it was clearly a tidbit of information her father didn't need to know about. That kiss out in the field had to remain her secret...and her fantasy.

Emily clapped her hands together, then banged them on the tray. "How has her fever been today?"

"Just a little this morning, but otherwise it hasn't come back. She's played more this afternoon."

Annabelle went to the pantry and pulled out a jar of baby food. "Never worry about calling me. I want to know if there's any problem with her or you."

Neil grabbed two plates from the cupboard and started filling them with homemade fried chicken, mashed potatoes, and corn. The homemade rolls had Annabelle salivating. She'd hurried through her glamorous lunch of a turkey sandwich so she could get back to work. Ranching was the fastest way she'd ever known to burn calories.

"Where's the puppy?" she asked, glancing around the kitchen.

"I put him outside in the fenced area to run around for a bit. He's a cute little guy, but a handful when I'm alone with the two girls."

Annabelle couldn't feel guilty about that. The situation they were in was part his fault, part fate.

As far as the dog was concerned, she should come up with a name for him soon. She wished the girls were old enough to decide, but at six months, they were just making random sounds and squealing.

Annabelle pulled a wooden kitchen chair over to the high chair and scooped up a bite from the jar. Emily pressed her lips together and turned her head.

"If that's green beans, I tried those for lunch. She hates them. Though Lucy was quite a fan. They're total opposites, except for their looks."

Annabelle chased Emily's mouth around with the spoon. "Yeah, well, I'd like a chocolate cake for dinner, too, but we can't all have that. Come on, little one. Veggies are good."

As she wrestled bite after bite past Emily's lips, Annabelle went over in her head exactly how to approach her father about the debt to Colt's family. It was more than the house, she was positive. Colt, surprisingly, hadn't been willing to throw her dad under the bus. But she needed to know what she was up against. She didn't have time to try to piece all these snippets together for the full story.

Maybe being blunt was the best approach. "Did you gamble against Colt's father before all of this happened?"

"What?" he asked, his fork clanging against his plate.

Annabelle shifted in her seat to face him. "Before now, had you borrowed money or gambled against Colt's father?"

Neil Carter's face tightened, his lips thinned. "Is that what he told you?"

Attempting to distract herself from the ball of tension in her stomach, Annabelle scooped up another bite for Emily. "He didn't tell me anything. That's why I'm asking you."

"There's nothing for you to worry about." He aggressively cut into his chicken. “I don’t like you working over there, Belle. You and I can move and start over. We don’t have to stay here, you know.”

Nearly everything she’d ever loved had been taken from her and as long as there was fight left in her and a chance this place could be hers again, she wouldn’t back down.

“If you want to go, then go.”

She knew he could never afford to live on his own. His addiction wouldn’t allow it. He didn’t have any savings, and everything she was bringing in would have to go to bills. There was no extra.

“We can find something inexpensive,” he argued. “I know your mother had this dream, but she’s gone and…”

“Well, I’m still here,” she snapped. “I will see this through with or without your help.”

Her father leaned back in his seat and raked a hand down his face. “Don’t let them come between us. You’ve been over there for two days and your attitude has changed already.”

Perhaps she had changed, but not because of Colt.

“I’m not the same person I was a month ago,” she informed him. She scraped the bottom of the jar and fought to get the last bite into Emily’s mouth. “Losing my sister and fiancé, then finding out they were having an affair pretty much destroyed me.”

“I lost a daughter,” he murmured. “I know how much it hurts.”

Yes, he was hurting, too. But, they were both feeling different types of pain. He’d lost a child, Annabelle had lost her future. They were going to have to lean on each other to get through this nightmare or she’d never make it.

“I need you here,” she told him. “I need you for Emily and Lucy so I can work. You need to get better for not just yourself, but for those babies who will look up to you one day. And I need you to work on making yourself the father I used to know because I can't do this without him."

Her voice caught on that last word. Tears clogged her throat as she blinked away moisture. Sometimes a girl just needed her dad.

"I'm trying."

Silence settled between them. Suddenly she wasn't in the mood to eat. She pulled Emily from the high chair and wiped her mouth with the bib before tugging it over her head. She dropped the dirty rag onto the tray.

"I'm going to give her a bath and then I'll come back for Lucy," Annabelle told her father. "If you can let the dog in and feed him, that would be great. I'll clean the kitchen later, after the girls are bathed."

"You're not eating?" he asked as she headed out of the room.

"I'm fine," she lied. But she didn't want to get into the mess inside her head. Especially not with her father.

Annabelle hugged Emily a bit tighter as she mounted the steps. "We're going to make it," she vowed. "You guys will have a stable home and never doubt my love. We're in this together."

All Annabelle had to do was make it through the next three months and she'd be free. She'd be able to push forward, take control of her life once and for all...and be rid of Colt Elliott.

Eight

"Hayes will be home next month."

Nolan laid the blanket across the horse he'd appropriately named Doc. Colt grabbed his own blanket and saddle and readied his stallion.

"I already asked Charlie to get the house ready and stock it before he arrives," Colt replied. "I'm sure he'll be ready to have some downtime to adjust to civilian life again."

Hayes had been in the service for the past fifteen years. He'd enlisted straight out of high school and now he was getting out for good. They'd thought he'd stay in a few more years and then retire, but Hayes wasn't the same man he used to be. He'd seen too much, things he'd never discuss, and there had been a haunted look in his eyes last time he'd been home.

Colt wasn't sure if Hayes would want anything to do with ranch life or if he'd like to explore other venues, but Colt would readily welcome him here for as long as he wanted to stay. Hayes had enough money that he'd never have to work a day in his life, but Colt intended to keep him a little busy so those demons didn't creep up and take control.

"Think Dad will remember him?" Colt asked.

Nolan hoisted the saddle across his stallion's back. "Depends on the day Hayes goes to see him. I stopped in earlier after my shift and he wasn't having the best day. He kept telling me to find Virginia because the dog had been hit by a car."

Virginia, their mother, had been gone for years. He still asked about her, still would question why she wasn't there. He may have dementia, but they had a love that would rival any fairy tale Colt had ever heard.

"That dog was killed when I was a baby," Nolan added. "So he's gone back pretty far. He thought I was Hank."

Hank had been their father's right-hand man at the stables, but he, too, had passed on. Their father was a prisoner in his own mind and he had no clue. All they could do was keep visiting, and hopefully he could grasp that he wasn't alone in his living hell.

"I'm going to see him tomorrow." Colt adjusted the saddle and patted Lightning's side before mounting him. "It's been a hectic couple of days."

When Annabelle had gone home an hour ago, Colt had been too keyed up to do anything. He'd just wanted to ride, but then Nolan had stopped in for some downtime.

"How's your new employee working out?" Nolan asked as he set off toward the back pasture.

Colt gripped the reins in one hand and tipped his hat down with the other. Who knew what truth his eyes would tell? He'd thought of little else since that kiss. Well, he'd thought of excuses to touch her again, because he was having a damn hard time *not* touching her.

"She's a hard worker. Josh and Ryan are impressed, too."

He rode parallel with Nolan, as they'd done so many times over the years. The inquisition was coming, Colt would bet the ranch on it.

"And you?" Nolan asked easily. "You're impressed."

He could still feel her tight body against his when he'd pressed her against the wall. Could still feel that warm breath brush across his cheek, his neck. She wasn't immune to their chemistry. She practically melted against him when they touched, and he couldn't wait until she was his.

"She doesn't complain about the heat or the work. She does her job and is prompt."

The sun, barely visible on the horizon now, cast an orange glow. The gorgeous summer nights never ceased to catch his breath. There was nothing more peaceful than a sunset on the ranch. There was nowhere else he'd rather spend his days than Pebblebrook.

"This is a hard life," Nolan said, giving Doc a gentle pat. "Think she'll be just as professional in three months?"

"She's determined to pay off her father's debt. She knows I want her land."

Nolan's disapproving sigh had Colt gritting his teeth. "Don't start," Colt warned.

"I didn't say a word. Sounds like the guilt is already getting to you."

That wasn't the only thing getting to him.

"I can't make decisions based on personal feelings, Nolan. This ranch is a business."

"Fair enough. So what are you going to do at the end of this, when the debt is paid?"

Colt rubbed the back of his neck. "I'm going to give them time to find another place."

"She's not going to be happy."

Colt pulled Lightning to a stop. "I'm not making friends. I'm pursuing a goal Dad had and I'm making sure it's carried out. How do you suggest I acquire the land? Because I asked multiple times to buy it."

Nolan eased to a standstill as well and glanced around

at the acreage stretching as far as the eye could see. "You know, I made a poor choice years ago that affected the rest of my life. I just don't want to see you doing something you regret."

Colt didn't need his oldest brother to spell out the mistake he'd made. Nolan had been in love, but when she'd pressured him to settle down, he'd gotten scared. Add an unexpected pregnancy and a miscarriage and Nolan hadn't been able to deal.

While Colt didn't know the entire story, he knew Nolan had never found that type of bond since. He flitted between the hospital and dates, occasionally working on the ranch when he could. But there was barely a weekend that Nolan didn't have someone on his arm…or in his bed. Of course, he never brought women back to Pebblebrook because that would be too personal.

"I'd regret if I let that land go," Colt stated simply. "I'm going to turn Pebblebrook into the greatest dude ranch the west has ever seen. I already have an engineer coming to draw up some plans for renovations on the house next door."

Nolan tugged his hat off and settled it onto the horn. "I wouldn't let Annabelle know that."

"She doesn't."

His brother's blue eyes bore into Colt. "You're starting to care for her. What are you going to do when you can't stop your feelings from getting involved with business?"

Colt snorted. "I want to take her to bed, if that's what you mean by 'care for her.' You should know something about meaningless sex."

Nolan nodded. "Touché."

"Besides, I want to settle down eventually. I definitely want kids to fill Pebblebrook with, but I want my dude ranch and my life in order first."

Laughing, Nolan shook his head. "There's no perfect

time to start a family and settle down. You need to do it when you find the one or you'll be left alone, trying to fill a void you caused."

Colt wasn't worried he'd fall for Annabelle. They wanted vastly different things and just because he ached to strip her down and have his way with her, didn't mean he was ready to monogram her initials on the plush towels in his master bath.

Tugging on his reins once more, Colt settled into an easy pace. "I've got a rancher from Oklahoma coming in two days to pick up forty head of cattle."

"Can't help you there. I'm on call for the next three days, starting tomorrow."

"Weren't you just on call?" Colt asked.

Nolan's horse jerked to the side before Nolan eased him back. "I was, but I picked up some extra shifts for a coworker. He's taking his wife on a surprise second honeymoon."

"You're going to work yourself to death."

Nolan cast a sideways glance. "I could say the same for you. But we're doing what we love, so it doesn't feel like work."

There was nothing else Colt had ever wanted to do. Nothing could pull him from Pebblebrook. He was anxious to have Hayes come back, and maybe he could help out for a bit until he decided fully what he wanted to do. Beau had been filming a movie in parts unknown for the past few months. Some action film where he would surely win the lady and save the day.

"Storms are coming in," Nolan stated, nodding toward the darkening skies.

Colt pulled on the reins. "We'll head back."

Colt couldn't recall the last time all four of them were together, but he was definitely going to call Beau and see if he could fly home for Hayes's homecoming. Maybe they could even all go visit their father. Better yet, maybe they could bring him to the ranch for a day.

Emotions threatened to overtake him at the idea of all of them there once again. Colt may be the youngest, but he had the most to prove. He wanted this property to thrive bigger and better than it ever had. He wanted his brothers to see just how hard he worked to make sure Pebblebrook remained the greatest ranch in Texas. And even though his father didn't always know what was going on in the world around him, Colt was going to honor him and personally see to it that his dude ranch came to fruition.

He'd set this dream in motion, so failing now would be a sure sign that he couldn't handle tough times. There was no way he'd let this scenario end without him getting the land and the house.

And letting Annabelle Carter appeal to his compassionate side was not an option. The only place he wanted her was in his bed.

"The truck?" Annabelle asked as she climbed into the cab. She set the basket from last night between them and reached for her seat belt. "Did I get a promotion?"

Colt dangled his wrist over the steering wheel and shot her a smile that shot straight to her heart. The instant response wasn't welcome, but she had no way of stopping it. At this point, all she could do was hang on for the ride.

"I need to run into town real quick and thought you'd enjoy a few minutes of air-conditioning before we hit it hard today."

Annabelle stretched her denim-covered legs out. "You're the boss."

"I do like how you keep saying that, sweets."

She let out a groan. "*Ms. Carter* still works fine."

Tipping his hat, he pinned her with his striking gaze.

"You've arched that sweet body against mine, you've kissed me, and you've imagined us as lovers. We're beyond formalities."

Annabelle's breath caught in her throat. She'd never met a man so blunt…and so dead-on with calling her out on her feelings. But she was a different woman than she was even a month ago and she wasn't about to be intimidated by Colt Elliott.

"That may be," she stated as she leaned closer, pleased when his eyes dropped to her lips. "But you've had the same thoughts, and you're no closer to getting me there than you were days ago."

Colt reached out, curling his fingers around the back of her neck. He captured her mouth, parting her lips, tangling his tongue with hers. The intensity of his touch, the urgency of the demanding kiss should have scared her, but Annabelle was too turned-on, too stunned at his actions to be frightened.

This was nothing like the sweet, delicate kiss he'd first given her. This was a toe-curling, body-tingling kiss like nothing she'd ever experienced before.

Annabelle fisted her hands in her lap, refusing to reach for him…but she wasn't going to deny she didn't want this to end.

Colt's grip on her neck softened as he trailed his fingers around to her jaw. Gently, he nipped at her lips before easing back. He stroked the pad of his thumb across her bottom lip and Annabelle couldn't stop her tongue from darting out and tasting him.

"I'd say we're one step closer," he murmured.

Annabelle was just digesting those words when he pulled back and reached over to start the truck. She had a snappy comeback, something snarky about his arrogance taking place of his ego, but when he extended his arm and waved, Annabelle cringed. She turned to see her father standing on the porch, cradling a girl on each hip, and from the look of his face, he'd witnessed everything.

Great. Nothing like having your father see you make out with the enemy. Just when she thought this situation couldn't get any worse.

Nine

At the end of the day Colt was still cursing himself for losing control with Annabelle earlier. Not that he regretted finally getting to taste those sweet lips again. No, he was more irritated with himself than the fact that he'd let her goad him. He did everything on his terms, his timeline.

The kicker had been looking up and seeing Neil on the porch, holding Emily and Lucy, that pup frolicking around his feet. Colt didn't mind that her father had seen them because he honestly didn't care what the old man thought. But he sure as hell didn't want an audience when his seduction of Annabelle was finally complete. He wanted to get her alone, to prove to her that they were indeed closer to intimacy. They'd been dancing around the subject for days and it was only a matter of time before they succumbed to what they both wanted. There was no way she could deny that, not after the way she kept responding to his kisses.

Colt had put Annabelle with Ryan today because he'd needed some time to think. When he was around her, he felt his control slipping by the second. He still had a ranch to run, and besides, he'd wanted to sneak away to visit his father.

Today had not been a good day for Grant Elliott. He hadn't recognized Colt at all. No matter what happened in Colt's life, nothing hurt more than looking into his father's blue eyes and seeing the blank stare, the confusion.

But his father had talked about a dude ranch. Colt had listened as his dad went on about all the things he'd incorporate onto the farm. The small cabins he'd build on the east side where the view of the pasture was breathtaking at sunset, the horses he'd bring in special for children who came to visit. He'd even mentioned having programs for physically handicapped riders who wanted to see what ranching was all about.

Colt knew his father was in there somewhere because he'd mentioned all of his original plans. Ranching had been so ingrained into the Elliott patriarch, that it was something Colt didn't think would ever be lost to this nightmare disease.

He had asked the nursing staff about the possibility of bringing his father home for one day when Hayes returned but, in the end, they decided to play it by ear. As much as Colt wanted his father at Pebblebrook, even for a short time, he would do whatever was best for his health.

Colt shut off the engine and grabbed his hat from the passenger seat. As he stepped from his truck, Colt headed toward the barn, but froze for a split second before taking off in a dead run. Annabelle lay on the ground just inside the structure, Ryan kneeling over her and patting the side of her face.

"What the hell happened?" Colt asked, skidding to a stop and dropping to his knees.

"She passed out, Boss."

Her color was off, perspiration dotted her forehead. He glanced at her body and noted that the white tank she'd worn was clinging to the dampness on her torso. He jerked his hat off and started to fan her.

"Get some water," Colt demanded, never taking his eyes off her pale face. He felt the pulse on her neck. Steady, thankfully, but he didn't like seeing her on the damn ground.

While Ryan rushed to the office, Colt eased his arms beneath her knees and her back. Carefully, he lifted her and stepped back to take a seat on a bench. Her lids fluttered as her head fell toward his chest. Ryan came back with a bottle of water and handed it to Colt.

"Want me to call Nolan?" Ryan asked.

Colt shook his head. "He's at the hospital. She's coming around."

Slowly, she turned her head, her brows dipping as if she was hurt. "What happened?" Colt asked again. "Were you in here when she fainted? Where's Josh?"

"Josh took off early because his daughter has some dance recital." Ryan pulled a handkerchief from his back pocket and wiped the back of his neck. "Ms. Carter and I had been out herding the cattle from the west field and we'd just gotten back. I walked around the side to turn the hoses on and when I came back in, she was all flushed. I asked if she felt all right, but she went down. I was fast enough to catch her before she hit her head, though. Scared ten years off my life."

Yeah, Colt was still trying to get his heart rate back under control after seeing her motionless on the ground.

"What else should I do?"

Colt shook his head and focused back on Annabelle. "I'd say she got overheated. It happens. Why don't you go ahead and tend to the horses and get them put away? I'll take care of her."

Ryan gave a clipped nod. "Yell if you need me."

Cradling her with one arm, Colt set the water bottle on the bench beside him and smoothed the stray, damp tendrils from her face. Her lids fluttered again and he silently pleaded for her to open them and give him hell for holding her.

He'd seen many cowboys go down due to heat and lack of hydration, but none of them had affected him like this. She'd worked herself to the point of exhaustion, and it was all his fault.

"Open those eyes, sweetness."

She fluttered once again. "You never ask nice," she murmured.

Relief spread through him as swiftly as a Texas storm in the spring.

Finally, those bright green eyes met his and for the first time in several minutes, he breathed a sigh of relief.

"Wh-what are you doing?" she asked, starting to ease up.

"Stay still." Damn it, he needed to hold her another minute. "You passed out."

One shaky hand came up to her forehead as she blinked in confusion. "I did? Where's Ryan? We were going to—"

"Forget it. He's outside tending to the horses and you're done for the day."

He helped her sit up, but kept a hold around her shoulders. Colt reached for the water bottle and brought it to her lips. "Drink."

She took the water from him and sipped, then swiped the bottle across her forehead. Condensation slid down the side of her face, down her neck, and disappeared into the scoop of her tank. He shouldn't be thinking how sexy she looked right now, but he couldn't help himself. He'd been away from her all day, then to come back and see this… his emotions were in overdrive.

"You have to take care of yourself," he stated, his tone much harsher than he'd intended.

With careful movements, she slid from his lap and set

the bottle down on the bench. "My welfare is none of your concern. I take care of myself just fine."

He came to his feet, going toe to toe with her. "Clearly not. And your welfare is my concern when it affects your work."

When she squared her shoulders, but rubbed her forehead as if her head ached, he felt like an ass. She was gearing up for a fight and he was just angry he hadn't been there to make sure she was fine.

"Damn it." He raked a hand down his face. "Get in the truck, I'll take you home."

"I'll ask Ryan."

Colt leaned forward, towering over her until she reached for his shoulders to stay upright. "When you need anything, I'll be the one to deliver it. Get. In. The. Truck."

Her eyes searched his face. "Something happened."

"Yeah, you passed out and scared the hell out of us."

She shook her head, her hands softened against him. "Something else. You're angry at me, but there's a sadness in your eyes I haven't seen before."

Colt hated how she homed directly in on the nugget inside him he tried so damn hard to keep hidden from the world. "Don't analyze me, sweetness. Unless you want to get into *your* secrets."

"I just thought…" She took a step away and swiped the back of her hand across her forehead. "Nothing. Forget I asked."

When she turned to head toward the truck, Colt grabbed her arm and hauled her side against his chest. "I had a bad day. That's all. It's nothing I want to talk about, but, thanks. I've never met anyone who knows what I'm feeling or thinking without me saying a word."

Those captivating eyes turned to him. "Maybe one broken heart recognizes another."

"Who broke your heart?" he whispered.

Her eyes went to his throat, as if she couldn't look directly at him. "Who hasn't?"

Those two words spoke volumes. She'd been broken, perhaps she still was, but she was a damn fighter. She stood before him ready to discuss what pained him when she was clearly just as shattered. But he wasn't asking, he couldn't. Getting involved on an emotional level was not an option. How many times did he have to remind himself of that?

Colt gripped her chin between his thumb and finger, tipping her head to capture her lips. Softly he caressed her mouth with his. His knees weakened the second she slid her hand over his forearm. The kiss was so innocent, definitely not the stepping-stone to sex he typically delivered. But this was the most relaxed he'd ever known her to be. Her body literally eased against his as she returned the passion so delicately.

"Maybe someday you'll trust me," he muttered against her lips.

Her hand tightened against him. "It's not my trust you're after."

Colt grazed her lips once again. "Maybe not, but if you trust me, then you'll be more likely to give me everything else I want from you."

Annabelle eased away as she blew out a sigh. "We both know that would be a terrible idea. I've still got months to go and we're already…"

"What are we? Because this could be so much better."

She glanced out the doorway. With the light breeze blowing in, strands from her ponytail danced around her shoulders. "I can't get involved with you, Colt. I already have to explain this morning's kiss to my father when I get home."

"You didn't go home for lunch?" he asked.

She shook her head. "I couldn't face him. After all that's happened—"

"Nothing has happened."

She turned her attention back to him. "Yet, right? You fully intend to keep this up until I give in."

Why answer such a rhetorical question? They both knew what was going on, they were adults. Colt wanted Annabelle and the feeling was mutual. He knew desire when it stared back at him.

"Come up to the house."

Those green eyes widened. "What?"

"For dinner. We'll talk." He held his hands out. "Nothing more. I swear."

Unless she wanted more, then who would he be to turn her down?

"I need to get home to the girls."

"Bring them."

What the hell was he saying? He never dated a woman with a baby, let alone twins. Never brought kids back to his home. But why shouldn't he now? It was no secret that he wanted Annabelle. Perhaps appealing to that side of her would make her come around.

Annabelle laughed. "Wow. You're letting your desperation show, Colt."

Yeah, maybe he was, but he wanted her trust, damn it. He was running out of patience. His body ached for her, responded to her when she merely cast a glance his way. He'd never felt this urgency toward one woman before.

"Give your dad the night off and bring your twins to the house. I know Winnie will have a feast prepared. She always does."

He could see her thinking, but refused to take no for an answer. "One dinner, darlin'. That's all. I think you could use a break."

"Fine," she sighed. "I'll bring Emily and Lucy in my own car and you will not touch me. Deal?"

Colt winked. "Sure thing, but what happens when you touch me?"

With an unladylike growl, she spun around and headed out the barn. "In your dreams."

"Every damn night," he muttered to her retreating back.

Ten

"You're not seriously going over there."

Annabelle slipped on her flip-flops and picked Emily up. "I'm only going for dinner. Anything I can do to stay on his good side and figure out his ulterior motive, I'll do it."

"I saw you doing it in his truck this morning."

The accusing tone, the knowing glare had guilt surging through Annabelle. She'd been home for nearly thirty minutes, long enough to change clothes and feed the girls, before he said anything. But she refused to allow him to turn this around on her.

"You're the reason I'm in this position," she countered, keeping her tone light since she held Emily.

"That's your excuse for kissing Colt Elliott?" Her father's silver brows drew in as he crossed his arms over his chest. "That man doesn't care about you, Belle. People like the Elliotts only care about money."

She swallowed back the hurt. Someday a man would be interested in her for no other reason than the fact that he liked, or even loved her. She'd been used and discarded too many times to care right now, though. Kissing Colt had been a pleasure, and she was going to steal those moments when she could. She was smart enough to know Colt wanted her in bed. And she couldn't deny she'd been fantasizing about it.

"Leave the girls here," her father stated.

Annabelle shook her head. She needed them as the buffer. "We'll be fine. Besides, I don't get to see them much."

"At least leave Emily since she's still been fussing."

"I'll take Lucy," she stated. She had to drive home to Colt that she wasn't the type to play around. She had a family she needed to look out for.

Finally, her father nodded. "I'm going to need some cash."

"What for?"

She'd taken over all finances, cutting him off since she'd been back. Until he proved himself to be addiction free, it was the only way for them to get his debt paid off in time.

"I'll go to the grocery while you're gone. We're low on diapers and we could use some milk and eggs."

Annabelle did the quick math in her head. Holding Emily on her hip, she crossed to her purse hanging by the front door. She pulled out a few bills and handed them to her father.

"Just put the change back in my purse," she told him. "I shouldn't be too long."

Before he could make another argument as to why she shouldn't go, Annabelle grabbed the diaper bag and her keys and headed out the door. Once she got to Pebblebrook, she pulled in to the large, circular drive near the front door. She'd only been in his office, so she had to admit she was curious about what the rest of the house looked like. Did any other rooms have that spectacular waterfall?

Annabelle unfastened Lucy from her car seat and headed up the wide stone steps. The small creek running in front of the home soothed her nerves with the trickling effect. She knew coming here was just another tactic of

Colt's to sway her into his bed. Little did he know nobody had been able to accomplish that in the past and she had a strong resolve built up. Well, she couldn't deny it was slipping, but she could hold out longer than him.

And she was pretty confident she was driving him insane. He wanted her and he was getting desperate. A thrill of power shot through her.

When the wide door swung open just as she hit the top step, Annabelle was a little surprised to see Colt in the entryway.

"I figured one of your minions would answer the door."

He held a hand over his heart and stepped aside for her to enter. "I'm crushed you think so little of me."

"You think enough of yourself for both of us," she countered as she stepped over the threshold.

The house was just as gorgeous as she remembered. Breathtaking. So far out of her league, she was afraid to take a step any farther. But she took her time in glancing around, taking it all in.

"Just one of the girls?" he asked.

Annabelle nodded. "This is Lucy. Emily stayed with my dad. I won't know how to act with just one. I'm always taking care of them both at the same time."

"Let me have the bag." Colt eased the diaper bag off her shoulder and set it on the accent table next to an enormous vase containing a spray of bright flowers. "Follow me. Winnie did indeed make a feast and she was thrilled to have someone enjoy it other than me."

"Where is she?"

"Oh, she's probably heading home," he replied as he led her down the wide hallway toward the back of the house. "She went to her suite earlier, but she's not staying."

Her suite. Of course. What chef didn't have their own suite?

Annabelle held on tight to Lucy, who had finally laid

her head down on Annabelle's shoulder. It had been a long day for everyone.

"How are you feeling?" Colt asked, stepping into the massive kitchen.

"I'm fine." Even if she weren't, she wouldn't admit it. She was still mortified she'd passed out earlier. But, the moment she'd woken up, she'd seen that worry on Colt's face. That was definitely something he couldn't fake.

Annabelle tried not to gawk, but she couldn't help herself. The massive center island dominated the kitchen. It featured a small sink and a second gas stove as well as an overhang stretching across the length of the island. There were even bar stools made from antique saddles.

Massive dishes of food had been set out: cornbread, potatoes, smoked sausages with peppers, and a pie. Apple. Her favorite. The spread on the island had her mouth watering.

"I should've worn my bigger jeans." Her stomach growled and she cringed. "And I shouldn't have skipped lunch."

His bright eyes narrowed. "No, you shouldn't have. You know how hard ranch work is and you need to take care of yourself."

Annabelle nodded. "It won't happen again. Believe me." Lucy let out a deep sigh. "I'm pretty sure she's fallen asleep."

Annabelle turned so the baby faced Colt. "Is she?"

"Oh, yeah. She's out."

Grabbing a plate off the edge of the bar, Annabelle started dishing up potatoes with one hand.

"I'll get your damn plate."

She eyed him. "No language around the baby."

Tipping his head, he pursed his lips. "She's already talking?"

"Well, no, but I don't want *damn* to be her first word, either."

"Fair enough, sweetness."

Rolling her eyes, she set her plate down and glared at him. "You've got to stop with the tacky pet names. I'm sure you've used those names on a number of other women, but I'm not falling for your charms."

"You think I'm charming?" That sidelong grin had her body instantly responding. "And I've never used *sweetness* on anyone else. Maybe that can be your name."

Slowly easing Lucy to her other side, Annabelle snorted. "I'd rather you not call me that, especially when we're working."

He put a piece of cornbread on the side of her plate and turned to face her, pinning her with that direct baby-blue gaze. "And when we're not working?"

She would not stand there and flirt with him. She had to cut that off before it could get started because she was losing ground. Her willpower was cracking and she couldn't afford to have it completely crumble.

Breaking his stare, Annabelle turned away. She headed toward the long, farm-style table in front of the floor-to-ceiling windows looking out onto the pool. Of course there was a pool house off to the side. She could only imagine what that looked like inside.

"Good evening." Annabelle jerked toward the doorway to see a beaming elderly woman. "I'm Winnie. I won't get in the way, I just wanted to introduce myself and tell you how amazing that cinnamon bread you sent back was."

Annabelle ignored the way Colt's gaze widened. "You're welcome. I love to bake and wanted to thank you for the dinner. I guess I should be thanking you for two."

She waved a hand. "It's no trouble at all. I'm happy to have someone else to cook for. I'd love for you to share that recipe, if you don't mind."

"I don't mind a bit," Annabelle replied with a smile.

"You made bread?" Colt finally asked as he poured two glasses of sweet tea.

"It was in the basket she sent back," Winnie stated.

"I had no idea or I would've dug into it." Colt crossed the kitchen and set Annabelle's plate and tea on the table. "This looks delicious, as always, Winnie. Did you eat?"

"I did." Her eyes zeroed in on Emily. "And who is this precious baby?"

"My daughter, Lucy." That still felt so strange to say. There were so many emotions tied to the fact the twins were legally hers. Emotions she'd not fully faced. "She and her twin, Lucy, are six months old."

"Oh, my. Two precious angels. Well, she's a doll with that red, curly hair. I can see she looks like you," Winnie stated with a confident nod and grin.

Of course they looked alike. Annabelle and her sister both shared the same skin tone, red hair, green eyes.

Winnie's gaze darted between Annabelle and Colt before she took a step toward him. "I thought about going to see your father, unless I'm needed here."

Annabelle took a seat at the table. The bench seating made for nice family-style dining, but she had a feeling Colt didn't host too many family gatherings. She didn't know the story behind his father, and he hadn't offered to give her details, so she tried not to pay attention to the conversation behind her.

She stabbed a potato with her fork and took a bite. In such a short time, she'd gotten used to doing things with one hand while holding Lucy or Emily with the other.

"We're good here," Colt replied. "Maybe, uh, why don't you take Dad some pie. Apple was his favorite. I don't know..."

This was the first time Annabelle had ever heard Colt even remotely sound unsure. And there was that sadness again. Colt may be a big, powerful rancher, but there was no masking the pain he obviously felt now.

"I'll take some," Winnie stated. "Let me just get that and I'll be out of your way."

Annabelle took a drink of her sweet tea and patted Lucy's back. She hated being caught in the midst of what was obviously a family moment. If anyone understood not wanting outsiders involved in a private affair, it was her.

"It was lovely to meet you."

Annabelle turned slightly, waving to Winnie. "You, too. And thanks for this wonderful meal."

"I hope you'll come back."

Before Annabelle could even reply, Winnie walked away with her container. Colt scooped hearty portions onto his plate and Annabelle stared at him, wondering what to say.

"Don't ask."

His firm command had her straightening in her seat. "I wasn't. I honestly don't know what to say. I don't know why I'm here."

Crossing the room, he set his plate down right next to hers and settled down onto the bench. "You're here because I'm tired of eating alone and I enjoy your company. You're here so you can see that you can trust me. And you're here so I can feed you."

When Annabelle reached for her fork, Colt covered her hand. Her eyes met his and he took the fork from her. When he scooped up a bite and held it in front of her lips, she froze.

"What are you doing?"

His mouth twisted into a half grin and Annabelle's heart kicked into a higher gear. "Making sure you're taken care of."

Annabelle took the bite he offered. Whatever Winnie had done to those potatoes was amazing, but it was difficult for Annabelle to concentrate with Colt sitting this close. His thigh rubbed against hers on the bench and it was all she could do not to touch it.

He fed her several more times, never taking his eyes off her as she closed her lips over the fork. Finally, she couldn't take it anymore.

"I can finish," she told him. "I'm used to holding her and eating at the same time."

"I'm getting to you."

"Yes." Why deny the truth? "Which is why I can't keep doing this."

Silence settled around them, save for the occasional clatter of their utensils against the plates. Annabelle only ate a little before she eased her legs around and came to her feet. She grabbed her plate and took it to the counter. She held on to Lucy and closed her eyes, willing some semblance of self-control to come back.

Coming here was a bad idea. She honestly didn't know what she wanted. Well, she knew, but she couldn't even go there. She had too much to worry about with her home, her father, learning about how to care for two babies. No wonder she was thinking of throwing every bit of common sense aside and letting Colt seduce her. She knew full well she'd enjoy it, that was never in question. The issue was what happened afterward? How would she work for him and try to keep the various aspects of their relationship compartmentalized?

Lucy started fussing and wiggling around. Rocking back and forth, Annabelle patted her back.

"You're really good with her."

Annabelle glanced up to see Colt standing on the other side of the island. "It's a learning process."

Wasn't that an understatement?

"What happened with the father?"

Colt's question took her completely off guard. Annabelle froze. "He's not in the picture."

"You said that, but I assume since you were engaged and now you're left alone with two babies, he wasn't man enough for the job."

Considering the father of this child and her fiancé were two different people, this could get tricky. But, she also wasn't about to get into the ordeal. She didn't intend to get too personal with Colt, and she didn't want him to look at her with pity, so there was no need to let him in on the truth behind the twins.

"The girls' father signed over all rights." That much was true. Trish had gone to him when she'd discovered she was pregnant, but he wasn't ready to be a daddy. "We're fine, though."

Because Annabelle wouldn't let them be anything but fine.

"I can't imagine any man not wanting to be with his children," Colt added, crossing his arms over his broad chest as he stared down at Lucy. "And if he was engaged to you, why would he just throw all of that away?"

"Stop," she murmured. "This isn't...I can't get into this."

Colt eased around the island and came to stand directly in front her. His eyes locked on to hers. "I'm trying to gain your trust, Annabelle. I want you to trust me when I take you to my bed."

"You're not taking me to bed," she insisted, though nerves in her stomach danced wildly at the thought.

"I am," he countered. "But I want to make sure it's my face you see, my name you say when you're there."

"Considering I've never said anyone else's name, that won't be a problem."

She hadn't meant to just blurt that out, but seeing the shock on his face was worth it.

“What?” he asked, shock lacing that single word.

She’d come this far. Might as well let him know what he was dealing with. Maybe he’d back off and get that ridiculous idea out of his head.

“I’m a virgin.”

Eleven

Very little in Colt's life shocked him. He'd traveled all over the globe, dealt with a variety of people and liked to believe he could think on his feet. But nothing prepared him for the confusing statement Annabelle had just dropped between them.

"How the hell is that even possible?" he asked. "I know the girls aren't adopted. They look just like you."

Annabelle patted the sleeping baby and nodded. "No, they're not adopted. My sister was their mother."

Her sister. The one who passed away.

Colt attempted to make things clear in his head, but he was at a loss. How the hell did he respond to that? She was clearly out of her depth with so much, having life throw things at her she wasn't ready for—motherhood…sex.

And he was an ass for being so forward, so blatant.

Well, he was a jerk for other things as well, but that was business.

In his defense, how the hell was he supposed to know she was so inexperienced? She had babies, for crying out loud, and the way she'd flirted, kissed…

"I don't know what to say."

Annabelle held his gaze as she rested her cheek against

the sleeping baby's head. "There's nothing to say. You needed to know what you were up against. Clearly, I'm not swayed by easy charms and sexy men. So, you'd probably be better off moving on to a woman who will actually give in to your advances."

Colt would've laughed had her statement held any conviction or had she not melted against him when they'd kissed. Annabelle was already giving in to his every advance, whether she wanted to admit it or not.

"You think because you're inexperienced that I'll move on?" he asked, taking a step closer until his chest brushed the arm she held Lucy with. "Baby, if anything, I want you more. To know I can be the one to show you everything, I've never been more turned on."

"Don't call me *baby,*" she whispered.

"When I get you into my bed, I'll call you your name and you'll damn well love every second of it."

She jerked back. "You're not seriously still interested in me. You just want the challenge."

"It's true I've never backed away from a challenge," he assured her. "But I want you, sweetness. I've wanted you from the moment you plowed into my fence. And you want me, too, or you wouldn't have stared at my bare chest so long that day."

Her eyes narrowed. "If I weren't holding Lucy, I'd smack you."

Colt believed she probably would. He couldn't help but laugh as he leaned close to her ear. "Save that energy."

"You're impossible." Annabelle took a step back, then shifted Lucy in her arms. "I'm going home. Tell Winnie thanks for dinner and I'll get her that recipe."

"Why didn't you tell me you like to cook?" he asked, the thought of her leaving suddenly unbearable.

"I never said I liked to cook," she retorted.

He leaned against the edge of the counter, feigning calm and giving her a bit more breathing room.

"You didn't have to," he stated. "You baked bread and brought it back. Someone who hates cooking wouldn't have done that."

Annabelle bit her bottom lip as if she were contemplating letting him into her personal life any further. She'd already dropped a bomb. What did it matter at this point?

"I actually love to bake," she told him. "Bread is my weakness. My mother always baked bread. Our house always smelled amazing. I guess I just want to keep up that tradition, and hopefully pass it down to the girls one day."

The importance of family traditions. That was definitely something he understood, something his father had instilled into each of his children.

"The girls are lucky to have you," Colt told her. "I'm sorry about your sister."

He'd already apologized, but knowing more about the situation gave him another tug on his conscience. Damn it.

"I don't want to talk about her."

There was something in Annabelle's tone that had him cocking his head and studying her. The sadness was there, but something else, too, something almost bitter or resentful.

"Do you want to lay her on the sofa?" he suggested. "We can talk while she rests."

"You just want to talk? Don't you think we've exhausted all the topics for the night? Unless you'd like to ask about my father's gambling. Better yet, why don't we talk about your father or why you have a limp."

The limp he could discuss, but he didn't want to talk about his father. He missed the man his father once was, and discussing him, given his current mental state, wasn't Colt's idea of a good time.

"Your father is a gambler and mine has dementia. That

sums up that topic." He pulled in a deep breath. "As for the limp, when a tornado ripped through Stone River last year, our main barn was torn up. I was helping to rebuild it when I fell off a ladder, shattering my hip bone and breaking my back. I'm still getting back to normal…if that's even possible."

Before she could offer pity, which he did not want, Colt opted to throw the focus back on her. He glanced down toward her half-empty plate. "You didn't eat enough."

Annabelle shrugged. "I haven't had much of an appetite lately."

"Which is why you passed out."

"You're not going to let that go, are you?"

Colt shook his head. "Not until I see you're taking care of yourself properly."

Annabelle wrapped both arms around Lucy as she turned and headed toward the patio off the kitchen. Colt followed, pleased she'd given up on the idea of just flat out leaving. For reasons he didn't want to examine too closely, he wanted her there, in his home. Annabelle took a seat on the sofa and laid Lucy down beside her. After making a wall with throw pillows, Annabelle settled against the cushion and tipped her head back.

"It feels so good to sit and do nothing."

Colt remained in the doorway, leaning against the frame. She looked so peaceful. Surprisingly, having Annabelle and Lucy there didn't feel awkward. The women he dated didn't have children, but Lucy was so damn adorable, it was impossible not to be lighter, happier in her presence. Both girls were precious and obviously so loved by Annabelle. She'd clearly do anything to keep them from harm.

But as Colt studied Annabelle, something shifted inside him. She was making him feel, she was making him want and that wasn't going to work. He didn't want to start thinking of her beyond business or the bedroom.

Maybe having her there wasn't the best idea. He still wanted her, that wouldn't go away until he'd gotten her out of his system. But he'd learned more about her, quite a bit, and she made him want to take care of her. She made it nearly impossible not to admire her acts of selflessness.

Annabelle Carter was one of the most amazing people he'd ever met.

And she'd just let out a most unladylike snore.

Colt stepped down onto the enclosed patio and stood over her. Her mouth was softer when she slept, her light lashes fanned out over her cheeks, her chest rose and fell so lightly, so steadily. She'd worn herself completely out.

Lucy whimpered and Colt's gaze jerked to the baby who was starting to wake up. Fear gripped him. He didn't want to wake Annabelle and he didn't want Lucy to start crying.

When Lucy started squirming even more, her eyes opened and she whimpered once again.

Colt instantly lifted her from the sofa. Throw pillows slid to the floor as he hurried from the room. Annabelle needed sleep, probably more than she needed to eat. But what the hell did he know about babies? Fussy babies at that.

As he headed through the kitchen and to the front of the house toward the diaper bag, Colt figured he was about to find out.

Annabelle woke with a start. She glanced around the large room surrounded by windows and filled with indoor plants. Then she recalled she was at Colt's house.

Her focus shifted to the sofa cushion beside her where Lucy had been. The pillow barrier had fallen to the floor.

Pushing her hair away from her face, Annabelle came to her feet and smoothed her shirt back into place. She had no clue how long she'd been out. The last thing she remembered was sitting down for a second and Colt leaning against the door frame. She'd wanted just a moment to relax before heading home.

After dropping the bomb about her personal life, she figured he'd be done with her, but apparently not. He said he wanted company, that he enjoyed talking with her. And she had to admit, as much as she hated owing him money, she enjoyed their talks, as well. Who was she kidding? She enjoyed more than their talks. She enjoyed the way her body tingled when he entered the room. Enjoyed the way his slightest touch fired up her every nerve ending. She only wished they'd gotten to know each other under different circumstances.

But this was the hand she was dealt. Unfortunately, she had no idea what card to lay down next.

Annabelle stepped up into the kitchen. Colt wasn't around. She headed through the wide hallway, not having a clue where he'd be. She wasn't worried, she knew Colt had a handle on Lucy or he would've woken her up. At least, she hoped that's what he would've done.

A wave of embarrassment swept over her. She'd obviously been even more exhausted than she'd first thought.

Glancing at a large wall clock at the end of the hallway, Annabelle realized she'd probably been asleep nearly an hour. She knew it had gotten later because the sun was setting, based on the pink and orange glow streaming in through the windows.

"Colt," she called out. She heard absolutely nothing as she peeked in various doors and headed down another hall.

When Annabelle stepped into the spacious living room, she stood in awe of an entire wall of bookshelves. The amount of cookbooks she could fill those with made her baker's heart speed up.

But she'd never be filling those shelves with anything. Pebblebrook wasn't her house. She'd do well to cling to the home she had.

As her eyes swept over the room, she stilled when her gaze landed on the set of patio doors leading out to the side yard. With the sun setting, the magical glow stretching across the horizon and cattle like little black dots in the distance, Annabelle's breath caught in her throat.

Colt stood beneath an old oak tree. He was cradling Lucy in one strong arm and feeding her a bottle. Annabelle had never witnessed a sexier sight than this man holding the child that had become her own.

Tears pricked her eyes as she gripped the handle of the patio door. She wanted to take in this moment, pretend that it wasn't fleeting. What would it be like if this were her home? If Colt wanted her for more than sex, more than her land?

He'd be an amazing father. Obviously he'd taken Lucy so Annabelle could sleep. How could that act of kindness not make her look at him a different way? How could she not find herself even more attracted to him?

But she was realistic. In just a few months, she'd have her debt paid off and he'd have no use for her. If she slept with him, well, she didn't know what would happen because she'd never been in that situation before. She obviously wasn't a casual-sex person, but nearly every part of her wanted to know what being with Colt would be like. She had a pretty good imagination.

Pulling in a deep breath and praying for strength where that man was concerned, Annabelle opened the patio door and stepped outside. When she started making her way across the yard, Colt turned and met her gaze. His smile nearly had her knees buckling. That man could do so much without ever laying a hand on her.

"I'm sorry I fell asleep on you," she told him as she drew closer.

"I won't take it personally." He glanced back down at Lucy who patted the side of her bottle with her chubby hand. “It got a little hairy when I was trying to hold her and read the directions on the formula can. I’m thankful you already had water in the bottle, so I hope I did everything right.”

Annabelle stepped closer, catching Lucy’s eyes. The instant their eyes locked, the infant smiled, milk streaming down the side of her mouth.

“Oops.” Annabelle laughed as she reached for the baby and the bottle. “She tends to get sidetracked easily.”

Colt swiped the dribble of milk from his forearm and shrugged. “I work with farm animals. I’m not afraid of a little formula on my arm.”

Annabelle took over feeding Lucy. She loved looking down into those green eyes. Loved seeing her sister’s reflection. For the past twenty-four years, Trish had been Annabelle’s best friend. At some point, she’d have to forgive her sister for her betrayal, but she wasn’t quite there yet. It was too fresh, too soon.

But raising her babies was easing the pain, it was bridging that gap even though her sister wasn’t there. Annabelle knew in time, she’d forgive Trish, because there was no way to care for those babies and still hold ill feelings.

“My sister and my fiancé were killed in a car accident.”

She didn’t know why she just blurted that out. Maybe she thought it would be therapeutic to get her feelings out in the open.

“They were seeing each other behind my back.” Okay, that didn’t make her feel any better at all. If anything, now she felt like a fool. “I didn’t know they were involved until the day of the accident. We got into an argument. My sister was crying, Matt was trying to justify their actions. Then they left and that was the last time I saw either of them.”

Colt took a step toward her, but Annabelle kept her gaze on sweet Lucy. She didn’t want to look up and see pity in Colt’s eyes.

"Annabelle..."

She smiled. "Now you use my name?"

"I'm sorry," he said, not a trace of humor in his voice. "I had no idea about this. I just knew your sister had passed away."

"It's crazy. For so long, I looked up to her, wanted to be like her. She was a wonderful mother to Emily and Lucy. I couldn't wait to get married and start my own family."

She'd have to wait a little longer for that. She had plenty of other things to get straightened out in her life first.

"After the wedding, I planned to come back here and get my business off the ground."

"What business?"

Annabelle shook her head, meeting Colt's worried gaze. "It's nothing."

He reached out, curling his hand around her shoulder. "It's something important enough to bring you back home."

It was everything. The dream her mother had had, the affection she'd had in her voice when she'd talk about opening the B and B, the people that would hopefully fill it and enjoy the beauty that Stone River had to offer.

"Tell me."

The command was delivered so softly, she knew he cared or he wouldn't pursue the issue.

"A bed-and-breakfast," she murmured, looking back down at Lucy. With the bottle nearly empty, Annabelle pulled it from Lucy's puckered lips and eased the baby upright. "It was a goal my mother had before she passed. She taught me how to bake, telling me that's what would be the heart of our business. People who came to stay with us would want good food. I couldn't wait to grow up and help her run the place. After she passed, I was nervous to do it all alone. But this past year, I got engaged and thought it was time to just go for it."

Holding Lucy on her hip, Annabelle looked out to the

horizon and forced her emotions down. She didn't want to break here, not in front of Colt.

"Over the past few months, these setbacks nearly destroyed me. But I know my mom wouldn't want me to give up, so I'm not. I'm doing all of this for her."

That last word came out broken as tears clogged her throat. Apparently she wasn't as strong as she thought.

"I don't know what to say," he murmured, squeezing her shoulder.

Annabelle turned her attention back to him. "There's nothing to say. Life sometimes has other plans for us. If I gave up each time I had a stumbling block, I would've thrown in the towel a long time ago."

Colt's bright blue eyes studied her and Annabelle wanted to know what was going through his mind. Did he see her as weak because she couldn't hold on to the life she'd wanted? Did he think she was pathetic because she had no real vision at the moment? Her life was in chaos and there was no clear picture in sight.

"You're one of the most remarkable people I've ever known," he stated.

Lucy tugged on Annabelle's hair and pulled some into her mouth. Annabelle eased the strands from the baby's clutches and pushed them behind her shoulders.

"Then you don't know too many people," she laughed.

Colt's hand trailed up to cup the side of her face. "I know people all over the world. None of them has half the tenacity for life that you do."

Such a compliment coming from Colt Elliott warmed her…as if she needed to be warmed in any more areas where he was concerned.

He leaned in, and Annabelle knew he was going to kiss her. She shifted Lucy slightly on her hip and tipped her head to meet Colt's lips. The gentle way he swept his mouth across hers while stroking his thumb along her jawline…yeah, that man was powerful without being forceful. He made her want things. Things that she would never have with him.

When he eased back, Annabelle knew she needed to go. If she stayed any longer, she'd start getting delusions that this life could be hers, that she could live on a sprawling ranch like Pebblebrook. That a man like Colt could fall in love with her. This wasn't a fairy tale. This was real life and she was crawling day after day to get hers back.

"I need to go," she stated, licking her lips to taste him once more. "Thanks for dinner."

He dropped his hand and stepped back. "I'm sure Winnie would love for you to come back again."

"And you?" She couldn't resist asking. "Would you love for me to come back again?"

Heat filled his eyes as he stared at her mouth. "I think you already know the answer to that."

Yeah, she did. And Annabelle knew if she came back for dinner, she would not be bringing a baby.

Twelve

Annabelle rifled through her purse before work the next morning. She needed a pen to jot down that recipe for Winnie, but she couldn't find one.

She also couldn't find the fifty dollar bill she'd had in there yesterday. She'd given her father some money for the store, and he'd put the change back like she'd told him to. She hated immediately thinking he took the cash, but she knew full well she didn't use it. Where had she been besides the barn, Colt's house and her house?

Dread filled her stomach.

Annabelle sank on the edge of her bed. She was going to have to confront him. She'd not only looked in her purse that had been on her bed, she'd looked all around the bed, beneath the bed, thinking maybe it had fallen out.

She should've known better than to leave cash around, but she'd sincerely hoped he was trying to be a better man, be the father she'd asked him to be.

Annabelle didn't know if she wanted to cry or throw her hands in the air and give up.

She grabbed her phone from the nightstand and texted Colt to tell him there had been an emergency and she'd drive herself over a little bit later. Shoving her phone in the pocket of her jeans, she cast a glance at Emily and Lucy, still sleeping in their cribs against the far wall. Both girls tended to wake once a night to eat and since they'd both gotten up at four and were wide-awake until six, they now opted to sleep in. Of course they fell asleep right when she needed to get ready to go to the farm.

The scent of coffee filtered up from the first floor—a sure sign her father was awake. She took a few minutes to compose herself before she went into full attack mode.

Pulling in a breath, Annabelle went downstairs and into the kitchen. Her father had his back to her as he poured himself a mug of coffee.

"Did you take money from my purse?"

His shoulders stiffened. "You gave me money for the store. I put the change back like you said."

The fact that he evaded her question told her everything she needed to know. Her heart sank—and her hopes weren't far behind.

"What was it this time, Dad? A ball game? A horse race? Online poker?"

Neil Carter dropped his head between his shoulders. "I'll pay you back. I know that investment will return—"

"It's not an investment, Dad," she all but yelled. "We have no extra money. I'm not only paying off this house, I'm trying to raise two babies now. When will you be a responsible adult? When will you see that this habit of yours is destroying us? Because it doesn't matter how much I want you to change, you have to want it, too."

Could he not see that this wasn't just about him or her anymore? Emily and Lucy needed them—they had no other family. No matter what happened with the farm, with the gambling, Annabelle vowed to hold strong. She would not fail those babies. She loved them like they were her own, and she wanted to honor her sister's memory, despite what had gone down in those final days.

Her father set the mug on the counter and turned to face her. "I do, Belle. It's just going to take time."

The subtle tap on her front door had Annabelle cringing. Colt. No doubt he'd shown up even though she told him she'd be late.

"Time is something we don't have," she whispered before turning away.

"Belle," he called after her.

"I have to go to work," she stated without looking back as she headed to the front door. "Someone has to hold this family together."

Considering she only had a few ones in her purse, she wasn't even bothering to take it. He could have her last dollar. What did it matter at this point? The money for the house wasn't even going through her hands. Colt was keeping her wages, so at least that was something. But she didn't have any extra and she knew she'd have to go to the store soon. Not to mention the bills would be coming due. Apparently, her father had no respect for such necessities as water and electricity.

Annabelle jerked the door open, causing Colt to jump back. She stormed past him, ignoring his questioning gaze. The sooner she got to the ranch, the sooner she could work out her frustrations.

"Hold up, sweetheart."

She whirled around on Colt. "Not today. Do not start with the pet names. I'm not in the mood."

The black hat shaded half of his face, but those eyes still managed to pierce her. "Care to tell me why you look like you want to kill someone?"

Annabelle closed her eyes and blew out a breath. "Not really. Just…get me out of here."

Colt opened his mouth to say something, but finally nodded. Annabelle turned and mounted Lightning before Colt got on behind her.

The instant his arms came around to grab the reins, Annabelle leaned back against his chest. She didn't care if this made her weak.

"Not a word," she muttered. "I just need this for a second."

"Lean on me all you want."

With a flick of his wrists, he set Lightning into a soft trot. Annabelle fought back tears. If her father didn't get his act together, she didn't know what they'd do. She couldn't pay off this house and keep them afloat if he was pilfering money. Annabelle had already hidden her mother's emerald ring. If her father found that, she hated to admit that he'd probably hock it.

"I was going to drive in a few minutes late," she told him after a bit.

"When you said emergency, I was afraid something was wrong with one of the girls. You didn't specify, so I went ahead and came anyway."

"I'm a mess, Colt. I'm more of a hindrance than help at this point."

He grasped the reins in one hand and wrapped his free arm around her waist, hugging her into his body. "Why this negativity? That's not like you."

"Just a morning dose of reality. And I haven't even had my coffee, yet."

She started to ease up when his arm tightened. "You're fine right here, darlin'."

"What did I tell you about the names?" she asked, the fight gone from her voice as she settled back against him.

"I think my nicknames are growing on you."

She couldn't help but smile. "Don't get too cocky."

They rode another moment in silence and her heart sank when they approached the barn. She could've kept riding, pretended nothing was going on in the world. For just a little bit she wanted to imagine her problems, her father's problems, weren't gnawing at her heels as she tried to outrun them.

"Something happen with your father?" Colt asked softly.

Annabelle sat up, mostly because if Josh or Ryan were in the barns, she didn't want them to see her nestled against their boss. Although she figured they knew something was up. It wasn't normal for a man to pick up a woman on horseback for work.

Funny how she'd not only gotten used to it, she actually looked forward to their rides.

"I'd rather not get into it," she stated as she focused on the stone building ahead. "What do you have planned today?"

"Something you've never done before," he promised. "You up for a ride on Genesis?"

"Sure. Anytime I get to ride is great."

Colt brought Lightning to a stop and dismounted before reaching a hand out to assist Annabelle. She let the touch linger. She'd take all the Colt she could get today.

"I left without grabbing a hat."

Colt patted Lightning as he looped his reins around the post outside the barn. "You won't need one today."

Confused, Annabelle blinked and crossed her arms over her tank. "I won't?"

"Nope. Go get Genesis ready. I'll meet you back here. I need to give some final orders to Ryan and Josh before we take off."

The man was intriguing, and she had a feeling that's exactly how he wanted to be seen. He wanted to keep her on her toes. Another reason she needed to be ready at all times for whatever he threw her way.

Colt didn't recall being nervous about anything in his life. He'd been angry and frustrated when Layla had left, he'd been hurt when his father slipped into a tragic state of mind and he'd been worried each time his brother Hayes was deployed. Even when his twin brother, Beau, had a movie opening in LA, Colt didn't have a bundle of nerves dancing in his stomach.

But today he was a mess. He was going to take Annabelle to a portion of the property that was rarely seen unless you specifically ventured back there. It was behind Hayes's house, stretching along the riverbank that ran on the edge of their property.

It was the most peaceful spot on the ranch. After Annabelle opened up emotionally at their dinner last night, he wanted to just relax with her. Forget the fact they were boss and employee. He wanted her to trust him.

Stupid of him really, considering his intentions hadn't changed one bit. But there was a part of him that wanted her to talk to him, to tell him her fears, her needs…her desires.

When he'd been in the yard feeding Lucy, Colt had been smacked in the face with a dose of reality. He did want a family, that wasn't news to him, but he wanted it sooner rather than later. Maybe his life didn't have to be in perfect order before he found someone to settle down with.

And he certainly wasn't saying he wanted Annabelle and the twins as his family. That would never work even if he'd had those thoughts. But holding Lucy just had him thinking and wondering if he could have it all and throw out the timeline he'd given himself.

Pushing his thoughts aside, he pulled out his phone and shot off a group text to Josh and Ryan. The edging around the landscaping needed trimming and the vet was due this afternoon to check on the steers once again. A fairly simple day, but Colt knew that not every day on the ranch could be predictable. Even if you had plans, sometimes livestock and Mother Nature had other ideas.

Just as he shoved his phone back into his pocket, Annabelle stepped out of the barn. Leading Genesis, she focused that bright green gaze on him. The punch of lust each time she looked at him never lessened. And to know she was untouched only made him ache for her even more.

How had someone so sexy, so damn passionate, gone all this time without giving herself to a man? More important, what type of man had been with her and not been able to pull out that desire? She practically dissolved in a puddle at his feet when he touched her, and he wasn't too proud to admit the feeling was mutual. She did something to him, something that made him want to possess her in a primal way.

"Where to, boss?"

He loved when she called him that. As if she surrendered to his power and fully accepted that he was in charge.

"Mount up and follow me."

He hated that he wouldn't reap the benefits of riding behind her, but she had no idea this little place even existed and he had to be the one to lead the way.

Colt pushed himself back up onto Lightning and set off to the east side of the land.

He called over his shoulder, "It will take us some time to get there, but I promise it will be worth the wait."

"No problem. I'm enjoying the view."

Colt sent her a wink. If she was going to flirt so blatantly, he sure as hell was going to return the gesture. He figured she was doing anything to forget what happened this morning with her father. Whatever had gone on, it must have been something major for her to be so angry when he'd picked her up. She seemed to want to stay mum about it so Colt would have to draw his own conclusions.

He just hoped like hell Neil Carter wasn't gambling again. Not now. Now when Annabelle was literally busting her ass to save his.

After about fifteen minutes, they reached Hayes's

house. It would be good to have his brother home for good. Colt only prayed he managed to adjust to being back and settling into civilian life.

"This is the house your father grew up in?" Annabelle asked.

"My grandfather had it built when he started ranching." Colt pointed to the old oak tree to the side of the house. "That tire swing has seen many years and every Elliott kid. It's just a neat location the way it's tucked between the river and the brook."

This house could tell stories. Colt figured one day Hayes would tear it down to rebuild, and Colt couldn't blame him, but he hoped he'd keep it and just put his home on another section of the ranch.

"I love this house."

Annabelle's wistful tone had him smiling. She appreciated the finer things, and he didn't mean expensive. She saw the beauty in everything. His ex, on the other hand, had had a taste for pricey, designer clothing, flashy cars, trips all over. He didn't mind pampering the woman in his life, but he expected he'd be her top priority…not his bank account.

"We can stop here." Colt made sure the horses were in the shade beneath one of the large oaks before looping the reins around the hooks. "We'll walk to the place I want to show you."

When he looked back, Annabelle was staring down at him, her head tilted in question. Colt crossed the distance between them and extended his hand.

"Trust me."

The two words were so simple, yet so complex, considering their relationship. She shouldn't trust him. She should hate him with every ounce of her being. He wished things were different, he wished she'd never come back into the picture because taking things from Neil didn't bother Colt's conscience one bit. But knowing he was going to take the land that was the foundation for Annabelle's dream…that twisted something inside of him that he didn't want to face.

Part of him couldn't help but wonder what his father would think. His dad had been determined to make this dude ranch a reality, but he was also a family man first.

Damn it. Colt couldn't think like that. He and Annabelle couldn't be more even if that's what he wanted. Once she discovered the truth, she'd hate him.

Annabelle slid her leg over the side of the horse and Colt gripped her waist to help her down. He stepped closer behind her, aligning their bodies perfectly.

"Is this why you brought me out here alone?" she asked, turning her face just enough for him see her half-grin.

"I've never brought a woman to my brother's house for sex." That much was completely true. "What I have to show you is in the back."

Without asking, he took her hand in his and led her around the side of the house.

"Oh, my word," she gasped. "It's beautiful."

The river curved around the property as if framing it with crystal clear water. An old stone outbuilding sat right on the riverbank at the edge of the property. The original stone wall ran along the edge of the property line.

"It's peaceful. I figured you could use some of that in your life."

Annabelle turned to face him fully, still holding on to his hand. "How do you know when I need anything? Dinner, a nap, a quiet place to relax. I'm going to get fired for not working if you keep this up."

He'd never fire her. And he wasn't sure he wanted to let her go at the end of this three-month period, either. She was a hard worker. Granted, she had her home as motivation, but he was going to hate to lose her.

And not just for the business. Cutting her out of his life would hurt and he'd have to learn to cope with the mess he'd made.

As Annabelle glanced back out onto the water, a strand of hair blew across her bottom lip, and before Colt could think better of it, he swiped it away. His fingertip grazed her mouth, sending a jolt of desire through him.

Her eyes swept back around and met his. "You did bring me out here to seduce me," she murmured.

Colt slipped his hand along her jawline, threading his fingers through her hair. "I didn't. But you've been seducing me since the moment you ran into my fence."

"I don't know what to do."

That whispered admission was the green light he'd been waiting for, the one he hadn't seen coming. But he sure as hell wasn't going to give her time to change her mind.

"Listen to your body," he told her, stepping into her. "What's your body telling you right now?"

A small smile spread across her lips. "That I want your shirt off again."

Colt laughed. "I can deal with that."

He tugged the shirt from his jeans and unbuttoned it, keeping his eyes on hers the entire time. Once he dropped it to the ground, he propped his hands on his hips. The approving once-over she gave him had him ready to rip off the black tank she wore. It was only fair.

"I've never known a man to look so hot in just a hat, jeans, and boots."

He didn't know what to say to that, so he slid his fingertips up her bare arms. "How slow do we need to take this?" he asked. "Because I don't want you scared and you deserve to get full enjoyment."

She shivered beneath his touch. "I'm enjoying this pretty well right now."

Oh, she was going to be so damn fun. His body trembled with need. He wanted this woman more than anyone he'd ever been with. He didn't know if it was the thrill of being her first or just the fact that this was Annabelle. Probably both. But he wasn't going to waste time in his head analyzing his every thought.

He had a woman to strip.

"Just…tell me if I do something wrong. Okay?"

Colt stilled. There was a hesitation to her voice that he didn't like.

"Are you sure about this?" he asked. "Because I don't want you to feel pressured. You have to want this as much as I do or we're done."

She reached down, tugged on the hem of her tank, and flung the garment over her head. Standing before him in a plain white bra and jeans with her hair around her shoulders, Colt had never seen a sexier sight.

"I'm nervous, but I know what I want," she told him. "So do what you want to me and I'll tell you if it's too much. Deal?"

Do what he wanted? Oh, hell yes, that was a deal.

Unable to wait another second, Colt slid his hands around the dip in her waist and tugged her until she was flush against his chest. Finally. Skin to skin. She was all curves and all his.

Colt captured her mouth and willed himself to slow down. He had an ache for this woman and he couldn't go into this like she'd been his every fantasy for days. He had to take his time, to make sure she got as much pleasure as he could possibly give.

Thirteen

Annabelle had never been so nervous and anxious at the same time. Colt's mouth magically moved over hers. There was an urgency in his kiss, yet she could tell he was restraining himself.

She eased her mouth from his and framed his face. "I'm not fragile. Don't hold back."

His eyes held hers for the briefest of moments before he picked her up. She couldn't help the squeal that escaped her. Instinct had her looping her hands behind his neck and wondering if he was shooting for romance.

This wasn't romance, though. This was nothing more than her finally giving in to a need she'd had for some time and it had never been stronger than with Colt Elliott.

For once, she was going to take exactly what she wanted, when she wanted it. Consequences be damned.

Colt carried her behind the house, his gait a bit off.

"Put me down," she told him.

"In a minute."

"You're limping."

He stopped, holding her so securely against him, and turned his focus to her eyes, her lips. "Sweetness, let me do this right."

Part of her wondered how many times he called other lovers by these names. He'd claimed none, but Colt was a natural charmer. Still, there was something that blossomed inside her at the idea that he only used those terms for her.

Annabelle closed her eyes and rested her head against his shoulder. What was she thinking? This wasn't the pivotal moment that would lead to a happily-ever-after for them.

Colt made her feel sexy and he wanted her. It was all that simple and that wonderful.

He started off again until he came to the riverbank. When he set her down, he nipped at her lips as if he couldn't get enough. Her chest rubbed against his and she couldn't help but arch against him.

"Wait right here," he muttered against her mouth.

He darted back around the house and Annabelle felt rather foolish standing there with her jeans, boots and bra. She waited a minute, wondering where he went, when he finally came back carrying the blanket that had been beneath her horse's saddle.

She couldn't help but laugh. "I figure you didn't plan this or you would've had something already set up."

"I really didn't plan this," he laughed. With a swift jerk, he fanned the blanket out over the ground. "But I'm damn sure not going to let this moment go."

When he turned back and raked his eyes over her, Annabelle had never felt such a jolt in her life. He may as well have touched her with his hands, his mouth. Anticipation curled deep in her stomach.

"Maybe you could help me undress, that would help." She went for the snap on her jeans. "Or maybe we should just—"

"No." Colt closed the space between them and eased her hands aside. "This belongs to me."

"Me, or getting me naked?"

He jerked the snap open, keeping his gaze on hers. "Everything."

Just as she processed his words, he reached behind her and flicked her bra open. Nerves fell away. Colt's intense stare, his passion and need, they all combined to make her forget she should be nervous. Ache replaced her anxiety and she wanted more.

Annabelle toed her boots off and watched as Colt reached for his belt buckle.

"Wait," she told him. "Shouldn't I get to return the favor?"

He shook his head with a laugh. "Honey, if you touch me right now, this will go faster than either of us wants."

"Maybe I'm ready for fast."

Where had that breathy voice come from? Was she seriously that girl? That flirty vixen? Apparently, with Colt she was another person, but this felt so right.

He slid his thumbs inside the waistband of her jeans. As his rough fingertips grazed her skin, Annabelle trembled. Colt jerked her pants down, pulling her panties with them.

When he dropped to his knees and removed the rest of her clothes, Annabelle pulled in a breath and willed herself to remain calm. She certainly didn't want to make a complete fool of herself right now. Between the ache and the nerves, she wasn't sure what to do, what to say.

But when she stood before him naked and Colt remained on his knees, sampling her with his heavy-lidded gaze, Annabelle knew for a fact that she held the control. He was giving her the reins, so to speak.

She dropped to her knees in front of him and curled her hands around his shoulders. "Touch me," she whispered.

Colt cursed his shaky hands. He finally had Annabelle naked before him and he was nervous. He'd never been nervous with a woman before, not even when he was a virgin. He'd always been about pleasuring his partner, being in control.

But with Annabelle, something was different. Something he didn't want to think about. He only wanted Annabelle, right here, right now.

Colt captured her mouth beneath his as he lowered her back to the blanket. Extending his arms to the ground, he caught himself before he could fully put his weight on her. Wrapping her slender arms around his neck, she threaded her fingers through his hair.

Colt pulled back, glancing down at the beauty laid out before him. He came back to his feet and quickly shed the rest of his clothes and boots. Annabelle's eyes roamed over his bare body. That passion he saw in her eyes only amped up his ache for her.

Despite the fact she told him to do anything, Colt had to have some semblance of self-control. He'd never taken an inexperienced woman before.

With her hair fanned out all around her, Annabelle reached for him. Colt grabbed his pants, pulled a condom from his wallet and covered himself. He dropped between her knees, took her hands in his, and stretched her arms above her head. She arched at the adjustment and it was all Colt could do not to devour her.

"You're driving me crazy," she stated through gritted teeth.

"At least I'm not alone," he muttered.

He used his knees to shove her legs wider. His free hand trailed up her inner thigh, instantly causing her to tremble beneath his touch. When he found her center, Annabelle's eyes drifted shut as she let out a moan.

Yes. That's exactly the response he wanted. Her hips tilted, urging him for more. He leaned down, placing his mouth on her stomach and trailing his lips up to her breasts. Her hands jerked beneath his grip as if she wanted loose from her restraints.

"Not so fast," he murmured against her heated skin. "I'm not done and you can't touch me just yet."

"I need…"

"I need," he agreed. "Too much."

So much, that he wasn't about to reveal everything on his mind. Hell, he wasn't even sure what he was thinking because he was trying *not* to think it.

When Colt removed his hand from between her legs, she let out a whimper. She was so ready and he…damn if he wasn't eager to show her what she'd been missing. He wanted to freeze that moment. To lock away this second of her staring up at him with such desire. He'd never felt so wanted before. Definitely not with…

No. He wasn't bringing any other woman into the picture, not even in his mind. Annabelle was perfection. She was his.

Everything else in the outside world didn't exist for him. Not the farm, not the potential dude ranch, not his brothers or even his father. There was nothing, no one but Annabelle.

Releasing her wrists, he placed both of his hands on either side of her face as he settled between her thighs.

"Tell me you're okay with this." Because if she wasn't completely on board, he'd stop. It would kill him, but she called the shots here. "You want me to keep going?"

"Don't even think of leaving me like this," she panted. "Finish what you started."

Music to his ears. Slowly, Colt joined their bodies. He kept his eyes on hers, waiting for a sign that she needed him to stop.

But her eyes merely widened as she bit her lower lip. Her hips jerked up to meet his and a low, sexy groan escaped her. Colt gritted his teeth. The agony of not claiming her the way his body needed to was excruciating. He wanted to gather her up and have her wrap those long, lean legs around his waist as he made her his.

Next time, he vowed. Because there would be a next time.

Annabelle lifted her knees on either side of him as she rocked her hips. "I told you not to hold back."

"I'm hurting you."

Her eyes held his as a smile danced around her mouth. "You're torturing me. I need this. I need you. Now move."

Colt nipped at her lips. "Whatever you say, sweetness."

"Don't—"

He crushed his mouth against hers as her arms looped around his neck. Colt quickened the pace, finally. He relished the sting of her fingertips on his skin. He wanted her to feel, to make him feel. They came together perfectly and she was certainly holding her own.

"Wrap your legs around me," he demanded against her lips. "Now."

As she circled his waist, locking her ankles behind his back, Colt pumped faster. Her little pants and whimpers spurred him on as she matched his rhythm.

"Colt."

"Right here, baby."

Her taut body beneath his trembled, then tightened. She tipped her head back and closed her eyes.

"Look at me," he commanded.

When that green gaze came back to his, Colt tried not to get lost in the depths there. Tried not to see exactly what was staring back at him, because it was definitely more than just sex. There were feelings. Feelings that he sure as hell didn't want to see.

Colt leaned down to run his lips along the side of her neck, across her chest. She cried out his name as her body stilled, her nails biting deeper into his shoulders.

Thrusting again, Colt shattered right along with her. This was exactly what he wanted, what he could control. All the feelings and emotions had no place here.

As her tremors ceased, Colt gathered her close, inhaling her jasmine scent. As much as his instincts told him to flee, he wasn't that big of a jerk. This was her time—he couldn't help if everything he saw in her eyes scared the hell out of him.

He prayed she didn't have some crazy notion that this meant anything more than just sex. He couldn't let her believe they had a future. Acting on their attraction had been inevitable, but he hadn't said anything up front about not getting involved. He had plans, damn it, and they didn't include getting wrapped up in those expressive green eyes.

But there was still that part deep inside him that could want more…with her.

Colt eased to the side, pulling her in his arms. He wasn't one to cuddle, but again, he wasn't about to be a jerk. He just needed to relax and consider his next step.

And that nugget of emotion circling his conscience could shut the hell up.

Fourteen

Colt was already having regrets.

Even though he hadn't said a word, he didn't need to. Annabelle lay against his chest, feeling his heart beat beneath her cheek and Colt was miles away—mentally at least.

His entire body was rigid and she knew he didn't want to be there. Didn't want to be holding her. The pity snuggle was not working for her and she refused to ever be made a fool of by a man again.

Annabelle sat up, causing Colt's arm to fall away. She smoothed her hair back from her face and attempted to radiate confidence she didn't feel. When it came to intimacy, she had zero experience, but her body was still humming… while he was silently stewing beside her.

If he was having regrets or doubts about what had happened, that was on him. Not her problem.

Coming to her feet, Annabelle purposely didn't look back at him. Bad enough she was walking around the riverbank retrieving her clothes, she didn't want to see guilt in his eyes.

What a fool. How could she think a man like Colt Elliott would actually want to be with someone like her?

He'd known exactly how to touch her, what to say, and just how forceful to be.

She'd relished every single moment.

Annabelle jerked her panties on, then wrestled back into her bra. Clutching her jeans to her chest, she whirled around to see him sitting up on the blanket watching her.

"If you're sorry this happened, just keep it to yourself."

Not a care in the world that he was as naked as the day he was born, Colt lifted a knee and propped an arm across it. "I'm not sorry this happened."

"Did I do something wrong?" she asked, heat flooding her cheeks. "Because you're not exactly giving off a vibe like you had a good time."

Like a panther, he rose and stalked toward her. "I had a good time, darlin'. I just didn't want you to get the impression that this meant more than what it was."

It took a second for his words to sink in, but when they did, rage boiled within her.

"Are you kidding me?" she asked, swatting her hand on his bare chest. "You think you show me a good time by the river on your family's property and I'm going to be head over heels in love with you? You do have quite the ego, Colt. I'm not going to start planning our wedding, so relax."

She hated to admit, even to herself, that she could see herself falling for him. She hadn't gotten there, yet, but it could happen. Still, the fact that he was afraid of it happening pissed her off. Like he was some gift to women because of his magical penis.

"Listen, if you have a problem, don't put it on me," she stated, still holding on to her jeans like a shield. "This wasn't what I expected when I left the house this morning, but it definitely got my mind off my problems."

"That's it?" he asked, one brow quirking. "You're glad I

could help you push aside your problems for a while? Don't downplay the joys of your first experience."

Strike one to that ego.

"The sex was great. Is that what you want to hear?"

He wrapped an arm around her waist and hauled her body to his. With his free hand he jerked her jeans away and flung them aside. That cool power and confident strength was too damn sexy.

"That's exactly what I want to hear."

Oh, that low tone could get her aroused in less than a second. And he knew it, too.

"We're going to do this again." He slid his mouth back and forth over hers as he spoke. "Whenever I can get you alone again, you'll be mine."

She had to grip his biceps to hold herself upright. "What makes you think I want to do this again?"

Colt eased his hand between them and palmed one of her breasts. His thumb raked back and forth over her thin bra. "Because I can have you squirming and panting in no time. And because we're not done with each other."

The moment was getting too intense and she needed to regain her composure. She patted the side of his cheek. "I'll let you have sex with me again, but if you go and fall in love, don't say I didn't warn you. I'm quite a catch."

The muscle in his jaw ticked as his eyes dropped to her mouth. She had no clue what was going through his head, but he clearly didn't like the idea of love. Well, that made two of them.

They dressed quietly and found their shirts around the front of the house by the horses. Colt threw her blanket back on Genesis before adjusting the saddle back in place.

As they rode back, all the issues awaiting her flooded her mind. If only life were as perfect as it had been moments ago on the riverbank. Annabelle couldn't even enjoy the euphoria because of the crap storm life had thrown her way.

Since her father was clearly gambling again, she had no idea how she was going to make everything work. He'd ring up more debts, and she'd have to bail him out. That was the cycle and she could only be stretched so thin. She knew gambling, as with any addiction, was a difficult habit to break. But she'd truly hoped losing a daughter and having to borrow money from the neighbor to pay off the mortgage would've slapped some sense into him.

Apparently not.

Annabelle's first priority was making sure Colt got every penny owed to him. She couldn't be her father's keeper and worry about his actions. "Once I get the house paid off, do you think I could continue to work for you until I find something else?"

Putting her pride aside was a bitter pill to swallow. The timing of her question was beyond tacky, but she had no shame at this point. She'd slept with her boss…what was the protocol?

"There's always work to be done on the ranch," he replied easily. "But I figured you'd want to take some time off to be with your girls."

Her girls. Yeah, they were hers. She'd come to think of them as her own and obviously Colt saw that, as well. And sure, in an ideal world where she wasn't broke she could take time off to spend with her family, but these weren't exactly typical circumstances.

"I've got too many bills to take time off."

Silence settled between them before he spoke up again. "Your father is gambling again, isn't he?"

Instantly, tears clogged her throat. She didn't want the world to know her father couldn't keep it together for his family. She despised that he was seen as weak and she resented having to clean up his messes. But the reality was, he had an addiction and she couldn't heal him.

"He took some money from my purse," she muttered, hating how saying those words made her heart ache—hating even more that she had to face the cold reality. "We argued about it this morning."

Great. She'd shared her body with him and now she felt it necessary to open her heart. She didn't want Colt, or anyone else, to know the details of her father's downfall.

She stole a glance at him, noticing his white-knuckled grip on the reins, the firm set of his jaw.

"Anyway, I've just got more on my plate than I'd hoped for," she went on. "But don't keep me at Pebblebrook out of pity. I'd rather be broke. Besides, I'm sure there are several places in town that are hiring. I worked at an upscale bakery before, so if I could do something along those lines, that would be—"

"You'll stay on at Pebblebrook as long as you want."

His low, commanding tone silenced her. Okay, then. At least that was something. It wasn't the position she dreamed of, but it paid and Colt understood her need to be near Emily and Lucy. If she could just get her bearings and keep her head above water, maybe she'd see the light at the end of the tunnel.

And maybe she'd quit thinking in cheesy clichés, as well.

"Tell me about your brothers," she threw out there. With all the intensity of the day, Annabelle needed normal. Just a simple conversation.

"I know their professions, but why don't they want to be cowboys like you?"

She kept her eyes on the horizon. Pasture as far as the eye could see. In the distance, the tip of the main barn near Colt's house guided their direction.

"Nolan loves the ranch," Colt stated. "He's swamped

with the hospital and he's always taking on more shifts. But he helps where he can."

"You have to be pretty proud of what all of your brothers have accomplished. And I'm sure they're proud of you for keeping all of this running so flawlessly. It's the greatest ranch I've ever seen."

Colt laughed. "I am proud, but it wasn't that long ago you were bashing me and praising them for being nicer and giving back to society."

A sliver of guilt spiraled through her. But, in her defense, that was before she'd developed feelings for Colt.

Oh, no. She was falling for her boss. Was *boss* even the correct term? Landlord? Virginity taker?

Regardless of the label, Annabelle's emotions were calling the shots and now she'd gone and slept with the man. But she wouldn't have been intimate with him if she didn't care for him. And she was starting to care. A lot.

"I think what you've done here at Pebblebrook is amazing."

His thigh brushed against hers as they rode side by side. "I can't take the credit for something my grandfather started and my father carried on."

"No, but you can take credit for keeping up the tradition and loving this land and these animals like they deserve."

She squinted against the sun and tried not to let that random touch throw her off. It was rather difficult to ride back to work like he hadn't just removed her wall of defense and changed her life. No matter what happened at the end of their agreement, or how long she stayed on at Pebblebrook, Colt Elliott would always be her first lover.

"If I owned this land, I'd never want to leave," she added. "It's so peaceful, so perfect."

"That's why I'm here," he told her. "I travel to get away, but I'm always eager to come back home."

As they neared the barn, Annabelle wondered how she

was going to be productive when her body still tingled. He'd blatantly told her that their encounter was not a one-time thing. Fine by her because she was more than ready to have that strong body pressed to hers again. When she'd pictured her first experience she'd been married, in a bed, wearing some sexy lingerie she'd purchased for just that occasion.

Instead, she'd been deliciously ravaged on a riverbank before her first cup of coffee.

"I like that smile on your face."

Colt's statement pulled her from her thoughts, and made her realize she had indeed been smiling.

"Makes me think you and I are both having the same thoughts," he added.

"I'm sure we are," she agreed with a slight laugh. "But right now I need to work so I can pay off the rest of my house. So, what are we getting into today?"

Colt's expression sobered. "Actually, I need to run an errand. I'm going to have you take it fairly easy today and clean out the stalls. I'll have Ryan pull down the extra hay from the loft."

"I can do that." How weak did he think she was? "I'm here to work, Colt. Stop coddling me."

He slowed Lightning down, so she pulled Genesis to a stop. When he tipped his hat up and flashed those killer baby blues her way, Annabelle's heart rate skyrocketed.

Is this how it would be each time he looked at her, now that they'd been intimate?

"I'm not coddling you, sweetness." He reached across and placed his hand high upon her thigh. "I don't want you worn-out because I have plans for you later."

Oh. That promise had her heart in her throat, her body responding. Yes, she was slowly falling for him when she had sworn she wouldn't. Sex clearly had messed with her mind.

"I won't be worn-out," she told him. "I'm sure Ryan has plenty to do without babysitting me and doing part of my job. I've got it covered."

A naughty smile crept over him. "If you're too tired, I guess I'll just get to do all the touching."

"Oh, I won't be that tired, cowboy."

And apparently sex made her a little saucier, too. Who knew?

Fifteen

Once Colt left Annabelle to take care of their horses and get to work, he sent a text to Ryan and Josh to check in on her throughout the day. She wouldn't appreciate it, but too damn bad. He couldn't worry about her and concentrate on this last-minute issue at the same time.

Colt drove a short distance from Pebblebrook and willed himself to calm down. He gripped the wheel, his knuckles turning white. There was too much anger, too much rage and guilt. That last one was on him, but the first two were on another man in Annabelle's life and Colt refused to sit back and watch her have to deal with more pain.

He glanced at the place that would soon be his and the guilt intensified. No, that was the sex talking. He was just feeling the aftershocks of having Annabelle wrapped all around him. He couldn't let those sultry eyes and passion-filled kisses deter him from reaching his goal. He would make sure she had a home, something nice and perfect for her business. But this one was perfect for this business he wanted.

Colt's anger still hadn't eased by the time he pulled up near the porch, but he would keep his head on straight, because Annabelle and her girls were the victims here.

Damn it. There was no way not to hurt Annabelle. But he could make the pain less intense.

He rang the doorbell and took a step back. After a minute, Neil Carter opened the old oak door, with the puppy right at his feet. He didn't offer to open the screen—as if that thin partition would keep Colt from business he had with the old man.

"We need to talk," Colt stated.

"Then talk."

He was going to be difficult. Colt didn't know why he thought this would be a simple trip. How could someone as sweet as Annabelle come from someone as cold and self-centered as Neil?

And there went that flare-up of guilt once again. Because Colt knew full well that he was self-centered...otherwise he wouldn't be so dead set on owning this property.

"I'm going to pay off your gambling debts," Colt announced. "Give me the names and contact information. And if I hear of you gambling anymore after that, I'll personally make sure Annabelle knows every last detail of how many times you've borrowed from my family over the years."

Neil crossed his arms over his chest, but before he could utter a word, one of the babies' cries sounded through the house. Neil turned from the door and marched away, the loyal pup on his heels. Colt wasted no time in letting himself inside. With his hand behind him, he caught the screen door before it could slam shut. The anxious puppy turned back around and ran toward Colt, sliding along the hardwood floors and bumping into the toe of his boot.

Colt reached down and petted the little guy and wondered if Annabelle had come up with a name yet. He'd ask her later, but right now, he had some unpleasant business to take care of.

Like any gentleman, Colt removed his hat and hung it

on the peg by the door, and then he proceeded to follow the cries into the living room. He walked slowly, careful not to trip or step on the bouncing dog.

Neil picked up one of the girls from some portable pen—Colt believed they were called Pack 'n Plays. They'd both been laying in their side-by-side, chewing on matching pink teethers.

Colt couldn't tell which twin Neil was holding, but he looked closely and thought it might be Lucy. One of them had thicker hair, but that was the only difference he'd noticed. Both girls were like mini-versions of Annabelle.

Lucy continued to whimper, but when she spotted Colt, she reached her arms toward him.

Okay. That was extremely unexpected. He'd held her the other night and fed her, but he didn't realize she'd already know who he was. Neil tossed a glance over his shoulder, reluctant to hand the baby over.

Colt stepped forward and took Lucy from Neil's arms. Her crying ceased as she sniffed and stared at his hair. He figured it was a sweaty mess between his morning activity on the riverbank and riding with his hat on.

"I see you've made an impression on my granddaughter, as well," Neil stated, clearly irritated. "And I don't need you or anyone else to take care of my debts."

"No?" Colt retorted, throwing Neil a sidelong glance. "Because as I see it, your daughter is busting her butt to pay off this house because you couldn't. And when my portion is paid back, she has to continue to work like a dog because she's still trying to save you and now raise twins on top of that."

Colt kept his tone somewhat light because he didn't want to scare the baby. One of her pudgy hands patted the side of his face and Colt couldn't help but smile at her. Those green eyes were going to bring a man to his knees one day.

"I don't need an Elliott taking care of my family," Neil growled. "And whatever you think you're doing with my daughter, she's smarter than to fall for your charms."

Colt wisely kept his opinion on that topic to himself.

"If you would man up, nobody would have to take care of your family."

Colt patted Lucy's back when she laid her head on his shoulder. The innocence of this child humbled him. One day he'd have a baby of his own, raise children on his ranch, and have a wife who shared his passion for the farm. A vision of Annabelle sprang to mind but he quickly vanquished it.

"So far, Annabelle is the only one working toward securing a future for all of you."

Neil's eyes narrowed. "What did she tell you?"

Oh, he wasn't throwing her under the bus. Hell, no. He was there to protect her from all angles…well, except his own agenda. That he couldn't help.

"She didn't have to tell me anything," Colt replied. "I can see how exhausted she is when she comes to the ranch. She gives it her all and then comes here to take care of you guys. There's only so much a person can take before they break and I won't see that happen to her."

"Is that so?" Neil crossed his arms over his chest and shifted his stance. "Why the sudden interest in my Belle? I won't have her hurt."

Something Neil should've thought of before he made the bargain with the Carter ranch and then signed documents he didn't fully read.

"You ever tell her about the jewelry?" Colt threw out.

"No," Neil ground out. "And you don't need to, either. That time has passed. I'm not proud of what I did."

"Passed?" Colt repeated. "You're telling me that you have completely stopped gambling? With no help at all?"

"How do you know I haven't had help?"

Colt merely raised his brows. Lucy's sweet breath tickled the side of his neck. From the steady rhythm, he'd guess she'd fallen asleep. What was it like to be so trusting and innocent?

Annabelle was exactly the same way. She'd trusted the wrong people: her father, her sister, her fiancé… Colt.

"Did you come here to berate me or just rub it in my face that you've gotten close with my daughter and granddaughters?"

"I came here so you'd realize what you have. You lost one daughter and your other one is here, ready to do anything to make her family work. Is that not enough for you to want to be a better man?"

Neil's lips thinned as he continued to glare at Colt. He didn't care if Neil was pissed, Colt was pretty much boiling since Annabelle had told him her father took money from her purse. Clearly, Neil had an illness, but Annabelle shouldn't have to endure the same struggle. She was trying to restore her life, yet she couldn't even move forward for worry over her father and his ongoing issues.

Damn it. He hadn't planned on getting personally involved. That plan obviously went to hell. Between that kick-ass attitude layered over vulnerability and her loyalty to her family, how could Colt ignore the tug of emotions Annabelle brought to life? But he couldn't allow those emotions to cloud his judgment.

His father had big plans, plans that Colt was to carry out. Colt always made good on his promises. With his father in the nursing facility, there was no way in hell Colt would let him down. Still, that niggle of doubt kept creeping up on him lately. Grant Elliott had always prided himself on being a family man first and foremost. Colt wanted that family life, but he couldn't sacrifice his promise to his father…could he?

If he'd met Annabelle under different circumstances,

gotten to know her, date her...but he hadn't. There was nothing but sex between them and when she found out about the legal documents, that would be gone. Even so, Colt would make sure she was taken care of.

Neil closed the distance between them and eased Lucy from Colt's arms. Lucy was indeed fast asleep, while Emily remained fully entertained across the room. Neil cradled Lucy against his chest and stared down at her.

"I'm doing what I can," he murmured. "And after this debt is paid, we won't need your help anymore."

Colt wasn't about to argue. He'd made his point and if Neil didn't want help, then so be it. But that didn't mean Colt wouldn't look out for Annabelle and her babies.

He let himself out the door and climbed back into his truck. He was on borrowed time where Annabelle was concerned. He couldn't go against his family and decades of wishes. Maybe on some level, she would understand that.

Regardless, he wanted her again. He wanted to see her, to touch her. He had a feeling today's workday might just be cut short.

Annabelle swiped the sweat from her forehead with the back of her arm. Ranch life was no joke. No wonder Colt had muscles like that of a calendar model. He'd earned each and every taut bulge.

Finally, the stalls were clean. As if anything in this immaculate barn was ever dirty. Still, she took pride in her position, in the animals. They were such beautiful creatures and deserved to be treated as such.

As she pushed the broom down the stone walkway between the stalls, familiar arms banded around her waist. Instantly she found herself hauled back against a broad chest.

"Sir, I'm working here and there are other employees that could see us."

"Those employees are nowhere near this side of the property and your boss sent me to find you," Colt whispered in her ear. "He said it's time for you to call it a day and meet him at the main house."

Annabelle dropped the broom and turned in his arms. "It's only two o'clock."

Colt shrugged. "Boss's orders, ma'am."

He stepped back and winced slightly. Annabelle reached for him, but he held his hands out.

"It's nothing," he assured her. "I've been riding more than usual and not soaking at the end of the day like I should."

"And you talk about me taking care of myself?"

"Touché."

"Seriously, I need to work. I've only put in about four hours today."

Colt shot her that side grin that never failed to curl her toes. Stupid charming man. Why did she have to be so easily swayed by a dashing smile and a sexy body? Hadn't she learned her lesson the first time a hot guy showed her attention? She'd ended up with his ring on her finger. That incident left her scarred, hollow. But Colt was different. He was loyal to those he cared for.

Never in her life would she have thought that she'd be half in love with an Elliott. Who knows, after this debt was paid off…maybe they could date and see where things went. She wasn't going anywhere and he obviously wasn't, either.

"This will count as a full day's work. You've earned it."

Annabelle reached down to pick up the broom and leaned against it. "Let's say I come up to your house."

"Which you will."

She bit the inside of her cheek to keep from smiling at his confidence, which made him too damn irresistible for his own good. "Let's say that I do. What about Winnie and Charlie? Where are they?"

Colt shrugged. "I'm not positive. I imagine Winnie is in the kitchen preparing some feast for the guys. Charlie is actually out at a ranch in Calhoun County because we're hoping to do some business with them. I sent him because his daughter knows the family there."

Annabelle weighed her options. If her tingly body would shut up, she'd be able to think a little clearer.

"So what do you tell Winnie when I come up to the house and…"

"To my bedroom?" he asked, quirking a dark brow beneath his black hat. "She'd probably throw a party, but to save your reputation, I can sneak you in the back door. She'll never know you're there."

He made things sound so simple, so perfectly tempting. Colt Elliott's bedroom was only a "yes" away and she stood here contemplating her move. What woman did that?

A woman who'd been burned and was falling in love.

Just that morning she'd made some grand speech on the riverbank, naked as a jaybird, about how she wasn't going to fall for him and he had nothing to worry about.

Liar, liar. It had only been a few hours and she'd analyzed their situation to death. He wanted her land, she wanted him. That pretty much summed up their crazy status in a nice, neat, jam-packed package.

"If you have to think that hard, maybe I didn't do my job earlier today."

Oh, he'd done his job…if his job was to make her fantasize about him all day and watch the opening of the barn for that familiar silhouette. Every time an animal shifted or she heard something, she'd jerked her gaze to that wide-open bay. It was rather schoolgirlish how quickly she'd become infatuated.

Was it the sex? She truly didn't think so. She'd been

turned on and intrigued by him since day one, when he'd been nothing but a shirtless stranger.

"Maybe you should show me again just as a reminder," she said, pleased when his bright eyes darkened with arousal.

Good. She wanted to affect him the way he did her. She hoped he thought of her today when they were apart. And, no, she didn't care if that was naive. She had to be honest with herself, if no one else.

"Where did you go today?" she asked.

Colt lifted one broad shoulder. "My day wasn't near as important as my afternoon is about to be."

Sixteen

Colt didn't bring women back to his home, and he sure as hell didn't sneak them through the back door and into his bedroom. The entire third floor made up his domain. He had a balcony off the front and back so he could see the acreage which had been handed down to him…which had been entrusted to him.

So the fact that Annabelle now stood staring out through the back double doors had Colt stilling in the middle of his suite. That long, red hair spiraled down her back. She typically kept it up, but sometime between their morning activities and now, she'd let it all down. He preferred it down, preferred it between his fingers and sliding over his skin.

"I don't know how you ever leave this room in the mornings. I bet the sunrises are amazing."

It was on the tip of his tongue to invite her to see it sometime, but that would require a commitment he couldn't make. Still, he could see it. Annabelle in one of his T-shirts and nothing else, standing just like she was now after a night of lovemaking. He was certain it was an image he would return to long after he revealed the truth and she cut him out of her life for good. Why was that thought becoming more and more agonizing?

Annabelle spun around, her hair dancing about her bare shoulders. She did amazing things to tank tops.

"I should warn you that I've been in horse stalls all day." She wrinkled her nose and damn if it wasn't the most adorable thing he'd ever seen. "I'm not sure what you got into, but you still seem fairly clean, like your deodorant is still working."

Colt laughed. He did that more with her than he had in years. She was unaware of her appeal, she spoke her mind and she was a hard worker. How could a man not find that charming and sexy?

"You're in luck," he told her as he crossed the room. "I happen to love the smell of my ranch."

She rolled her eyes. "You're really a terrible liar."

Actually, he thought he was a stellar one…which was where that guilt kept creeping in from.

He took her hands in his and squeezed, pulling her against his chest. "You're also in luck that I have a shower built for twenty with jetted sprays and three rain heads."

She raised her brows. "A shower? You mean…you're going to shower in the middle of the day?"

"With you," he added, with a smile as her mouth fell open and her eyes widened. "You need to clean up and I need the heat on my hip. It's a win-win."

"I've never…I mean, that just seems so intimate and…" She narrowed her eyes. "Are you laughing?"

Colt pursed his lips and shook his head. "Not at all."

"Terrible liar," she muttered.

"Then maybe I should use my mouth for more important things."

Before he could ease forward, she took a step back and let go of his hands. "Seriously, Colt. I'm not feeling very attractive right now."

Heat speared him. "You spent the day working on my

ranch, tending to my animals. That's the sexiest thing I've seen in a long time."

She tipped her head to the side, her eyes softening. "You take so much pride in this place. It shows."

"It's my life," he stated simply.

When a sadness swept over her features, Colt wasn't having any part of that. Not here, not now, when he wanted her with a need he couldn't even identify.

Reaching behind his back, he jerked his T-shirt up and over his head. There. That's what he wanted to see. Annabelle's eyes locked on his bare torso. Needing to keep her in the moment, he went for his belt buckle.

"If you really want out of those smelly clothes, you could remove them," he suggested.

Her hands shook as she reached for the hem of her tank. Even after this morning she was nervous, or maybe in spite of it. Colt figured she knew exactly what to expect now and fear was getting to her.

Damn it. That was worse than seeing her slip into unhappiness about her current life situation.

"Tell me what you want, sweetheart." He toed off his worn boots and shucked his jeans and boxer briefs. "I'm here for you."

Annabelle finished undressing until she was standing before him just as bare as he was. "I want to see this promised shower that will fulfill my every need."

Colt reached out, snaking an arm around her to pull her into his body. "That would be my job. You have a need, I'll be the one meeting it."

"You might want me to rinse off before you join me," she stated, placing her hands on his shoulders.

Colt turned her toward his bathroom and smacked her rear end. "I'll be the one to wash you, darlin'. Now let's go."

* * *

Annabelle's jaw dropped. "This should have another name besides something so simple as a shower."

The walk-in area could indeed hold twenty, she was positive. His bathroom was the size of her entire living room. The all-glass shower with glass tile floor was something from a magazine, as was the rest of his home. How was she ever going to just move on like none of this ever happened?

Colt stepped inside and turned on all the various sprayers. Good grief. Who thought up such necessities? And this was a necessity. She'd give up nearly anything to have a shower like this one.

Annabelle followed him inside and instantly groaned at the glorious heat spraying her from all angles.

"Okay, now I know for sure I'd never leave this room if I lived here. The shower, the view. If I could get food delivered, this would be my very own domain."

"Winnie would be more than happy to—"

She whirled around, shoving her wet hair back from her face. "Winnie will not know I was here in the middle of the day."

Colt laughed as he reached for her. "I'm a bit sore, so you may have to take the lead."

Wrapping her arms around his waist, Annabelle was surprised how easy this felt. How right.

But it wasn't right, was it? He wanted her land, she wanted to fulfill her mother's dream. So they were at a standstill.

"Tell me what to do," she murmured, focusing on the here and now.

Colt grazed his lips along her jawline and up to her ear. "Listen to what your body wants. I guarantee it will match what mine is telling me."

She went up onto her toes to kiss him. Curling her

fingers around his shoulders, she backed him toward the bench running along the back wall. His mouth devoured hers and it was all she could do not to climb all over him.

Everything between them had escalated at an alarming speed, but she couldn't stop…didn't want to stop. Colt had becoming a craving and she wasn't going to deprive herself. She deserved happiness, even if it was only temporary.

Annabelle eased her mouth away and pushed on Colt's shoulders, silently urging him to have a seat. As he sat, he raked his hands down her sides, grazing her breasts as he went.

She stepped back out of his reach and glanced around. She spotted the soap and shampoo on the built-in shelf on the adjacent wall. An idea sparked and then fully engulfed her mind. She was going to be daring and seductive, she hoped. If she could drive him out of his mind half as much as he had done to her, this afternoon shower session would be a success.

Annabelle grabbed the shampoo and squirted some into her hand. As she lathered her hair, she made sure to get a good arch in her back, thrusting her chest in Colt's direction…and she was pretty sure she'd heard a groan escape him.

Tipping her head back, she rinsed the shampoo away, suds gliding down her body. She shot him a wink and a smile as she went back for the soap. With no washcloth in sight, she squeezed some soap into her hands and lathered them up before sliding it over her arms, her legs, her torso.

Each slow stroke was like torture. She wanted his hands on her, but the way he was squirming on that bench, his piercing gaze locked on her every move, Annabelle knew it was only a matter of time before he snapped.

Anticipation flooded her.

"Enough."

Colt's harsh demand had Annabelle jerking around to

face him fully. His body was tight, shoulders squared, jaw set, and those eyes held hers as if he'd reached out and touched her.

"Come here."

Water hit her from all around as she made her way back across the shower. Annabelle came to stand between his legs, and his hands instantly gripped her waist.

"I think you're clean enough for what I have in mind."

Arousal spiraled low in her belly.

"I didn't bring any protection in here with me," he told her. "But I've never gone without and I guarantee I'm clean."

Even though she'd been a virgin up until this morning, she'd been on birth control since she was twenty.

"I'm safe," she assured him.

His eyes darkened as he raked them over her bare chest, her torso, between her thighs. As his gaze traveled back up, she shivered and braced her hands on his shoulders. Colt urged her forward and she placed her knees on either side of his hips.

"I want nothing between us," he muttered.

Slowly, Annabelle joined their bodies. At the onslaught of sensations, her head fell back. Colt reached around, gripping her wet hair and pulling just enough. Her body went into action as she couldn't stay still another second.

As he tugged on her hair, his mouth closed over one breast and Annabelle didn't know how long she could hold out. The sprays hit her from the back, the side, and Colt's hands and mouth were assaulting her in the most delicious ways.

"That's it," he urged.

Apparently he knew her body better than she did because she instantly tightened around him as pleasure tore through her.

Colt flattened his palms against her back, captured her

mouth and crushed her entire body against him as if he wanted to completely absorb her. The tip of his tongue parted her lips, and everything inside Annabelle exploded. Colt stiffened beneath her as he tore his mouth away and rested his forehead to hers. His fingertips dug into her back as his own release consumed him.

Moments later, when the trembling had ceased and the water continued to caress them, Annabelle kept her eyes closed. She didn't want to face reality. She didn't want Colt to look in her eyes because of what he'd see. She'd fallen for him. Completely. She had no idea how she would continue to work for him and keep this secret.

But she had no choice. They were on opposite ends of life's spectrum and he'd made it clear that this was nothing more than sex. Too bad her heart didn't get that memo.

Seventeen

"I was engaged before." Colt laid that declaration between them as they dressed after the shower. "You're the only other woman I've ever had in this house."

Annabelle squeezed her hair into a plush towel, but her eyes remained on his. "I didn't think you were a monk, Colt. Besides, this is just physical, right? I don't need to know your history."

Wearing only his jeans, Colt crossed the spacious bathroom until he stood before her. He pulled the towel from her hands, grasped her hair, and proceeded to rub the dripping ends of crimson.

"I believe we both know this escalated into more than just sex." As much as he didn't want it to, and as much as these damn emotions complicated everything, there was no denying the fact that Annabelle had gotten to him. "I don't know what to call it, or if we even need a label, but I like being with you even outside the bedroom."

"Like on a riverbank?" she asked, a half smile curving over her swollen lips.

Tossing the towel aside, he curled his fingers around the back of her neck and brought his forehead to hers. "Everywhere. I like you in my barns, on my horses, the way you look at my land. I just, I don't know how to explain it all."

Annabelle looped her arms around his neck. "I've only really known you for less than a week," she stated. "I knew Matt for a year, was engaged to him, but I never felt like this."

His ego, which she'd claimed was inflated, grew even more at her words. Warmth spread through him, knowing that there was a strong undercurrent of emotions running through her, as well. But how the hell did he go about this without totally screwing everything up? How did he keep the land and the woman once all was said and done?

Maybe she never had to know about the documents. Perhaps now that their connection was growing deeper, he could use that momentum.

This was crazy. One of the most reckless decisions he'd ever made, but in order to have it all, it was his only option.

Colt framed her face, tipping her head up so he could see those gorgeous green eyes. "Move in with me."

Her chest pressed against his as she pulled in a gasp. That unpainted mouth dropped into a perfect O. He wasn't going to give her a chance to turn him down.

"You can take your time finding a job you like or keep working at Pebblebrook," he went on. "I don't care. But I want you here in my house, in my bed."

"But...but I have six-month-old twins," she muttered, as if thinking aloud of reasons she shouldn't agree.

"I didn't expect you to come alone. There's even plenty of room for your dad if he wants to join us. I have eight bedrooms on the second floor. The master is plenty large enough for cribs."

What was he saying? Was he really willing to play house to ensure that her land remained his and she would never know what he'd done?

Yes. And in his defense, some of his motives were completely selfish, but he truly wanted to spare Annabelle any more hurt. She'd been through so much, too much, and all at the hands of people she'd trusted.

And she trusted him with the most important aspect of her life. No way could he betray her now. Seeing her in pain, knowing he'd caused it, would be like a knife to his heart.

She closed her eyes and blew out a sigh. "Colt, this is all so much to take in. I don't trust my feelings right now."

Colt took her hand, placed it over his bare chest and flattened it with his own. "You feel me, feel us. I'm not asking for anything more than you to live here and give this a shot."

"I'm adjusting from so much," she whispered, tears pricking her eyes. "I lost my sister, a man I thought I trusted. My finances are a joke and I'm learning how to be a mom."

"All the more reason for you to come here. Finances will never be an issue." Colt would make it his personal mission to keep her father out of trouble. "And Winnie would be happy to help you care for the girls. In fact, she'd love it."

"And you?" she asked, her eyes hopeful.

"I've always wanted a family and kids." That was absolutely true. He just never thought they'd land in his path like this. "This place was made for children."

"You want kids of your own?" she asked, then shook her head. "That was a silly question. You asked me to move in, not bear your children."

An image of her pregnant with his baby ripped something open in him. Yeah, he did want children and if he had them with Annabelle, he knew they'd be strong-willed, independent kids who could take on the ranch in the years to come.

Was he…no. He wasn't falling in love. Was he?

He'd vowed to keep deeper emotions separate, but that

simply wasn't possible anymore. Still, she couldn't find out about the paperwork her father signed. Colt refused to be the one to destroy her life once again.

"I don't want to get hurt."

She blinked back her tears, and Colt knew in that moment, he'd do anything to keep her safe.

And he also knew then that he had fallen for her. How had this happened? Within days he'd gone on such a roller coaster ride of emotions with her, Colt didn't know when his control had started to slip.

Perhaps all of his power transferred over to her the moment she plowed into the fence and stared at him as if she wanted to mount him right in his driveway. Because from the start, Annabelle had held the proverbial reins. She'd pulled him into her world and he knew now that he wanted to stay.

"If you need to think about it, that's fine," he told her, knowing someone like Annabelle didn't make rash decisions. "I'm not going anywhere."

"I need to pay off my father's debt," she told him. "How would we work that out? I mean, I'd feel a little weird paying you and sleeping in your bed. Assuming that's where you'd want me."

Colt wrapped his arms around her waist, filling his hands with her backside. "My bed is the only option for you."

When she went up onto her toes and covered his lips with her own, Colt knew she'd already made her decision. She may not have voiced it yet, but she would.

He would have everything he wanted and nobody had to get hurt. A burst of relief spread through him as he captured her lips, but a shrill ring from the bedroom broke the moment.

Annabelle pulled away and rushed in to answer the call. Colt grabbed his shirt and pulled it over his head.

"I'll be right there."

He noticed Annabelle's worried tone as she slid the cell into her pocket. "I have to go," she told him.

"What's wrong? Is it the girls?"

She shook her head, glancing around the room for her boots. Pulling one from beneath the bed skirt and one from the other side of the bed, she hopped on one foot then the other to pull them on.

"Dad didn't say. He just said he needed me home right now."

Fear pushed through him as he grabbed his own phone from his dresser and followed her out of the bedroom. They hurried out the back door of the house, just the same way they'd come in. Silence accompanied them as he drove her back home in his truck.

Colt had barely pulled to a stop in front of her porch when he recognized the silver SUV in the drive. His heart sank.

"Annabelle, wait."

But she was already out of his truck and running toward the door. That future he'd just secured only moments ago in his bedroom was about to blow up in his face.

And that vow to keep Annabelle from getting hurt by his actions? Well, he was getting a front row seat to an epic debacle and there wasn't a damn thing he could do about it.

"What's wrong?" Annabelle asked the second she stepped through the front door. "Where are the babies?"

She took in so much at once. Her father stood in the middle of the foyer with a stranger. The puppy was bouncing between everyone like he'd just found new friends.

"I just laid them down for a nap," her father replied. "It seems this engineer was hired by Colt to do some work on the house."

"I'm only here to take a quick look around," the stranger

replied as he turned his attention toward her. "My name is Sam Stevens. I work for the Elliott family. They gave me this address and I just came to do a quick survey. I wasn't aware people were living here."

Confusion settled deep as she tried to grasp what was happening. And all of this was on the coattails of Colt asking her to move in with him.

Annabelle crossed her arms over her chest and addressed Sam. "What exactly did Colt ask you to do here?"

The engineer had a clipboard in his hand and held it up for her to see a long list of items. "Various renovations. But I can come back at a better time."

"We don't need you to come back," Neil chimed in.

"I'll take care of this."

Annabelle turned to see Colt standing in the doorway. She was still perplexed at why this man was here, but the guilt written on Colt's face painted a clearer picture.

"Sorry, Mr. Elliott." Sam tapped the clipboard against his side, drawing the puppy over to his feet. "When we talked the other day, I figured you were ready to move forward with this project so I wanted to come out and get your estimate—"

Colt held up a hand, cutting the man off. "I appreciate your work. But for now, let me handle this. I'll be in touch."

Annabelle watched as the engineer nodded obediently, then sent her and her father an apologetic smile. Once he was gone, her father scooped up the rambunctious pup.

"Let me put him out back and then I want to know what the hell you're doing, Elliott."

Annabelle watched her father walk away, not wanting to glance back to Colt. She didn't want to know the truth, didn't want her fears to come to life. Surely he wasn't the monster she was imagining right at that moment.

"Darlin'," he began.

She held up a hand. “No. Don’t start that. Tell me what that man was doing in *my* house.”

The muscle in his jaw ticked as he raked a hand over the back of his neck. His hair was still damp from their shower, as was hers. She jerked the band from her wrist and pulled her hair back into a loose bun. Only a short time ago she was in his arms, coming apart, and then he was opening up to her about his feelings, his hopes for a future with her.

And now he stood before her a total stranger.

“Sam works for me.”

“We got that,” her father said, coming back to stand next to Annabelle. “What the hell was he doing here on your orders?”

Annabelle watched as Colt waged a war with himself. Her stomach tightened as she leaned against the banister on the staircase for support. She met his gaze from across the foyer. “The truth, Colt.”

“I was going to have some work done on the house to get it up to the standards I needed.”

A piece of her heart broke, fell at her feet and shattered.

“Because?” she asked, thick emotions welling up in her throat.

“Because this house is going to be part of my dude ranch.”

“The hell you say?” Her father was on the verge of exploding. “I paid off my loan to the bank and this house is mine.”

Colt cleared his throat, his chest puffed out as he drew in a breath. “Actually, the house and the land belong to me.”

“What?” Annabelle gasped. “How is that possible? I’ve worked myself to death for the payments coming due.”

Honestly, she didn’t want to know the answer. He’d deceived her. He’d lied to her face, made a joke of her and she’d given him her virginity. How naive could she be?

Baby cries echoed over the baby monitor in the living room. She'd come to tell them apart and this was definitely Emily. Annabelle turned toward the steps, but her father held up a hand.

"I'll go." He threw a glance to Colt before turning back to her. "See what this mess is all about."

Once they were alone again, Annabelle sank onto the steps. The fight was leaving her. She'd been hit so hard, so often lately, she wasn't sure she could keep standing for the final knockout.

"Just tell me," she stated as she wrapped her arms around her knees.

"I want to explain why—"

"No." Annabelle held up her hand. "I don't care about the why. That part is obvious. You're a selfish bastard, only looking out for your family, your precious land and not caring who you hurt in the process."

"Yes. That was the case at first. But then you came into the picture."

Annabelle laughed. "Seriously? That's the route you're going to take for the defense? You were dead set on having my childhood home, but then you saw me and the error of your ways shone bright. Am I close?"

Suddenly she felt like fighting. The burst of anger surged her to her feet. It felt good, and kept the hurt at bay. "So let's hear it. How do you own this? Because when you gave Dad the money, he paid the bank. Now we owe you and he signed a paper with you… Oh, no. What did he sign?"

Any minute she'd wake from this nightmare.

Colt took a step toward her, but she held out both hands. Emily's cries echoed once again over the monitor, along with her father's soothing words. This house meant everything to her and she wasn't about to let Colt take it away. Surely there was something she could do.

"When he asked for the money to pay off the loan, I offered to buy the place for more than market value, all cash. He turned me down. So when I gave him the money to pay off the loan, I had everything put in writing. My attorney drew up a document stating the amount due back and how it should be split into payments."

Annabelle shook her head. "Wait. Why would Dad come to you for the money anyway? I've wondered that from the beginning."

When he hesitated and glanced away, she threw her arm in the air. "Oh, come on. It's a little late to protect me now, isn't it? You've taken everything from me, just say it."

Colt dropped his head between his shoulders and stared down at his worn boots. "That's not the first time I've loaned him money."

She couldn't have heard him right. "What?"

"He's borrowed before," Colt stated, bringing his bright gaze up to hers.

"And…has he paid you back?" she whispered.

Colt shook his head. "That's how I knew I could have this place. He was so desperate for the money, he didn't read what he signed. It states that after the debt is paid back to me, I will be the sole owner of your property, the house, and all outbuildings."

The wind literally was knocked out of her as if he'd punched her in the gut. She reached out, placing a hand on the newel post, and looked out the window toward the large oak tree in the front yard.

How could this day be so bright and sunny when inside her heart was black and stormy? There was nothing left. She literally had nothing but a gambling father and two babies depending on her.

"Annabelle."

"Don't say my name. Don't talk to me and don't ever touch me again." She jerked and took a step backward.

"You made a fool of me. You used me on your ranch, worked me like one of your minions, purposely seduced me and made me feel…I hate you for that most of all."

Dampness tickled her cheeks, and she swiped the backs of her hands across her face. "Get out. Get the hell out so I can figure out what to do now."

The harsh reality slapped her in the face. "I can't order you out of your own house, can I? Damn it. Can you at least give us a few days to find someplace to go? We need to pack…and my mother's things are in the attic…her dishes, where will I store all of that?"

She was thinking out loud, muttering really, because she certainly wasn't talking to the devil disguised as a cowboy.

"You can stay here," he told her. "I wasn't going to just kick you out. I will buy you someplace to stay. You can pick it out."

Tears flooded down her cheeks and she didn't even care at this point. Pride be damned. She had nothing left to lose.

"I don't want a thing from you," she growled. "I don't ever want to see your face again. I don't want to hear your name. We'll be out by Friday. Tell your precious engineer he can return then."

He continued to stare at her, and she had to be hallucinating because she could've sworn she saw pain in his eyes. But men with cold hearts and no souls didn't hurt.

"Everything that happened between us was real," he told her. "I have feelings for you and I wanted you to move in so we could try—"

"So I wouldn't find out what a lying jerk you are?" she asked, another realization hitting her square in the chest. "My eyes are wide-open now. You only wanted me at Pebblebrook so I wouldn't learn the truth. But you got your wires crossed with one of your minions, exposing you for the worthless man you are."

Why did looking at him hurt so badly? Those blue eyes

that had captivated her for days, held her when they made love…

No. They hadn't made love. They'd acted on their attraction and used each other for sex. Nothing more. No matter how much she thought she'd been in love with him.

"I care for you," he told her, and his tone might have been convincing had she not known the truth. "I want you happy, I want to help your family. Let me find you another house."

A humorless laugh escaped her. "I'd think you of all people would understand the importance of family tradition and loyalty. I don't want another place and I most definitely don't want you paying for it. I'd live on the street before I took a dollar from you."

It may come to that. But she'd figure something out. An inexpensive apartment in town could always serve as backup.

"Annabelle—"

"Leave, Colt. You've got the house, the land. That's what you wanted, right?" She bit down on her quivering lip and swallowed. "You have everything now."

His eyes misted. "Not everything."

Then he was gone, leaving Annabelle to sink back to the steps. After all the fighting, all the hurdles she'd jumped, she had been defeated by a man she'd fallen for in a whirlwind affair.

Her broken heart would have to wait. Right now, she had a house to pack and a future to try to piece back together…a future without any dream coming true.

Eighteen

Colt slammed his office door and cursed the moment he'd decided to back Neil Carter into a corner.

The land was his. The debt wasn't fully paid, but the end result was inevitable since Neil signed the papers. For years Colt had dreamed of this moment. He'd waited for the day when he could tell his father that they had secured the land next door and were ready to move forward with Pebblebrook Dude Ranch. The extra home and barns would be useful space. Added to that, the other property carved into the corner of Pebblebrook and now their ranch would be complete.

But instead of texting his brothers the news or rushing to the nursing home to tell his father, Colt went straight to his bar and poured himself a tumbler of bourbon. He downed it, welcoming the familiar burn.

Getting drunk wouldn't solve a thing. It sure as hell wouldn't turn back the clock and give him the chance to handle this whole ordeal differently.

But he truly didn't know what he'd change. He wanted the land, that was obvious. Hurting Annabelle was never part of the deal. She'd come to him broken, ready to slay any dragon in her way to save her family. He'd admired her from day one and had instantly set out on claiming her.

Well, he'd done that, as well. So now what? He had the land, he'd slept with Annabelle, and now she held his heart. How the hell did he get himself into this mess and how could he work his way back out without doing more damage?

Damn it. He hadn't expected emotions to botch up the triumph of his success.

His office door jerked open and Colt barely raised his gaze to his brother in the doorway.

"Not in the mood," Colt growled as he poured another round. Nothing like toasting your failures with yourself and having your oldest brother, the miracle surgeon, as a witness.

"I saw you tear in here like your world just ended." Nolan didn't take the not-so-subtle hint that Colt wanted to be alone. He crossed the office and stopped on the other side of the bar. "I assume this has to do with Annabelle."

Colt tipped back the glass and closed his eyes before slamming the empty tumbler back onto the mahogany bar top.

"The land is ours and the engineer will be moving forward with drawing up some plans and getting us an estimate."

Nolan braced his hands against the grooved edge of the bar and leaned forward. "Which is what you've always wanted, so I'm assuming Annabelle knows that she no longer has a home."

"She knows everything."

Well, not everything. There was one more thing he could do for her that might lessen her pain. She'd still hate him, he couldn't change that, but he owed her.

"You care for her." Nolan let out a low whistle. "I didn't see that coming. But I can tell you from experience, if you want to be with her, fight. No matter what you've done, you can't let her go."

Colt shook his head. "She doesn't ever want to see me or talk to me again. Those were her parting words."

"And you're just giving up? You fought for years for this property, but when you find a woman you care for you opt to drink and will the pain away?"

Wasn't that what any cowboy did?

"She deserves for you to grovel, to show her that she means more than this dream of yours," Nolan went on. "But only if she does mean more. I could be reading you all wrong, but you look like hell."

Colt had never second-guessed a business decision he'd made. Confidence was key to maintaining a successful ranch. But right now, he wanted this pain to go away. And he knew if he was hurting this much, that Annabelle was miserable. She was still trying to pick up the pieces of her shattered life and all he'd done was throw more shards into the mix.

"There's no fixing this," Colt stated, pushing away from the bar. "I can make the process a little easier, but she doesn't want my help. I offered to buy her another house."

Nolan laughed and raked a hand through his dark hair. "You don't get women at all, man. She doesn't want another house. She wants the one she grew up in. We don't need that property to grow, Colt. We have five thousand acres. Use some of the east side to build cabins. You want the girl, go get her. If you're content with simply keeping the property, stay here and drink your day away."

Nolan started back toward the door before stopping and glancing over his shoulder. "Don't make the same mistake I did."

Colt knew Annabelle didn't want to see him. He needed to give her time before he approached her again and explained his side, and maybe then she'd understand.

But if he wanted to nudge her in the right direction, then he needed to take something to her, something that rightfully belonged to her.

There was no denying the truth any longer…he loved Annabelle. In a short time, she'd captured his heart. Oh, she'd fought the attraction, but he'd pursued her and he wasn't sorry. How could he be? She was the greatest thing that had happened to him and he'd destroyed their chance at happiness before it could even get started.

He had to prove to her that he wasn't an unfeeling jerk.

Colt headed to his master suite to retrieve the box he'd had hidden for nearly two years. Doing the right thing at this point was rather moot, but he couldn't let Annabelle believe he was the monster she claimed.

"I'm sorry, Belle."

If she only had a dollar for every time her father had said those words just this evening alone…

Annabelle cradled a sleepy Emily and swayed back and forth on the porch. "There's nothing we can do now. We wouldn't have the money to fight that document anyway. But I am going to demand to see it. I know Colt wouldn't have allowed for any loopholes, but I won't take his word for it."

From the start, she'd known he had an agenda, but she'd thought most of it was getting her into bed. She had a clue he wanted her land, but she never dreamed he already owned it.

She heated all over again when she thought of how foolish she was, how much of a laughingstock she must've been each time she showed up for so-called work at the ranch.

From here on out, she was focusing on her girls. Annabelle needed to go out first thing in the morning and find a job, and then she'd look into housing.

The thought of packing up the only place she'd ever

wanted to be hurt almost as much as Colt's betrayal. Just his name in her mind had her heart aching.

"We'll get through this," she told her father. "But when I say no gambling, I mean it. This can't go on. I don't care if it's one dollar or one hundred. No more."

He stood up from the swing, sending it rocking on its own in the breeze. "I'm going to do everything I can. I know we need to do this together. I'm trying."

"I know." He was always trying, but this time he had to stick to a plan and now that she was back, maybe she could watch him more closely. "Go on to bed," she told him. "I'll come in later. I just want to hold her a while longer and enjoy the silence and the fresh air."

She wanted to sit on this porch swing with Emily and Lucy, just like her mother used to do with Annabelle and her sister. Leaving the memories behind would be the hardest part. Seeing the inside of this home bare would quite possibly break her.

"I can take Emily in and lay her down if you'd like. It's rather late."

Annabelle nodded. "I know, but she can sleep in my arms. She calms me, gives me peace. I guess I'll have that time to spend with my babies after all until I find another job."

Considering the hell she'd been through, Annabelle needed peace. She needed to focus on her family, on piecing the broken hearts back together.

"We're going to rebuild our lives," he told her. "With your mother and Trish gone…"

His voice caught and it was all Annabelle could do to hold it together. Her father never broke down in front of her.

"Now that they're gone," he said on a shaky breath. "You are all I have. You and those sweet girls. I want to be a better man for you guys and I want you to know I'm going to help by getting a job. We'll do this together."

She truly hoped so because she wasn't sure she could do it alone. "I love you, Dad."

He crossed to her, kissed the top of her head, and headed inside. Annabelle patted Emily through the cotton sleeper and made her way to the swing. Wherever she ended up, Annabelle vowed to own a porch with a swing. It may not be this porch, it may not be this swing, but it was a tradition she could take with her.

Tears slid down her cheeks as she pushed off the porch with her toes to set the swing in motion again. Emily clutched onto Annabelle's T-shirt as she drifted off to sleep. Trish's precious babies were counting on her to provide protection, stability, a future, and she planned to deliver.

So much had happened today and Annabelle was still trying to wrap her mind around the fact that she was still in love with a man who had hurt her so deeply, she didn't know if she'd ever recover.

But he'd told her all along that family was everything to him. He hadn't been lying.

He'd cradled her in his arms after making love and told her his father's ultimate goal when he'd been in charge. Now Colt was pushing forward with those plans no matter who was run over in the process. A part of her knew where he was coming from, realized the importance of clinging to a parent's dream.

Still, it didn't cancel out what he'd done. He'd stolen her home. From the moment she met him, he knew exactly what the outcome of this situation would be and he chose to play with her life anyway. Those actions were unforgivable.

Headlights swept up her driveway and Annabelle came

to her feet, tightening her hold on Emily and pulling her into her chest.

Colt's truck came to a stop and Annabelle braced herself. If he was coming to beg for forgiveness, he could take his shiny, expensive vehicle and get the hell off her…

It was his land. He had every right to be there.

The soft glow from the porch cast enough light for her to see that he was carrying a box. As he drew closer, she recognized that box. Her mother's.

Annabelle went to the edge of the porch and met his eyes when he stopped at the base of the steps.

"I'm not staying," he told her. "I just thought this should be returned to you."

There was no holding back the tears, making it difficult to juggle a sleeping baby while swiping at her eyes with the back of her hand.

"Why do you have my mother's jewelry box?"

Colt held the box between his hands, his attention never wavering from her. "Because your father needed money. He knew there wasn't anyone around who could afford to buy this, so he came to me."

She'd known her father had sold the jewelry, but she hadn't known to whom and she never dreamed she'd get it back.

"Is it all in there?" she dared ask.

"Every piece," he confirmed. "I had no use for it. I always figured if Neil got straightened out, he may want this back. But you deserve it."

She didn't know what to say. He could've kept this box and she never would've known. Clearly, her father wasn't going to say anything.

Annabelle stepped aside. "Can you set it on the table over there?" she asked.

Colt stepped up onto the porch and placed the box on the side table next to a rocking chair and potted fern. The breeze kicked up, bringing Colt's familiar woodsy scent with it. The same scent she'd been up close and personal with in his shower earlier.

When he turned back around and locked his eyes on hers, Annabelle froze. "Don't," she whispered.

"I know you hate me. I know you think I'm the worst person you've ever met."

In the pale glow, those blue eyes glistened with unshed tears. She didn't want to believe he had a heart. She didn't want him to have feelings. He'd done all this to himself, to her and her family.

"But everything that happened with us was real. I didn't want it to be," he added. "I wanted to keep things business and physical. You showed me there was so much more. I know you don't believe me, but I had to tell you that I'm not the man you think. I'm just a guy who put his father's wishes above all else. I'm a guy who wanted to prove himself to those people he loved most."

Colt pursed his lips, but Annabelle didn't miss the way his chin quivered. Her heart ached for him, but again, she hadn't done any of this. All of his pain was self-inflicted.

"And in the end, I hurt the woman I'd fallen in love with."

Annabelle had barely processed the words when he turned and walked off the porch. That limp, a little more prominent this evening, only reminded her that he was human. That he made mistakes, he wasn't perfect. But he'd hurt her and now he just wanted to turn her world on its side once again with those words?

She clutched Emily and turned, going down the steps.

"You can't drop that bomb so conveniently and then just leave," she called.

"Too late. But there's little I can do to make you believe me," he told her as he opened the truck door. "I just want you to know…"

He shook his head and glanced toward the starry sky before looking back at her. "I just want you to know that those moments I spent alone with you were some of the best of my life."

Colt hopped into the cab of his truck and backed away, not looking in her direction again. Emily slept through the entire encounter and Annabelle envied her for it.

Colt had brought back her mother's box, the box Annabelle remembered playing with as a little girl. Oh, there were plenty of real pieces in there, but her mom had also kept costume jewelry, too.

Annabelle sat in the rocker beside the box and nestled Emily into the crook of her arm. With her free hand, Annabelle lifted the lid and was instantly swept back in time. The emerald earrings that matched the ring Annabelle had were safely in their divider.

All of the other familiar pieces were there, too. Memories of her mother wearing each one came rushing back.

Closing her eyes, she rested her head against the back of the rocker and longed for answers. What was she supposed to do? How could she move on when it would be so easy to give up?

And how did she process Colt's announcement that he'd fallen for her? That wasn't fair. She wanted to continue hating him, but he'd sounded sincere. Those tears he blinked away were certainly not fake, but how could he feel that way about her and still treat her like he had?

Unless…

Annabelle needed to think. She needed to clear her head and dissect all that had transpired in the past few months. She couldn't just do what her heart told her to because there was no way she was following that advice anymore.

She had to be smart about this and make the best decisions for her and the twins. And that started with marching over to Pebblebrook first thing in the morning.

Nineteen

Hard work made a man forget, or at least that's what he'd told himself when he came to the barn at five that morning.

Colt had intentions of working until his muscles burned and he temporarily forgot how much his heart ached. He'd only meant to take that box to Annabelle last night, but then he'd seen her holding Emily and his mouth just opened, pouring emotions out.

And in that moment his future became so clear. Family, above all else, was the most important thing in life. His father had never put anything above his family…not even business. The Elliotts were all successful because they'd put integrity and loyalty first.

Annabelle may still hate him, but he wasn't giving up. He may have been determined to get her farm, but that was nothing compared to the motive he had to get her back. She was…everything. She was absolutely everything he'd ever wanted and he hadn't even known it.

Colt had texted Ryan and Josh, telling them to start work on the west side near Hayes's house. Not only did Colt want that place perfect for his brother's return in a few weeks, but he wanted the guys away because he was not in the mood for chitchat.

He'd taken Lightning out first thing and tried to clear his mind, but all he kept seeing was the hurt on Annabelle's face when she realized he'd lied to her. He'd not only lied, he'd stolen the one thing she'd held dear to her heart since she was a child.

As soon as he'd come back from his ride, Colt had gone straight into his office in the barn and fired off an email. He may never get Annabelle back, but he sure as hell wasn't about to continue the process of taking her home.

Guilt had gnawed at him into the wee hours. But there was so much more. That moment on Annabelle's porch last night had turned the final click on his heart, proving that he didn't only love her, he loved the image of her and those babies being his, living on Pebblebrook.

He loved her more than he'd thought possible and had completely crushed her.

All his own doing and his brother tried to tell him. Hell, his employees had, too.

But Colt had been stubborn. Now he'd have to do damage control. His father wouldn't have approved of Colt letting the woman go only to have the expansion. His father would be disappointed in how Colt had handled everything. But that wasn't the only reason Colt decided to fight for what he wanted.

A car door slamming caught his attention as he tossed another bale of hay from one side of the loft toward the opening near the ladder.

Stepping over hay, he crossed to the small hinged door and swung it open wide. Glancing down, he saw the most beautiful sight: Annabelle in a pair of fitted jeans, a green tank that matched her eyes and her boots. She pulled a stroller out of the trunk and slammed the lid. Then she opened the back door and removed Emily and Lucy from their car seats.

He watched as she strapped them into the stroller and

then looked around the open area. She was there to see him, but why? Had his words affected her last night? Was she willing to hear him out and maybe start over?

He hadn't had a chance to rehearse his speech in his head. He wasn't ready to face her when his emotions were so raw and vulnerable. But there was nothing more he wanted than to believe she came there to forgive him.

He was asking too much, he knew, but he still wasn't ready to give up. Maybe spouting off his profession of love last night had been wrong, but if it got her thinking, he wasn't sorry he'd exposed his weaker side.

"Up here," he called.

Annabelle jumped, a hand over her heart as she glanced toward him. Her eyes landed on his bare chest. "Oh, um… I need to talk to you."

"I'll come down."

He didn't bother to grab his shirt from the hayloft. It had been hot as Hades up there so he'd shed it early. As Colt climbed down the ladder, he didn't care that he was playing dirty by going at her half-dressed. He'd do anything to remind her of just how good they were together.

"I want to see that document my father signed."

He'd barely put his boot on the ground when she came up the walkway pushing the twins. The girls were bright eyed today and Lucy was chewing on some stuffed cowboy doll. The sight of those expressive green eyes clutched his heart.

He focused back on Annabelle. "I have the print copy in my office at the house."

She nodded. "Then let's go there."

"We can go into my office here and I can pull up the document in email format that I sent to my attorney."

She kept trying to look him in the eye, but she failed. Every few seconds her focus shifted down to his bare chest.

"That's fine. I want to know what I'm dealing with and if there's any way to get out of it."

"The document is binding, darlin'."

"Do not even start with that," she told him, her eyes now locked on his. "I want to know something and I want you to answer honestly."

He crossed his arms and nodded. "I have nothing else to hide."

She gripped the handles of the stroller and tipped her head. "When you asked me to move in with you, was that because you wanted me or because you were trying to cover your tracks so I wouldn't find out about the property? I assume you were hoping I'd fall madly in love with you and we'd just merge and live happily ever after. Am I right?"

Colt swallowed. "Yes."

When she lowered her lids over those mesmerizing green eyes, Colt felt as if the day had dimmed. Her light was gone and he'd put it out. He had to explain himself and then she could decide what to do.

"I asked you to move in because I was serious about wanting to try for something deeper with you." He took a step closer. "I asked because if you fell in love with me and we did this whole happily-ever-after, then you'd never have to know what your father or I did." Another step brought him toe to toe with her. "But I wanted to spare you the pain, I wanted you to start a new life without the heartache. The last thing I ever wanted was to hurt you."

She opened her eyes, tilting her head so she could meet his gaze. "You didn't want to hurt me? What did you think would happen? Did you seriously think I'd never find out about this form my father signed?"

Colt watched as Emily turned the toy over again, then put it back in her mouth. "After I started falling for you, I did what I could to keep you safe. I wanted to protect you.

I was trying to find a way to keep my father's wishes and hold on to you at the same time. What I didn't realize was that my father would rather see me happy and settled than to have the extra land for the dude ranch."

"How can I believe you?" she whispered.

She was breaking down. Now all he had to do was catch her.

"Because this place is better with you. Because my life is brighter with you here. I've always wanted a family and the moment I held Lucy out in the yard, I started falling. I had a weak spot for you, and getting to know your girls more only made the trio even more appealing. I want you all here, Annabelle."

She'd left her hair down today. The soft curls lay over her shoulders and he remembered the deep shade of red her hair turned when wet. He'd give anything to have her back in his shower again, in his bed, in his life.

"I messed up," he went on. "I'll freely admit that I should've been honest with you from the moment you came, but I didn't know you and I only wanted to fulfill my father's wishes…I guess the same as you did with your mother."

Annabelle's soft smile clenched his heart. "That bed-and-breakfast was her only goal."

"Then you can do it," he told her. "Take your house and do whatever you want with it."

Her brows drew in. "What?"

"I emailed my attorney this morning regarding the legal agreement. It will be reversed and the land will remain in your name."

Emily started fussing and threw her toy on the ground. Colt picked up the cowboy as Annabelle came around to lift the baby from the stroller. With Emily on her hip, Annabelle turned to face him once again.

"Why?" she asked simply.

Colt shrugged and held the toy up to Emily. "Because it's yours. I only want you and if I can't have you, then I sure as hell don't want to take your home."

There was an emptiness inside him that had existed since he left her house last night. He needed it filled, but only Annabelle had that power.

"You're just giving it back?"

Emily reached a hand toward him and instinct had him taking her into his arms. At least he still had one of them on his side. Lucy remained silent in the stroller and stared up at him as if assessing her own opinion.

"I'm giving it back with access to my engineer and contractor. You have an unlimited budget to do the bed-and-breakfast like you want."

Annabelle's eyes instantly filled. "Colt…but, what about your dude ranch?"

This was the tricky part. "I'm hoping I can still open it. I'm hoping we can do this together. That land can stay in your name, you can have complete control over what happens with your house, but there is something I want to merge."

Her eyes widened.

"I want you to have my name. Marry me, sweetness. Not for the land, or the house. I want your happiness and I hope that means you'll be with me and give me a second chance."

"You're serious?" she asked, blinking back tears.

"I've never been more so."

A shaky hand covered her mouth as she shook her head. Hope stilled inside him. He wanted it to grow, he wanted some sign that she was giving in.

"I want to," she whispered behind her hand. "I'm so scared."

Emily laid her head on his shoulder. Colt reached out

and wrapped an arm around Annabelle's waist, hauling her against his side.

"I'm terrified," he admitted. "This is insane for both of us, but I know what I want."

With a watery smile, she reached up and cupped the side of his face.

"The land stays in my name. I'll move in with you and let's see how things go."

Relief swept through him as he hugged her tighter against his side. "That's more than I deserve. There's one more thing."

"What's that?"

"I'd like to pay to have your father get some help. He can't do it alone."

Now she burst into tears. "You're going to take on so much with me. You must be serious if you're on board for all my baggage."

He nipped at her lips. "I'm more than on board, sweetness. I want you here more than I've ever wanted anything."

Lucy started fussing and Annabelle reached down to unfasten her. Once the baby was on Annabelle's hip, she instantly calmed.

Colt wrapped his arms around the family he'd finally found.

Annabelle smiled. "I have the perfect name you can call me."

Colt laughed. "What's that?"

"Yours."

Epilogue

Nolan hadn't had the best night at the hospital. This was the time of day when he couldn't go straight home to bed, he needed to ride to unwind.

Just as he rounded the corner to the main barn, he came up short.

Colt had his arms wrapped around Annabcllc and her girls. Apparently he'd come to his senses and gone after the family he wanted.

Nolan swallowed and stepped back, so as not to be seen. He was happy for his younger brother. Nolan always figured Colt would be the first to settle down. He was a little jealous, though. Nolan would be lying to himself if he didn't admit that he wanted a family of his own. He was tired of coming home to an empty house. When he'd built it, he'd had every intention of filling it with a wife, with children.

But he'd let that dream go. Years ago, he'd let go of the only woman he'd ever wanted. He'd hoped he'd move on and someone would come along and fill the void in his life.

As Nolan headed back to his SUV, he realized that there was only one woman he would ever care for.

Pepper Manning. He'd let her go without a fight. They'd

been through hell together, but when it came to the time she needed him most, he hadn't been there. He'd messed up, but that was something he'd had to live with because there was no way to erase the past.

Living with that heartache was a battle he'd always face. He devoted his life to saving others, but he hadn't been able to save the one person he loved from heartache.

So, yeah, Nolan was jealous that his brother had found love, found a family. Because if Nolan had it to do over, he'd never let Pepper go.

But there were no second chances…right?

* * * * *

"Stop doing that."

"Doing what?" He offered a smug grin. "Cleaning up after you?"

"No. Making me lose control."

"Is that what I do to you?" Damn, but he hoped so.

Her breathing deepened, her chest expanding with her heavy breaths. "Yes."

Things were progressing right on track. "Good. I think you need to lose control, Red."

"No, I don't. That's not a good thing." She pushed against his chest but the gesture seemed half-hearted.

"I think it's a very good thing."

"Ha. You would. You're a man." Her eyes glittered like whiskey in a cut-glass tumbler. "I think *you* need to lose control."

To prove her point, she wrapped her hands around the back of his neck and tugged his face down to hers.

* * *

Redeemed by the Cowgirl
is part of the Red Dirt Royalty series—
These Oklahoma millionaires work hard
and play harder.

REDEEMED BY THE COWGIRL

BY
SILVER JAMES

First Published in Great Britain 2017
By Mills & Boon, an imprint of HarperCollins*Publishers*
1 London Bridge Street, London, SE1 9GF

ISBN: 978-0-263-92813-6

51-0317

Our policy is to use papers that are natural, renewable and recyclable products and made from wood grown in sustainable forests. The logging and manufacturing processes conform to the legal environmental regulations of the country of origin.

Printed and bound in Spain
by CPI, Barcelona

Silver James likes walks on the wild side and coffee. Okay. She LOVES coffee. A cowgirl at heart, she's been an army officer's wife and mum, and worked in the legal field, fire service and law enforcement. Now retired from the real world, she lives in Oklahoma, spending her days writing with the assistance of two Newfoundlands, the cat who rules them all and the characters living in her imagination.

To Clary. You know why.
And to my dream editor, Charles.
You know why, too.
Also to Stacy and Tahra, and the whole
fantastic Harlequin Desire team!
Y'all are made of awesomesauce.

One

Cash Barron was a man who understood duty—especially to his family. Unlike his brothers. Staring out the window of his twin's apartment on the fiftieth floor of Barron Crown Hotel and Casino in Las Vegas, he did his best to stuff his anger into a corner of his mind. He'd watched his three older brothers turn their backs and walk away from the very thing that made them Barrons—their loyalty to one another. Even his twin, Chase, had chosen a woman so completely unsuitable that Cash could barely comprehend their marriage. And now Chase and Savannah were about to celebrate the first anniversary of their quickie Vegas wedding.

A sharp rap on the door jerked his attention from the vista outside the window. Bridger Tate, his cousin and second-in-command, entered without invitation. He didn't like the look on the man's face.

"What?"

"Last night's video from the casino floor has been analyzed."

A series of curse words ricocheted through his brain but he refrained from speaking them. "Is it them?"

Bridge looked angry but resigned. "Yeah. Tucker isolated images of the Rowland clan on the casino floor."

Tucker Tate was Bridger's brother and vice president of Barron Entertainment, the media and hotel conglomerate that was Chase's domain. They'd been dealing with a security problem at the casino for almost a year. As president of Barron Security Services, all problems—from the security detail for his brother Senator Clay Barron to the theft of oilfield pipe from a Barron Energy drilling site—landed on his desk. The occasional missing cow from the ranch, the odd employee embezzlement, the more frequent crackpot sending threatening emails—these bucks all stopped with him. It was his job to protect his family, even from themselves.

"Cash?"

Glancing up, he realized he'd tuned out Bridger's play-by-play. "Sorry. What were you saying?"

"Tuck did a good job isolating the Rowlands."

"Are they all present and accounted for?"

"Yup. Max, Alex and Ajax, Braxton, Dexter. The king of cons and his larcenous princes. I had IT highlight their positions in each of the videos."

Cash huffed out a breath that was a thinly disguised sigh. He strode to Chase's in-home office, settled heavily at the desk and called up the info on the giant monitor. He leaned back, eyes tracking the glowing orbs highlighting faces on the screen.

Bridger settled a hip on the corner of the desk and twisted his head to see the monitor. "I have our IT team checking footage from Scottsdale, Nashville, Miami and New Orleans."

"What's their objective?"

"Who knows? Seems they really like Barron properties, though."

"Jolly."

"Yeah, figured that would please you."

"Are we the marks or is it a guest?"

"Probably both."

Cash closed his eyes and rubbed the back of his neck. Could it get any more complicated?

Roxanne Rowland lined her lips with red pencil before adding bright red gloss. The woman in the mirror staring back at her was a stranger. Dragging fingers through her red hair, she fluffed the waves, startled anew by the bright color tipping her nails. She wasn't used to the manicure, either. Dark, smoky shadows fringed her eyes, making them sparkle like amber. She refused to wear the tinted contacts sitting in a case on the counter.

Smoothing down the borrowed body-hugging black dress, she opened the bathroom door and collided with her older brother. His fingers gripped her biceps none too gently. "Time to go, Rox." He studied her a moment. "You didn't wear the contacts."

She winced at the accusatory tone in his voice. "They hurt and make my eyes water. I had to redo my makeup three times before I gave up."

He squeezed her arm as he strode away, pulling her along. She wobbled on the stiletto heels and teetered for a moment as she scrambled to find her balance. The high heels were as foreign to her as the rest of her getup. She wore jeans and boots. Not haute couture. Especially not a dress that cost close to a month's salary—a dress she'd been told to tuck the tag inside and not to get dirty. That meant it would be returned to the store for a credit.

"What's going on, Dex?"

"You don't need to know, little sister."

"Yes, I do."

"Max is working."

Maximilian Rowland—her father and sire of her four older brothers, Lex, Jax, Brax and Dex—whom they never called "Dad."

"That doesn't explain why *I'm* here. I don't work with him."

"You do now." His voice remained implacable as he ushered her out of the hotel room. "This is big, Rox, and you'll do your duty to the family. Or else."

Or else? What did that mean? Dex didn't enlighten her as they rode down in the elevator. When he'd picked her up at Las Vegas's McCarran International Airport, all he'd said was that their father needed her help, and it was time to take her place in the family.

"Stop fidgeting."

"I can't help it."

Dex cut his eyes in her direction and smirked. "What's wrong, your feet hurt?"

"As a matter of fact." Her feet didn't just hurt, they ached like someone was shoving cold needles into her toes and hammering her arches with rusty nails. "You try wearing these shoes for five minutes."

"I'm a guy. I don't wear heels."

"So?"

"So, you're a girl. You do."

"No, I don't. I—" She didn't get to finish her argument. The elevator doors opened and Dex grabbed her arm, jerking her out into a swirl of color and noise. He guided her into a corner, his gaze fixed on the ceiling.

"Stand here until one of us comes to get you."

"What? No—"

"Shut up, Roxie. Do as you're told."

"You are not the boss of me, Dexter."

"Tonight I am. Shut up and listen. There's a man at the blackjack table. He has a propensity for redheads. Tall, curvy redheads." He flicked the strap of her dress so it sagged off the curve of her shoulder. "When the time comes, you will sashay that sweet ass of yours to Max. You will ignore Max but you will make nice to the man next to him. Understood?

"No."

"Tough. Just do as you're told. You flirt. You distract. And you get him to take you up to his room. You get him naked and we'll do the rest."

"Now you wait just a minute, Dexter Row—"

He pushed her back into the corner, eyes hard. "You've had it easy all your life, baby girl. Time to pay up. We told Max he screwed up sending you off to those snooty schools instead of teaching you what you needed to know about the business. That ends tonight. Starting now, you'll do your duty to this family."

Dex draped a heavy necklace around her throat. Colored diamonds and old gold. He bent to her ear. "There's more where this came from—all hidden where you won't find the evidence, but the cops will. You try to walk away or turn us in? They'll know just how deeply involved you are."

"That's blackmail." Her voice remained remarkably steady despite the fear zinging through her.

"Welcome to the family, little sister."

With those parting words, he disappeared into the crowd bustling around the entrance to the casino floor. When they'd arrived at the Crown Hotel and Casino that afternoon, she'd been excited. The resort was one of the jewels on the Las Vegas Strip. Like the naive twit she evidently was, she thought she was coming for a vacation at the luxurious hotel. Yeah, no.

She slipped her feet out of the heels and almost whimpered in relief when the thick rug cushioned her toes. She wasn't sure she believed Dex's threat. He'd always been something of a bully—a fact she'd put down to him being the youngest brother. Sibling rivalry rolled downhill. Alexander—Lex, her oldest brother—had always been aloof. He'd been thirteen when she was born, and they had nothing in common. By the time she'd turned five, he was already traveling with Max. Ajax, two years younger than Lex, was the next oldest. Tall, handsome and gregarious, Jax was a charmer. He'd always attracted the opposite sex. He and Braxton were what were sometimes referred to as Catholic twins—barely nine months apart. Brax was the scholar, always reading and studying. Wickedly intelligent, he had an innate ability to plan. Then there was Dex. He'd been five when Roxie came along, and he'd pretty much hated her from the beginning.

Roxie jerked her thoughts away from her family and concentrated on how she could get out of this mess. She didn't doubt for a minute that Dex would carry through with his threat and not only set her up but make sure she took the fall. She knew that from experience. At the moment, she had no choice but to follow orders until she could figure out their endgame and how to avoid involvement.

"Get your shoes on, girl."

Startled, she retreated deeper into the corner and squinted at Lex. At 35, he was debonair and aloof, and he scared her just a little. Okay, if she was honest, a lot. He might have been absent—like Max—for most of her childhood, but when he was around, he was as much a father figure as Max had been.

"I don't want to do this, Lex. Whatever *this* is." She made air quotes for emphasis.

"Don't care what you want, Roxanne. You're doing it. Get your shoes on and get out there. You make that smart mouth of yours pouty, bat your lashes and get the mark up to his room."

"Or else? Dex already threatened me with that. I'm not impressed."

He slid his big hand around her throat, and she gulped but raised her chin. "Not telling you again. Get to work." Squeezing his fingers for good measure, he didn't let her go until she had both shoes on her feet and was wobbling into the throng of vacationers.

She was terrified of falling flat on her face, arms and legs akimbo, her tush displayed in the air and her thong hiding nothing from the crowd of onlookers. "Slow down," she hissed over her shoulder at Lex. He didn't, the hand at the small of her back pushing her harder. "If I fall off these darn shoes and break my ankle, the great con will be a bust."

Cash rubbed his eyes, a dull headache caused by staring at the bank of security monitors throbbing at the base of his skull. Tucker handed him a cup of coffee and a bottle of painkillers. He tossed back a couple of the pills and chased them with the hot black liquid.

"When did you tumble onto their presence?" Cash didn't take his eyes from the live footage.

"Yesterday when they checked in. That new facial recognition software you had installed works like a charm. I have footage if you want to see." Tucker watched the monitors, too.

"Just give me the rundown."

"Max arrived first. Had reservations for a mini-suite under the name Grant Franklin."

Cash scrubbed at his forehead with the heel of one hand. "And his sons?"

"Alexander and Ajax checked in together. Another mini-suite. Hamilton and Jackson Grant."

"Please tell me you're joking."

"Nope." Tuck's voice hardened.

"Great. Go on."

"Braxton checked in about an hour later. Lincoln Washington. And then Dexter checked in this afternoon. Reservations were for Mr. and Mrs. Franklin Cleveland."

Cash sat up straight, whipping around to stare at the other man. "Hamilton, Jackson, Grant, Lincoln, Washington, Franklin and Cleveland. Now they're just rubbing our noses in it." His cousin looked confused so he laid it out. "Those are presidential last names. All of them. Except Franklin. But ol' Ben's still on the hundred-dollar bill."

"It's all about the money."

"Yeah. Wait. Dexter brought a woman?" Cash pushed out of the chair. "Do you have a picture of her?"

"No. He checked in alone, was up in his room for about forty-five minutes and then left in a cab he caught at the front entrance. He hasn't been back since."

"You sure of that?" Cash walked to a monitor and tapped it. "That's Dexter at the roulette table."

"How the hell—"

Bridger walked up to them and cut his brother off. "We have a gap in the security surveillance somewhere. We'll find it, Tuck. Sorry I'm late for the party, Cash. I was ouble-checking footage."

"I want eyes on all of the Rowlands. Max is at the high-stakes blackjack table. Alex walked out about five minutes ago, after Dexter tossed him a high sign. Ajax and Braxton are roaming around on the slot machine floor." Cash returned to his chair and swiveled it around. "I want our guys on them, Bridger." He held up a hand to stop Tucker's rebuttal. "Your security is good. Heck, we hired and trained them, but they look like casino security. My guys won't."

Bridger offered a feral grin to Tucker. "Little brother, you pick my guys out, I'll buy you the biggest steak they have at the Barron House."

The radio at Cash's elbow hissed. "I have target two in sight. He's with a woman. Redhead. Black dress. Lobby entrance."

Cash's eyes swept the bank of monitors until he picked out Alex Rowland. His eyes locked on the woman preceding the thief. She was tall but not slender. No, she definitely had curves in all the places a woman should, but she still looked sleek in the short cocktail dress. Her auburn hair was a mass of wavy curls, but he couldn't tell the color of her eyes through the grainy camera lens. He stared at her, a memory swimming in the back of his mind. He knew her from somewhere.

Alex peeled away and Braxton took his place, herding the woman toward the table where Max sat, relaxed and cheerful. She stumbled and Cash found himself reaching forward as if to catch her. Braxton made no move to assist, and it was a stranger who offered a steadying hand. He managed to read her lips, the words and expression easy to translate. "Pardon me. I'm so sorry," she mouthed before Braxton swept her along in front of him.

"Bridge, pull in some markers. Find out when the Rowlands added a woman to their crew. I want to know who she is."

"On it."

Cash continued to study the woman. She looked…uncomfortable. Unsure. If it was an act, it was a good one.

She ended up squeezed between Max and the man next to him at the table, all but sprawled in the man's lap. Something hot and angry lanced through him. Keying the camera on her face, he could see that she looked young and scared despite the getup. That didn't fit the Rowlands' MO at all. That odd sense of recognition continued to niggle at him and he sorted through memories of all the women he knew. He'd figure it out sooner or later.

He'd been so intent on the woman—girl—he'd lost track of the other Rowlands. "Where's Alex? And where did Ajax and Dexter disappear to?"

Various scenes flickered on the monitors mounted to the wall in front of him and a lot of cuss words filtered into muttered conversations as Chase's security staff combed the screens for a sighting. Something popped, and then there was a hum like a generator winding down. Moments later, lights dimmed, monitors died and the room was plunged into darkness.

Cash was out of his chair and headed toward the door as backup lighting kicked in. He tapped the emergency code into the keypad and had to shove the door open when the lock clicked. He heard Bridger shouting behind him.

"Lock down the counting room and the vault. Deploy personnel to all the exits."

Knowing Bridge would take control of the security room, Cash sprang into action. He needed to get his hands on one of the Rowlands. And he definitely wanted to get his hands on the red-haired woman.

The lights went out and the packed casino floor erupted into pandemonium. Women squealed. Men shouted. Other voices rose, yelling above the melee in an effort to restore order. Lights from cell phones added ghostly illumination to the scene as emergency lighting flickered on.

Someone gripped Roxie's arm and jerked. She attempted to pull away but hearing her name growled shocked her into compliancy. Max. She tripped after him, trying to stay upright. Blasted shoes. She hobbled in her father's wake, then he shoved her at Dex with a muffled, "Get her undercover."

The next thing she knew, she was tossed over her brother's shoulder like a sack of flour, and no amount of beating against his back made him release her. She tried to kick her legs but his arm was an iron band across her knees. When they reached one of the exit doors, he set her down and backed her against the wall. A moment later, the door slammed open, missing her by a hair.

She watched a tall man sprint through the exit. Dark hair, broad shoulders, a shadowed jawline. His suit was likely hand-tailored. Roxie wondered who he was as Dex disappeared into the stairwell and the door closed. She pulled on the handle, panicked now that she was alone. The door didn't budge. She had to get away.

Roxie turned, feeling the blood drain from her face. She recognized the man now. Cash Barron, standing there, bigger'n Dallas. She whirled to run the other direction only to be brought up short by two security guards who could play middle linebacker for the Dallas Cowboys. She pivoted very slowly to face the man she'd never been able to get out of her fantasies. She was in so much trouble now.

"Well, well, well. What do we have here?"

Two

As soon as Cash saw her up close, he remembered who she was—or who he thought she'd been. Anne Landerson—a slightly clueless student who'd been involved with the theft of some jewels and fine art from his great-aunt Elizabeth. He reached out to snag her but she charged, ducking under his arm and diving into the crowd milling around the lobby. He plowed after her but she was gone, running right out of her shoes. He was left with a pair of killer stilettos in a color his sisters-in-law described as "Do-Me Red." Like a whiff of smoke, she was gone.

Two hours later, he was no closer to capturing any of them. Despite the lockdown, the Rowlands had escaped, as had the girl. Frustrated at every turn, Cash threw in the allegorical towel and returned to Oklahoma City.

Cash spent the week chasing shadows, but no concrete leads had popped up. Neither had the Rowlands. Frustrated, he sat in his office staring at the designer high heels displayed on his desk. How the hell did a woman walk on stilts like them? Then he remembered the stumbling gait of the woman in the security footage. A woman dressed to the nines, with makeup meant for seduction, wearing a black cocktail dress that hugged her curves like a lover. A curious dichotomy. He'd pulled the file on his aunt's case, one of the first Barron Security had handled after he took over.

The girl had claimed to know nothing about the stolen goods—only that she'd received a package in the mail and the items had been inside. She'd been scared, panic and apologies reflected in her huge amber eyes—eyes Cash hadn't forgotten in the six years since the incident. The school's headmistress and the lawyer who'd showed up had met with the prosecutor and a deal had been worked out. Seemed the kid was probably an innocent dupe so Barron Security signed off on community service and recovery of the property.

Now he had another problem. He'd run a search on Anne Landerson. She didn't exist. There was no record of her in any databases his team could access. Bridger was calling in favors to check those they couldn't without special dispensation. In the meantime, he had to focus on the Rowlands. He was no closer to discovering why they were targeting Barron properties and what their endgame could be.

Twice now, this girl had been in the Rowlands' crosshairs. Why? Was she with one of the brothers? That created a tangled knot of thoughts. For reasons he couldn't identify, Chase didn't like the idea of her belonging to someone.

A brusque tap on his door had him looking up as Bridger entered.

"Please tell me you've found something."

His second-in-command shook his head, a hangdog expression on his face. "Nothing with FBI or Treasury. We even checked Interpol. The Rowlands are everywhere, but the girl? She's a ghost, at least under that name."

Cash leaned back in the massive leather desk chair and

scratched at his cheek. His dark stubble was becoming a beard, a decision he made after he'd impersonated his twin in an attempt to make Chase and his wife separate, and realized how simple it was. "Maybe we're looking at this wrong."

"How so?"

"Could she have been the mark?"

Before Bridger could answer, his phone pinged. He checked the screen and a huge smile creased his cheeks. "Bingo. We found her."

Bridger pressed some buttons on his phone and a second later, a link popped up on Cash's computer monitor. He clicked on it and waited as the tab opened. There she was. Sort of. His brow furrowed as he stared at a face familiar yet that of a stranger. He read off the information.

"Roxanne Rosetta Rowland. Bachelor's degree in history, followed by a master's in museum studies." Cash continued skimming the information. "She graduated from the University of Central Oklahoma?"

"Yup. And with that information, we should be able to find out where she's currently living and working, and why there's no record tying her to the Rowlands, especially since she's using their name."

"I want to know everything there is to know about her." Cash rubbed his chin. Oh, yeah. He wanted every last detail about Roxanne Rowland, especially where she'd been and what she'd done since that interview at the Fairfax Police Department. Man, but he'd been a fool to believe her sob story and not follow up, despite assertions from the school that she was a victim. Innocents didn't use fake names. Now he'd have the facts before the day was out.

Roxie paced the confines of her cluttered office. No one in her family had contacted her. She'd managed to get to her room in Vegas, grab her stuff—sans the blackmail items—and run. Ha! She knew all their tricks, and had found the incriminating evidence and deposited it in the lost and found box on a maid's cart on her way out. She'd caught the first flight out of Las Vegas, then made her way home.

Every time her phone dinged with a text message, she jumped. Was it one of her brothers? But there had been no phone calls. No emails. Nothing. Aggravated, she'd put her research skills to work. What she'd discovered about her family left her worried, feeling stupid and more than a little angry. She'd guessed they walked the wrong side of the line. Con men. Grifters. But like an ostrich with her head buried, she'd had no clue how illicit their activities were. Her father and brothers were wanted by the FBI and Interpol for fraud, theft and questioning in a murder.

"What have y'all dragged me into?" she muttered as she paced. And what did the Barrons have to do with it? Nobody took on the Barron family and won. Everyone at Reade-Cannon-Mansfield was in awe of the family people called Red Dirt Royalty. She wouldn't be surprised if the advertising firm had originally coined the phrase. While she really wanted to work in a museum, she loved her job as corporate archivist for the ad agency. She didn't want to jeopardize her position by tangling with the Barrons.

So what could she do? Going to the police was a bad idea. One, she had no clue what her family had done—if anything—and two, she'd likely be considered an accessory. If the police got involved, she could kiss any chance of a career goodbye.

She clutched her cell phone in her hand and stared at it. Should she call Max and ask him what was going on? Would he tell her? She bit her bottom lip in indecision. Scrolling to his name on her contact list, her thumb hovered over the call button. When the phone vibrated in her hand, she almost dropped it. Fumbling and juggling, she got it back in her grip and stared at the text message from Brax.

FORGET U EVER WENT TO VEGAS

She texted back frantically. What's going on?

NOT A WORD TO ANY1 ROX BAD THINGS HAPPEN IF U TALK

I want to know what's happening!

WILL CALL WHEN WE NEED U JUST REMEMBER FAMILY IS EVERYTHING

Family is everything? That was rich. Growing up, she spent every Christmas alone at boarding school. The one time they'd remembered her birthday, it had been to hide their ill-gotten gains. And graduations? Ha! Their idea of family and hers were oceans apart.

She stared at the screen. Wait. Bad things would happen if she talked? What did that mean? She panicked for a moment, sinking onto her chair and putting her head between her knees. When she stopped seeing stars, she straightened. Her father and brothers were criminals. And they were up to their necks in something involving the Barrons—something they wanted her in the middle of. That was so not going to happen.

"What to do, what to do?" she mumbled, standing to pace again. One of the open tabs on her computer browser caught her gaze. A web search for "Barron Companies."

Dropping into her chair, she scooted it up to the desk

and began investigating. Five minutes later, she had a phone number for Barron Security Services, at the helm of which was CEO Cash Barron. She hadn't known who he was back when she was sixteen and he'd stood in that dingy interview room at the Fairfax Police Department. But she'd never forgotten him. He'd starred in some of her more…lurid fantasies over the years. Should she call him? What would she say?

She needed a plan.

Cash put his best tracer on Roxanne Rowland. The information they'd discovered did not mesh with what he knew about the rest of the family. The girl lived in a cheap apartment in the northwest part of town and worked at Reade-Cannon-Mansfield, the premier advertising firm based in Oklahoma City. He'd made some phone calls to the Barron account executive at RCM to get a rundown on her. According to his investigation of the Rowlands, Max and the boys lived the high life. From the French Riviera, to the luxury hotels of Dubai and Hong Kong, to the Gold Coast of Florida, the Hamptons, Aspen. Every playground of the rich and famous had been a hunting ground for the larcenous clan. None of that jibed with the information they'd dug up on Roxanne.

His door burst open and Bridger stood there with a shit-eating grin. "You aren't going to believe who's on line one." His cousin nodded toward the phone console on the desk.

Cash arched a brow, waiting for Bridger to fill him in. He didn't have to wait long.

"A woman wanting to speak to whoever is in charge of casino security. The call was routed to Cheri. When she asked the caller's name, the twit gave it to her. Roxanne Rowland."

Suspicious by nature, Cash reined in the surge of adrenaline spiking through him at the news. "What are the odds, Bridge?"

"High enough I wouldn't lay a bet on 'em. That said, we don't have anything to lose. I've already started the trace on the call. I can keep her on the line long enough to pinpoint her location."

Cash motioned him closer, and before hitting the line to put it on speakerphone, said, "You take the call."

"Bridger Tate. How can I help you?"

"Um..." Several muffled breaths puffed through the speaker. "Uh...hi. I...are you the one in charge of security for the Crown Casino out in Las Vegas?"

"Yes."

"Uh...you said your name is Tate?" The voice on the other end sounded hesitant.

"That's right. Bridger Tate. I'm vice president of BSS."

"Oh. Okay. That's okay then. I guess."

"Is there a reason you're calling, ma'am?"

"Oh. Roxie. Er, Roxanne. Roxanne Rowland. You don't know me or anything."

Cash made a circling motion with his hand, indicating Bridger should move things along.

"Should I know you, Ms. Rowland?"

"No." The word came out forcefully. "I mean, no." Softer this time. "I don't think so. I...look, I'm sorry. This was a bad idea."

"Don't hang up!" Cash's order cut through the air. "This is Cash Barron."

"Oh." The single syllable all but trembled as it sighed through the speaker.

"Why are you calling, Ms. Rowland?"

"My family...you see, they..."

They what? he wanted to shout. Her father and brothers were criminal scum and she had to be calling on their behalf. What sort of scam were they trying to set up? "I don't have all day, Ms. Rowland. There must be a reason you're calling. Get to it."

"Oh, okay. Yes. Well, see…I'd like to meet with you. Explain in person." Her voice grew a little stronger. The woman was a helluva actress.

"Explain what?"

"Can we meet somewhere?"

"I'll be happy to set up an appointment here in our offices." And he'd have the cops on speed dial to take her into custody.

"I…I'm not sure that would be a good idea." She inhaled deeply and blew out the breath. "Oh, never mind. This was a stupid idea. I'm sorry to have bothered you."

"Ms. Rowland," Cash snarled. "Roxanne."

"I don't know what's going on. I don't know what they're doing. Only that it's bad. I'm sure of it. It was stupid to call you. I just… When I saw you in Vegas, and recognized you…I thought maybe…oh, heck. I don't know what I thought."

"Come to my office, Roxanne. We'll talk."

"No. I don't know if they're following me."

"Who?"

"My…never mind. I…look, I'll be at the…at the—" She cleared her throat. "Cyrano's. At Thunder River Casino. You know where it is, right? Eight o'clock tonight." Muffled voices sounded in the background. "I have to go. I'll be there. For an hour."

The dead line hummed over the speaker. Cash hit the button to end the call. Oh, yeah. He knew where the nightclub was all right. He stared at his cousin. "What's your take on this?"

Bridger lifted his shoulders and dropped them, his expression perplexed. “Your guess is as good as mine. I do find it interesting that we hit pay dirt with our search on her and she just happens to call. Out of the blue.”

“Don’t trust coincidences?”

“Nope.”

“Neither do I.”

“Then again, Cash, maybe we shouldn’t look a gift horse in the mouth.”

“Maybe. Maybe not.”

“You’ll meet her?”

Cash curled his lips into a sarcastic smile that didn’t reach his eyes but coated his voice. “What do you think? I mean, gift horse and all that.”

“Yeah, I figured. I’ll arrange backup.”

Backup was easy. Barron Security was the authority in casino operations, and in addition to the Barron family properties, they had contracts with most of the tribal entities in Oklahoma. Meaning they’d have their own security force in place at Thunder River.

After Bridger walked out, Cash studied Roxanne’s driver’s license. Fresh-faced, her red hair a tangle of wisps and waves, eyes the color of the aged whiskey he liked to drink. With a click of the mouse, he displayed the clearest photo he had of her from the Barron Casino. Smoky eye shadow smudging her lids. Kiss-me red lips. Heightened color on her cheeks. The girl in the first photo appeared sure of herself, almost cocky, but with a sweetness under the surface. The second? She looked like a kid playing dress-up. Who was the real Roxanne Rowland? Cash planned to find out. And would in a matter of hours.

He couldn’t wait.

Three

Cash studied the monitors in the Thunder River Casino's security room. He'd manually added photos of the Rowland clan to the facial recognition program. He didn't trust Roxanne and trusted her family even less. That slip of the tongue indicating she might be followed could be paranoia, real fear or calculated intent. He leaned toward calculation. She'd certainly played him when she was a teenager.

He almost missed her when she walked in. This was *not* the woman he'd seen in Vegas. Everything about her was toned down—hair, makeup, clothing. He had to look twice to be sure. Then he checked her ID photo. Yes. Same woman. He wondered again who the real Roxanne Rowland was. The ID and the woman waiting at the hostess station in Cyrano's, or the femme fatale in a little black dress and four-inch designer stilettos. Tonight, she wore tight jeans tucked into blinged-out Western boots and a body-hugging sweater belted with leather and silver.

"Keep your eyes open for any of the suspects," Cash ordered the security supervisor.

"Yes, sir. Monitor three is the camera for her table."

Cash's breath came quick and sharp as he watched the hostess escort Roxanne to the table. Concentrating, he leveled out his nerves. This was business. Nothing more. He needed to stay focused. Moments later, a waitress arrived, took her order, then delivered what looked like plain iced tea.

Over the next hour, Roxanne nursed the tea, declined several offers from men and fended off increasingly impatient attentions from the waitress. She became jumpy, staring at the entrance and coming to attention every time someone entered, and constantly checked her watch. Interesting. She looked at her watch a final time, finished the tea and left a tip far larger than the cost of the drink.

Cash smiled, feeling predatory. Showtime.

Roxanne was looking over her shoulder when she plowed into him just outside Cyrano's entrance. Reflex made him grab her arms to steady her, but something far more perverse had him hauling her up against his chest. She held still for a long moment, then pushed her arms between them and attempted to shove him away. He allowed only enough room between them that he could look down into her face.

Those amber eyes of hers widened and she wet her bottom lip with her tongue. He corralled his libido and pasted a disinterested expression on his face. Snagging her hand, he tugged her along as he returned to the security area. Two uniformed guards waited at the secured door and escorted them to a small interview room. Roxanne's hand tightened convulsively on his as he led her inside. Interesting.

"Have a seat, Ms. Rowland." He held out a chair for her and waited until she sat down before asking, "Why are you here?"

* * *

Roxie did her best to curb her panic. She hid her hands under the table, gripping her thighs to control their trembling. Swallowing around the lump clogging her throat, she prayed her voice remained steady. “Why am I here?”

“Easy question, Roxanne.”

“No, not really.”

“So enlighten me.”

Enlighten him? Easy for him to say. She needed to understand what was happening—*why* it was happening to explain her reasons for contacting him. “Do you have a couple of hours?”

He arched one brow, and darn if that didn’t set hummingbirds loose in her stomach. He was just as dark and sexy and…no, not debonair. He was too intense for debonair, too cynical. Cash didn’t say anything. He didn’t have to. His piercing gaze and that oh-so-eloquent eyebrow spoke volumes.

“You probably don’t remember me.” Why would he? She’d been a gangly teenager, just turned sixteen, with wild red hair and more than her share of freckles. Mortified, she’d sat in that interview room for almost twenty hours until a fast-talking lawyer in a cheap suit had shown up with the headmistress. Sometimes, Cash had sat across from her, never speaking, just watching. Other times, he’d stood in a corner, shoulder braced against the wall, legs crossed at the ankle and arms either crossed over a very muscular chest or shoved into the front pockets of tailored slacks. Her teenage self had totally fallen for him. Her grown-up self was torn between that remembered hormonal hero worship and total terror.

She huffed out a breath, placing her fisted hands on the table. “My father is a thief.” She didn’t expect the sharp burst of laughter her statement evoked.

"There's no need to be rude, Mr. Barron." Heat suffused her cheeks but she ignored it. "I didn't have to call you."

"We would have tracked you down eventually."

"I'm not that hard to find."

He slid a hip onto the corner of the table and stared at her. "Last time we sat in a room like this, your name was Anne Landerson."

Her lips pursed at that and she quickly smoothed them out to a hard line as his eyes focused on her mouth. "That's the name I was enrolled with at that school. My father told me it was for security reasons."

Cash laughed again, but this time, the sound was dark and derisive. "Oh, this ought to be good. Spell it out for me, Red."

"Don't call me that."

And there went his eyebrow again. "I…didn't spend much time with my father or brothers growing up. I was left with a family called the Millers until I was old enough for boarding school. I had…" She wondered how to phrase this part. "I was told not use my real name and had a false birth certificate. I had no clue what my father did. I only knew that he traveled, was very dashing and mysterious, and on more than one occasion, I imagined he was an international spy."

His other eyebrow rose, accompanied by a twist at the corner of his mouth. Cash's expression caused her to feel dumb about those childish fantasies. What little girl wanted to believe her father was a criminal?

"On my sixteenth birthday, a box arrived. As I'd never received a gift from my father before, this was a momentous occasion."

"Yeah, I bet."

Ooh. The sarcasm fairly dripped from those three

words. “For a girl who had little contact with her family, who had never celebrated birthdays or Christmas, it was.”

He shifted off the table, moved to the corner and assumed a posture she’d grown familiar with. Something jiggled his jacket pocket. He reached in and withdrew his cell phone, presumably to send and receive texts. She couldn’t keep herself from admiring his long, nimble fingers, even though her blush deepened as her thoughts wandered down completely inappropriate paths.

Cash Barron was fantasy-inducing. Tall, broad-shouldered, with long legs, a slim waist. She could attest to the muscularity of his chest from her stolen moment of weakness earlier that evening. She couldn’t help but be struck by the black hair, brown eyes the color of dark-roast coffee and a sculpted face that would make a fashion model jealous. When she’d looked up his bio before calling, Roxie had been shocked to learn he wasn’t all that much older than her. At sixteen, she’d been a starry-eyed girl and he’d been very much a man. Confident, handsome, strong. She’d sat there in that room, dreaming about kissing his full lips, about falling into his arms, about… Jerking back from the sexy images, she deep-breathed through a slight panic attack when she discovered him watching her intently. The glint in his eyes was…unsettling.

“So, you received a gift from your mysterious father.”

Right back to business. This was good. She should concentrate on business, not…other things. She centered her thoughts. “Yes. I was excited when I opened it. I found what looked like costume jewelry, which I thought odd, given my age and the fact that we’d had little interaction over the years. And then I found the little picture. I thought it was a print—ballerinas in tutus, and I was thrilled. I wanted to be a ballerina at the time, despite the school’s dance master rolling his eyes whenever I attempted to dance in toe shoes."

Cash snorted and she glared at him. "I was a lonely girl with no particular talent, Mr. Barron. I was touched because I believed the picture was my father's way of acknowledging my dreams. I didn't read the note attached to the package until later, when it was too late."

"Okay. I'll bite. What did it say?"

And why did her thoughts go right back down that dark road to sexy city? Biting was a big no-no. She cleared her throat. "My father told me to stash the box and keep it safe. I was never meant to open it. It never even occurred to him that I might mistake it for a gift. He didn't remember it was my birthday."

Roxie lifted her head, her gaze colliding with his. "I discovered on my sixteenth birthday that, not only was my father a wanted criminal, but he had so little regard for me that he couldn't be bothered to remember my birthday. As you know, the jewelry turned out to be real and that sweet little print of the ballerinas turned out to be an original Degas, scammed from an eighty-year-old woman by a smooth-talking stranger, according to the police." She dropped her hands to her lap and wiped her sweaty palms on her jeans before continuing. "The next day, I returned to the Millers. I used my birth name after that."

"Want to explain how you ended up here?"

She contemplated that question for a moment. "*Here* here or here in general?"

"In Oklahoma. In Oklahoma City. Why did you go to UCO?"

"Oh. I took online classes and got my GED when I was seventeen. I checked out a directory of American colleges and universities from the library, closed my eyes, opened the book and stabbed my finger on the page."

His dubious expression said it all. “That’s the truth, Mr. Barron.”

“Why were you in Vegas?”

“I don’t really know.” She canted her chin at a stubborn angle as her hands gripped the edge of the table. “The itinerary, hotel reservations and boarding pass showed up in my inbox. A weekend jaunt in Vegas, all expenses paid. The email said I’d won a contest. I checked with the airline. The ticket was real so I had no reason to think it was a setup until my brother Brax met me at the airport. I was given a bag of clothes from a high-end boutique, told to—and I quote—doll myself up. On the way down in the elevator, Brax told me I was to…” Her voice faltered and she swallowed down a wave of nausea. “They had a mark. Max was working him on the casino floor. I was supposed to…to be *nice* to him.”

“What does that mean?”

She clasped her hands and stared at them, unable to meet Cash’s gaze any longer. “They wanted me to get him to his room, to…” She had to swallow again.

“I get the picture.” His voice sounded gruff but she still couldn’t face him.

“The lights went out and then…”

“And then I almost caught you.”

“Yes.”

Cash almost believed her—that lonely little girl act was guaranteed to play on a man’s protective instincts. If this were a movie, he’d nominate her for an Oscar. She was one terrific actress. The blushes, the swallows, the trembling hands fisted together were all perfect touches.

“Why is your family targeting Barron properties?” He moved closer, then dropped into the chair across from her.

Roxanne’s head jerked up and for a fleeting moment,

he wondered if he'd taken her by surprise. A look of consternation quickly followed the one of shock created by his question. Cash had interviewed a lot of people in his life. Instinct insisted this girl was exactly what she seemed—a sweet kid too naive for her own good. But experience persisted in believing her to be as big a con as the rest of her family.

Maximilian Rowland was a consummate thief and scoundrel who had raised his sons in his own mold. Why would such a man not utilize every tool he had—including his beautiful daughter? He shoved the parallel to his own father and brothers to the very back of his mind.

"I…didn't know they were." Her eyebrows pulled into an intriguing vee above the bridge of her scrunched-up nose. She looked cutely perplexed. "I suppose that rather falls in line with why I contacted you."

Leaning back in the chair, he waited for her to continue.

"My father is a…criminal, Mr. Barron. We've been mostly estranged my entire life, but especially since that one incident. My brothers have contacted me periodically, checking up on me, occasionally sending money—which I sent back." She hurried to add that bit of information and again, he almost believed her. "Anyway, the trip to Las Vegas was a complete surprise."

She blinked at him, still portraying her innocence. "So you had no idea you'd be…" He searched for a word. "*Working* with them?"

"No! None at all. But…" Her voice trailed off and she wouldn't look directly at him.

"But what?"

"I have the feeling they aren't done with me." She leaned forward, her expression earnest. "To be perfectly honest, Mr. Barron, I want nothing to do with them. I like my job. There are things I want to do with my life and they do not include jail time." She inhaled deeply, huffed out the breath and plastered a serious look on her face. "I have a proposal for you."

Cash watched, making sure there was nothing on his face for her to read. "A proposal."

"Yes." She nodded enthusiastically and leaned even closer.

He glanced down, just to see what she was "offering." Nothing. Her sweater remained sedately in place. He was almost disappointed. Then her pursed lips caught his attention.

"You see, as I stated, I don't want anything to do with them, but if you—or the police—can catch them, then I get to keep my life."

"And keeping your life is important to you?"

She tossed him a cute expression meant to convey "duh."

"Exactly. Look, I'm a museum curator by education. I want to work in a museum. Being the corporate archivist for RCM is interesting, but I really want to use my history degree. My father and brothers? They'll ruin everything."

"And your proposal?"

"Oh! I thought I'd said. I'm pretty sure they plan on dragging me into whatever their scheme is. I can pretend to play along, notify you, and you and the police can swoop in and arrest them."

"Swoop in."

She nodded enthusiastically again. "Exactly."

Cash didn't believe her, but he admitted things were getting interesting. "Tell me what you do know."

She rambled along, either filling in blanks or making stuff up as she went. She was an imaginative little thing. He was busy texting Bridger. She had a proposition? He had the beginnings of a plan.

"Um… I still have the dress."

"Dress?" He looked up from his phone.

"Yes, the one I told you about. The one I wore to the casino? It still had the tags when I wore it and I was told not to tear them off because my brother planned to return the dress for credit. Or he shoplifted it and just told me that."

"Uh-huh."

"I want to send it back to the store…or at least find out if someone actually paid for it. I might keep it if Braxton did. He's a pig."

Somewhere along the way, Cash had lost control of the conversation, though the flurry of texts he exchanged with Bridger had been enlightening. According to their account rep at RCM, Roxanne Rowland had been hired as an archivist—basically a glorified librarian charged with cataloging and preserving ad campaign material. They were thrilled to have her, she'd been a model employee, and was there a problem?

He wasn't quite sure when—or why—he made the decision he did, but with one final text, he put his plan into motion.

"Okay, here's the deal. You're moving in with me."

Roxie's face registered shocked denial. "What? No!"

"I don't think you understand, sweetheart. Until this situation is resolved, we're joined at the hip."

"First, I am not your sweetheart."

"Boy, ain't that the truth." He muttered the sentiment under his breath.

"And second, I can't. I have work."

"That's been taken care of. You're on loan to the Barron Companies."

"Wait…I…that can't be! I'm in the middle of a project. You…what in the world will I do for the Barron Companies?"

"The same thing you do for RCM, Red. Bottom line, I'm not letting you out of my sight."

Color tinted her cheeks, and her eyes glinted like bright sun shining on a broken whiskey bottle. "Oh? Really? How does that work, precisely? Are you going to handcuff me to the toilet when you shower? Tie me to the bed?"

"That can be arranged."

Four

Evil. He was just pure evil. Roxie's temper flared even as a wave of unadulterated lust surged through her insides. It had nothing to do with being tied to Cash Barron's bed and everything to do with the man himself. And she needed to murder her girlish fantasies immediately or she'd never survive this debacle intact. She chanced a look in his direction. His expression remained resolute but was that a twinkle of mischief in his eyes?

"Let's go."

"I'm not going anywhere with you. My car is in the parking lot."

"I'll have security drive it home for you."

"I'm perfectly capable of driving myself."

"You're riding with me. We'll go by your apartment, you can pack, then we'll head to my place."

"What part of *no* do you not understand? I have responsibilities. I—" She felt her eyes widen. "I have someone waiting at home for me."

"Who?"

"Um… Harley."

"Who's that?"

Cash's gaze narrowed, and did he sound suspicious or was it something else? Something…intriguing. Like jealousy? Ha. Roxie was just a means to an end. *Jealous* was not a word she would ever associate with Cash. "He's my…roommate." Well, technically speaking, that was true. Harley lived with her. "And I sort of have to take care of him."

Cash leaned closer and peered at her, his gaze sharp and assessing. "What's that mean—you have to take care of him?"

Roxie forced herself to meet his gaze despite the jitters skipping through her. "He's…um…immature. He can't really look after himself."

"Uh-huh."

He totally was not convinced. But there was no way she could leave Harley home alone. "I'm telling the truth, Mr. Barron."

"Uh-huh. C'mon. Let's go meet this guy and see what he has to say about all this."

He latched on to her hand and tugged her along after him. Roxie was suddenly reminded of what walking with Harley was like. She tried to plant her feet, but the leather soles of her boots skidded over the smooth flooring. She attempted to jerk her hand free, but Cash simply tightened his grip and kept walking. She finally gave up and trotted to keep up with his long-legged stride.

When they reached the entrance, there was a dark gray Range Rover waiting, and a man in a black suit, starched white shirt and black tie held the passenger-side door open. He tucked his chin as he extended a hand palm-up and said, "Ma'am, we'll need your keys."

"No, you don't. I'm driving myself home."

The security guard quickly turned his attention to Cash, looking for guidance.

"Give him your keys, Red."

"Gah! No. Get it through your thick head, Mr. Barron. Just because I agreed to help you does not mean you can tell me what to do."

Cash stalked around the vehicle toward her and she stepped back, right into the bulk of the security guard—who didn't give an inch. "Give the nice man your car keys, Roxanne, and get into the Rover."

He glared daggers at her and his mouth was a tight line. This guy definitely meant business. She'd been an idiot to call him. Still, if she ever wanted control of her life back, she needed him. Darn it. She huffed out a breath, dug in her purse and pulled out her key chain.

Cash watched as Roxanne meticulously removed a key from the jumble of metal consisting of more keys, a flashlight, at least ten plastic loyalty tags for various restaurants and stores, and other dangly things like weird jewelry. She passed the key to the guard, then that mess of a key chain disappeared back into the bag hitched over her shoulder.

"Get in the car, Roxanne."

She stuck out her tongue but settled into the front seat. He closed the door and gestured for security to remain there so she couldn't escape. Once he was behind the wheel, he glanced at her.

"Buckle up, buttercup."

Her upper lip curled into a kittenish snarl and he almost laughed. Roxanne Rowland was turning into something totally unexpected. Deep down, Cash wondered if he was getting played. The woman dressed in comfortable clothes and wearing no makeup with a sprinkling of freckles was not the woman he'd watched on the security monitors in Vegas.

The trip from the south end of the metro to the northwest side was made in silence. If she was surprised when they turned into her apartment complex, she didn't show it. He couldn't wait to meet this imaginary roommate. Bridger had checked with the complex's management. Roxanne had a one-bedroom studio and was the only one listed on the lease. If she'd sneaked in a boyfriend, she was in violation.

He parked in a slot near her ground-floor apartment and watched her. She appeared irritated rather than nervous. "Getting out?"

"I was waiting for you to open my door, but you obviously aren't a gentleman." With that, she popped her door open and started to get out—only she was snagged by the seat belt.

Pressing his lips together to keep from laughing, Cash hit the release button to free her. Was she really this klutzy, or was it all an act meant to disarm him? Act or not, she was doing just that.

Stomping up the walkway to her apartment, she inserted her key, pushed the door open and stepped to the side. Cash had about fivc scconds to prepare for the hairy monster launching in his direction. He braced himself, one foot forward, shoulders lowered, and found his arms full of furry energy intent on slobbering all over his face. He muscled the gigantic dog to the ground and glared at Roxanne. She was doubled over, laughing.

"Thanks for the warning. I'm assuming this is Harley?"

She inhaled deeply and bit her lips for a long moment while she regained her composure. "Yes."

"I'll make arrangements to have him boarded." He recognized his tactical error a second too late. Both woman and dog turned on him.

"Harley is not going to some smelly old kennel! He goes where I go!" The dog barked, an echoing *woof* that rattled windows.

"Oh? What did you do with him while you were in Vegas?" He had her there.

Her face scrunched up into an adorably perplexed expression. "Um… Leo."

"And who is Leo?"

"I'm Leo and girlfriend, you did not tell me you had a date with a fine, *fine* man like this one."

Cash looked up at the man leaning over the balcony above them before returning his attention to Roxanne. "So let Leo take care of him."

"Uh-uh. Not happening. I have company comin' and I won't have time to be traipsing back and forth to let that creature out every time he thinks he needs to sniff the bushes."

Roxanne turned those golden eyes on him. "Harley suffers from separation anxiety. You're the one who is so insistent I move in with you."

"Whoa! You've really been holdin' out on me, Miss Roxie-anne." If Leo leaned any farther over the railing, the man would fall into the very bushes Harley now sniffed.

As if he knew he was the subject of conversation, the big mutt lumbered over, sat right in front of Cash and put a massive paw on his thigh. The dog *whuffed*, a sound too similar to Roxanne's echoing sigh. He resisted throwing up his arms in surrender.

"Fine, but that thing better be housebroken."

Squaring her shoulders and raising her chin, Roxanne leveled what he supposed was an insulted glare on him. "Good." She turned away and muttered under her breath, "Oh, yeah? I bet you aren't housebroken, Chase Barron."

For the next hour, Cash sat on the couch with the massive furball. The dog sprawled next to him, huge head on his thigh. Roxanne puttered around, packing suitcases and grocery bags full of dog food, toys, brushes and other pet paraphernalia. He was far too amused by her, discovering he was smiling at odd times.

"Okay, I'm ready."

Cash checked her over. Roxanne had tucked her hair up into a messy ponytail and stood in the midst of a pile of stuff. He stared at her, then stared pointedly at the boxes and suitcases around her feet. "Should I call a moving van? We can load up your furniture, too."

"Ha-ha. Not funny. I'm trying to be nice in a difficult situation."

He eyed all the gear. "Nice?"

"Yes. I figured you wouldn't want to be running back and forth between your place and mi—"

Cash's cell rang, cutting her off. He shoved the dog away and stood, phone to his ear. He listened to Bridger without giving away the gist of their conversation, his gaze glued on Roxanne.

"Otto Baer is a whale, according to Tucker. He's never stayed at any of the Barron casinos before the incident with the Rowlands."

He considered that information. A whale, also referred to as a high roller, bet large amounts of money. Casinos offered them lavish "comps," such as free private jet transfers, limousine access and use of the casinos' best suites, to lure them onto the gambling floors.

"What was the deal?" Cash asked the question with careful words.

"That's what's really weird, coz. Tuck checked with Chase and with their concierge. They didn't even know the guy was there."

"Interesting."

"I thought so. He stayed two days, lost some money but not a huge amount, won a little of it back and then took off for Tahoe." Harley bellowed out a bark, and a startled Bridger added, "What the hell was that?"

"One of my new houseguests."

"Do I want to know?"

"Probably not. See what else you can find out. I'm headed to my place as soon as I can get all of Roxanne's stuff loaded in the Rover."

"Roxanne's stuff. Loaded in the Rover. Uh…huh. Care to explain?"

"Executive decision."

"Oh, boy. Can't wait to hear this story. Will I see you at the office in the morning?"

"Yes." Cash clicked off the call before Bridger could ask any further irritating questions. He centered himself and said, "Let's go."

Ignoring the huge wet spot staining his slacks—a splotch that resembled slug slime—he gathered up an armful of boxes and a suitcase. It took them two trips each to stow all of her odds and ends in the cargo area. When it came time to load Harley in the backseat, Cash balked.

"Those are leather seats. Claws and drool do not mix with leather."

Roxanne harrumphed and rolled her eyes. "Fine." She marched back inside and returned quickly with a blanket. "Here, Mr. Fuddy-Duddy."

He was not a fuddy-duddy. He just appreciated fine things, and that included leather seats in his vehicles. "You already owe me a cleaning bill for these slacks. I figured you wouldn't want to add replacement seats to your tab."

"Replacement—" Roxanne's jaw snapped shut and her golden eyes sparked.

Cash had a perverse streak, obviously. Pushing this woman's buttons was far too much fun. He watched her avidly while she bent over, reaching into the vehicle to smooth the blanket over the backseats. He caught a few of her muttered imprecations.

"...made of Corinthian leather...male-chauvinist moron...cheapskate...cars that cost more than some people's houses...hates my dog."

He glanced down at the huge black dog sitting beside him. "Does she always talk to herself?" The animal gazed up with solemn brown eyes and sighed. Cash tilted his head to get a better look at Roxanne's very lovely butt. She backed out of the vehicle and whirled, catching him in the act.

"Really?" she demanded, then muttered, "Add jerk-face to the list."

Biting his lips to stifle a burst of laughter, Cash snapped his fingers at the dog. "Get in the car, mutt."

"He is *not* a mutt. Harley is a full-blooded, pedigreed Newfoundland."

He figured the inside of his mouth would be bloody before they got to his place. "Fine." He snapped his fingers again. "Get in the car, full-blooded, pedigreed Newfoundland mutt."

Harley bounded into the backseat, apparently unconcerned that Cash was dissing him. Roxanne threw her arms up as her anger simmered. She clambered into the front seat and slammed the door. Cash could no longer hold back his laughter. She was cute and feisty and he was far more turned on by that than he should be, given their circumstances. He just managed to choke off his laughter as he got into the driver's seat.

"It's not funny," Roxanne huffed.

"It is from where I'm sitting."

Five

"You have white furniture?" Roxie's voice squeaked. What man in his right mind would have white furniture—white *leather* furniture? Harley took one look at the big couch, jerked so hard she let go of his leash, and leaped. He romped all over it, snuffling, and then finally settled on one end. He sat there as proud as punch.

She glanced over her shoulder. Cash had put down his load and returned to the car for a second one. Snatching the moment of privacy, she waggled her finger at the Newfie. "Harley, get down. Bad dog. Bad, *bad* dog!" The big goof rolled over on his back and offered his belly for rubs. "You are going to cost me a fortune," she groused, but obediently petted the beguiling animal.

"I'll put the damage on your tab."

She whirled to face the other half of her torment. "It's not my fault that you live in a sterile environment, and I will remind you, *you* are the one who insisted on this arrangement."

His dark brown eyes glinted and she was reminded of dark ale in a glass. "You're laughing at me."

He arched one devilish brow and said, “Am I?”

After nailing him with her most fierce glare, she gestured to the stuff piled in the entry. “Where am I supposed to put all this?”

Roxie could almost see the thoughts whipping through Cash’s mind as he glanced down a hallway. She’d bet that way led to danger—in the form of the master bedroom. When she drew her gaze back from that precipice, her eyes collided with his. Her whole body ignited from the half-lidded look and sexy grin he lavished on her. She was far too young for hot flashes, but darn if this man didn’t make her want to peel out of her clothes and dance in the sprinklers to cool off.

“Your room—” Cash cleared his throat and she wondered why he’d need to “—is that way.” He pointed to an arch next to the kitchen. “Guest bedroom. Attached bath.” He pointed to a curtain beyond the open dining room area. “Doors to the patio. There’s a little grass. You’re responsible for picking up after the dog. The kitchen is tiled. Leave his food and water bowls there. There’s a walk-in pantry to store the rest of his stuff.”

She nodded at each instruction, half listening while she perused the room. Roxie wasn’t quite sure what she’d expected but this condo hadn’t even been a faint blip on her radar. Bricktown properties weren’t cheap, but this complex? It was one of the most expensive in the area—not that she was surprised. The Barrons were rolling in money. Still, this place was probably the largest unit, with its huge open living room flowing into a high-end chef’s kitchen and large dining area.

The floors were hardwood and Harley’s nails would leave scratch marks, if not gouges. Rugs were scattered under the furniture. The place looked like the set for an HGTV series. Cash had mentioned that the condo also had outdoor space, and she could just imagine what she'd find out there. The guy probably had a private lap pool. In addition to all the public space, the condo contained at least two bedrooms and baths. And every piece of furniture and artwork was designer unique. That all added up to expensive with a capital *E*.

This man was too rich for her blood. Not that Cash would give her a second look if her family hadn't dragged her into whatever nefarious scheme they were working.

Roxie jumped when Cash touched her chin and closed her gaping mouth. He'd caught her gawking at her surroundings and daydreaming about the man himself. She couldn't afford to lose focus like that. She had to keep her wits about her. Cash Barron did not like her, and had a real issue with her family. Okay, *she* took issue with her family, too, but that was different. They were hers. He was an outsider and he was pushy. A jerk. Aggravating. Exasperating. Sexy. Hot. Smelled like heaven.

"Earth to Roxanne."

"What?" She reacted sharply, embarrassed that she'd floated off again.

"Your dog wants out."

"You can't walk across the room, open *your* door and let him out into *your* backyard?"

"Not my dog, buttercup."

Muttering dark thoughts under her breath, Roxie snapped her fingers and marched over to the curtained door. She had to fumble through yards of material before she found the handles for the French doors hiding behind the draperies. The lock took concentration and more than a little finesse to open. Of course, it would. The man was president of a major security company. This entire place was probably wired for sound and video. She froze.

Harley, impatient to get out, used his 150 pounds to

push her out of the way and she grabbed the curtain to keep from falling to the floor. Only the fabric ripped, and the whole wall of material cascaded to the floor, pooling around her where she sat on her tush.

Cash didn't even try to hold in his laughter. All but slapping his knees, he was learning that a person *could* laugh so hard they cried. He had to wipe moisture from his eyes and every time he started to calm down, he'd look at Roxanne, and hilarity once again ensued. Once he convinced himself he was under control, he started across the room to help the girl up.

Harley charged through the back door and must have decided that finding his mistress sitting on the floor was a new game. The giant dog pounced, taking Roxanne down, slobbering all over her face. Her shrieks of protest only incited the mutt to more mayhem. The dog fell off Roxie, tangled his feet in the yards of silk fabric and proceeded to roll up in it.

There'd be no salvaging the curtains and Cash admitted to feeling a sense of relief. The condo had been decorated by one of his father's mistresses and she'd used it as a showroom until Cash came home early from a trip to find her in bed with the guy who'd laid her tile. Glancing around, he discovered the place *was* sterile and stark. The walls were white, the furniture white, the rugs white. The only splashes of color came from the framed art photography on the walls. Most of the prints were black-and-whites but some had odd dashes of red—an umbrella in one rainy-day photo, lips on the pouting female model in another.

He contrasted his space with the one Roxanne had left behind. Her stuff was what some would call shabby chic, or thrift-store vogue. The place looked and felt lived-in—like the houses his older brothers all shared with their wives. Different styles but the same sense of…home.

Jerking his thoughts away from that quagmire, Cash focused on the situation at hand. Roxanne still sat in the floor—either crying or laughing silently. He couldn't tell. He edged around the large granite-topped dining table and stared at his houseguests. Harley pawed at Roxie with both front feet, paddling against her thigh. Her red-rimmed eyes didn't bode well. He clicked his fingers. "Enough, Harley."

The Newf stood up and shook. Hard. Silk curtains and slug slime flew. Cash refused to laugh, though he had to turn around for a long moment to regain his composure. Not that Roxanne noticed. She'd pulled some of the silk over her head.

"Just kill me now, okay?" Her mumbled words elicited a *woof* from Harley, then he danced around her, nosing through the material.

"Harley!" This time he barked out the dog's name and the beast came to sit obediently beside him. Cash glanced down at the woman. She was glaring at the dog. "Need a hand?" he offered.

"No," she snapped at him, pushed the material off and stood. She craned her head to look toward the ceiling where the valance and jalousies had once hung on a brass pole. She heaved a huge sigh. "Let me guess. Real silk, right?"

Cash lifted a negligent shoulder. "Probably."

"Criminy. I'm going to owe you my firstborn at this rate."

Everything stopped for a heartbeat and he stared at her. His rational brain insisted she was simply borrowing a figure of speech to describe her predicament. But that part deep inside he hid from everyone—from his brothers, his twin, even himself—wondered for that brief moment in time what it would be like to hold his child.

"Cash?"

Reality crashed back. "Don't worry about the drapes, Roxanne."

"Um..." She stretched a hesitant hand in his direction. "Are you...okay?"

"I'm fine." Okay, he'd been a little short with her, but whatever. She wasn't his girlfriend. She wasn't his houseguest. She was a suspect in an ongoing investigation. "I'll help carry your junk to the guest room."

He turned on his heel and headed back to the entry hall.

"What about this mess?"

"Leave it." Yeah, definitely short.

"If you say so..." She didn't quite put a period on the end of that sentence.

"I say so. It's late. I have an early morning. That means you do, too."

"Well, all righty then, Mr. Sociable."

With Harley doing his best to trip him, Cash ferried the remainder of Roxanne's belongings to her room. She managed one load, fell over the dog, then wisely waited in the bedroom to direct him where to put the bags, boxes and luggage. After the last load, he paused at the door. He should have said something to her but he wasn't quite sure what.

Cash eventually settled on the tried and true. "Good night, Roxanne."

He shut the door firmly and retreated to the kitchen. Grabbing a beer from the fridge, he headed to the media room. He clicked on the giant-screen TV while waiting for his laptop to power up. He'd catch the OKC Thunder game while checking his email.

After drinking the beer and dealing with a few problems from the office, he was still restless. It was pushing midnight and he needed to sleep. Pausing outside the guest room, he listened at the door. The only sound he caught was a jingling noise—probably the tags on Harley's collar. The Newf was scratching. Great. He probably had fleas.

He tiptoed away and paused in the kitchen long enough to deposit the beer bottle in the trash. In his bedroom, he stripped down to his boxers and stretched out on his bed in the dark. Cash didn't sleep well on the best of nights. Having others in his space perturbed him more than he wanted to admit. The rhythm was off—different noises, different feel to the atmosphere. He wasn't used to a woman sleeping under his roof.

Two hours later, he was still staring at the ceiling. He got out of bed and wandered out. The living room looked brighter than normal, and he remembered there was no longer a wall of curtains blocking the French doors and windows in the dining area. Security lights and the moon cast a grid pattern across the floor. He couldn't decide if he liked the openness or not. One more thing that was different. And unsettling—as troublesome as the thought of Roxanne sleeping not fifty feet away.

He wasn't hungry or thirsty—not for anything in the refrigerator anyway—so he bypassed the kitchen. The media room was empty. The guest room wasn't. He should have gone back to bed but he didn't. He stood outside the door, breathing shallowly and listening to the indistinct noises on the other side. Two additional sets of breathing sounds—one whispery soft, the other a sonorous snore. Curious, he eased the door open and peeked in.

Roxie lay spread-eagled on her stomach under the sheet and a light blanket. In the low light, her hair created a glowing nimbus against the white pillowcase. The black dog was a dark stain across the foot of the bed. The animal raised his head, snuffled, sighed and dropped back into sleep.

Something knotted up inside Cash but he didn't want to examine the feeling too closely. This woman was getting under his skin and he didn't like that idea—or maybe he liked it *too* much. He closed the door as carefully as he'd opened it and padded barefoot back to his own room. He still felt unsettled but he climbed into bed. After some tossing and turning, he dropped off. Exhausted, he barely noticed the dip of the mattress as a warm body joined him.

Six

Something heavy lay on Cash's chest and hot breath fanned his face. A clammy glob of…something nasty pooled on his bare skin. What the blazes? Something cold and wet nuzzled his face. He pressed his head into his pillow and opened one eye. Big brown eyes, a shiny black nose and trails of slug slime filled his vision.

Harley. The damn dog was gazing at Cash like he was the critter's new best friend—or breakfast. It was hard to tell.

"Get off." The big goof *woofed*, rolled over and burrowed into Cash's side. Laughing despite himself, he shoved the animal off the bed. "Not what I meant."

Cash sat on edge of the mattress and grabbed his watch—all while ignoring the sad-faced dog. Six a.m. It might be Saturday but he had things to do. When Harley shuffled to the door, he figured letting the dog out was probably the first thing on the agenda.

While Harley wandered around sniffing everything in sight inside the enclosed patio, Cash slipped down the hallway. He was more than curious how the dog had gotten out. The door was ajar just enough for a 150-pound dog to amble through. He nudged it with his foot and peered in.

His guest was still sprawled under the sheet, face covered by a web of tousled hair, and she was making soft puffing noises with each exhalation. Roxanne appeared to be dead asleep. Either Harley was Houdini in disguise or Cash hadn't closed the door all the way when he'd spied on the girl earlier.

Ten minutes later, he was doing his best to forget the girl and her dog. Cash had things to do. First up, his daily five-mile run. While he normally used running time to order his thoughts and plan his day, he was failing miserably this morning. Thoughts of tousled auburn hair, golden eyes, pouty lips and an innocence that couldn't be real intruded.

What were her intentions? Why was her family after the Barrons? Where did she fit into the scheme of things? Which Roxanne was the real one—the sexy siren or the adorable klutz? How did he find the answers he needed? The questions beat in his head in time to the thud of his running shoes on the pavement.

The woman was a menace—from her curious offer to help nab her family to his perplexing reaction to her. Especially the latter. He didn't want to think about her as an attractive woman, or the way her skin felt when he touched it. Messy hair should just be messy hair. It shouldn't make him wonder how it would look after a night of hot sex. And he definitely shouldn't be thinking about having sex with the delectable Ms. Rowland. She was nothing more than a grifter, born into the life and raised on the long con.

Wasn't she?

Cash had learned early on to rely on his gut reactions to situations and people. He was seldom wrong. Everything he knew about the Rowlands pointed at Roxanne being smack-dab in the middle of things, right up to her beguiling whiskey-colored eyes.

He pounded the pavement but came no closer to answering the questions circling his brain. And the only answers he had pointed in opposite directions. Roxanne Rowland was an enigma—a woman allegedly raised away from her family, sentenced to boarding schools, whose one brush with the law involved Cash's great-aunt. To cross paths now, six years later? With her father and brothers on the prowl in numerous Barron properties?

In Vegas, the house always held the advantage and the odds. Working security, Cash had learned to watch for the long shot and plan accordingly. That outlier would jump up and bite you in the butt nine times out of ten. So what did that make Roxanne? A puzzle—and one he would solve sooner rather than later. He had no choice. He had a duty to his family to do so, and his father would expect no less from him.

He jerked his thoughts away from his father. He'd molded his life to his father's expectations after his first career lecture. He'd been seven and wanted to join the military like his cousin Hunter Tate. *Barrons aren't soldiers,* his father had said. *They're generals.* As a child, he'd only understood that he'd done something wrong—just as it was wrong when he wanted to join the police force.

Ever since his mother had been killed in a car accident, Cash wanted only to protect his family, wanted to keep them safe from harm. And he'd wanted his father's love and approval. One was just as elusive as the other. As an adult, the need to protect was still strong. Everything he'd done, either at his father's direction or of his own volition, he'd done with that desire in mind.

He wanted his head clear but his thoughts were convoluted this morning. That was the problem. Cons. Questions. Puzzles. Family.

Cash altered his morning routine slightly. He'd programmed the coffeemaker before leaving on his run but on the way back to the condo, he stopped in at Sugarbaker's to pick up breakfast. The place catered to residents in the Deep Deuce/Bricktown area. Part coffee shop with amazing pastries, the store also carried gourmet groceries and takeout for lunch and dinner.

With hot muffins and a few staples, like milk, cream and sugar in tow, he jogged the two blocks to his condo. Harley waited at the door—right where he'd been when Cash left—looking both mournful and miffed. The mutt had attitude and wasn't afraid to show it.

In the kitchen, he found a bleary-eyed Roxanne wearing a thin-strapped camisole and low-riding yoga pants. Cash had never appreciated yoga pants more than he did at that moment. Shifting the grocery bag to hide his reaction, he frowned at her puzzled expression.

"Roxanne?"

She turned to him with a yawn as she bent her arms to her shoulders for a big stretch. A stretch that bared her stomach and gave him a peek at a perfectly formed belly button. Refrigerator. He needed to put the milk and cream in the fridge.

"I need coffee."

"Coffeemaker."

Her gaze slid from him to the machine on the counter. "Coffee?"

She sounded a bit bewildered, and he stifled a laugh by sticking his head in the stainless steel fridge to deposit the perishables. "You get a mug from the cabinet, pick up the carafe, press on the lever and pour."

"Mug?"

He looked at her from behind the fridge door. He pointed to the cabinet above the coffeemaker. "In there." She didn't move. "Roxanne?"

"Yeah?"

"Are you all right?"

"I need coffee." Bewildered tipped over into totally mystified.

"You said that." He stepped closer and she stepped back. Herding her in the opposite direction, he got her around the granite breakfast island and installed on a bar stool. Harley shadowed every step he took.

Roxie plopped her elbows on the cool stone and propped her chin in one palm. Her sleepy eyes tracked every move he made from beneath heavy lids. Snagging two mugs from the cabinet, he glanced over his shoulder. "Black?"

She yawned again, a jaw-cracking widening of her mouth that squinted her eyes shut. "Cream and sugar?"

"Yes." Cash couldn't resist teasing her.

"Huh?"

"Yes, I have cream and sugar. Or milk."

"You drink your coffee with cream and sugar, too?'

"No, I take mine black."

"Then why did you…never mind. Can I have cream and sugar in mine?"

"If you're capable of adding it yourself." He poured coffee into both cups, his to the brim, hers with a little room for additives. Retrieving the carton of cream from the fridge, Cash took pity on Roxie and opened it for her. He placed everything in front of her, including a spoon, before leaning his hips against the counter to watch.

Harley immediately sat in front of him and pawed at Cash's thigh before looking pointedly at the closed pantry door. Did the dog want food? With another swipe of his paw, Harley shuffled to the pantry and stood waiting.

Obliging, Cash opened the door and grinned when the mutt grabbed a box of dog bones in his massive muzzle and backed out. Cash took the box and instead pulled out the large rawhide bone he'd also picked up that morning. Harley happily settled on the kitchen floor mouthing the big chewy and leaving a puddle of drool.

Roxie nursed her coffee and savored it like it was a rare vintage wine. "He likes you," she muttered, and Cash caught a hint of jealousy in her tone.

"How long have you had him?"

She finished the coffee in her mug and pushed it toward him with an *Oliver Twist* "more please" look. He snagged the carafe and filled her cup. After she doctored it and took a sip, she answered. "He was a rescue. I think he was two. Maybe three. That was a couple of years ago."

Then Roxie sighed and all but buried her nose in the coffee mug as she gulped the remaining liquid. When it was empty, she held it out a second time.

Cash choked back his laugh and attempted to look serious. "You aren't a morning person, are you?"

Roxie suppressed a snarl but forced her eyes to open wide. She blinked, then stared at Cash, giving the sexy man a long, slow perusal. She took in his broad shoulders, the sculpted chest outlined by a damp cotton T-shirt. Tapered waist, lean hips encased in form-fitting—and, oh, what a form they fitted—running pants that showcased his muscular thighs to perfection.

"And you are, I'm guessing." She dropped her gaze to focus on adding cream and sugar to her coffee.

"I am." The smug amusement in his tone was almost more than she could take this early in the day.

She gulped more of the hot liquid and choked as the sum of his outfit worked through her now caffeine-soaked brain cells. Sputtering, she managed to swallow and not spit out coffee. “Oh my gosh! You run!”

Okay, that came out as an accusation but she didn’t care. Runners were…insane. Bordering on evil. Did he do this every day? Would he make her get up and go with him?

“I do.” Now he *was* laughing.

A paper towel appeared next to her cup. She wiped her mouth, studiously avoiding looking at Cash, with his lean runner’s body that she wanted to press up against and do bad things to. A huge muffin, resting on a small plate with warmth still radiating from it, appeared in her peripheral vision.

“That one is buttermilk spice. If you prefer blueberry or lemon poppy seed, I have those, too.”

Buttermilk spice was her favorite muffin in the whole world. It tasted the way she thought family holidays should, not that she had any real idea. Only as an adult, during college and while starting her career, had she any inkling of how normal families—real families—celebrated Thanksgiving and Christmas and…birthdays.

Roxie picked at the edge of the muffin overlapping the paper baking cup. A small piece crumbled into her fingers and she popped it into her mouth. The flavor burst on her tongue—cinnamon, ginger, nutmeg. This might just be the most delicious muffin she’d ever eaten. Peeling back the paper, she picked up the treat and took a real bite. She prevented her eyes from rolling back in her head but she couldn’t quite stifle the soft moan of appreciation.

Cash moved, quickly putting the island between them. She lifted her gaze and let out a startled *eep* when she saw his face. His eyes were glued on her and she tried to decipher the look on his face. He edged along the far side of the island and all but dashed across the dining area, his back to her. "I need a shower. Enjoy your muffin and I presume you are now capable of pouring your own coffee?"

"Uh-huh." Her mouth was dry from the quick glimpse she'd caught of him before he turned away. Those muscle-hugging running pants left nothing—*nothing*—to the imagination and oh boy was her imagination doing cartwheels, shaking pompoms, and jumping up and down screaming, "Do me! Do me now!"

No. NononoNO! Roxie reined in her thoughts and concentrated on her muffin. The delicious, her-favorite-kind muffin. Thinking about that man, with that body, naked in the shower? Nope. Not going there. Bad idea. Dangerous road ahead. Slippery when wet. Watch for falling rocks.

Back in control, she finished her muffin and got up to pour one more cup of coffee. She was about to take a drink when Cash stepped out of the door to his bedroom. Wearing. Nothing. But. A. Towel. A towel slung low on his hips. Her fingers stopped working as her brain stuttered to a halt.

Cash held up his cell phone. "There's been a change in plans."

The mug in her hand dropped and shattered on the tile floor.

Seven

Roxanne stared at him, eyes so wide Cash could see the whites circling her irises. Unfazed by the broken crockery, Harley happily slurped up the coffee pooling on the kitchen floor.

"Change in plans?" Did Roxanne just lick her lips?

The towel hitched around his waist stirred. He really needed to get control of his reactions to her. "That's what I said. Harley, stop!" At his sharp order, the dog stopped licking the floor and let out a disgruntled huff. Cash turned his attention to Roxie. "Back out of the kitchen so you don't cut your feet."

She glanced at the floor, as if she'd just realized what had occurred. "Oh. Oops. I'll clean that—"

"You're barefoot. Back out carefully. Go get ready. We need to hit the road ASAP. I'll clean up the mess as soon as I'm dressed."

Roxie's expression waffled between determination and uncertainty. "Um, where are we going?"

"To the ranch."

Her face lit up and she all but danced over and around

the shattered mug. “A ranch? Harley! Did you hear that? We’re going to a ranch! Horses! I love horses! We’ll have a blast. C’mon!”

The dog barked happily and followed his mistress as she jogged to her room.

Cash stood flat-footed and confused. When had he lost control of this situation? He’d had no intention of taking the blasted dog, but Roxie automatically assumed the mutt would be welcome on this trip. He took a couple of minutes to collect the broken pottery and toss it in the trash. He wet a paper towel to mop up the remaining coffee.

With the sound of the shower splashing from the guest bath, Cash finished cleaning the floor and headed to his bedroom to get dressed. He was on a conference call with two of his agents when Roxie appeared, Harley prancing alongside her.

She had donned well-worn jeans that hugged her in all the right places and Western boots. Her sweater was a color that reminded him of peaches. With the sterile white of his living room as a backdrop, she looked like a ray of sunshine bouncing across a cloud. Her confidence was back in full force. She *looked* like a cowgirl. Walked like one. The ditzy girl was gone and in her place was a lovely woman whose golden eyes glinted with excitement.

He ended the call and prepared for an argument over Harley. He surrendered when he saw the dog sitting next to the door to the garage, leash in his mouth, brown eyes begging. Cash had always been a sucker for big brown eyes.

Once in the Range Rover and headed north on I-35, Roxie broke the silence. “Can I ask how long it’ll take to get to this ranch?”

“Since you just asked, I suppose you can.”

She huffed a breath and rolled her eyes. “Are you one of those grammar Nazis?”

"Only where you're concerned." He cut his eyes in her direction to judge her reaction.

"Gee, don't I feel special. So, how long?"

"To get to the Crown B? About thirty minutes."

"Oh." She shifted in her seat. "Is there like…a restroom there?" She cleared her throat and added by way of explanation, "I drank a lot of coffee this morning."

He smirked. "Well, we've had indoor plumbing for at least a year or so."

Roxie slapped at his arm. "Do not make me laugh."

"I can pull over and you can find a tree."

"Hardy-har-har. I'm not Harley. I'll wait, thank you very much."

Harley, upon hearing his name, pawed at Cash's shoulder and whined before looking wistfully at the window.

"Fine." Cash hit the button to lower the window just far enough for the dog to stick his head out, muttering, "Idiot mutt."

Harley, in doggy heaven, nosed into the wind, his ears streaming behind him, along with long ribbons of slime. Cash made a mental note to wash the Rover before the toxic stuff dried and ruined the custom paint job.

Cash should not enjoy sparring with this woman as much as he did. And he should not be working so hard to hide his smiles, because he hadn't smiled this much in months—years, if he were being honest with himself.

Leaning forward, Roxie fiddled with the sound system. She punched through his preset radio stations, apparently dissatisfied with his choices. Admittedly, he had mainly news and sports talk channels programmed, but he also had a few music stations. When she started twisting the knob, he preempted her and pressed the steering wheel controls for the sound system. A moment later, his cousin's voice crooned a ballad.

"Who is that?" Roxie stared intently at the dashboard as if she could divine the identity from the dials.

"Deacon—"

"Tate!" She all but bounced in her seat. Cash should have been used to women reacting this way but it still stung a little. "I *love* Deacon Tate and the Sons of Nashville. I don't recognize this song, though."

"It hasn't been released yet."

"How did you—"

"We run security for Deke's tours, and he's my cousin."

"He's…of course he is. Duh. I remember when Senator Barron announced he was running for president. Deacon played for the crowd."

Roxie settled back into her seat and studied him, her expression serious. "Your family is…wow. You guys really are red-dirt royalty."

He resisted the urge to shrug. Cash hated the term but it was just one more thing to deal with for the privilege of wearing the Barron name. In his business, low-profile was better—a difficult proposition given his identical twin's history of appearing weekly on supermarket tabloid front pages.

Exiting the interstate, Cash navigated the country roads to reach the massive rock-and-iron entrance to the Crown B. He followed the meandering drive toward the cluster of homes, ranch buildings and the big house that was the center of the Barron family.

"Oh…wow," Roxie sighed at her first glimpse of the ranch house. "It's gorgeous."

Cash eased on the brake and the Rover rolled to a stop. He looked at the place, trying to see it through fresh eyes.

Roxie continued to gush. "It's…it's like a movie set. A fantasy. This is where you grew up? Oh my gosh, how lucky you and your brothers were to live here!"

Except they hadn't and they weren't. This house had been remodeled, added on, partially rebuilt as it evolved from the functional original ranch house built by his great-grandfather just after the Oklahoma Land Run in 1889. Alice, Cash's dad's first wife and mother of Cash's three oldest brothers, had loved the ranch and remodeled it. Upon her death, Cyrus had moved his sons to a house in Nichols Hills, an exclusive suburb of Oklahoma City.

Cash remembered that house the most, and the touches *his* mother had tried to add before her death. Then it had been Big John and Miz Beth who looked after the house, the ranch and the Barron brothers. As they got older, the ranch had been the place that became home because that's where Big John and Miz Beth lived.

He glanced at Roxie and almost told her that there were no fantasies in that house, no magic in growing up there, but he'd be lying—at least a little bit. He remembered the summer skinny-dips in the cool, spring-fed lake. Fishing on the river. Riding the ranch. Hunting in the fall. The older boys always included the two "stragglers." And they all circled the family wagon whenever Cyrus brought a new stepmother or mistress home.

Shaking off thoughts of his brothers and his father, he drove toward the house again. He was the outsider now and he needed to remember that. It was his job to protect the others, whether they wanted it or not.

Cash kept going rather than pull into the circle drive at the house. He recognized the Ford Explorer parked near the door. Jolie, Cord's wife, was here, which probably meant that his nephew, CJ, was around. The last thing he wanted was for Roxanne to meet any of his sisters-in-law.

He stopped at the ranch's office building. Roxie was unbuckled and out of the Rover before he could kill the engine. She ran-walked to the door and ducked inside.

Harley, sensing a chance to escape, vaulted into the front seat and followed her.

Dusty, the Crown B's ranch dog, charged off the porch, barking wildly. Great. The last thing he needed was a dog-fight. Harley let out a rumbling *Woof!* Dusty skidded to a halt, almost somersaulting in his haste to stop.

Harley was about twice Dusty's size and Dusty was a big dog—a combination of breeds ranging from sheltie to rottweiler with a bunch of others in the mix. The two critters sniffed each other cautiously, tails stiff but wagging. Then in the mysterious ways of dogs, they became best buds and charged off to explore and mark bushes.

Ranch manager Kaden Waite, and Manuel Sanchez, the ranch's stockman, were waiting in the office when Cash walked in. He glanced around. Both men pointed toward the hall that led to a break room and the bathroom. Roxie hadn't been kidding.

A curvy Latina emerged from the hall, grinned and threw her arms around him. "Yo, Cash. Long time no see."

He couldn't help but smile at the woman while Manuel scowled at him. Manuel had worked on the Crown B for as long as Cash could remember, and the cowboy had raised his family in one of the houses on the property. His oldest daughters, Rosalie and Selena, had taught Cash and his twin, Chase, to French kiss during a particularly steamy game of spin the bottle played up in the hayloft of the big barn.

They'd been caught by Big John. He and his brother had been thirteen. Selena had been the same age and Rosalie two years older. They were lucky Big John found them instead of Manuel. All four of them had been grounded and at the end of the semester, the girls had been transferred to a Catholic school.

Rosalie was now a pediatric nurse practitioner married

to a firefighter. Selena had stayed on the ranch, married one of her father's cowboys and now worked for Kade as the ranch secretary. The girls were the closest things to sisters the Barron brothers had.

"How's it going, Leenie? Your cowboy still being sweet to you?"

She threw back her head and laughed. "You know it, *hijo*!" Selena glanced toward the hall. "You been holdin' out on me?"

"What?" It took Cash a minute to figure out she was referring to Roxie. "Ah. No. Business."

"Whatever." Selena didn't sound at all convinced but when her father growled, she backed up, still grinning. "Funny business if you ask me." She waved at her father and her boss. "Yeah, yeah. I'm working."

Kade laughed and patted Manuel on the shoulder before his expression sobered. "We have a problem, Cash."

"So you said." He gazed at the man who might or might not be his half brother. "Explain it to me in detail."

It was Manuel who spoke. "I went out to the north pasture at dawn. We always have a few early calves drop. I found the fence cut. Tracks. They had horses. Took the herd through to the road. Cattle hauler, from the tire tracks I found in the mud."

Cash cut to the bottom line. "How many did we lose?"

"Close to a hundred. All prime heifers ready to calve."

Looking at Kade, Cash waited for the real bottom line. The ranch manager rubbed his hand through his long hair. "Given they were all first years? We're looking at close to seven hundred thousand dollars."

His old man was going to have a cow—figuratively and literally. Cash pulled out his cell, punched in numbers and typed out a text.

"What did you do, Manuel? Step by step."

"I took the Gator out. It has heat. I'm too old for cold mornings on a horse. The herd was scattered. They shouldn't have been. I checked the fence, found the cut. I followed the tracks. I called the sheriff. I called Kade. He called you. And here we are." The older man looked uncertain for a moment. "Should I have called you first, Mr. Cashion?"

Cash shook his head and he, too, clapped Manuel on the shoulder. "Just Cash, Manuel, and you did exactly right. The sheriff's office will get the word out to check all cattle haulers." Dan West had been Oklahoma Highway Patrol before an accident cut his career short. Now he was the newly elected sheriff of Logan County and Cash had the man's cell on speed dial, which he was currently keying in.

"Been waiting for your call," an amused voice answered.

"Seven hundred thousand, Dan."

"Ouch. We put out APBs statewide. Without a description, beyond red mud on the tires and a load of pregnant heifers, we don't have much to go on."

Cash muttered a few words under his breath. "They were slick. I'd bet they have paperwork that looks all nice and legal. I have my team on it. Those cows carry the Crown B brand. Every sale barn within a thousand miles has been put on alert."

The sheriff's laughter rolled from the speaker. "Then why did you drag me out of bed on a Saturday morning?"

"Misery loves company. I owe you a beer. Thanks, man."

"We'll stay on top of things, Cash. And yes, you owe me a beer *and* a burger."

Ending the call, Cash looked up to find Kade and Manuel looking at something behind him. Roxanne. He pivoted and sucked in a breath at the excitement etched on her face.

"Cattle rustlers? Really?" She was all but bouncing up on the tips of her boots. "Are we going to saddle up and go after them? I love riding horses."

Kade smothered a snicker and Manuel cleared his throat. Selena shot Cash a look and mouthed, "Seriously?"

He gave in to the urge and shrugged. "No horses. We'll take the Gator."

"What about Harley?" Roxanne looked around the room.

"What about Harley?"

She waved her hands, her face paling. "Where is Harley? Oh, no. Did you leave him in the car? No, no, no. That's bad. He eats leather seats. I can't afford to replace your seats."

"Breathe, Roxanne. He's not in the car. He got out when you did."

"Got out? Got out!" Her voice rose almost to a screech. "He's a city dog. He doesn't know anything about the country. About cows or horses or…or…"

"He's with Dusty. He's fine."

Color came back into her cheeks and she breathed deeply several times. Cash did his best to ignore the obvious amusement shared by the room's other occupants.

The office phone buzzed and Selena snagged it before the end of the first ring.

"Crown B Ranch… Miz Beth?… What?… Calm down, Miz Beth, I can't understand—" Selena clapped her hand over her mouth but laughter still escaped. She managed to say, "Cash is here. Talk to him."

Cash grabbed the phone. "Miz Beth?… What?…I… Miz… Fine. We'll come up."

Four people were totally focused on him. "Big John fished Harley out of the pool, but he'd left the back door open."

Roxanne sank onto the nearest chair. "Oh…no." She

gazed up at Cash. “Harley’s a Newfoundland. A water dog. And his coat…the outer layer…it sort of sheds water unless he’s submerged. And when he gets out, he…shakes. A lot.”

Well, hell. Cash’s chin hit his chest and he rubbed the back of his neck, chasing the knot of tension forming there. Miz Beth was furious. Could this day get any worse?

Eight

Roxanne could still hear the guffaws from the three people in the ranch office. When she'd burst in the door, the two men and one woman had looked up in surprise and she'd asked for the restroom. The woman had pointed and she'd sprinted. She *knew* better than to drink that much coffee before a road trip. But in her defense, she hadn't known there would be a road trip.

Or that Cash would just let Harley run wild. Because the Newf loved water. And could find it faster than an ant could find a picnic. But she hadn't mentioned that to him. Still, what sort of idiot would let a dog out of a car in strange territory and just leave him? Only this wasn't strange territory to Cash and, wait, he'd mentioned someone named Dusty. Had Harley jumped in after this Dusty person had fallen in the pool? The Newfie had a tendency to do that, whether the swimmer needed saving or not. It was instinct.

"Who's Dusty?"

"What?"

Cash seemed distracted and she looked around in time

to realize they weren't taking the main drive to the house. He was driving up a gravel road that was little more than a path and headed toward the back of the house.

"Dusty. You said Harley was with Dusty. Is he one of your cowboys or something?"

He cut his eyes her direction. "Or something."

Roxie arched a brow and widened her eyes to indicate she was waiting for the rest of his answer.

"Dusty is our ranch dog."

"A…dog?" Cash had to be the biggest idiot in the world. Who let two strange dogs run off together? To a pool? And some woman named Miz Beth was on the warpath because Harley had gotten out of the pool and run into the house. The main house that was probably as luxurious as everything else the Barrons owned. If she wouldn't strangle herself with the shoulder harness, she'd thunk her head on the dash.

"You've never owned a dog before, have you." She'd meant that to be a question but her sarcastic tone turned it into a statement.

He pulled up before a series of garage doors and parked. "Save the lecture, Red. You have to get in line."

Cash exited the Rover before she could snap her jaw shut. She jumped out and followed him through a wooden gate set in a stone wall and across a landscaped patio with an outdoor kitchen and large pool. She had no time to stop and admire the view as she watched Cash's broad shoulders disappear through a door into the house. She trotted after him and walked into pandemonium.

"That…that beast ate my roast!" An older woman held a rolling pin in one hand and a metal spatula in the other. The front of her apron was soaked and Roxie could see splatters on the cabinets, stainless steel appliances and the tall man standing off to the side. A little boy stood in front of Harley and a large black-and-white dog almost as big as the Newf.

"He didn't mean to, Miz Beth."

The woman shook the spatula at the child. "Don't you be taking up for that monster, CJ, and get away from him. He's foamin' at the mouth. Probably has rabies."

She pushed past Cash to defend her dog. "No, he doesn't. He's a Newfoundland. They…drool. And if he had rabies he wouldn't be dripping all over your kitchen because he'd be afraid of water."

The woman eyed her with hostility. "And who are you?"

"She's with me, Miz Beth." Cash stepped toward them.

The woman turned to glare at him. "Well, that just figures. You owe me a roast and a clean kitchen, Cash Barron." She thrust the kitchen utensils into his hands, shed her apron and waggled a finger at the older man. "Don't you laugh, John Sanders."

"Honey, I just can't help myself. You do make a picture standing there mad as a wet hen."

"That's because I *am* wet, you big galoot. What kind of dog jumps into water in the middle of winter?"

"A Newfoundland bred for water rescue in the North Atlantic," Roxie murmured under her breath.

Miz Beth whirled around to glare at Roxie before returning her attention to the dogs and the little boy. "You get them dogs out of my kitchen, Cordell Joseph. Now scat!"

The kid didn't stick around to argue. He grabbed the black-and-white dog's collar and tried to drag him out. The dog didn't move. Cash whistled, one sharp note.

"Out. Both of you." Cash pointed to the open door. The dogs made a dash for it with the boy hard on their heels.

Roxie was about to ask Miz Beth where the cleaning

supplies were kept when the other woman advanced on Cash, stabbing her finger against his chest, eyes narrowed.

"And you, Cashion Matthew Barron. This is all your fault."

Cash backed up a step so Miz Beth couldn't grab his ear. That had been her MO when he was a kid—first the finger and then the ear pinch. Which hurt. A lot. He was settling in to let her tirade run its course when Roxanne waded into the middle of the fray.

"This isn't Cash's fault. Well, not all of it, anyway. Harley is my dog and I insisted we bring him so he could have a day in the country, only I didn't know it would include a pool and a mangy ranch dog—"

"Hey now, Dusty isn't—" Big John began a defense of the ranch mascot but Roxie rolled right over the top of him.

"And who leaves gates and doors open? You all might live out in the middle of nowhere but there are wild animals out here. What's to keep a herd of coyotes from wandering in and moseying right through that door and stealing your roast?"

Roxanne had her own finger in motion now. Cash took cover with Big John and the two of them wisely let the "women folk" go at it.

"A herd of coyotes? Where are you from, girl? Are you from up north? Dear Lord, we don't need any of your kind around these parts." Miz Beth turned away from Roxie to stare at Cash. "You bring a stranger into my kitchen, Cashion? You've done nothing but stir up trouble and now you bring this…woman and that monster dog of hers—"

"Harley's not a monster! And don't be so hard on Cash. This isn't his fault!" Roxie's cheeks were flushed a becoming pink and her hair almost looked like it was on fire.

Cash glanced at Big John. Yup. He'd caught that flash

of triumph in Miz Beth's eyes, too. Miz Beth's reaction to this situation had been totally out of character and now Cash was suspicious of the woman's actions and motive. Then he glimpsed someone attempting to stay out of sight just around the corner in the family room. Jolie, CJ's mom and his brother Cord's wife, her cell phone pressed to her ear as she talked almost as fast as Roxanne.

Crap. He walked on eggshells whenever his sisters-in-law were around. They all pretty much hated him and he believed deep down that his brothers only tolerated his presence because he was the one who kept everyone safe and cleaned up all the family messes.

"You could have handled the situation, Big John." Nodding in Jolie's direction, he didn't keep his disappointment out of his voice. "Roxanne and I didn't have to come up here."

The man who had practically raised the Barron brothers shook his head, but his blue eyes were twinkling. "You have to admit, there's a lot to admire about the way that woman's mind works."

Cash muttered something under his breath that would have gotten his mouth washed out with soap had he been a kid. John guffawed and clapped him on the shoulder. The women, now including Jolie, ignored the men.

"Beth saw you drive around to the office and saw the girl with you. You never brought one out here before. She just wants you to be happy, Cash. She worries about you. We all do."

He glanced sharply at the other man. "What's that supposed to mean?"

Big John's expression turned sad. "Someday, your old man and I are gonna have words, Cash, for what he's done to y'all."

"Leave my father out of this."

Too late, he realized the three women had stopped talking and his declaration dropped into a heavy silence. Fed up, he stomped into the walk-in pantry, grabbed a mop and other supplies. Without a word, he returned to the kitchen and began wiping up the pool water Harley had tracked in. Silently, Roxie took the roll of paper towels and spray cleaner.

When they'd cleaned up the mess the dog had made, Roxie returned the supplies to the pantry while Cash pulled out a money clip. He peeled off a hundred-dollar bill and laid it on the counter. He stared pointedly at Miz Beth while he did it. "To replace the roast."

Roxanne slipped past him and headed for the door. He followed her. On the patio, he whistled sharply. Both dogs came running and CJ stared at him, his mouth forming a little *O*. Cash paused to pet Dusty's head and direct him back to the boy.

"Look after Dusty, will you, CJ? Make sure he doesn't chase the car?"

The child nodded, looking solemn, but didn't speak.

"It'll be okay, bubba. Miz Beth is mad at me, not you."

CJ huffed out a breath as he glanced over his shoulder. "They're all mad at you, Uncle Cash."

"I know. It's okay."

"No, it's not. I know the secret, Uncle Cash. I tried to tell Mom and Dad but they wouldn't listen to me."

Cash didn't breathe for a minute. "There is no secret, CJ."

"Yes, there is. I know why you took me."

Before Cash could react, CJ charged, colliding with his thighs. The boy wrapped his arms around Cash and he wondered when the child had gotten so tall.

CJ leaned his head back so he could look up. Cash obliged by tilting his head down. "Thank you, Uncle Cash.

Without you, I don't think Mom and Dad would be my mommy and daddy."

Before he could respond, the boy turned loose and ran across the yard, yelling for Dusty to follow. Cash didn't speak as he took Roxie's arm and pulled her toward the gate. Even if he knew what to say, he wouldn't be able to get words out around the lump in his throat.

The kid didn't know a damn thing. He hadn't gone with the Oklahoma County deputies to remove CJ from Jolie's home with the plan of getting Jolie and Cord together. He'd been doing his best to break them up, and to secure Cord's rights as CJ's father. That act had been one more nail in the coffin containing his brothers' love. Hell, when it came right down to it, what did a Barron know about love anyway?

Except Cord and Jolie *had* gotten together and married. They now appeared to be living their own happily-ever-after. What a stupid phrase. Except every one of his brothers had found someone who made him happy. And every one of those women was totally wrong for his brothers. His father knew that and Cash knew that. All that happiness made his skin feel tight and itchy. Barron men weren't meant to find true love. Just look at his old man.

His phone rang while he was herding a still-wet Harley into the backseat of the Rover. Speak of the old devil himself. He'd barely said hello before his father started in.

"What are you doing to get my cattle back, boy?"

Yeah, his dad was having that predicted cow about now. "Law enforcement has been alerted. My livestock agents are combing the area sale barns. The fence has been fixed and the remaining cows were moved closer to the home place."

"Who's the woman you moved into your condo?"

That was a question Cash hadn't been expecting but

he wasn't surprised his father knew Roxanne was at his place. "She's someone I need to keep an eye on in regard to another situation."

"You turning into your twin now, Cashion? I'm not surprised. I've been waiting for you to betray me just like they did. Disappointment doesn't even come close—"

"I told you, Dad. It's a case. That's all. Look, I have to go. I've got a call coming in. It might be about the cattle." He cut off the call.

After the chewing-out from Miz Beth, Big John's insinuations and now his father's outright accusations, he'd had more family than he could stomach. He climbed into the driver's seat and noticed that Harley seemed unnaturally subdued, as if the dog was picking up on his mood. Backing out of the drive, he glanced at Roxie. She was subdued, too.

Great. Just…great. What a craptastic day and it wasn't even midafternoon. Time to do something different.

Nine

Most Saturday nights, he'd be out somewhere. Either Donovan's, the midtown pub where he usually went, or one of the nightclubs in Bricktown where the party girls hung out looking to hook up. The quiet woman at his side precluded both of those things. For some crazy reason, after that call from his father, he'd driven back to the ranch office and barns and saddled two horses. He'd made the excuse that a trail ride would give Harley time to dry, because who wanted to drive with the stink of wet dog filling the air. Roxanne had all but glowed with excitement and she'd turned out to be a better rider than he'd anticipated. Harley had frisked like a puppy and Cash had sort of felt the same way.

Now they were headed back to Oklahoma City and he had no idea what to do with his guest and her furry companion. Donovan's didn't seem her kind of place—not that he had any idea of what she liked to eat or do. Still, the idea of fish and chips and a Guinness held appeal.

"How's the furball in public?"

Roxie furrowed her brow. "What do you mean?"

"Do you like fish and chips?"

Her whole face squished into an "I'm totally confused and what was that segue anyway" look. He swallowed his chuckle. "I'm hungry. There's a pub with the best fish and chips in the state. Can Harley be trusted to lie under the table and not make trouble?"

"They'd…let him in?" Confusion morphed into shock before settling into speculation. "Because I happen to love fish and chips."

"Guinness?"

She scrunched her nose. "Harp."

"Close enough."

"Close? Harp is nothing like Guinness."

"Still Irish. Close enough."

Roxie sputtered and looked like she was going to argue but Harley picked that moment to stick his head between the seats and bark furiously at the semi-truck in front of them. The clamor covered Cash's laughter.

An hour later, Harley was installed on the floor of the back booth at Donovan's, happily gnawing a bone, Roxie was licking malt vinegar off her fingers, and Cash thought he was going to lose his mind if she didn't stop. Her tongue could be a lethal weapon—in more ways than one. In that moment, Cash knew he would seduce her. And he would start as soon as he got her back to his place.

She glanced up and sucked in a breath, holding it a moment before exhaling. He studied her from beneath hooded eyes and didn't even try to hide his slow smile as her cheeks flushed. Reaching across the table, Cash snagged her hand and tugged it toward him. He used his own tongue to clean her fingers. The tart, malty taste of the vinegar coupled with the texture of her skin turned his thoughts to tasting her in other places.

"Finished eating?" His voice was little more than a growl.

Roxanne didn't speak, just nodded, as she stared at him with wide eyes. She tugged her bottom lip between her teeth, alternately nibbling and wetting it with the tip of her tongue. He was about three seconds from embarrassing them both. Cash was honest enough to admit that he liked sex. A lot. And he was going to enjoy teaching this woman just how much he liked it.

Tab, dog and woman were handled—one paid, one called, one led by the hand outside to his Rover. Cash helped Roxanne into the passenger seat and leaned across to buckle her seat belt. He enjoyed her quick inhalation almost as much as her exhale. Her breath whispered across his cheek with just enough force to ruffle his hair.

Cash plotted on the way to his condo. Just sex. Roxanne was amenable—as evidenced by the vibes she was putting off. He'd make no promises to her, there would be no flowery words, no declarations of anything more than what this was. Sex. Plain and unadulterated.Two consenting people attracted to each other, with no commitment.

Perfect. Just the way he liked it.

Twenty minutes later, he had Harley locked out on the patio and was pouring Roxanne a glass of wine. He carried the glass to her, waiting until she'd sipped and swallowed before he moved in. Without touching her with his hands, he leaned forward, his gaze focused on the prize—her lips. A light brush of his against hers, a long pause. Then more pressure and a curious lick with his tongue. She sighed, parting her lips, and that's when he gathered her close, angled her head and kissed her deeply.

Roxie's heart jittered against his chest and it occurred to him that his own drummed out the same erratic beat. This woman definitely turned him on. The calculating part of his brain that never shut off considered the implications. She definitely wasn't his type. In fact, Roxanne Rowland was not a woman he would ever pick out of a crowd, yet he could find her in a sea of faces without a moment's hesitation. The woman he'd watched on security cameras at the Crown Casino was an actress playing a role—poorly, as it turned out. The woman standing here in his living room was a contradiction.

The Roxie he held in his arms was nerdy, a little accident-prone, but seemed…real. She had a temper to match her hair. As clichéd as that was, it was still true. And now it was time to see what else Roxie Rowland was made of. The neck of her sweater was wide, so he eased one side over her shoulder so he could kiss and nibble her skin. She sucked in air and held it. Good. She liked that.

Cash brushed her cheek with his and whispered in her ear. "Drink."

"Are you trying to get me drunk?" Her question came out in a rush of breathless words.

"No. Just relaxed."

A nervous giggle and then, "I don't think I want to be relaxed." Still, she gulped the rest of the wine. While Roxie was doing so, Cash nibbled along her collarbone.

"I love the feel of your skin."

A delicate shiver danced through her and he felt her muscles slacken. Her fingers lost their grip on the wineglass and it dropped toward the floor. He snatched it in midair.

"Stop doing that."

"Doing what?" He offered a smug grin. "Cleaning up after you?"

"No. Making me lose control."

"Is that what I do to you?" Damn but he hoped so.

Her breathing deepened. "Yes."

Things were progressing right on track. "Good. I think you need to lose control, Red."

"No, I don't. That's not a good thing." She pushed against his chest but the gesture seemed halfhearted.

"I think it's a very good thing."

"Ha. You would. You're a man." Her eyes glittered like whiskey in cut glass. "I think *you* need to lose control."

To prove her point, she wrapped her hands around the back of his neck and tugged his face down to hers. Balancing on her toes, Roxie stretched up to kiss him. He let her have control for a moment, then claimed her mouth, greedily tasting her with his tongue. It could have been five seconds or five minutes when he finally broke contact. Cash stared down at her, surprised that his breath was hitching in his chest, just as hers was.

"I'm going to make love to you, Roxanne. Sooner or later. Personally, I think it should be now."

Her heavy-lidded eyes ticked up at the corners to match her smile. "That's pretty much sooner, don't you think?"

"Yes."

"Okay."

Cash took her mouth again, holding her tight against him as he walked her backward toward his bedroom. He didn't stop until the backs of her legs bumped up against the mattress. "Last chance, Red."

A languorous sweep of her lashes hid her eyes. When she opened them, he found resolve in her gaze—and longing. Need. Desire. She wanted him. Good, because he wanted her more than— He halted that thought in its tracks. This was just sex. He needed to discover her motivations, what her family's plans were. That's what this seduction was about.

Roxanne reached for the hem of her sweater but he stopped her with a gentle touch. "I'll do that." He trailed a fingertip along the silky skin edged with peach from shoulder to shoulder. “Let me.”

“Help yourself.” The words sighed out as another shiver danced along her skin, chasing his finger.

Slowly raising the hem, he pulled the sweater off over her head. Cash forgot about professionalism. He forgot this was just sex, didn’t even consider the emotional distance he should keep between them. He forgot about everything but her. Standing there in a lacy pink bra, her skin flushed from his gaze, her lips swollen from his kisses, Roxanne was beautiful. The band holding her hair disappeared with her sweater and dark auburn waves caressed her shoulders.

He gripped her hips, pulled her close and kissed her again. The soft, silky texture of her skin felt incredible beneath his fingers. He could taste the sweetness of the wine splashed with tart, malty vinegar. Just like her: sweet and tart. Her perfume—something subtle with hints of cinnamon and jasmine—went straight to his head.

She twined her arms around his neck, leaned into him. She was… His brain short-circuited. Everything about her—the texture of her skin, her scent, the taste of her lingering on his tongue, the heat surrounding him… She enveloped him. She was everything he could want or need or imagine. His hands found her belt buckle before his brain caught up.

This was a mistake. Taking her, making love to her. No. Sex. This was just sex. She whimpered softly as his knuckles brushed the bare skin of her belly and wanting her morphed into an abiding need. Who was he kidding? This wasn’t just sex. He truly wanted to make love to her. As the enemy, she should be forbidden. But that just added an irresistible layer of attraction.

He tugged the buckle apart, undid her jeans, set his teeth on the flesh of her shoulder as he pushed her jeans down her thighs. Her head fell back on a deep sigh and he nibbled his way toward the little moan caught in her throat.

"Something to be said about now," he murmured. Easing her down on the bed, he dropped to his knees to remove her boots, socks and jeans. Then he went back to whisk off her panties. "I'm definitely a here-and-now kinda guy."

"I've heard that about you." She fumbled as her fingers attempted to unbutton his shirt.

Cash leaned back just out of her reach and ripped the shirt over his head without bothering with the buttons. The T-shirt he wore under it disappeared in the next instant. Standing in one smooth motion, he toed off his boots and stripped out of the rest of his clothes.

Roxanne's expression softened. She liked what she saw. Then her gaze sharpened, running over him much like that of an appraiser faced with a piece of fine art. Her tongue appeared, teasing her bottom lip, and his body reacted. That earned him a slow, knowing smile.

"I hope we don't need to call 911," she teased. "I may not survive this."

Bending to snag his jeans, Cash pulled out his cell phone and tossed it on the bed. "You're going to need this."

Her peal of laughter stirred things deep inside him—emotional things he didn't want seeing the light of day.

"Promises, promises."

"Just remember, Red. I never break a promise." He stalked closer and she scooted backward across the bed. Cash snagged her ankle and tugged her back to the edge. "Did I give you permission to move?"

Her jaw dropped and Cash was delighted to discover that when her temper rose, her entire body flushed. He was pretty sure the sight of her sitting on the side of his bed all pretty and pink was going to keep him company for a very long time.

"My bed, my rules, Red." He lowered to his knees once more and with his hands on her inner thighs, began to spread her legs. He worked slowly, drawing out the process, his eyes locked on her face. When her knees were wide enough to fit his sides, he leaned forward. Only then did he drop his gaze to fully take in the sight of her.

"Beautiful."

Her skin darkened, transforming from pink to a dusky rose. She was embarrassed and Cash found that oddly endearing. Roxie reached for him. One finger traced the line of his jaw, her nail scraping lightly over his five-o'clock shadow. His body tightened in response.

"I should say something," she murmured.

Cash raised a brow but didn't reply.

"Something…memorable or sexy…or something." She sucked in a deep breath and held it as her eyes roamed over him. "But it's really difficult when I don't even have the ability to breathe."

"Give it a shot."

"Wow?"

"That works." He didn't fight the chuckle that followed.

She trailed her fingers down his chest, brushed through the dark hair there. "No one has ever looked at me like you do."

He furrowed his brow. "Oh?"

"I think I like the way you look at me. At least the way you're looking at me now."

"Then lie back, Red, and let me look my fill."

Roxie shook her head. "No, I don't think so. You want to touch me."

"I do." He enjoyed the way her skin quivered. "I'm going to touch you." He cupped one breast. "Here." His other hand moved lower. "And here."

Roxie's tongue played peekaboo again and he darted

forward to catch it with his teeth, giving her bottom lip a little nip in the process. Her eyes closed and she swayed slightly. "You could seduce me with your words alone."

"Where's the fun in that?"

She blinked and studied him, her head tilted slightly. He moved in to kiss the soft spot just under her ear, now that he had easy access.

"What do you see?"

Her question startled him so he leaned back. "What do you mean?"

"When you look at me, like you're looking at me now. What do you see?"

Cash's first thought was to give her a platitude but something in her expression stopped the cliché on the tip of his tongue. He studied her—her apparent wide-eyed innocence, her playfulness, the pouty mouth he wanted to kiss again. "I see a woman who doesn't know who she is."

He could see that his words stunned her, and likely hurt. He hadn't meant to be that honest, and truth be told, he wasn't sure where the statement had come from.

"I know who I am." She wouldn't meet his gaze.

"No, Red, I don't think you do." He cupped her cheek, urged her gently to look at him. "I see a woman who thinks she knows, but she's just now discovering how amazing she can be."

And where the hell had those words come from? Though he wanted to deny them, he knew them for the truth. "I watch you even when you think I'm not looking."

"That's a little unnerving."

"Maybe. But that's who I am, Roxanne. I study people. It's my job. I can't step away from it. Some people are meant to see others. I'm one of them. And I see you for what you are."

Did he? Wasn't she supposed to be an enemy? Someone

he needed to keep an eye on, to protect his family from? But it was him who needed protection. She was burrowing under his skin with her wide-eyed innocence, her expressive face and those damn lips calling to him, demanding he kiss her.

"You don't trust me." She pushed at his shoulders for a fraction of a moment. Then her fingers curled over them and tightened. "You don't trust me," she repeated. "But I don't care." And then she crushed her lips to his.

Cash grabbed what she was offering, tilting her head so he could deepen their kiss. This woman did things to him, sent jolts of excitement sizzling through his system, short-circuiting his brain. He'd started this evening with the intent to seduce her but now found he was the one being seduced—beguiled by her innocence, her blatant desire. A flood of anticipation washed through him.

He wanted to be reckless, to take something *he* wanted for a change. To ignore everyone's needs but this woman's and his own. He wanted to drink her in with greedy gulps, to live and act only in the moment, to taste the pleasure and the passion they could share.

When he scooped her into his arms without breaking the kiss, she arched against him, hooking her arms around his neck. She made needy little whimpers in her throat and he could feel her pebbled nipples against his chest. He'd planned to take his time, to taste and tease, to elicit long, shuddering climaxes from her before finally sinking into her warm depths and giving in to his own pleasure. Later. There would be time enough later for that. He wanted her now.

Settling Roxanne on the bed, her head and shoulders cushioned on the pillows piled against the headboard, he reached blindly for the nightstand drawer. He didn't want to break the connection between them, but instead fed at her mouth, caressed her from the slope of her shoulder to the curve of her hip while he dug out a condom. Her breathing stuttered when his hand slid between her thighs. She arched her hips, a husky moan vibrating against his throat as he found wet heat. A hot wave of pleasure seared him. All of this was for him. He had no need to arouse her further. She was ready.

Cash managed to get the package torn open and the condom on. They were tangled together on the white comforter, touching, lips searching, in their desperate struggle to taste, to caress, to somehow get closer than they already were.

Roxanne's magnificent hair splashed across the white pillows like a mass of silken fire. He ran his fingers through it just to see if the waves would burn him. They didn't, but his skin felt scorched anyway. Her scent deepened, grew richer, and he happily filled his lungs with it, drowning in the spicy sweetness.

"Please," she muttered against his mouth. He lost the battle against his greed. He wanted her. The depth of their need would drown them both if he didn't act. His body knew what to do and a moment later, he slid into the wet silk of her center. Propped on his elbows, he looked down at her. Her lips were parted and damp from her tongue. Her skin remained that dusky rose and her nipples puckered, calling his attention to them. He dropped his head and feasted on her. She moved under him, arching her body, her hands on his hips urging him to move with her. He did, with a long, slow withdrawal that left her whimpering.

"More," she demanded.

He surged inside her and she gasped, but her hands [illegible]enched him, her nails scored his skin, telling him he was [illegible]g it right. He tortured them with another slow retreat. [illegible]uscles clamped around him and he was completely lost. He pounded into her now, rougher than he'd intended, all in a desperate search for more. More of her. More for him. More of them.

His lungs screamed for air and his heart hammered against his ribs. Her skin radiated heat so intense it rivaled the sparks of fire in her hair. He made an effort to gentle his hands but he was ravenous. He'd never get enough of this woman, of Roxanne. He demanded everything from her, he wanted *her*—all of her—now. Right this moment. With a hand cupping the sweet curve of her butt, he changed the angle of his entry. Driving into her, he listened to her gasps, felt the shudders gathering as she arched and opened for him. She cried out, her eyes clouded with passion, topaz replaced by something closer to burnt amber.

Roxanne reached for him blindly, her palms cupping his face before her fingers traced its lines and hollows. Again her nails rasped across his shadow beard and his skin twitched as his muscles tightened in response. She breathed his name, dropping her hands to clutch his shoulders as she drove herself against him, grinding until her inner muscles fisted him, throbbed around him, milked him. He gritted his teeth, continued to pump inside her. "Now, Roxie. Now!"

"Cash!" she rasped. And when she fell apart in his arms, shudders racking her body, he buried his face in the curve of her neck and followed her over the edge.

"Shh, baby. Shhh," he said around his own ragged breathing.

Little aftershocks rocked them both and they clung to each other. Her breath hitched each time one hit and C[illegible] was egotistic enough to enjoy the hell out of the fa[illegible] he'd brought her to this state. He raised his head [illegible] kiss her cheek. When he moved, his sweat-drenched skin glided over hers. She inhaled deeply and sighed.

"Wow," she managed to say after wetting her lips. "Definitely wow."

She struggled to open her eyes and when she managed to do so, Cash looked into deep pools of sated pleasure. "You certainly are. I think I need the phone now."

"The phone?"

"So I can call 911."

Ten

Cash was laughing—probably at her, but she was too happy and too comfortable to care. His weight on her, the sensation of him still inside her felt…right. She shouldn't go there—shouldn't even stick a toe over that line. His affairs might not make the entertainment news or social pages, but he was a Barron. If his little black book were a digital file, it would probably take up a terabyte of space. He was that darn sexy. He'd melted her bones and they hadn't done anything but the basics. What would he be like— Nope. She was *not* going down that rabbit hole.

"How you doin' down there?"

"Just peachy." His brows quirked and he looked disgruntled. She hurried to add, "I mean that in a very good way. My brain hasn't switched off auxiliary power yet."

That startled another laugh out of him and oh man did that do funny things to her insides. She tightened her thighs and contingent muscles and Cash cut the laugh short. She squeezed again. Did his eyes roll back in his head, and was he getting hard again? How was that even possible? Roxie pressed her head back into the pillows so she could see his face without crossing her eyes. She was about to say something when the bedroom door burst open. She managed a shouted, "Oh, no!" before Harley bounded onto the bed.

The Newf barked happily, licking both of them with abandon. Roxie was trying to fend him off with little success. She was laughing too hard to tell him no. Cash didn't have that problem. He put a muscled arm around the dog's neck and wrestled him to the mattress. They uncoupled in the process and Cash managed to shove the dog onto the floor. He followed with a graceful roll that put him on his feet. Roxie caught a glimpse of his tight butt before he disappeared into the adjoining bath.

As soon as the door closed behind him, Harley was back on the bed, all four feet in the air, tongue lolling from the side of his mouth. She rubbed his belly and choked back her laughter.

"I swear I locked him out in the back."

She hadn't heard Cash leave the bathroom and as she glanced at him, Roxie was disappointed that he'd pulled on a pair of low-riding gym shorts.

"Yeah…about that. I probably should have named him Houdini. If I'd known about his tendency to escape, I probably would have."

"Why did you name him Harley?"

Feeling a bit sheepish, Roxie tucked her chin against her chest and wrapped her arms around the dog's neck. "Because he's big enough to ride and when he snores, he sounds like a motorcycle."

"He snores." Cash's voice was flat. He closed his eyes. "Great. Just…great."

Sunday had been spent lounging—watching movies, lots of kissing, more than a few sessions of steamy sex followed by steamy showers and an evening topped off with wine, pasta and a bubble bath. But now it was Monday. Normally, she'd be in her office digitizing files, moving boxes, searching for this piece of advertising art or that archived article. Today?

Today, she would be stuck in Cash's office. With Harley. Why Cash insisted the dog come to work was a question she had no answer for. The dog was perfectly happy staying home alone all day snoozing. No one in the building looked a bit surprised when she, Cash and Harley boarded the elevator in the parking garage. They got off on the thirty-fourth floor.

A somber receptionist looked up at the *ding* of the elevator, acknowledged that the big boss was in the house, arched a brow at Roxie and Harley, then answered a phone that might or might not have rung, since Roxie didn't hear a thing. The reception area was backed by a wall of polished black granite. Brass letters, lit from behind, spelled out BARRON SECURITY SERVICES. Cash didn't say a word as she followed him down a hallway covered with carpet so thick she could see Harley's footprints. At least it wasn't white. She couldn't afford to replace it, either. The thought made her smile. Cash hadn't mentioned her debt lately.

They passed office doors—some closed, some not. Curious faces appeared in the open offices and she could bet that the office grapevine would be humming the moment Cash stepped into his inner sanctum. The rumor mill in her office would definitely be on overtime if she'd walked in first thing on a Monday morning with Cash Barron in tow. The difference was that these people had no clue who she was. At RCM? They *all* knew the Barrons on sight.

At the end of the hall, they entered an open space. A woman of about forty, with stylish dark hair and dressed in a dark pin-striped suit, occupied a huge circular desk that was flanked by matching file cabinets. A space-age-design computer with the largest monitor Roxie had ever seen sat on one end, a telephone system and files cluttered the other. Three doors opened into private offices. One said Bridger Tate, Vice President of Operations. She remembered talking to him on the phone—before Cash had jumped into the conversation. One had no nameplate. The other simply said, Cash Barron. Yeah, no need for titles where the Barrons were concerned.

The woman's expression didn't change as she handed a stack of message slips to Cash. Roxie glanced at her nameplate. Cheryl Carter.

"No fires, Cash. You can work your way through as time allows."

"Thanks, Cheri."

Only then did the woman's gaze flicker to Roxie. "Want me to hold your calls?"

He looked up from reading the top slip and frowned at his administrative assistant. "Why would you do that?"

Cheri raised both eyebrows and tilted her head in Roxie's direction.

Cash glanced from one woman to the other. "Oh. No. Beep me if I need to handle something."

"Of course."

Still riffling through the messages, Cash headed into his office, Harley and Roxie dogging him. At one point, Roxie slipped out to inquire about coffee. Five minutes later, a young man wearing jeans with knife-edge creases and a starched Western shirt appeared with a drink carrier holding two large Styrofoam cups. "Two creams, two sugars," he said as he passed one to her. He set the second cup on Cash's desk.

"Coffeemaker will be installed after lunch, Mr. Barron."

Cash looked up at that and nodded. "Thanks, Nick."

Roxie was about to say something when her phone pinged. She stared at the text on the screen and blanched. Her eyes rose to meet Cash's gaze. She didn't like the way her voice quavered when she announced, "It's Dexter."

Cash was beside her an instant later. She angled her phone so he could see the message, sent all in caps.

WHY AREN'T YOU AT WORK?

She steadied her breathing and willed her thudding heart to slow down to a normal rhythm. "What do I say to him?"

He studied the text before glancing at her. "Tell him the truth. You're working on a special assignment."

She typed out the reply in normal syntax and it had barely been sent when Dex's reply popped up on the screen.

YOU AREN'T IN YOUR OFFICE.

Conscious of Cash's perusal, she typed out, No, I'm on site.

YOU'RE A LIBRARIAN.

Roxie could all but hear the hostility and dismissive tone of her brother's voice in that text. The corner of her mouth curled up in snarl and she narrowed her eyes at her phone. WRONG. I am NOT a librarian. I'm an archivist. There IS a difference. I'm on site curating a client's collection.

I WAITED HOURS FOR YOU IN THE GARAGE.

She eyed Cash as she typed but he already had his phone out and was punching in numbers. Moments later, his door swung open and a man looking very similar to Cash walked in, his own phone glued to his ear. His hair had more russet and his eyes were a clear blue, but the bone structure of their faces was similar.

You're here? Why are you in Oklahoma City?

NOT FOR LONG. CHECKING UP ON YOU BECAUSE YOU NEED TO BE WHERE WE CAN FIND YOU.

Her temper spiked and she typed furiously. Seriously? I have a job, Dexter. A real job. Get lost.

Cash growled at her so she held up a finger. "Just wait. I know my brother."

Thirty seconds later, her phone rang. She tossed a smug I-told-you-so smile in Cash's direction and made sure the man standing next to him saw it, too. She pressed the speakerphone button. "I don't have time to talk to you. Go away."

"Now you listen to me, little girl. This is about family. You ran out on us in Vegas—"

"*I* ran out on *you*? Ha! That's rich. You left me to take the fall, Dexter. Did you tell Max that? I bet you didn't. I bet you told him I got caught and you barely escaped trying to save me."

"That's over and done, Roxanne. You know Max has something big working."

"I know nothing of the sort."

"Well, he does—"

"What, Dex? What does he have working? What are you all dragging me into?"

"It doesn't matter, Rox. We're family. You do as we say, when we say it."

"Oh? Family, are we? So family is all about leaving me

hanging like when I was sixteen? I had a blast sitting there in an interrogation room. Just awesome."

"If you hadn't opened the boxes—"

"Whatever, Dexter. I'm not doing this. Tell Max I'm done."

"Doesn't work that way, sister mine. Your last name is Rowland. That puts you in the crosshairs just like the rest of us."

She couldn't breathe for a moment and turned her back on Cash and the other man. "What does that mean, Dex?" She didn't quite manage to keep the quiver out of her voice.

"That means next time you won't have a lawyer show up to bail you out." His voice was muffled by some background noises—or maybe it was the buzzing in her ears. Her hands trembled. "I gotta go. You be where we can find you. One of us will call when you're needed. You come, Roxanne. Or else."

Her phone went dead and Roxie felt as if all the blood had drained from her body. She thought she was breathing but she wasn't sure. She couldn't think. No matter what, her father and brothers would always drag her down into the mud.

"Damn, Cash. And I thought Uncle Cyrus was a piece of work." Cash's colleague scrutinized Roxie before he smiled and extended his hand. "Bridger Tate. And you would be the infamous Roxanne Rowland."

Eleven

Cash was exasperated as texts from his security team filled the screen of his phone. Dexter Rowland had slipped through his fingers again but what infuriated him was the look the jackass had put on Roxanne's face. He'd hurt her feelings and threatened her, but then she got angry and wasn't that a sight to see. Now she was sputtering at Bridger, and Cash inhaled deeply to center his temper and calm down.

"Infamous? Infamous! Are you freaking serious? *Gah!*" She threw her hands in the air and stormed around his office like she was looking for something to pummel.

Harley raised his head, huffed out a growly groan, stretched and thunked his head back on the carpet. If her dog wasn't upset, she must melt down like this periodically. He wisely stayed out of her way and motioned for Bridger to do the same. They retreated to Cash's desk and both of them leaned against the front, their legs stretched in front of them, arms crossed over their chests as she ranted.

"I hate him. I really and truly hate my jerk of a brother. *If I hadn't opened the boxes...*" She managed a fair imitation of her brother's voice. "So that whole mess in Virginia when I was a kid was *my* fault? I can't believe these people. They ignore me all my life and then they think they can just snap their fingers and I'm going to heel? I'm not a dog."

At that word, Harley raised his head again and grumbled.

"No offense, Harley." Seemingly satisfied, the dog lowered his head but now his expressive brown eyes tracked her every move.

So did Cash. Her rant continued, replete with sweeping gestures and voice extremes. He especially enjoyed it when she walked away from him. Her hips swayed in time to her marching stride. He'd always been a butt man. And legs. Hers were curvy and muscular. Breasts were nice, too. He liked the way hers fit the palms of his hands. His fingers curled at the remembered feel of her nipples pressing against his skin.

Bridger cleared his throat and then elbowed Cash. He focused on Roxie. She stood about four feet away, cheeks glowing, eyes sparking, hands fisted on her hips, lips pursed and damn if he didn't want to kiss her. He uncrossed his legs and stood straight in hopes of hiding the evidence of his misdirected thoughts. They had a situation—one that negatively impacted his family and their resources. The last thing Cash should have been doing was standing there mooning over this woman.

"You are such a guy, Cash!"

He blinked, having no real reply for that. He *was* a guy, and being typical of his gender, he replied, "Yeah, and?"

Roxie took two long steps and thumped her fist against his chest. "I know where your mind went. We don't have time for that."

Unable to resist, Cash curled his mouth into a grin and hooded his eyes. "There's always time for *that*, Red."

Coughing now, Bridger backed out of the way. "I think my work here is done."

Cash cut his eyes to his cousin and stopped him with a look. "Actually, she's right. We need to discuss what just happened." He refocused on Roxie, too aware of her closeness and wanting to shift his feet to make adjustments for the increasing discomfort behind his zipper. Duty, he reminded himself, and sidled away to avoid her, ducking behind the relative safety of his desk. Settling in his chair, he scooted forward so he could put his arms on its top and keep everything from the waist down hidden.

Bridger, taking the unspoken hint, dropped into one of the guest chairs. Roxie continued to pace the room. Cash gave her a couple of minutes to calm down. When she didn't, he called her to task.

"Roxie. Sit."

"Sit? I repeat, I am not a dog. I do not come when I'm called—"

Choking back laughter, Cash lifted a brow, giving her an "oh, really?" look.

Flustered, Roxie sputtered a series of incoherent words in protest until she managed, "Shut up, Cash."

He lifted his shoulders in a smug gesture. "The truth is my defense, Red."

"And stop calling me that."

"If the name fits..."

"Argh!"

Cash had set her off again and he watched in amusement as she circled the room in what could pass for a stomp dance. After several circuits she stopped in front of his desk. "Okay, fine. I can tell you have questions. So ask." She dropped into the empty chair and stretched her legs out, her butt perched on the edge.

"You have an interesting way of handling your brother."

Roxie rolled her eyes. "I bet you do, too."

"My brothers aren't the issue here. Yours are. How did you know he'd call you?"

"I didn't. It was a calculated risk. While I don't spend any time with my family, they do drift in and out of my life periodically. And Dex is the next oldest. He's the youngest of the boys." She tilted her head and eyed Cash speculatively. "Just like you. He has a chip on his shoulder. Do you?"

He ignored his instinctual response to the gibe and said, "We aren't talking about me. He wants to prove himself so he acts the major jerk, especially with you."

"If the boot fits," she said under her breath.

Cash didn't appreciate the sentiment. "Stay on target, Roxanne. Why did you try to piss him off?"

"Ha. Shows what you know. I don't have to *try* to piss off my brothers. I do that just by existing, especially Dexter. But knowing what he's like—and knowing he has to get in the last word and be all up in my face about being the boss of me—I knew I'd get him riled if I jerked his chain. You should be happy about this."

Roxie resisted the urge to prop her feet on the front edge of Cash's desk. It was that or fist pump. While she wasn't quite sure how to read his expression, she knew she'd scored some sort of point.

"I should be…happy? Care to explain?"

"Sure. I just guaranteed that they'll include me in whatever they have going on." She had the entire focus of both men, and a small part of her brain curled up. These men were wolves and she was a bunny. Roxie opened her mouth to speak but nothing came out. She cleared her throat and still no words. She gazed at her feet. "Um, can you guys not stare at me like that? It makes me nervous."

She peeked up from under the sheet of hair covering the side of her face. They were exchanging looks. "Hey, not my fault you guys are so scary. For some reason my father wants me involved in this deal. I have no clue why. I have no clue what I'm supposed to do. That whole deal in Vegas? Yeah, that was an unmitigated disaster. I'm still not sure if I was set up to take the fall again. It's not exactly like I was raised in the family business, you know."

"Why do you think they're after the Crown Casino?"

She cut her eyes to Bridger, fully cognizant that Cash's gaze remained fixed on her. Roxie could admit to herself that despite sleeping with Cash—and having the most mind-blowing sex ever—he still intimidated the heck out of her. "Look, you want intel on what they're doing, right?" They nodded and she sat up a little straighter. "Well, since I've spent most of my adult life avoiding their schemes, if I suddenly got all on board with this deal, do you really believe they'd trust me?"

Cash and Bridger exchanged another look. This one she read more clearly.

"So I have to play hard to get. Eventually, they'll need to tell me what's going on. Hopefully, with enough time, you people can be ready to catch them. If not, then I hope you guys can roll with it because we may be improvising out the wazoo."

"We?" Roxie was amazed at how much unhappiness Cash could pack into that one syllable.

"Well, unless one of you two is dressing up in drag, I pretty much need to be there."

Harley picked that moment to stand up, do a downward-dog stretch and start sniffing the furniture. Roxie catapulted out of her chair. "No! Don't you dare, Harley. Bad dog." She snatched the leash on the coffee table near the couch and attempted to hook it to his collar. Harley dodged her and trotted over to lay his head on the arm of Cash's chair. She blew air out with enough force to tousle her side-swept bangs. "Uh, a little help here? He needs to go out. Like now."

Cash ruffled the fur on her dog's head, and checked his watch with a lazy arrogance that grated on her nerves. "We'll break for lunch."

"Roof?" Bridger looked far too nonchalant for Roxie's peace of mind.

A slow smile spread across Cash's face and she almost shivered. The man had devious written all over him.

"What?" She asked the question in her mind out loud and wished she could have called it back. There was clearly something going on.

"Definitely roof. You take Roxie and grab a table. I'll deal with Harley." Cash pushed the Newf away so he could stand. He snapped his fingers and her traitorous dog fell into perfect heeling step with the man.

Roxie turned to the couch to grab her jacket but Bridger shook his head. "You won't need it. We won't be eating on the patio." He took her arm and tugged her toward the door Cash and Harley had just disappeared through.

She and Bridger caught up to man and dog at the elevators. If she hadn't known better, Roxie would have thought Harley was a well-mannered, and obedience-trained, dog. The big double-crosser was sitting next to Cash, his nose all but pressed to the man's hip, as pretty as you please. She curled her lip at the dog to show him she was wise to his shenanigans. The ride up to the fortieth floor was short. When the elevator opened, Bridger led her toward wide mahogany doors while Cash and Harley disappeared around the corner in the opposite direction.

"Where's he taking my dog?" She was so busy looking over her shoulder to catch a glimpse of the two, she tripped and had to grab the back of Bridger's shirt to stay upright.

"Outside."

"On the top floor of a forty-story building?" Okay, she didn't mean to screech it. Not really.

"There's outdoor space that direction. And the restaurant has a patio area they open in nice weather."

"Restaurant? I didn't know there was a restaurant in Barron Tower." She racked her brain trying to remember if any advertising material had crossed her desk.

"It's not open to the public. Only to Barron employees and the building's occupants and clients."

As they reached the massive double doors, one side opened to allow them entry. A rather austere man in a black suit offered a regal nod to Bridger. "Mr. Tate. Will Mr. Barron be joining you for lunch?"

"Yes, Bentley."

"This way, sir."

The maître d' led them to a round table overlooking the city. A girl in a black dress and starched white apron appeared at his elbow with a— Roxie sucked in a breath. The pitcher looked like real silver. The server filled crystal glasses with water and disappeared without a word. Rox was having a hard time reconciling the five-star atmosphere with a restaurant on top of a building in Oklahoma City. New York? Absolutely. Here? Not so much. Oklahomans were more about casual comfort and friendliness than the whole snooty mystique.

There were no menus. According to their waitress, a starched scarecrow of a woman, "Chef" prepared daily specials, each one unique.

"Beef, chicken, pork, fish or vegetarian."

Cash dropped into the chair next to Roxie as Harley crawled under the table. A minute later, the water girl returned carrying a large stainless steel bowl and her silver pitcher. The girl placed the bowl on the floor and filled it. Then, just like before, she disappeared without saying a word. Cash glanced at Roxie. "I know you aren't a vegetarian. She'll have fish. Two beef for me, one rare, one medium rare."

"Beef," Bridger confirmed. "Medium."

The waitress executed a perfect military pivot. Roxie reached for her. "Wait. Excuse me." The woman looked at Roxie's hand on her arm, then lifted her head for a haughty stare. "What sort of fish? What sort of any of these meats? How are they prepared?"

The woman gaped at her as if Roxie had lost what little of her mind was left. "Chef decides. It is always a delightful surprise when his dishes are presented."

For a brief instant, Roxie wondered if Cash and Bridger were pulling a prank on her. The four businessman who were seated nearby made one-word orders to their waiter, so this wasn't a joke. What sort of crazy chef ran this place? She never would have believed that Cash would put up with such nonsense.

"Ahem."

Roxie looked up. She was still touching the waitress. Oops. She dropped her hand to her lap. "Okay. Fine. Fish. But I'm allergic to tomatoes. And strawberries."

"I'll make note of that, madam."

Madam? Yeah, Roxie might as well crawl under the table and snuggle up with Harley. Before she could carry through with that urge, other patrons turned their attention to the front door as a man entered. Roxie recognized him immediately. The man scanned the room, his gaze stopping on their little group. Cyrus Barron took two long steps and then bellowed, "Cashion!"

Twelve

As the Barron patriarch stormed toward their table, Bridger leaned close to Cash and said, "Please tell me you pooper-scooped after the dog."

Cash, without taking his eyes off his father, muttered out of the corner of his mouth. "Was I supposed to?"

Roxie panicked. In a furious whisper, she hissed, "Please tell me he's not coming over here to yell at me about Harley."

In almost one voice Cash and Bridger said, "He's not coming over here to yell at you about Harley."

"Probably," Cash added.

As if hearing his name was a siren's call, the topic of conversation emerged from beneath the table just as Cyrus Barron arrived. Roxie had moments to grab her napkin and muzzle the beast before he could shake his head. He'd drained the bowl and streamers of slug slime decorated with drops of water trailed from his jowls. She fell out of her chair, napkin flapping, and managed to get one arm around the dog's neck. Too bad she was a fraction of a second too late.

To her horror, the scene unfolded in slow motion like that Tom Hanks movie with the drooly dog. Harley twisted his head from side-to-side, ears and jowls flapping and drool flying. Roxie could almost hear her voice distorted by time slowing down as she dragged out the words, "Ooohhhh noooo." Mr. Barron stepped backward, a look of total disgust on his face. She caught the brunt of the flying slime but a few strands splatted on Mr. Barron's tailored—and probably massively expensive—slacks. She held up her napkin before realizing it was covered in dog goo.

Mr. Barron harrumphed and focused his attention on Cash. Roxie wasn't sure that was a reprieve. "We have things to discuss. Come to my office."

Cash motioned for the waitress, who was carrying a loaded tray, to approach. "After I eat."

"Don't make me come looking for you, boy." Mr. Barron did an about-face and marched out of the restaurant.

Roxie peeked over the edge of the table. Cash was rubbing the center of his forehead with the heel of his palm. She could almost see the headache forming and figured she was probably the cause. She felt awful for creating all the drama. In a muffled voice, she said, "Sorry?"

She caught movement from the corner of her eye—Bridger getting out of his chair to help her up while the waitress waited for them both to get seated before serving their meals. She shook off his assistance, regaining her composure while she glared at her dog. He didn't look contrite in the least. In fact, he looked pretty darn proud of himself.

The waitress placed two plates in front of Cash. One looked like steak tartare, and the other was a crusted filet served with grilled new potatoes and asparagus spears, drizzled with a creamy white sauce that might be hollandaise, but Roxie suspected it was nothing so "mundane."

Bridger also had beef—small medallions braised with a thick, dark roux containing mushrooms, green onions and… She leaned over to get a closer look. Coffee beans? His sides consisted of potatoes, sliced paper thin and layered with Parmesan cheese and butter, and what appeared to be brussels sprouts lightly breaded and sautéed. Her own plate included a lobster tail, grilled and topped with an orange-colored sauce, a nest of julienned potatoes and carrots sprinkled with blue cheese and a side of snow peas.

The silent water girl appeared in the waitress's wake, refilling glasses. Once the serving staff faded away, Cash bent over, snagged Harley's empty bowl and shoveled some all-but-raw meat into it. The dog nosed in and ate with great gusto while the humans sitting nearby watched. Roxie should have felt too embarrassed to eat but her stomach rumbled and the food was too delectable not to enjoy. And she did. Every last bite. If there had been any of the delicious hot yeast rolls left, she would have mopped up the remaining orange sauce on her plate and called it dessert.

As she chewed and swallowed the last bite and reached for her water glass, she looked up. Her gaze collided with Cash's and heat washed through her. He looked like he wanted to eat *her* for dessert. Feeling her skin flush, she swallowed hard and just avoided licking her lips because… company. She could hear Bridger making muffled noises behind his napkin.

When she returned her focus to Cash, he was lounging nonchalantly in his armchair. "Did you enjoy your meal?"

Ooh! He looked so smug and cocky, and she knew exactly what he was thinking. Despite her best efforts, she flushed more and her breathing quickened, because her brain recalled what that man looked like sprawled naked in bed with that same expression on his face. Roxie mentally shook herself. She could not let Cash get under her skin, even though he'd gotten in pretty much everywhere else. He was a player and she was a convenient mark. Once he caught her father and brothers, he'd be done with her. She needed to remember that, especially whenever she got starry-eyed about this whole situation.

As if Cash recognized where her thoughts had turned, he pushed back from the table and stood. "Bridger, take Roxanne back to my office. Cheri can babysit her until I'm done with my father."

Roxanne also stood. "I don't need a babysitter. I'm sure your assistant has far more important work—" She cut off her sentence when she felt the eyes of the other patrons drilling into her back. "We'll discuss this on the way to your office. How much do I owe you for lunch?"

Cash dismissed her question with an insolent wave of his hand. "More than you want to pay, Red."

His cryptic answer stunned her enough that she almost missed Harley, but this time, when the dog stuck his head out from under the table, Roxie managed to snap the leash on his collar *and* wipe his muzzle. She reached within for a false sense of calm and forced a nonchalant expression on her face. Head high, the dog's leash tight in her hand, she followed Cash out, Bridger right behind her.

When Cash kept walking, Bridger very gently circled her biceps with his hand and tugged her to a stop. "We're going down."

"But—"

Cash raised one hand in the air right before he disappeared around the corner.

"He needs to deal with Uncle Cyrus before he can do anything else. C'mon. I'll take you down to Cheri before I get back to work."

She was still arguing with Bridger when the elevator doors opened on the thirty-fourth floor. "Look, I don't need someone—" She clamped her mouth shut as the receptionist's head came up. The woman gave Roxie a steely-eyed stare. Waiting until they were in the common area between Cash's office and Bridger's, she started in once more.

"See? Cheri isn't even here. She's probably at lunch and despite her near-OCD need to keep her desk pristine, I'm betting she's a very busy woman. And you said yourself that you have your own work to do. In fact, I don't even know why I'm here. I could be at my own very busy office doing the work my employer is paying me to do but that isn't getting done because I'm standing here arguing with you about why I can't go back to my apartment, my job and my life."

She paused to take a breath and noticed Bridger staring at her, his expression bemused. "I can tell you aren't from around here originally."

"What's that supposed to mean?"

"It means you said a whole mouthful of things, bouncing from one topic to the one that's really stuck in your craw, all in one breath. I'm amazed, country boy that I am, that I could keep up."

"Har-dee-har-har. You're a real comedian. Why can't I go home?" Bridger frowned so she rushed on, "Or least to my own office. I have projects due, Bridger, and I can't afford to lose my job. Besides, I *like* my job."

"You need to be where we can keep an eye on you."

Roxie blew out an angry breath, counted to ten and worked on putting a patient smile on her face. From Bridger's wry grin, that last ploy didn't work. "Why? Why do you need to keep an eye on me? If you'll remember, I'm the one who called you people. I'm the one who offered to help." Harley tugged against the leash and she dropped it. He wandered over to a leather couch, climbed up and flopped down.

"Let's just say we haven't figured out your long game."

"My long game?" Roxie gave him a hard stare but remembered to keep her mouth closed so she wasn't gaping. "This isn't a game, Bridger. This is my life. I've worked hard to separate from my family. I don't want to be like them."

"So you say."

Bridger stood there, calm, collected, looking perfectly reasonable as he accused her of…dishonesty. Double-dealing. Being untrustworthy. Cash had spent the weekend seducing her and now his top henchman was insinuating that she was…unworthy. Roxie didn't know whether to be angry or hurt.

"Wow." She said the word with no inflection but she was shaking inside. "Guess I know exactly where I stand with you and Cash…er, Mr. Barron. Fine. I'll need to walk Harley soon. Can you arrange for one of your minions to accompany us?"

"I'll have someone come up."

"Awesome." Now she let the sarcasm loose. She moved to the couch and dropped down beside the Newf. The big dog lolled over on his side, his head plopping on her thigh in search of petting. She rubbed his ears, pointedly ignoring the big jerk who was using Cheri's desk phone to call her prison guard to duty.

Roxie sighed and ripped the earbuds from her ears. Three weeks she'd been stuck in this office. Granted, it was bigger than her own, but she had things to do back at RCM. Files to scan, research to be done, items to be preserved and cataloged. Here, she had an empty desk and her cell phone. And a love seat, which Harley currently occupied as he snored contentedly.

She needed to be busy, because idle thoughts? They led

to trouble. The first week had been an adventure—getting to know Cash both publicly and in private. Oh, yeah, especially in private. She'd given up any pretense of believing she was staying in his guest room. Her clothes maybe, but not her. Sleeping with him—and yes that was a euphemism for some very good times between the sheets—was becoming much too necessary to her well-being.

Life had settled into a routine. Cash ran every morning, taking Harley with him. She slept in and was happily awakened to 150 pounds of exuberant dog, 180 pounds of sexy man and something sweet for breakfast. Then they came to the office. Where she spent endless hours being bored to tears—and daydreaming about Cash and all the things she wanted to have with him but couldn't.

She tried to explain her need to stay busy to Cash but he brushed her off. How could a man be so attentive when they were alone and so adamantly stubborn and recalcitrant when it came to her getting back to her job? She'd suggested picking up her work and bringing it to his office. Nope. He even stood there listening whenever she had to call her office to explain things to her assistants.

It wasn't like they'd made headway in the search for her family. The investigation was stalled and every morning, she figured that would be the moment when he said, "We need to talk." And that would be the end of it.

Harley groaned and stretched. It was time for his midafternoon walk. She stuck her head out of her temporary cell. Cheri was talking to the receptionist but Roxie caught the older woman's attention. "It's that time."

"I'll take care of it, hon."

Roxie huffed out a disgruntled sigh. "Tell whoever's coming that I really want to stretch my legs. Harley and I are going to Bricktown to walk the canal."

Ten minutes later, a man in the requisite dark suit

knocked on the door. He looked fit, dangerous and highly capable. Which made her want to laugh. She was tied by the leash to a 150-pound dog that ambled. She couldn't outrun Cheri in her stylish suit and elegant pumps, much less a trained security…agent? Guard? Private cop? Whatever. She never knew what to call the parade of men who escorted her on these outings.

"C'mon, Harley. Let's go do your business."

The receptionist was back at her desk as Roxie and her tagalong arrived. The woman looked up from her phone, gave Roxie a spiteful look and then resumed texting as the doors closed, hiding her from sight. They had a straight, express-level ride to the first floor. Still ignoring her escort, Roxie headed out. Harley needed the exercise; she needed away from the tower looming behind her *and* all the people in it, so she set out on the four-block hike to the Bricktown Canal.

She'd just descended from street level to the canal, her shadow trailing her by a few feet, when three women walked toward her. Roxie shortened Harley's leash and scooted over to give them room to pass. They didn't. They stopped right in front of her.

"Miz Beth is right," the brown-haired woman in scrubs said. "He *is* a monster."

The blonde laughed and ruffled Harley's fur. "Naw. Not a monster. A big ol' teddy bear." She bent over to cup Harley's head and croon, "Who's a good boy? You. You're a good boy."

Roxie stood there dumbfounded before realizing that the third woman—a very attractive Native American with gorgeous black hair—remained aloof while giving Roxie the once-over.

"Huh," the raven-haired woman said. "There's no accounting for some people's taste."

Roxie didn't know what she was referring to. "Who the heck are you people?"

The first two laughed, the blonde flashing a wink directed toward the guard at Roxie's back. "I'm Cassidy Barron," she said.

"Jolie Barron." That from the dark-haired nurse.

"Savannah Barron. I'm married to Cash's twin brother."

Roxie backed up a step and bumped into the large man behind her. From the way she spat out Cash's name, there was evidently no love lost between Savannah and her brother-in-law. She wondered what Cash had done to earn that sort of scorn.

"Okay then. Well, nice to sort of bump into you." Roxie tugged on Harley's leash and moved to duck around the women. Two things happened—Harley refused to move and the women stepped forward to cut her off.

"So," Jolie drawled. "You're living with Cash now."

What? Roxie frowned at them. "No. I'm not."

"And he took you to the ranch," Cassidy added. "Several times."

"So?"

She looked at Savannah, waiting for her comment. Savannah just stared back.

"Look, you three might have time for fun and games but I don't. You want to know why I'm staying with Cash, you ask him. Now, if you'll excuse me, I need to walk my dog so I can get back to the Tower of Doom and relieve the Hulk here of his duties."

This time she jerked Harley's leash and he lumbered after her. If she thought she was getting away, she was wrong. The trio fell into step with her.

"So," Cassidy coaxed, "it's been almost a month since you moved in?"

Roxie kept walking, head down, doing her best to ignore them. Knowing Cash and Bridger, they'd probably arranged this little tête-à-tête as way to trap Roxie into revealing something. What, she had no idea.

"I can't believe he'd take her to the ranch," Savannah said from behind her. "In fact, I can't believe he went out there, especially knowing you and CJ were there, Jolie."

Harley stopped, sniffed a bush next to the walkway and did his thing. Roxie pulled a plastic sack out of her messenger bag and cleaned up after him. Still ignoring her entourage, she walked to the nearest trash can and dropped the refuse inside. Pivoting, she headed back the way she'd come.

"Aren't very friendly, are you?" Savannah stood right in front of Roxie, blocking her way.

"Look, I don't know any of you. The three of you swoop down like crows on fresh roadkill and ask questions that are none of your business." She pointed at Savannah. "I get the distinct impression you don't even like Cash, so why do you care what he does, what I do and what we might or might not do together? I repeat, it is none of your business. And your little crack about taste? Yeah, I'm not rich. I'm not gorgeous. But I'm not a bimbo either. Here, I'll make it easy on you. Call your brother-in-law if you want gossip." She glared at Savannah and felt her temper rise. "Now get out of my way."

Harley picked that moment to bark loudly and jerk against the leash. He yanked it out of her hand and bounded down the sidewalk, stopping when he reached the angry man striding toward the group. Cash. And he looked like he wanted to kill Roxie.

Thirteen

Cash wasn't sure who he was mad at. His fingers curled into Harley's ruff while he attempted to regain control. When a text had come in from his security guard Alan, he'd just finished up another round with his father and was feeling the stress. According to the old man, he'd done nothing right in the past month. Despite the lack of incidents. Despite the new security contracts the company had signed. Despite Cash himself doing everything his father demanded.

And now this.

"You know, Roxanne, you look like a nice girl. Why would you hook up with someone like Cash?"

He watched Roxie blanch at Savannah's question, her eyes glued to his face.

"Roxanne." At his voice, his sisters-in-law whirled.

At least Cassidy and Jolie looked a little guilty. Savannah just looked resentful. A part of him understood why they disliked him. Another bit mourned the division between him and his brothers because of his actions against these women. He hadn't even known his twin was in town.

But this was his reality. Cash had doubted each one of them and their motives for being with his brothers. And he was still trying to wrap his head around Clay giving up a chance to be president to be with Georgie.

Then there was the part of him that was jealous his siblings had found such happiness. The cynical part kept waiting for shoes to drop and cracks in their relationships to widen and drive them apart. Besides, their father hadn't been a great role model when it came to relationships.

"If you three have questions, ask me, not Roxanne."

"She's living with you and you haven't bothered to introduce her to the family." Cassidy was never one to back down.

"She's staying with me because she's part of an ongoing investigation."

"So…you aren't sleeping together?" Savannah threw him a skeptical look.

"That's hardly your concern, Savannah." Cash stared at each of the three women—catching and holding their gazes for a long moment. "The only thing between Ms. Rowland and me is business. Once the investigation is concluded, she'll be returning to her own residence."

"So the two of you aren't involved?" Jolie looked thoughtful as she asked.

"Beyond the investigation? No. We aren't involved."

Cash caught a glimpse of Roxie but he couldn't read the emotion flitting across her face. Consternation? Misery? She glanced away and a wooden facade settled in its place. Only then did he recognize that he might have hurt her feelings. He'd explain himself later. Right now, he needed to get her away from the wives.

"Look, I know y'all enjoy these little sneak attacks but Roxie is not my girlfriend so leave her out of your schemes."

Cassidy and Jolie exchanged a guilty look and Savannah scuffed the toe of her cowboy boot against the sidewalk. He was just glad that Clay and Georgie were in Washington so he didn't have all four wives ganging up on him. As he watched the women, he saw discomfort morph into alarm as they all looked past him.

He heard three sets of footsteps coming their way, footsteps he recognized.

"Cassie." Chance appeared on Cord's right but didn't approach his wife.

"Oh, hi, darlin'."

Jolie pasted a big smile on her face. "What are you doin' here, Cord?"

Cash glanced at his older brother, who'd halted on his left. "I thought you said you couldn't get away for lunch, Jolie." Was that humor in Cord's voice or was he chiding his wife?

Savannah pasted a stony expression on her face and glared at the man who'd once been Cash's mirror image. After the incident that almost separated his twin and his wife, Cash had started wearing scruff instead of shaving daily.

"Savvie?" Chase brushed past Chance and approached his wife. "Want to explain what's going on?"

Savannah didn't back down. "What? Did *he* call you to come rescue him?"

"No, Cash didn't. So why are y'all here?"

"I'd like the answer to that, too," Chance chimed in.

"I don't know about Cass and Jolie but I wanted to find out what kind of woman would fall for him. We kinda... got a text saying she'd be here," Savannah said.

"We were just curious," Jolie chimed in. "After seeing them at the ranch and then finding out they're living together..."

That caused his brothers to scrutinize *him*. "She's part of my investigation," Cash reiterated. "Those incidents with the hotels and casinos."

"Using that for an excuse again—"

"Enough, Savannah." Chase jumped to Cash's defense, surprising him. "Cash is handling some serious problems that threaten the family business." Chase studied Roxie and that perturbed Cash for some reason he couldn't pinpoint. His twin offered his hand. "Ms. Rowland? You don't look much like the woman I saw on the security cameras. Barron Entertainment appreciates your assistance with this matter."

Roxie pinkened and ducked her chin but she shook Chase's proffered hand. "I just want to help so I can get back to my life."

"Understood." Chase released Roxie's hand and snagged Savannah's. "You and I will talk later, Savvie."

"I still don't know how y'all knew we were here," Cassidy threw in.

Alan cleared his throat. "That would be my doing. After I notified Mr. Barron, I notified your husbands."

Cassidy linked her arm through Chance's and winked at Jolie. "Busted!" She pushed up on the toes of her boots to kiss her husband. "You can't blame us for trying. We were curious about the woman in Cash's life."

"Speak for yourself," Savannah muttered darkly.

Cord snagged Jolie and dropped a kiss on her head. "Don't play matchmaker, sunshine."

"We were concerned, since he'd moved her into his place but hadn't introduced her to anyone." Now his three brothers all exchanged looks and Jolie elbowed Cord in the stomach. "Y'all knew?"

While the three couples devolved into a teasing argument, Cash approached Roxie, Harley's leash in his hand. "C'mon. I'll walk you back to the office."

She executed a precise about-face and marched back the way she'd come without comment. Cash had no trouble matching her stride. They'd climbed the steps to street level and were halfway to Barron Tower before he spoke.

"Don't pay them any mind."

"Why does your twin's wife hate you?"

"She has her reasons."

"That's not an answer."

Resisting the urge to rub the back of his neck, he rolled his shoulders instead. "That's the only answer you're going to get."

"Oh. Because we don't have a relationship. Because I'm just *business*. Despite the fact I've been sharing your bed for almost a month. Fine. I get it. Shutting up now." She lengthened her stride and pulled away from him.

"Roxie? Roxanne! It's not like that." He caught up to her. "I just said that so they'd leave you alone."

She stopped abruptly and he almost plowed into her. She faced him, her eyes shadowed with misery. "They're your family. Why would you want them to stay away from me? Are you ashamed of me or something?"

Her question caught him flat-footed and she was half a block away before he moved. Tugging Harley into a rolling gallop, Cash ran to catch up.

"Wait, Roxie." He snagged her arm and gently stopped her. "It's not like that."

"Oh. So how is it? Because if it's not those things, it's so much worse."

"Wait…no." He paused to gather his thoughts. "Look, I just wanted to keep you away from them."

"So that's not worse than them leaving me alone?"

"You don't know them."

"You're right. I don't. You never bothered to introduce me, so how could I? And you didn't introduce me because I'm just some…person involved in your investigation who just happens to be warming your bed on a nightly basis. Yeah, I can see why you'd want me separate from your family life."

"I don't have a family life, Roxanne." The bitterness coating those words surprised him. So did the truth of them. "My brothers' wives don't like me. They have reason not to. Anyone I might care about would be fair game for their prying. I didn't want to subject you to that."

"You keep saying they have reason to dislike you. Tell me what you did."

"It doesn't concern you, Roxanne. Just…leave it be. Okay?"

"No, not okay, but whatever." She walked off again and he followed with Harley. Once at the office, they went their separate ways.

She hid out in the spare office and he didn't see her again until the end of the business day. Only he needed to remain at the office for a conference call with a company in Sydney. He tagged Alan to drive Roxie and Harley home and to stay with her until he arrived. He went to the office where he stashed her when he needed privacy and explained. She gathered up her things and leashed Harley without a word.

Cash didn't get home until almost midnight. Alan was on his feet and gave his report immediately as soon as Cash entered the house.

"We had takeout for dinner, which we picked up after the dog's evening walk. She went to bed shortly thereafter and hasn't stirred since."

"Thanks, Alan. I'll see you in the morning."

Locking the door and setting the alarm after the man's

departure, Cash didn't put off facing Roxie. He quietly opened the door to his bedroom—and found an empty bed.

"What the—" He jerked off his tie and suit coat, dropping them on the armchair on his side of the bed. Harley met him in the hallway with an aggrieved *woof.* Cash put the dog out onto the patio and then stalked to the guest room. Roxie didn't belong in the guest room. He should have found her in his bed, where she'd been for—

Cash cut those thoughts off. Given what he'd said that afternoon, her retreat to the guest room shouldn't surprise him, nor should it sting, but it did. He crept into the room and stretched out beside her on the bed. Kissing the back of her neck, he whispered, "Red?"

"Don't call me that."

"Are you still upset?"

"What do you think?"

He curled his arm over her waist and snugged her back against him. "Would it help if I say I'm sorry?"

Roxie rolled to face him and he noticed the circles beneath her eyes. She looked tired. And troubled.

"Will you mean it?"

"I *am* sorry you got dragged into my family drama, Roxie." He realized *he* felt as tired—and as troubled—as she looked.

"Will you tell me about it?"

He considered opening up to her, but twenty years under his father's direct tutelage stopped him. "It's just family, Rox."

"And I'm not family. I get it."

She attempted to roll away but he stopped her by cupping her cheek in his hand. "No, Red, you don't. My family is a hot mess. You don't have anything to do with them, with…things. I can get away from all that when I'm with you."

A tiny smile hovered around the corner of her mouth. "Well, that's a start on the groveling."

"Oh," he teased, his voice growing rougher. "You want groveling." He kissed her and cupped her breast. "My bed is bigger," he hinted.

Roxie was buried under the covers, snug and warm and floating on the last wisps of a dream—a dream of Cash and her living in a beautiful house with little Harleys weaving between their feet. She tripped—klutz that she was—and Cash caught her, laughing as he kissed her.

She'd decided to forgive Cash last night. Yes, he'd hurt her feelings, but the look on his face when he admitted he had problems with his family had almost broken her heart. They were two of a kind in that regard. Her family was no prize, but a little thought niggled at the back of her brain. Cash admitted his sisters-in-law had reason to feel as they did. It was just as obvious that he accepted their dislike and the estrangement it must cause with his brothers as if he expected to be ostracized. That hurt, too.

While she often found him emotionally frustrating, standoffish and cold upon occasion, when he took her into his arms and kissed her? When he made love to her? Her world narrowed and focused, and for the first time in her life, she felt like she might just belong somewhere—belong to someone.

Snuggling back under the covers, she stretched, deliciously stiff and beard-burned in sensitive places. Cash had shown her in so many ways how good he was at *groveling* and, boy, did her body enjoy it. She was about to drop back into sleep when someone started pounding on the door.

Roxie blinked, now fully awake, and sat up. Whoever it was pounded and rang the doorbell like it was a noisemaker on New Year's Eve. Tossing off the covers, she shivered in the cool air and looked around for something to put on. Just because Cash locked himself out when he and Harley went for a run was no excuse to answer the door naked.

A slow smile curled her lips. Maybe that was a good idea after all. If she answered the door naked, maybe Cash would take her back to bed and they'd be a little late to work. Okay, *he'd* be late to work. She'd be late to twiddling her thumbs. With that thought souring her desire, she snagged the shirt Cash had been wearing the night before. He'd dropped it on the chair rather than tossing it in his hamper. Stark white with French cuffs and an impossibly high thread count, she slipped her arms through the shirt's sleeves.

"All right already! I'm coming. Keep your shorts on." She rolled up the sleeves but didn't bother to button the shirt. She turned off the alarm code as Cash had shown her—a guest code he'd delete after she was gone, and wasn't that a depressing thought. When the panel beeped at her, she unlocked and opened the door.

"What? You forgot—" Words dried in her mouth and she scrambled to button up the shirt in the face of Cyrus Barron's disapproval.

The man barged in and pushed past her. She got the door shut but didn't lock it or put the alarm back on as she jogged after him. "Uh…excuse me? Cash isn't here right now—"

"I can see that."

"Well, I'm not sure when he'll—"

Mr. Barron looked her up and down, and his disapproval tipped over into disdain before morphing into outright derision. "I'm surprised my son left one of his bimbos here alone. I thought I taught him better than that. I'll add that to the list of things we need to discuss."

Cash's father stalked toward the kitchen as if he owned the place and once again, Roxie scrambled after him. "Um..." She couldn't say any of the things she was thinking, like "Go away!"

With absolute confidence, he grabbed a mug from the cabinet above the coffeemaker and poured himself a cup. He turned to face her, his eyes as sharp as a hawk's, his mouth pressed into an arrogant sneer. "Cash always did go for the brainless ones."

Brainless? She had a master's in museum studies and was seriously considering going back to school for her PhD. She'd graduated summa cum laude with a 4.0 grade average—for every degree she'd earned. And this dried-up old fart was calling *her* brainless? She bit back what she wanted to say and muzzled her temper. "We've never been introduced, Mr. Barron, and you have no idea who or what I am, and since we've said no more than a few words to each other, I will forgive your natural propensity for antipathy." Then added under her breath, "This time."

The man stared at her like she was something stuck to the bottom of his shoe. Whatever. She'd managed to haphazardly button Cash's shirt so none of her naked bits were showing. She made a mental note to put a robe in Cash's room and start wearing underwear to bed.

Inhaling, she proceeded. "And since you don't know anything about me, I will explain so you understand." She arched a brow. She'd been working on her haughty expression for dealing with her minions—the two interns and three assistants who worked under her supervision in RCM's archives. The old man didn't look impressed so it probably needed more work. Still, she persisted. "My name is Roxanne Rowland and I am the corporate archivist for—"

The front door slammed open and Cash's yelling cut her

off. "Dammit, Roxie, what have I told you about leaving the door unlock—" He turned the corner, saw his father, and stopped moving *and* speaking.

Harley, on the other hand, barreled across the living room, hit the tiles in the kitchen and slid sideways as he tried to turn the corner of the kitchen island. With scrabbling claws, the dog kept his feet and his momentum, nailing Mr. Barron with his nose, just below the belt. Roxie never had a chance to stop the collision—not that she was too inclined to try, given the circumstances.

Cash had to shift gears fast. The last person he expected to see standing in his kitchen was his father. The next to last was Roxie, wearing his shirt and nothing else, chewing out his old man. He'd thought the voices he heard from outside were from the TV. And then Harley pulled an end run that all but took his father to the floor. His temples began to throb.

"Ah, Roxanne? Clothes, maybe?"

She glanced down, seemed to realize her state of attire and nodded. "Good idea. And Cash, just so you know… there won't be enough coffee in the world today." She offered his father a scowl before disappearing down the hall to the guest room, calling for Harley to follow.

"What is she doing here, Cashion?"

"Staying in the guest room, Dad."

"Wearing your shirt?"

Cash shrugged. "My sex life has been off the table for discussion since I turned eighteen. Why are you here?"

"I want to know about that phone call you made to Sydney. We discussed this a month ago. I don't want us doing business with those people."

"*We* aren't, Dad. Barron Security is."

"Splitting hairs."

"Am I the CEO of Barron Security?"

"For now."

"Is that a threat?" Something inside Cash tore a little. He'd sat back and watched his father make the same threat to each one of his brothers. They'd all stood up to him, knowing that Chance had them covered under the family trust. Except Cash knew he wasn't protected. There'd been reasons—viable ones—to leave Barron Security outside the trust's umbrella. BSS had clients from around the world and beyond the scope of the Barron umbrella of companies. The company needed autonomy that being in the trust wouldn't provide.

And now he was sweating bullets because the one thing he could do for his family was shield them through the auspices of his company. If that was taken away? Cash had to face the possibility.

"If it needs to be."

That little rip ruptured, becoming a chasm. He clamped down on his emotions and faced his father. "We'll discuss this at the office. I need to shower and dress."

Cyrus emptied his untouched coffee into the sink and set the mug down with a clink. "You bet we will. And we will be discussing that woman. Get her out of your house, Cashion. Dump her and get your mind back on business." He stopped before getting to the front door. "I'm well aware you've had her stashed in your office, along with that ridiculous dog, and you've taken her to the ranch. That ends now. I know who she is. The Barrons don't associate with trash, boy. You'd better remember that."

Fourteen

Cash should have gone to Roxie, soothed her by telling her everything would be all right, explained that his father often spoke without thinking. Except all of it would be a lie. Nothing was right and his father always said exactly what was on his mind. He heard water running from the bath off the guest room. So much for sharing their morning shower, as they normally did. Harley brushed against his leg and he glanced down. Even the dog looked accusatory.

"What?" he growled. "Dad's right. I shouldn't have gotten involved."

And he was. Very involved. Cash didn't do relationships and, before Roxanne, the thought of a woman sharing his space would have left him laughing. Not that Roxie didn't make him laugh—but in a good way that made him feel warm inside.

Later, when it was time to leave for Barron Tower, Harley refused to get off the couch. No amount of entreaty from Roxie or Cash's commands moved the dog. Frustrated, Cash stormed out of the condo and sat in the Rover until Roxie appeared a few minutes later. As the weather had a tendency to do in early March, winter had come back with a fierce blast of cold. He had the heater cranked up and the seat warmer on high.

Roxie slid into the car, buckled up and never once looked at him. He lasted until they pulled into the parking garage. Leaving the car running for warmth, he twisted to look at her. “You shouldn’t have opened the door.”

She finally flipped out. “I shouldn’t… You… He…I thought… You… What he said…” Then she slugged him. In the shoulder. Harder than he would have given her credit for. “I thought you’d forgotten your keys and it was cold out and you were only wearing those ridiculously sexy running clothes. You are the world’s biggest jackass. No. Wait. I apologize to mules everywhere. And I’m wrong. Your father is the biggest. You? You’re just…just…” She threw up her hands in frustration. “I’m trash? Is that what you believe? Is that really how you feel?”

Cash grabbed her hands, holding them gently despite her efforts to pull away. “Shh, Red. That’s not how I feel. You aren’t any of the things my father implied.”

She inhaled deeply and quit fighting his grip. “Then why didn’t you say something?”

That was a fair question. How did he explain? Could he explain? How did he summarize twenty-five years of the messy, broken relationship between father and son? “It’s…complicated.”

“Complicated.” Roxie leaned away from him. “Easy excuse, Cash. You don’t want to talk about it? Fine.” She glanced at the clock in the Rover’s dash. “You’re late for work.”

They exited the vehicle, rode the elevator in silence and he dropped her at the door to the empty office without a word. Yesterday had been rough, though last night’s sweet make-up sex had mitigated the situation with his sisters-in-law. Today? Today just made him want to run away. Like to the top of Mount Everest. Instead he was met by a stack of urgent messages.

At 6:00 p.m., Cash emerged from his office for what seemed like the first time all day. Lunch had been delivered to his desk by the ever-present and efficient intern Nick and it felt like his phone was permanently attached to his ear. The niggling headache his morning had started with was now a full-blown head-pounder. Roxie was sitting on the couch across from Cheri's desk, now occupied by Nick, her booted feet propped on the hand-carved wooden coffee table. A part of his tired brain noted that she had a magazine under her feet, probably to keep from marring the polished surface.

"Ready to go home?"

She pulled her earbuds out and studied him. "I've been ready to go home for a month now."

Cash realized his slip immediately but something twinged inside. He'd begun to think…no. He wouldn't go there. He lived in his condo, but it wasn't home, except with Roxie there… No. He couldn't think of that. He studied her the way he would a suspect. Her nonchalance was forced, as was the bored look. He noticed the white-knuckled grip on her phone and the nervous twitch of the toes of one boot.

"You can head out, Nick," he ordered. Once they were alone, Cash sat down beside her, stretched his legs out and planted his boots next to hers. She frowned and he wondered what caused it—him sitting there or his boots on the bare wood. Roxie had funny ideas about furniture and art. He supposed it was her training as a museum curator.

She folded her arms across her chest but refused to look at him. "What?"

"I'm sorry I was too busy to see you today."

Roxie jerked a little and cut her eyes in his direction. He'd taken her by surprise. Good. "And I'm sorry my father dragged you into our family drama."

She didn't respond for almost a minute. "I have no room to talk when it comes to family drama. Mine sort of dragged you into theirs."

He nudged her shoulder with his own in a show of fond solidarity. "How 'bout we head ho—to my place. We'll stop, grab some steaks. I'll grill."

"It's too cold to grill, though Harley would growl at me for saying so. He's a steakaholic."

Cash chuckled. "I'm a man. It's never too cold to grill. C'mon, Red."

He surged to his feet and tugged her up after him. Slinging his arm around her shoulders, he kept her close all the way to his car. The crisis seemed to have passed for the moment.

Harley, full of prime beef, was sprawled on the couch imitating a dead cockroach, except for the snores that too closely resembled a set of untuned motorcycle pipes. Cash waited for Roxie to step into his bedroom before shutting off the lights in the main part of the condo. He followed her a moment later.

Walking up behind her, he stopped her from taking off her sweater. "I'll do it."

She glanced over her shoulder, her expression concerned. He had sounded gruffer than he'd intended but he needed to be in control tonight. To take charge. To do things his way. Residual resentment from his father's actions lingered, but he refused to allow thoughts of the old man to intrude into his bedroom.

Cash yanked the sweater over her head and tossed it away. As he stroked her bare belly, her silky flesh felt smooth against the calloused tips of his fingers. She shivered beneath his touch and tried to turn in his arms.

"No." He whispered the order against her temple, one arm banding her in place. With his free hand, he captured her wrists and locked them together, his grip firm, unyielding, yet gentle.

"I'm taking you." His voice was clogged with something he didn't want to name. It couldn't be need. He wouldn't let it. "I'm taking you the way I want to."

"I want—"

"No, Red." She struggled a little and he tightened his hold on her. "You'll get what you want. I promise." He unfastened the center hook of her bra and teased the straps off over the points of her shoulders. "But I get what I want first."

At the moment, he wanted her naked. When he dropped his arm to undo her belt buckle and jeans, her bra fluttered open, the straps catching on her elbows. He brushed the hair off the nape of her neck with his chin and nuzzled. He murmured his next command against her skin. "Lose the boots, Red."

"Let me go."

Cash felt his rumbling chuckle all the way through her body. He slid his hand into her jeans, teasing her over her panties. "Boots." He tightened his grip when she twitched.

He scooped her long hair and draped it over one shoulder, kissing his way along her jaw. He captured her chin and turned her head so he could claim her lips, slipping his fingers inside her panties as he did. Teasing her mouth open with his tongue, he did the same with his finger, both plunging into her at the same time. Her body went limp and he swallowed her tiny whimper of need.

Dazed, she leaned against him, tried to toe off one boot, then finally managed and kicked it away. She rubbed against him as she worked on the other boot. He slipped a second finger inside her. She was wet, hot, her sex clamping around him as he stroked her. She shuddered and gasped as a mini-orgasm hit. He didn't give her time to recover, instead urging her forward.

"On the bed, Red. Facedown."

She did as she was told and he stripped her socks and jeans off. Kneeling next to the bed, he rolled her panties down, leaving kisses in the path of their removal. He knelt behind her and spread her knees. Cash intended to take his time, to touch, to taste, to wring every bit of passion from her. When his mouth clamped over her, she erupted.

He held her down on the bed with a forearm across the small of her back. She bucked and writhed, her moans stifled by the thick comforter as she pressed her face against the bed. He feasted on her, tempering his tender assault with kisses along her thighs and cheeks.

Cash glanced up and smiled. Her hands had fisted the comforter and her eyes were squinted shut. Her back heaved with each shuddering breath she sucked in.

"Please," she cried. "Please. I can't. No more."

Heat radiated from her and her skin was tinted rose. He was so hard he had to clench his teeth. He wanted to be inside her so badly he was about to go insane but he held on. He wasn't done with her. "You can. You will."

Cash's fingers filled her, teased her, pumped into her. She could barely breathe, much less speak as his tongue worked her into a frenzy. She begged, sobbing, but still he wouldn't stop. She spiraled higher and higher, and when she shattered, she couldn't control the shaking. A moment later, he was beside her, naked, warm, turning her over and sliding inside.

If she'd had enough breath, Roxie would have screamed

from the pleasure of it all. She managed to keep her eyes open, fixed on his face, and what she saw there melted her heart. She'd fallen for Cash, was in-over-her-head in love with him. She clutched him, arching into his body as he made love to her. When she fell the third time, he went with her.

There was a breathless moment of his weight, his warmth, holding her down before he rolled off. He pulled her to him, cuddled her.

"Breathe, Red," he commanded with a pleased chuckle.

She gulped in air, expanded lungs starved for oxygen, found her voice. "Yeah, easy for you to say."

Cash didn't respond and she opened her eyes, tilting her head on his shoulder so she could see his face. He looked infinitely sad and she cringed, the bliss welling inside her popping like gossamer soap bubbles.

Roxie had no pet name for him. No *honey* or *sweetheart.* Nothing as maddeningly endearing as *Red* but calling him by name in this moment seemed…out of sync. Almost harsh. She laughed at herself for even having enough brain cells to rub together after three mind-blowing orgasms. Sliding her cheek against his skin, she curled her fingers through the feathering of dark hair on his chest.

"Thinking too hard, Red."

Cash's voice grumbled beneath her cheek.

"What's wrong?"

"You're the one thinking. I should be asking you that question."

"Worried for you."

"Not worth worrying over."

"Yes, you are."

And that was the root of the problem. Roxie caught a glimpse of the lonely man he hid from the world before Cash shuttered his expression.

"Cash?"

"I'm fine, Roxanne." He rolled into her, claimed her mouth for a deep kiss, and she knew he was trying to distract her.

When he broke the kiss to nuzzle her breast, she tried again. "What's the deal with your sisters-in-law?"

A low growl emanated from the back of his throat. "I've got your nipple in my mouth and you want to talk about them?"

"Yes. They don't like you much."

"Duh."

"I'd like to know why...and don't give me that family drama excuse. Your brothers came when Alan alerted them to save you from them."

"Hardly. They came to see the show." He sighed and settled on his back, one arm tucked behind his head, his other still curled around her. "Look, Barron men aren't exactly lucky in love. And there were unpleasant circumstances surrounding each of the women my brothers fell for."

"They seem happy enough now."

"Yeah." He stared at the ceiling. "Look, I did the job I was given. I served legal papers on Cassidy. I made sure Cord could claim the son he had with Jolie. I..." Cash closed his eyes. "I tried to save Clay from living through the illness and death of another woman he loved."

"Another?"

"His mother, when he was a kid. Then Georgie."

"But Georgie didn't die."

"I underestimated her strength. And his."

"And Chase?"

"No."

"His wife really dislikes you."

"Yeah."

She stroked her fingers along the dips and curves of

his chest and abdomen, continuing even when he spoke again. "They…when they got married, they didn't love each other."

"How could you know that?"

"They'd known each other for all of forty-eight hours when they eloped."

Something in his voice alerted her to more underlying currents. "Do you feel…left out?"

Cash glanced at her sharply. "Why should I?"

"I have the impression that the five of you used to hang around together. A lot."

"Clay is twelve years older. We never hung around. And he's been in Washington for years. Chance is six years older, Cord eight. We didn't hang with them either."

"Maybe not as kids, but as adults. I mean, you all work in the same building. Well, except Clay. Surely you did lunch occasionally or went out for happy hour? And there had to be times at the ranch—" The expression on his face dried her mouth up and no more words came. As quickly as she stopped speaking, he shut down, his eyes glinting with cynicism, those full lips that could work such magic on her pressed into a hard line.

"Leave it be, Roxie. You can't change things. They are what they are." He kissed her forehead, to take the sting out of his harsh tone, she suspected.

She raised her face to his and claimed a real kiss before murmuring, "Tomorrow is another day."

Fifteen

Cash was exhausted. He'd had meetings with his father every day this week. They'd recovered half the stolen cattle, and a situation at one of the hotels in Florida had been resolved without a lawsuit thanks to his investigators, but there was still no sign of the freaking Rowlands. Today, he'd dodged a bullet; his father had gone off on some tangent that didn't involve him. Still, every meeting had ended with the same question, "Have you gotten rid of that woman yet?"

And he'd stalled. He told himself he didn't need Roxie in his life. Part of him didn't want her there, yet there she was, day in and day out. And nights in his bed, even if he was too worn out from stress to do anything but hold her while he slept. She was always just…there. Smiling. Occasionally making him laugh. Always ready for his kisses—and more. Since he was being honest, he also liked having her big, goofy dog underfoot, too.

He paused in the lobby to send Roxie a text.

Meet me in my office. Two stops to make, then we'll sneak out early.

They'd go home, change and then he'd take her to Donovan's. He thought Roxie would enjoy listening to the Irish folk group slated to perform there. With April almost here, the weather had turned mild and the band would be playing on the patio, so Harley would be comfortable.

Cash got off the elevator at the thirty-sixth floor and dropped a file off at the reception desk for Barron Exploration. There'd been a situation involving embezzlement by a BarEx employee. The file held the evidence of the investigation Cash had run. Next stop, Barron & Associates to drop off a copy for Chance.

He didn't bother waiting for the elevator, opting for the stairs since he was headed down only two floors. Pushing through the fire door, he all but knocked Nick down.

"Hey, boss!" The kid grinned at him while glancing at the file. "If you need to deliver that, I can take it."

"Yeah, thanks." He passed off the paperwork and headed back to the elevator. Cash felt wound up tight, and he very much wanted to get out of his corporate skin to spend time with Roxie. The elevator opened and as soon as he saw his father, he knew all bets were off.

"Cashion."

He resisted the urge to slump his shoulders in defeat. Posture stiff, he stepped into the elevator. "Not here, Dad. My office."

Cheri looked up as they walked in and her smile faded. Then his assistant's face twitched as an elaborate and unreadable set of expressions danced across her face. He didn't have time to decipher them today. He wanted to get rid of his father, grab Roxie and get the hell away from the office. He pushed his door open and led the way into his inner sanctum, closing the door behind his dad.

"I'm tired of waiting, Cashion."

"For what, Dad?" He did his best not to sound as tired as he felt.

"For you to get rid of that woman. She's still in your house."

"My private life isn't up for discussion."

"When it involves women like her, it does. How much are those criminals costing us?"

"I'm on top of the investigation, Dad. Let me do the job you hired me for."

"And that's the operative word, isn't it? Or have you forgotten I'm the one who signs your paycheck?"

"Kinda hard to do that when you're in my face reminding me every five minutes." Cash wanted to retract those words the second they left his mouth.

"I expected better of you, Cashion. The older boys were too coddled by their mother. And Chasen was too erratic. I put all my hope in you, boy. You were to be my legacy. My one true son. And look what you're doing to me."

"What, Dad? What am I doing to you?" The beast that was his temper had escaped its cage. "I'm doing exactly what you ask of me. No matter the damn consequences. I've done everything in my power to protect this family, to make sure our companies run smoothly, to make sure no one can mess with us."

"But that woman is still in your bed."

"So what, Dad? How many bimbos have you bedded for the sex? Because that's what this is. Roxie is the key to prosecuting her family and if she wants to put out while we wait for the next move, how is that any different from the women who warm your bed?"

He headed toward his desk, then faltered. The snow globe that normally occupied a spot near the one photo he allowed in his office was missing. His gaze swept the desktop. The framed photo, of the Barron brothers sitting on a fence at the ranch at Christmastime, was untouched. He and Chase had been eight the year they received antique snow globes from their mother, two weeks before she was killed by a drunk driver.

"Are you listening to me, boy?" Cyrus grabbed his arm, spun Cash around. "I've had all of the foolishness I can stomach. It's time to get rid of her and move on. I need your full attention. I've written off your brothers but I expect you to live up to your obligations."

His father stalked to the door and pushed it open. "I'm disappointed in you, boy."

Cash followed him out into the private reception area. At least Cheri was nowhere to be seen, so no one would see his fall from grace. It was all he could do to maintain his equilibrium. He'd built his whole life around pleasing this man, around getting his respect and acceptance. And now his father was threatening to rip it all away because he'd allowed his desire for a woman to overshadow his duty. He should have known better.

"Get rid of her, Cashion, or you will both be sorry. You know what I'm capable of."

Cash stood stock-still, a burning ache knotting his stomach. He knew exactly what his father was capable of. Remaining outwardly calm, he said, "Why are you threatening me, Dad?"

Cyrus stepped up to him, circled. Cash turned to keep his father in front of him until Cash's back was to the open office door.

"You were my protégé, the one I spent years grooming. And now you betray me. Over some woman. You're no better than *them*." Cyrus waved a hand in the direction behind Cash before he pushed past and stormed away.

A hand landed on Cash's shoulder. "Welcome to the club, bro."

He shook off his twin's grip and faced his brothers. Why were all of them here? Clay stayed in Washington and Chase traveled constantly. Though Cord and Chance occupied their offices on a daily basis, Cash didn't often interact with them, hadn't since they'd married. Each of his brothers wore an expression of pity. Pity for him. "Screw you, Chase."

Cash didn't need this BS. He'd always put the family first, done what was right for the Barron name. He reminded himself that Roxie was only in his life because of a threat to the family. And it wasn't like anything was going on between them. Besides the sex. Which was, admittedly, some of the best he'd ever had. But she was just a means to an end. He didn't have feelings for her. None. She was simply a distraction, like his father insisted. He didn't want her. Certainly didn't need her.

In fact, he couldn't wait to move her and that damn slobbering beast of hers out of his condo. He wanted life returned to normal—ordered, calm, collected. No more lacy bras hanging in his bathroom. No slug slime on his tailored slacks. No muddy footprints on the leather seats in his Range Rover. No more sexy woman sharing his bed.

Chase threw his head back and laughed. "Yup, dazed and confused. She must be some kind of woman to make the last Barron brother bite the dust."

"You aren't nearly as funny as you think you are." Cash glared at his brothers. "Some reason all of you are hanging around here? If you're just waiting for Dad to hand my ass to me again, too late. Show's over and you can get on back to your lives."

He stormed into his office and jerked the door shut, ignoring the soft protests he left in his wake. Cash had more important things to do—like get rid of a woman he should never have been involved with.

Sixteen

Roxie managed to keep her breathing controlled and quiet. Ducking under Chase's desk had been a monumental mistake, especially since his father had followed him in and shut the door. Their argument raged over her head and she hadn't missed a word. The same with the confrontation Cash had with his brothers. When the door slammed, she remained in hiding, her heart hammering in her chest.

The fact that it was still beating surprised the heck out of her. The things Cord said didn't break her, they shredded her. And made her angry. She was such a fool.

"You can come out now, Roxanne." Cash's voice sounded flat.

She crawled out from the kneehole and used his luxurious leather desk chair as a prop to climb to her feet. Facing the windows, her back to the room, she did not want to turn around, did not want to face Cash's anger. The argument had been terrible and personal and she was an interloper who had no right to have been a witness, but she was angry, too.

Swallowing her emotions, she turned to confront the

man she'd come to love. His expression broke her heart, her anger dissolving in the face of his pain. His normally tan skin held a gray pallor. His full lips—which were quirked into a sardonic smile more often than not—drooped at the corners. His eyes were empty, bleak. His pain was almost visceral.

Her eyes filled with tears as she faced the despondent man—a man determined to hide his feelings, as desolate and lonely as that action might make him. Roxie wanted to run to him, wrap her arms around him, hold him. Tell him how she felt. She did none of those things. Anything of the sort would be rebuffed. She could tell by looking at his stiff posture.

"I'm sorry." She all but swallowed the last word trying to get it out around the lump in her throat.

"For what? For sneaking into my office?" Life came back into his eyes and they sparked with temper. "For watching me get eviscerated by my father? Mocked by my brothers?"

Anger, no matter how bitter or directed at her, was better than the defeat of a devastated man who looked like he'd been abandoned by his last friend. She stepped around the desk, wanting to be closer to him.

"I didn't sneak into your office. *You* asked me to meet you here and your assistant showed me in."

"Why the hell did you hide?" He stalked toward her but stopped after a couple of steps. His fists clenched at his sides and he was all but swaying with the effort to regain control.

"Uh, duh? You were with your father."

Cash frowned. "So?"

"After my last little run-in with the man, I figured it was better for us if he didn't find me in your office."

He scrubbed at his forehead with the heel of his palm

and Roxie could almost see the headache forming. She wanted to make him sit down so she could rub his temples, massage his shoulders, kiss him. Something. Anything. Whatever it would take to make him understand he wasn't the worthless son his father accused him of being.

Cash, with studied casualness, skirted her location as he moved behind his desk and sank into the chair. "Sit down, Roxie," he said without looking at her.

She obeyed, sinking onto the edge of the nearest visitor's chair as Cash swiveled so that his back was partially to her and he could look out the window. Oklahoma City was spread out below—a blend of old and new, greenery and concrete, a place the Barrons considered their domain.

Silence stretched between them. She would have given anything to know what Cash was thinking. He was worlds away from the man he'd been the night before. The sex was always good, but last night had been special. He'd been tender. Loving. He'd shared his feelings with her. Today, that man no longer existed and her gut twisted up in greasy knots as she feared the worst.

"You shouldn't have hidden, Roxanne." Cash's voice was toneless.

"So, I should have stood here and defended our relationship?" Her chest was tight and her nose burned with tears threatening to appear. She knew what was coming, braced herself for his words.

"We don't have a relationship."

Cement solidified in her lungs, and she went cold as all her emotions drained away.

"I'll have Bridger arrange for someone to accompany you to the condo to pick up your things, take you and Harley home."

Roxie sat there too staggered by his proclamation to

move. "You can't be serious. You're going to break us just like—" she snapped her fingers "—that? Are you joking?"

Now he turned to stare at her. His eyes held nothing but disdain. "I never joke, Roxanne. It was fun while it lasted but there was never any *us* to break. At this point in time, I don't need your assistance any longer, nor do I want you in my bed."

She was all but sputtering now. "My assistance? My *assistance*?" Her voice climbed in pitch and volume. "Is that what last night was? What the last few weeks spent in your bed, on the floor, in the shower, were?" Damn her red hair—for her temper and the way her skin colored when she was angry.

"I am not a prostitute, Cash. And you just made me feel like one. Maybe your father was right after all, because from where I'm standing? The apple didn't fall far from that tree."

She ducked around the desk, grasped the back of his chair and spun him around. Leaning down, she pinned him in by placing her hands on the arms of the chair. Spitting mad, she swallowed and narrowed her gaze on his eyes.

"You, Cashion Matthew Barron, are a major jerk. And you want to know something else? I think you try to be a major jerk. Look at your brothers. Clay is the leader. Cord is the responsible one. Chance is the smart one. Chase is the lovable rascal. And you? What is left for you? Being the jerk. In fact, I think you cultivate this whole persona because deep down, you're just a scared kid who—"

Cash grabbed her arms and shoved her backward as he surged up. Less than a second later, her back was pressed forcibly against the window glass and she was on her tiptoes. A mishmash of emotions suffused his face—anger, shock and, when his eyes dropped to her mouth, lust.

"Leave my brothers out of this."

"No. They are as much a part of this as your father is."

"You don't know anything about my family. About them. About him." He was growling the words and when he stopped to breathe, his chest pressed against hers. His whole body was vibrating from his barely-leashed anger. "And you know nothing about me. Nothing at all, Roxanne Rosetta Rowland."

Now his entire torso was pressed against her, chest to hips, and she was shocked to discover that Cash was aroused. A weird, detached part of her brain wondered if that was the reason angry make-up sex was so good.

"Let me go, Cash."

"No."

His grip on her biceps tightened and he lifted her high enough that her feet no longer touched the floor. Cash was scaring her a little but, positive she'd both touched a nerve and hit on the truth, Roxie pushed her luck. Cupping his face in her palms, she softened her voice.

"I know more than you think, Cash." She closed her eyes, let her own pain, her own fears, well up so they'd show. Then she raised her eyelids. "I know what having a bullying father is like, what it's like to have brothers who think you're nothing but a means to an end."

Cash loosened his fingers and her feet hit the floor. She dropped her hands when they started to tremble. Her voice was thick with suppressed hurt as she continued.

"You at least had your brothers, Cash, when you were growing up. You had Miz Beth and Big John after your mom died." He squeezed her arms again and his look turned fierce, but she wouldn't be deterred. This was too important. *He* was too important, and if they were ever to have a chance, she had to convince him of this.

"You had people who cared. I didn't. I never knew my mother. My father was a stranger and my brothers treated me like a stray puppy." She swallowed the spit that pooled in her mouth as she considered what she would reveal next.

"When I was five, my brother Dexter accused me of murdering our mother, of depriving the rest of them of her love. She died when I was born, you see." Roxie dropped her gaze, watched cars crawling along the street thirty-four floors below. "The next day, Lex—who was barely eighteen, by the way—loaded me into a car with one little plastic suitcase and drove me to a boarding school. He left me standing alone at the gate. I clutched my suitcase and watched the taillights disappear."

She dashed tears from her eyes, tears that blurred her sight when she really needed to be able to see Cash, to see his reaction. "You aren't the only orphan in this room, Cash. You aren't the only one who worries you aren't good enough to be loved."

"You're full of crap." He let go with one hand and ran it through his hair. His gaze moved from her to the vista outside the window. "I don't believe a word of this. You're as big a con as the rest of your family. Lies come out of your mouth as easily as you breathe."

Her heart was shredded into tiny pieces but at least her tears dried up from the force of the anger that overrode her anguish. "You don't get it, dumbass. Your father is a piece of work—as bad as mine, only yours claims to be legitimate in his feelings for you. That man wouldn't know love if Harley was covered in it and bit him on the butt. He's egotistical, hard, uncaring and a right royal bastard. Just like my father. Max Rowland lives for the game. The con—long or short. Using people and discarding them is his stock in trade. And I'm just one more asset to be used up and discarded. He has you in his sights and you know what? Despite everything you've said to me, I'll still do my best to protect the Barrons." She brushed her sleeve under her nose to avoid sniffling.

"I made a promise to you. To help you stop him. To stop my family, even if it means sending them to prison. And I will, regardless of what you think of me, or what you believe my motives to be."

Roxie jerked her other arm free and ducked away from Cash. "But there is a difference between your family and mine. A huge difference. My brothers only want to use me. But *your* brothers? They love you. A whole lot by everything I've seen. Mine are as bad as my father. They'll use me up and abandon me just like they did when I was five. Just like they did when I was sixteen. Just like they did in Vegas. You have a chance, Cash. A chance to be part of a family. A chance to be loved. Go make up with them while you can."

Cash's expression didn't change. She marched to the door, pulled it open and paused. "I'll get out of your life, but dude? Throwing me out is one of the biggest mistakes you'll ever make. In case you ever wake up and realize what an idiot you are, you know where to find me. Maybe you'll get lucky and I'll still love you. But you'd better be ready to crawl back. Groveling always works best."

She walked out, closed the door gently despite wanting to slam it. The darn thing was hung wrong for a dramatic exit. Placing her hand against the door in a final farewell, she called softly, "You can do it, Cash. You *can* find your family again."

Seventeen

Cash didn't remember covering the distance to the door. He leaned his forehead against it and heard Roxie's murmur. "How am I supposed to do that?" he asked the closed door.

Straightening, he wandered to the window and stared out. Taking a moment, he sent a text to Bridger. Any of the men hanging around the office could deal with Roxie, with getting her out of his life, but he didn't trust just any of them to do it right. He didn't hate her. No, he reserved that emotion for himself. Loathing what he'd become, he'd done what was needed. He knew all too well what his father's ultimatums meant.

Orders given, he remained at the window, ignoring both his phone and the pings coming from his computer whenever an email hit. He was done with the world for today, so he watched shadows grow, the spiked silhouette of the Barron Tower acting as a sundial. Roxie would be packed by now, her clutter cleared out of his condo. He wondered if Bridger had assigned Alan to her, then shoved those thoughts away.

He was a busy man. He didn't have time to moon over what might have been. Roxanne was the enemy; the Rowlands were out to harm the Barrons. She had to be in on it. Forget the sweet noises she uttered as he made love to her. Forget the way she made him laugh. Forget—

Cash banged his fist against the window hard enough to bruise the side of his hand. She was wrong! He couldn't fix things with his brothers. He was his father's son, through and through. His gut churned when he thought of the things he'd done in the name of family. Despicable. That's how Chance's wife, Cassidy, had described him, and she'd told the truth. He'd done everything his father asked of him. Everything. It didn't matter that he hurt the women his brothers loved. He hadn't cared that he'd betrayed the four men who deserved his absolute loyalty.

Family is the only thing that matters. How often had he heard his father spout those words? More importantly, when had he swerved from that premise to blindly follow his father's orders? He'd stopped questioning and just accepted that the old man was doing what was right for the family—for everyone *in* the family.

He paused his pity party long enough to text Bridger. He didn't get a reply.

A few lights flickered on below him. The Barrons pretty much owned everything within sight. But historically, what they had in business prowess, they lacked in their personal lives. At least that was the case for him and his father. Roxanne was wrong. His brothers didn't love him. They couldn't. Not after what he'd done. Because no matter what, Cash was his father's son. Cyrus had shaped him. Trained him. Molded him into the son he thought he wanted, only to discover Cash was a flawed creation.

By the time he left the office, hard dark had fallen and city lights painted an urban glow against the night sky.

Cash should drink himself into a stupor. Yet going to a bar, even a quiet pub like Donovan's, didn't appeal and the thought of a nightclub filled with noise and crowds curdled his stomach. He should have just gone to his place but the thought of facing the empty space troubled him. He headed toward the ranch instead. He needed something—anything—that felt like home, and his vacant condo wasn't that. It would be filled with the lonely echoes of Roxie's presence, filled with what-ifs and what-might-have-beens.

Who was she to lecture Cash on the meaning of love? Or family? Her brutally honest recitation outlining her own childhood meant she had no more insight—and probably less—than he did. The families of her fellow boarding school "inmates" hadn't inspired confidence in families and love, either. But through it all, she'd remained a cockeyed optimist when it came to love. Love existed. Families supported one another, took care of one another.

Roxie caught glimpses of it from time to time, and since being in Cash's sphere of influence, she'd gotten firsthand experience. Miz Beth and Big John had been married fifty years and they were still as much in love as they were the day they pronounced their vows. Cash's brothers tended to avoid him, as did their wives. She hadn't forgotten the confrontation with three of them that time in Bricktown. While the women appeared angry, she still had the sense they were sad about the estrangement—that their husbands missed their brother. The Barron brothers seemed close-knit, at least the other four. Did Cash purposely hold himself apart from them or had they segregated him, like her brothers had her? She knew all about being the odd one out. She'd watched her brothers from afar, had seen how they all seemed so bonded, a pack of puppies tumbling around the feet of their father. And there was never time for her—no place for her in their testosterone-laced circle. She definitely had no right to spout off about family dynamics.

As she packed her things, to the accompaniment of Harley's soft grumbles, she tried not to think. Yeah, like that would ever work. Maybe this was a good thing, Cash sending her away. Her heart was growing way too fond of him, her dreams far too focused on a future with him. But there would be no future now. Or ever. Her fleeting hope of forming a family with him, of finding the kind of love she saw shared by his brothers and their wives, was just a pipe dream.

People like her weren't made for relationships. Evidently, neither were people like Cash. Harley, on the other hand, didn't want to leave. She understood his reluctance. She didn't want to go, either. Still, it was time. She couldn't stall any longer.

Roxie sat stiffly in the front seat of the Ford Expedition. The man who'd taken her to Cash's condo loaded the vehicle with her things and Harley, then drove with a reckless abandon that had her clenching her jaw more than once. And she didn't miss the side glances he angled in her direction. He'd rolled down a back window and now the Newf had his head stuck out, jowls and ears flopping in the wind.

Tired of the strained silence, she shifted in her seat to face Bridger Tate. She hadn't known him long and the taciturn man flummoxed her. She had no clue what he thought of her, of the way things had shaken out between her and Cash.

"Get it off your chest."

Bridger braked the SUV and idled at a stoplight. "Got nothing to say."

"Really?" She gave him the stink-eye. "Could have fooled me."

"He's my cousin, Roxanne. Family. What am I supposed to say?"

She flung out her hands. "I don't know. *You* must like him..." She studied his expression. "Or is it just because he's your boss?"

He glared at her so long the car behind them honked. The light had changed. He tromped the gas pedal and the big SUV jerked forward. "Yes, Cash is my boss. He's my cousin. He's also my friend."

"Huh." She packed a lot of sarcasm in that one syllable.

"What's that supposed to mean?"

"Seems like you and me are the only two around who actually like him."

"I'm not discussing this with you."

"Ah. Gotcha. I'm the outsider. The one he kicked out of his bed when his father snapped his fingers."

"That's not true."

"Were you there?"

Bridger stopped for another red light. Anger sculpted the planes of his handsome face. "No."

"Well, I was."

His head whipped around so fast she was worried he'd pull a muscle or something. "What do you mean? Uncle Cyrus threw his tantrum in front of you?"

She could actually feel the blush crawl up the skin of her throat and face. "Not exactly."

"Explain. Exactly." He sounded like a cop—or a drill sergeant.

"I was waiting for Cash in his office and I was sort of... um...looking at some stuff—"

"What stuff?" Bridger's eyes turned the color of a natural gas flame burning blue hot.

Roxie would have backpedaled if they'd been standing in a room. As it was, all she could do was press harder against the door to eke out extra space between them. Then she figured out why he was upset. "Oh! No, not *that* kind of stuff. No…no. I wouldn't…I wasn't spying. He has this really cool snow glo—"

"His mother gave that to him. He and Chase both had one. Chase broke his. It's the only thing Cash has left that belonged to Aunt Helen."

She pressed her lips between her teeth to help rein in her emotions. "That was his mother's name?"

Bridger nodded. "Yeah. Did he tell you how she died?" After she shook her head, he continued. "Drunk driver. She was DRT."

"DRT?"

"Dead right there. And it's weird, but I think Uncle Cyrus really was torn up by her death. At least according to my mom. He was still an SOB about things, but Mom says he mourned her."

"Huh. I think I might be surprised."

"I know, right?" Bridger winked as he divided his attention between her and traffic. "So…the snow globe?"

"Oh! Right. It's an intriguing piece, maybe even historically significant. I'd have to do some research to be sure—"

"Roxanne, I don't care. Get on with the story." She could hear the exasperation in his tone.

"Oh, right. So, I'm being nosy about the globe and I heard voices in the hall. I hadn't closed the door all the way when I got there because…well, you know the reason. I'm aware that none of you trust me. But the globe was so interesting and—"

"The voices, Roxanne." Bridger jerked her back on topic.

"Voices. Yes, outside. I…panicked. And hid. Under Cash's desk. By the time I realized I should not be there, and did not want to hear what Cash and Mr. Barron were saying, it was too late. Announcing my presence would be far more awkward than just staying under the desk. I thought—hoped that Cash would leave with his father and I could sneak out, pretend I'd never been there and didn't hear a thing."

"But."

"*Huge* but. I suspect Cash knew I was there but I can't figure out how."

"Not that my cousin is OCD or anything but he knows with one glance whether someone has been in his office. You moved the globe."

"I did. In fact, I took it under the desk with me. Oh dear! Do you think Cash thought I was stealing it or something? I wasn't. Truly. And I put it right back in its spot on his desk when I stood up."

"No, Roxanne. I don't believe Cash thought you were trying to steal his snow globe."

"So he just…hates me now." Her insides were curled up like a ball of rattlesnakes and she didn't want to move, knowing she'd get all sorts of bites that would really hurt.

"I wish I could say you're wrong, Roxie, but I just don't know." He parked the SUV in front of her apartment and looked at her, his expression surprisingly sad. "I thought Cash might have a chance with you."

"A chance? I gave him all the chances in the world."

"That's not what I meant, hon. I meant that if my cousin smartened up, he'd take what you were offering. He needs what you could give him. I'm sorry he turned out to be an idiot."

He exited the vehicle on those words and silently unloaded her things, stacking them up on the small patio area next to her front door. Harley happily darted back and forth, following Bridger, then diverting to sniff the bushes.

Bridger set the sack of dog food down on the step and retreated without saying anything. He got in the driver's seat, started the SUV and backed out. Before pulling away, he stopped and rolled down his window. "You might have brought him back, Roxanne Rowland. It's a damn shame because you're right. I'm about the only one in the family who understands him—understands why he does what he does. And that makes me the only one who will stand for him when shit hits the fan. Take care of yourself."

Stunned, Roxie worked her mouth but no words came out. By the time they did, he was long gone.

"That was not the same man you left home with, sugar britches." The voice of her neighbor floated down from on high. "How many times have I told you that you come home with the one that brought you?"

"Hi, Leo." She sounded as deflated as she probably looked as she stepped closer to the parking lot so she could see him.

Leo eyed her pile of belongings from his perch on his balcony. "Oh, honeybun." He sighed. "Please don't tell me that you blew your chance with that grade A prime piece of man."

"Okay. I won't."

"Girl, I thought I taught you better. How did you manage to screw things up?"

"I wish I knew."

Eighteen

Roxanne stared into her coffee cup. How could she have been so totally wrong about Cash?

"You're giving up on him." The chiding tone of Miz Beth's voice whipped across her nerves like an electric wire. The woman had shown up on her doorstep and Roxie hadn't known how to politely send her away.

"Do I have a choice?"

With her eyes closed, Roxie bent her head back in a vain attempt to ease her cramped neck muscles. "He threw me out, Miz Beth, and frankly? The things I've heard about what he did to his sisters-in-law?"

"I thought better of you, Roxanne."

She tossed her hands up to emphasize her exaggerated shrug. "Why am I the bad guy here?"

"Do you love him?" Miz Beth was relentless.

"I don't know. I thought I did, but after what he said about me, about us? I thought I knew him, Miz Beth, but I don't know him at all."

"Neither do his brothers, or their wives." The woman sniffed, her displeasure apparent.

Roxanne was dismayed. "How can you defend him?"

"Because I see what everyone else ignores." Miz Beth settled into her chair. "I see the lonely boy who only wants to be loved."

"He has a funny way of looking for love."

"His brothers believe he is without remorse. Their wives think that not only are his actions despicable, but that he actually enjoyed hurting them." Miz Beth's gaze softened. "That boy feels far more and far deeper than the lot of 'em."

Confused, Roxanne worked through the meanings behind the older woman's words—the woman who was his surrogate mother, the one who'd told Roxie not long ago that she loved every one of "her" boys. Everything she'd learned about Cash's brothers pointed to the fact that they loved their wives, loved one another. Deeply. All four couples shared an abiding loyalty, with Cash standing on the outside. Like she and her family.

"Right or wrong, Cash does what he does out of a sense of duty. He decided at some point that he has to protect them all. Sometimes from themselves, but more often than not from their father."

"Would Mr. Barron do something terrible to them?" Cyrus Barron was a force to be reckoned with but Roxie didn't believe he'd actually carry out his threats on his own blood.

Miz Beth sipped her coffee, and sadness settled around her like a shawl made of shadows. She ignored Roxie's questions. "Those terrible things Cash has done? Would you like to know why he did them?"

Roxanne nodded, her throat closing in reaction to the expression on Miz Beth's face.

"Because Cyrus Barron decreed they had to be done, and Cash took the tasks upon himself to save his brothers from having to do them."

"I…don't understand."

"Everything Cash did, it was at Cyrus's orders—orders he'd given to the other boys first. Cash stepped in and did the things his brothers couldn't stomach, and he didn't do it because he's a bad man. He did it to shield his brothers from their father's wrath. In fact, that boy has taken the brunt of it—from Cyrus and every last one of his brothers."

"Why would his father…? I'm not following, Miz Beth."

"Cyrus wants to control his sons. When Chance first defied him, that vile old man would have destroyed him. But Cash stepped in."

"So Chance didn't have to—and…" Roxie's brain whirled through the possibilities. "Chance would have destroyed any possibility of a relationship with Cassie."

"Precisely. I knew you were a smart one." The woman pushed away from the table, stood and went to retrieve the coffee pot. Miz Beth refilled her cup, offering one to Roxanne, who shook her head. She wasn't sure she could swallow around the lump in her throat.

Miz Beth sighed. "They were all so angry at him." Her soft *humph* was both sad and telling. "No one ever accused the Barrons of having easy tempers. Ever last one of 'em goes off like a firecracker. Cash wants his father to love him. He's never figured out that it's a lost cause like the other boys have. They got smart, decided it didn't matter. But when Cyrus decided to stop his sons from falling in love, Cash stepped up to shield his brothers. Every time. Cash is the one who feels the duty to be a good son the most—no matter what terrible things Cyrus orders him to do."

"They've all but cut him out of their lives because of that, haven't they?" That knot clogging Roxanne's throat grew bigger.

Miz Beth's eyes glistened with tears. "They may not

mean to, but they do. Every day. In little ways. Ways they don't realize, but he does. He feels their rejection. Those boys just… They broke his heart. He stood there in my kitchen, hiding from the rest of the family the night his own twin renewed his marriage vows in front of the whole family. Cash hadn't been invited, had been told by Cord and Chance to stay away, given what he'd done in an attempt to break up Chase and Savannah."

Roxie had to blink her own tears away. "That's…" She inhaled and exhaled in an attempt to ease the constriction in her chest. "I don't know what it is."

"It's sad and cruel. But he came, slipping in at the last minute. He stood in the shadows and listened and wished his brother well. And just as fast, he disappeared again. We had a big Christmas at the ranch but Cash wasn't present. He wasn't welcome in his own home. Then or now. I've seen him turn around and leave when he comes up the drive and sees one of the others is there."

"That's…that's just mean and…and…"

"Don't get me wrong, Roxanne. Cash isn't an angel. Heck, none of those boys are. Cash, though? He listens to his father way too much, and while his actions are bad, his heart truly is in the right place—as he understands things. Trying to take Cassie's inheritance. That whole custody kidnapping of CJ. Setting up Clay and then Chase so Georgie and Savannah thought their men were cheating on them. It wasn't right. I think Cash knew that but his concept of right and wrong is skewed thanks to the old jackass who sired him." Miz Beth dumped her coffee in the sink. "You have a lot of thinking to do, girl. And it's a long drive back to the ranch."

The woman was right. Roxie did have a lot to consider. "Thanks for coming by, Miz Beth."

"Any time, sugar. Any time at all."

They'd reached the door when Miz Beth spoke again. "Roxanne, if ever a man needs to be loved—deserves to be loved, it's Cashion Barron."

Those parting words played over and over in her mind. Cash deserved to be loved, and she did. She didn't know exactly when, and sure couldn't figure out how, given his prickly personality, but she loved him with all her heart.

Nineteen

Cash braked for the stoplight, angry that he couldn't even enjoy lunch at Donovan's without memories of Roxie intruding. His phone pinged and he checked the caller ID, then answered. "Hey, Bridger, did you get—"

"Cash." The dire tone of Bridger's voice saying only his name had him maneuvering into the parking lot of a fast-food restaurant. He stopped haphazardly and shoved the Rover into Park.

"What's going on, Bridge?"

"It's…your father. I found him. In the parking garage. It's bad, Cash. I couldn't call before now. I was doing CPR."

CPR? Cash went cold but his skin prickled from nerves and dread. He couldn't speak and Bridger filled in the silence.

"Fire department got here fast. The ambulance just left. They're taking him to the ER at OU Med Center. It… I'm sorry, Cash. They're still doing CPR. The defibrillator didn't get a blip when they zapped his heart. You need to meet me there. Okay?"

"Okay." The word came out flat, robotic. Cash couldn't feel a thing.

"I'll call your brothers."

Something sparked in his brain, shoving aside his shock. "No. I should call. I'll…I'm on Western. I'll be there in twenty minutes. Less."

"I can send someone to pick you up." Concern coated his cousin's voice.

"No. I'm okay. I…I need to call Chase. The others. I'll see you at the hospital." He ended the call to Bridger, then scrolled through his contacts. He started at the top.

Clay's phone rolled over to voice mail. Cash managed to keep his voice level. "Clay, it's about Dad. He's at OU Med. I don't know what happened. Bridger did CPR before they transported him. Probably his heart. I…thought you should know. Thought you might want to come."

He called Cord, got voice mail and left the same message. Ditto with Chance, but with each successive call, it was harder to keep his voice steady. Under normal circumstances, he would have called their administrative assistants, knowing they'd delegated contact with him to their employees. But this was far from normal and he couldn't—wouldn't—do that to his brothers. They might not want to talk to him, obviously didn't want anything to do with him, but he would not tell them their father was most likely dying through the filter of an employee.

Breathing became hard, his chest tight and aching. He didn't love his father—not in the sense most sons did, but the man had sired him, raised him, taught him hard lessons. All he'd ever wanted was to have his father's respect, his acceptance. Cash knew, deep down, that Cyrus Barron was incapable of loving anyone but himself, but Cash had always held out hope that someday, he'd do something to make his father proud.

Cash had one more call to make. He punched the link for his twin. This time he got a live person, but not the one he wanted.

"Cash. What's up?"

"I need to talk to Chase, Tucker. Please?" The last word came out as a plea.

"He's…busy. I can pass him your message."

Busy. His twin brother wouldn't even talk to him. Cash closed his eyes, rubbed them with his fingers, ignoring the moisture dampening his fingertips. He'd never felt so isolated and alone in his life.

"Cash? Is there a message?"

"Tell him…tell him I…" He swallowed so many words that wouldn't come out. What could he say? *I'm sorry*? *Dad's dying*? *I'm as big a bastard as our old man and maybe I should be the one the doctors are working on*? *I love you*? He heard his cousin breathing. No help there. "Tell him Dad is at OU Med. I'm headed to the ER. It's… not good. Bridger had to do CPR. I…thought everyone would want to know."

Silence. Yeah. No one in his family would give a rat's ass that his father was in the ER, fighting for his life. His cousin's lack of response was far more telling than any comment. "Sorry I bothered y'all, Tucker."

He ended the call, inhaled and held his breath until his hands stopped shaking enough that he could drive. Twenty-two minutes later, he walked into the ER. Bridger stood off to the side of the waiting room. For the biggest ER in the metro area, the place was almost eerily quiet. His cousin's face pretty much said it all.

"The doctors are working on him," Bridger said as Cash walked up. "I have a security team coming. It's just a matter of time before the media get wind of this."

Yeah. The media. Vultures of every stripe would be circling soon. "Your mom?"

"I called her. She's in Belize but headed home now." Bridger waited a moment before adding, "Your brothers?"

Seemingly of its own volition, Cash's head bowed. He rubbed the back of his neck and mumbled, "I left voice mails. No one was answering. I did talk to Tucker. Chase—" His voice broke. "Chase was too busy."

Embarrassed by his lapse in control, Cash walked away. He had too much pent-up energy to sit, but pacing just drew unwanted attention. He dropped into a chair in the far corner of the ER waiting room and hunched over, his elbows resting on his thighs, head bowed. Wrapping his misery around him as if it would make him invisible, Cash stared at the floor and tried not to think.

Roxie stopped in the break room to refill her travel mug with coffee. Four coworkers stood staring at the TV mounted to the wall and she stopped to listen to the breaking news.

"Oklahoma City billionaire Cyrus Barron was rushed to OU Medical Center ER this afternoon in unknown condition. Witnesses stated that a member of Mr. Barron's security team found the businessman unconscious in the parking garage of Barron Tower and began CPR. A hospital spokeswoman will only confirm that Mr. Barron was admitted to the ER." The perky blonde went on with her recitation but Roxie had tuned everything out.

Mr. Barron was in the ER? They'd done CPR? Cash. He'd be there all alone. She didn't stop to think. Dumping her cup in the sink, Roxie whirled and headed for the exit. More people had gathered to watch the report, blocking her way, and the VP she reported to was already in crisis mode.

"We'll need to put a package together—photos and

video of his life for media release. Contact Chase Barron or Tucker Tate. They'll have the obit and other information." He pointed at Roxie. "Good. You're here. You can pull up the file documents faster than the rest of us—"

"No." Roxie had no idea where the strength to stand up to her boss came from but she was fairly vibrating with it. "I can't. Get one of my assistants to do it. I have to go."

"Go?" The man looked flummoxed.

"Cash. I have to get to the hospital." He might not want to see her, would probably try to throw her out, but she was not going to let him sit there all alone waiting for word on his father. "I…sorry. I have to go," she repeated.

"They're dating," she heard someone explain as she ducked through the door and jogged toward the elevator. That wasn't true. They'd never…*dated*. But when she'd been moved into his condo and he'd informed her bosses he needed her for a "special" project, they'd leaped to an obvious conclusion. They'd be horrified to discover that Cash had only wanted information about her family. Well, that and sex. What he hadn't wanted was her falling in love with him. Too bad. For both of them.

Roxie stopped in her office long enough to grab her purse and keys, then made the dash to the medical center complex on Lincoln Boulevard. She gave up on the ER parking lot, driving around to the garage complex on the back side of the hospital. All four local television stations had live remotes going outside the ER doors and two uniformed policemen stood just outside monitoring anyone going in or out. Knowing what she'd learned about Barron Security, Cash would have a team inside the ER to protect his family.

She waited, watching people come and go for a few minutes. The police didn't stop anyone unless they looked like media. She was fully prepared to lie her way inside, up to and including faking an injury or illness. Turned out, all she had to do was keep her head down and look puzzled at the reporters all doing live feeds. The officers gave her cursory glances, she dipped her head in acknowledgment of their presence and scurried through the automatic doors.

Bridger Tate stood across the room speaking into his phone, his eyes darting between the door and a spot in the far corner. A man in a dark suit stood a few feet away from him. Roxie wondered for a minute if Senator Barron got Secret Service protection. Bridger eyed her speculatively and she offered a tentative smile even as she picked out two more men and a woman, all in various types of civilian clothes and spread throughout the room.

Her gaze came to a rest on Cash and she forced air into her lungs. He looked so lost and forlorn. She was already walking toward him before her brain caught up with her instincts. The woman came to her feet and moved to intercept, but a sign from Bridger waved the female security guard off. Roxie sank onto the chair next to Cash. She didn't speak, didn't touch him though she was desperate to do both.

"Go away, Roxie." Cash didn't look at her and his voice sounded like a rusty nail being yanked out of wood.

"You shouldn't be alone."

He glanced up and his upper lip curled into a snarl. "Does it look like I'm alone?"

"Except for Bridger? Yes."

"Goes to show what you know."

And as if in answer to his rebuttal, the entrance doors whispered open. Two angry Barron brothers ate up the distance and stopped in front of them.

"What the hell, Cash?" Cord demanded.

Roxie was about to choose discretion over valor when

Cash stood and brushed his older brother back. “Dad had a heart attack. They’re working on him.”

Before Cord could respond, Cash pushed past him and moved to the opposite corner. The two elder Barrons exchanged looks but didn’t follow him. They ignored Roxie, walking instead to Bridger, where they spoke in low tones she couldn’t overhear. She was still sitting there hunched in on herself when the ER doors opened and the doctor stepped through. The Barrons gathered around him.

Roxie watched Cash crumple, then straighten. He shook off his brothers and stormed out into the night. Wearily, she pushed out of her chair and headed after him. Bridger stopped her halfway to the door.

“Let him be, Roxie. For now at least. I know Cash. He’ll want to be alone.”

She turned her tear-streaked face to the one other person in the room who cared about Cash. “But isn’t that the problem? He’s always alone.”

Roxie slipped into the funeral home hoping for the chance to see Cash before the service started. Wandering down a hallway, she heard voices coming her direction. Finding an alcove with a drawn curtain, she ducked behind it, planning to wait until the people moved on. When the group stopped right in front of her hiding place and she recognized the voices, she cringed.

“I did not appreciate finding out my father was in the hospital after suffering a massive heart attack when my wife called to tell me it was the lead story on all the news channels. Georgie had us packed by the time I got home from the Senate building.”

“I caught a report on the radio coming back from a rig. Jolie wasn’t on duty at the hospital so she had no idea.”

“I was in court. One of the court clerks brought a note to

the judge and he called an in-camera hearing at the bench. The damn judge knew before I did."

Clay, Cord and Chance, in that order. She'd seen Cord and Chance at the hospital, knew they'd gotten word fairly quickly to get there when they did. Far too curious for her own good, Roxie peeked around the edge of the curtain.

The three stared at Chase, who appeared thoughtful. "Did any of you check your missed calls or your voice mails?" The older brothers exchanged looks. "I'll admit I haven't wanted to deal with Cash, and that includes talking to him even with all this BS going on with the Rowlands. I had his calls forwarded to Tucker's cell." A look of sadness settled on Chase's face—a face so like Cash's Roxie's heart broke all over again. "Tuck answered. Cash… he was broken up. Hurting. Tuck didn't know what to do so he didn't do anything. Didn't say anything. When Cash ended the call, Tuck called me immediately." He rubbed the back of his neck, a gesture so achingly familiar Roxie almost cried.

Clay, Cord and Chance went for their phones and started scrolling. Then they each listened to the message left by Cash. At least they looked remorseful now.

"What are we going to do?" Cord glanced around the circle, but rested his final gaze on Chase.

"We do what this family has always done," Clay said. "We present a united front. Then, when we're in private, we'll figure it out."

Their wives arrived and Roxie faded deeper into the alcove. They walked away, en masse, presenting their united front. Only Cash wasn't with them. A Garth Brooks song played in her head, the words so fitting. Yeah, Cash was standing outside the fire. And he was facing his world all alone.

A few minutes later, after no sign of Cash, she settled

in the last row of pews in the chapel. The family entered from the right and filled the first several rows, the four Barron brothers and wives in the first pew with Miz Beth and Big John. The next few rows were filled with cousins and Mr. Barron's sister. Still no sign of Cash. Then Roxie caught movement on the opposite side. Cash entered from the left and sat down in the empty front pew, as far away from his family as he could sit.

Roxie grabbed the box of tissues sitting on the seat next to her and pulled out a handful as tears spilled over. She'd never seen anyone look more dejected—and *rejected* than Cash Barron at that moment. The service and eulogies went on interminably. She heard the disparaging whispers about Cash from those sitting around her.

When it was finally over, Cash slipped away once more. She waited in the reception hall, just in case, but Cash never appeared. Oh, but his brothers were all there, accepting condolences. They'd finally retreated to a spot away from the remaining crowd. When she saw Chase laugh at something Cord said, she lost her temper.

Roxie didn't stop to think, didn't consider her actions. She marched right up to the lot of them and snarled, "You know, for seemingly intelligent men, the four of you are pretty damn stupid."

The wives bristled, moving to stand with their husbands, and Cassidy scowled at her. "Now wait just a minute—"

In no mood for their resentment, Roxie cut her off. "You have no clue what Cash has done for you, each and every one of you. And what did you do? You turned your back on him. You never once asked him why he did the things he did. You just assumed he was the bad guy. You ostracized him." Her temper was riding her hard and her nose was running from unshed tears. She whirled on Chance.

"Want to know why Cash served those legal papers? So you wouldn't have to, so your father would get off your back and you'd have a chance with Cassidy because you were the good guy."

Roxie pointed a finger at Cord and Jolie. "And you two? You should talk to your little boy. He has some mighty interesting ideas about his uncle Cash's motives. You know what they say, out of the mouths of babes.

"And no offense, Senator, but who do you think your staff called to arrange to get you back to Oklahoma so fast? It was Cash who made the arrangements. And it was Cash who installed a discreet guard at the hospital the whole time Georgie was a patient. To make sure she stayed safe."

Clay glowered at her, his mouth pinched. "How do you know all this?"

"That's not important. What *is* important is that you all wake up! Cash did all the dirty work your father wanted each of you to do. He *protected* you. He protected you so well that he walked away from me to keep that rotten old man happy. He loves you four so much he won't let himself be loved because somebody has to be the bad guy. And bad guys don't deserve to be loved. Not by anybody."

Blinking hard and breathing around the ache in her chest, she fixed her gaze on Chase. "You didn't even invite him to your wedding."

"Well, no one was invited—"

"Not the one in Vegas. The one at the ranch. Did you know—" she paused to glare at Cord and Chance "—that your brothers warned him to stay away. Insisted on it, in fact."

Chase paled while his brothers exchanged guilty looks. "But I saw him there, in the kitchen."

"Yeah, he sneaked in the back door. He stood there in the shadows of the kitchen watching you exchange vows with the woman you loved, because you're brothers. Because he's your twin and no matter what he's done or said, he freaking loves you. All of you. Not that you deserve it."

She sniffled and swiped at her cheeks. Tears fell freely now. "I thought my family was pretty messed up but you Barrons? I don't have an adjective vile enough for any of you."

Wheeling, she managed one step before a firm but gentle hand snagged her arm. "Ms. Rowland? Roxanne, please…a moment?"

Shaking with anger, she held still but refused to look at Cash's twin.

The hand on her arm remained, as if Chase needed a connection to her when he asked, "Do you love him?"

Her lips trembled and her chin quivered as she tried to form words. She finally managed a whispered, "Yes."

"Then go find him and tell him."

Twenty

After the funeral, Roxanne had no contact with any of the Barrons. Cash ignored her repeated attempts to contact him. Life settled into an unsettled routine. Harley missed Cash almost as much as she did. He slept on her bed and while he was almost as big and far warmer, he was a poor substitute. Almost a month had passed and she was in a meeting when the text came. She didn't reply for an hour, waiting until she was safely back in her office. Then she typed a one-word reply.

NO.

Her phone rang almost immediately and she answered with, "What part of no don't you understand, Dexter?"

"You want to keep your boyfriend safe, you'll use the tickets, Rox."

"He's not my boyfriend." She was proud her voice didn't waver, even though her heart was pounding. Cash was out of her life for good but the idea of him being hurt because of her? Unthinkable. She didn't doubt for a minute that

Dexter would do something awful to Cash. Besides, she'd made a promise to keep the Barron family safe.

Putting all her acting abilities to use, she put steel in her voice. "I'm done with Cash, with all the Barrons, Dex. And I'm done with you."

"Yeah, but you care about the pretty boy so you'll come. Info's in your inbox." Her brother hung up.

Opening her email, she scanned the message, extrapolating what Dex actually meant from what was said. Then she picked up the desk phone and dialed.

"Where's Cash?" she asked when Bridger answered.

"Vegas."

"Of course he is." Her family knew that. They were putting the plot into action, and she had her own part to play. "It's time. I'll send you the details."

"Good."

Good for the Barrons. Not so good for her. She would fulfill her promise but then even the tenuous link she had with Cash would be gone. Time to say goodbye to the future she'd barely dreamed of before her hopes were crushed. Once a con, always a con. Isn't that what her family said? "It's in your blood, Rox. It's in your blood."

Cash occupied a seat at the small bar against the back wall of the Crown Hotel and Casino's main floor. The scotch on the rocks in front of him had remained untouched so long the "rocks" had melted. He caught the stir near the entrance to the slot machine room and stiffened.

She walked in like she owned the place and every man in the room came to attention. Including him. Shifting his hips in his chair to give his rapidly growing erection a little breathing room, Cash watched the sea of bodies part as she sauntered toward him. Roxanne Rowland fixed him with a sultry stare. Gone was the klutzy girl. This was the woman only hinted at on the security footage he'd watched months ago. She wore red. And sparkles. The dress barely covered her, the floaty material swirling around legs made longer by red stilettos.

Part of his brain wondered, not for the first time, which Roxie was real. Had he made a mistake about her? He remembered something Roxie said the first time he questioned her in his office. "Takes a con to catch a con." The muttered reminder didn't make him feel any better.

He should have stood up, intercepted her, but Cash didn't move. He sat, alert and focused, watching her weave through the crowded room, her gaze holding his. *Eye on the prize*, he thought. She arrived in front of him, placed her hands on his knees and applied a little pressure to open a space for her to stand between them. Her hands slid up his thighs as she leaned in. Her lips grazed his cheek on their way to his ear.

"I've missed you," she murmured.

"Missed you, too."

Roxie gave no indication she heard him, so maybe he hadn't confessed that out loud. He could barely admit it to himself, much less expose his weakness to her.

"I'm supposed to seduce you and lure you to a room upstairs."

"I see."

She pressed closer and he widened his legs until their lower bodies touched. Her swift intake of breath was a sure sign she'd felt his arousal.

"You've been their target all along. I don't know why, but if you'll come with me, we'll find out."

Cash slipped an arm around her, anchoring her against him. "And I should just trust you?"

He felt the hitch of her breath as her body tensed. "No,

I suppose you shouldn't. I'm a Rowland, right? But you can trust your family. Trust Bridger."

She brushed glossy red lips across his mouth. "I'm sorry." The words whispered across his skin. Her fingers twined with his resting on her hip, and she twirled away, tugging him to his feet.

Unable to resist, he followed her. Cash heard the murmurs as they passed. "Lucky SOB." He didn't feel lucky; he felt more like a lamb being led to slaughter. They entered an empty elevator and he recognized Bridger's hand in that. Once the doors closed, she dropped his hand, pushed a button and moved to the far corner, putting as much distance between them as possible.

"Smile for the camera, Cash, so they know I haven't drugged you or something."

He expected her to sound bitter—or sarcastic. She sounded resigned. Glancing up at the camera, he pretended he didn't miss her warmth, the touch of her hand. As the elevator settled to a gentle stop, she returned, slipping under his arm and plastering herself against his side.

"They'll be watching," she said by way of explanation.

The back of his neck prickled as they exited. Cash didn't see anyone but he didn't doubt her. They strolled down the thickly carpeted hallway arm in arm. Stopping at the door to a suite, she produced a key card from the soft folds of fabric covering her breasts. Cash shifted uncomfortably. This wasn't about the sexy woman standing next to him. This was business.

The lock clicked and he pushed the door open all the way. She stretched to whisper in his ear. "We have to make it look good. Just go with it, okay?"

More curious than apprehensive now, he wondered if this was some elaborate ruse Roxie had cooked up to get close to him. He followed her into the living area. She turned and one crystal-encrusted strap dipped off her shoulder. She wet her lips and he almost groaned. She looked wanton and he wanted her more than anything he'd ever desired in his life.

"You got me up here, Roxanne. Now what?"

"Now we make a deal." Max Rowland stepped out of the bedroom.

Cash did his best to look surprised, then he raised a sardonic eyebrow. Someone knocked on the door and Max added, "Get that, Roxie girl. It'll be your brothers."

"What deal, Rowland?"

"You and my sentimental daughter cost me a great deal of time, money and annoyance six years ago. It's taken me this long to get plans in place."

"Ah. I see. You're still holding a grudge because I recovered everything you swindled from my great-aunt."

"I don't hold grudges, Barron. I get even."

Cash moved away as Roxanne returned, followed by her brothers and…his intern, Nick? What the hell?

Max wore a Cheshire-cat smile. "I see you recognize my youngest son, Nixon."

He glanced toward Roxie. Her face had drained of color and she looked devastated. There was no way she could fake the emotions warring on her face. She didn't know. And his own vetting process had failed. There'd been no record of any other Rowlands when they were trying to track down Max and his sons.

The college intern Cash knew as Nick England had fooled them all. The guy didn't look much like his brothers and looked nothing at all like Roxie. She'd locked her knees to remain standing but he could see the hands clasped in front of her tremble. He wanted to cross to her, hold her, but he couldn't. Not yet.

"So you wasted all these years just to put a mole in my

organization? Why? Nick—Nixon didn't have access to anything confidential that would do you any good."

"Au contraire, Cashion," Max said in a perfect imitation of Cyrus's voice. "I'd say things are a little strained at the moment."

"What do you want?"

"Twenty million. Transferred to an offshore account."

Cash snorted in disgust. "And what do I get out of it?"

Nixon approached with a thick file. "You get to save your family one more time."

Accepting the file, Cash moved toward the built-in bar. He snagged Roxanne's hand as he passed and drew her along in his wake. Settling her on a bar stool, he put the file on the granite bar top and flipped through it. He should have given Nick more credit. The kid was good. He'd dummied up deals, laid a trail of under-the-table payments, double accounting books—all things the IRS and Justice Department would kill to get their hands on.

Cash raised his head to stare at Max. "Nice little web you've built here."

"Twenty million makes it all go away."

"For how long?"

The Cheshire cat once more, Max grinned. "Until we need more."

"And if I say no?"

"Copies will inconveniently show up several places—the government, rival media outlets. I wonder what the Senate ethics committee would make of this? Nevada gaming commission? EPA?" Max's eyes cut to Roxie. "And my daughter will be implicated as your coconspirator."

Her sharp intake of breath was almost silent but Cash heard it, and then felt her stiffen, then collapse next to him. Yeah, she was right. His father had been a cold and vicious piece of work but her father was ten times the monster.

"So you're saying Roxanne had nothing to do with this?"

Max and his sons all laughed, but it was Dexter who explained. "The stupid twit is too sentimental and honest. We set her up just like we did you. If she'd just hidden that stuff all those years ago, we'd all be in the clear."

Cash's frigid smile rivaled Max's. "That's all I needed to know."

Before anyone could move, hotel security and Las Vegas cops poured through the door. Within moments, the Rowlands were handcuffed and marched out. Cash stood frozen in place as he realized all of his brothers were there. It was Chase who approached.

"An apology is pretty meaningless, Cash, even when it comes from the heart. I'm sorry. For everything. I had no idea…" Chase gestured toward their other brothers. "*We* had no idea, but we should have. We knew what the old man was like, how he could twist things. And we left you hanging."

A moment later, Cash was swallowed in Chase's hug, then the rest of his brothers stepped up to offer their own apologies and hugs. Family. He'd found his again and he had to blink back tears. A flash of red caught his attention. Roxie. She slipped out the door without a word or a backward glance.

Chase chuckled and clapped him on the back. "Go after her, Cash. And when you're ready, I just happen to know a Liberace impersonator who does weddings."

Cash caught up to Roxanne at the elevator. "Where ya goin', Red?"

The door opened and he stepped in with her, keying in the code for the top floor. She eyed him warily and he couldn't blame her. "I'm sorry." Apologies never came easy and he was surprised the words didn't stick in his throat. "I'm sorry your family betrayed you. I'm sorry I…" Now it got hard. "I should have trusted you. And I was wrong. I need you, Roxie. And I want you. What do I need to do to get you to forgive me?"

She silently got off the elevator with him when it stopped. He led her to his suite and ushered her inside. He smiled, remembering her parting words. "How much groveling will it take?"

That startled a laugh out of her, and he saw the insecurity, saw her own need for acceptance and love. She was everything he wanted and didn't know how to find. She had so many layers and he wanted to spend the rest of his life peeling them back, discovering the fascinating woman she was. She fit him in ways no one else ever had, or ever would.

Fingering the sparkly straps of her dress, he slipped them off her shoulders, pushed the silky dress down, found the clasp under the crystal-covered brooch at her hip and watched the dress float to the floor around her ankles. He cupped her cheeks, kissed her gently despite his overwhelming need to take her, conquer her, claim her. He needed to be gentle.

"I want to make love to you."

She nodded and slipped out of her heels, stepped over the puddled silk. He picked her up, carried her to the bed. She watched him strip out of his clothes, then he joined her. Cash drew her to him, stroking her hair back from her face. An unfamiliar emotion welled up. Love. This must be what love felt like. He kissed her, cupped her, stroked and petted until she sighed, the long, contented sound of it a balm on his wounded heart.

He vowed to cherish her because no one ever had. It was easy to be tender, to put the dreamy look in her eyes he now enjoyed. He would spend his life proving how precious she was to him—if she'd give him the chance.

Using all his skill, he teased her until she was begging.

"Please, Cash. Inside me now. Please!"

"Not yet. Not until you say you'll marry me."

"Marry you?"

"Yes. Marry me."

"That's blackmail."

"A man's gotta do what a man's gotta do."

Roxie laughed, as if she couldn't help it. "Yes." She giggled, then her breath caught as he slid deep inside her. "Oh, yes," she moaned. "Just like that."

He rocked against her and caught a glint of mischief in her golden eyes. "What?"

"I should tell you something."

"Oh?" He pulled almost free of her.

"Yeah. The only reason I said yes is because Harley likes you."

"So...if that walking furbag didn't like me, you would have said no?" He held still, hovering, barely holding their connection.

"I would have agreed to a mad affair." He reached between them, found the spot guaranteed to drive her wild. "Maybe agreed to be your mist—aah." She sucked in her breath, quivering as she arched her hips against his touch.

"You love me. Admit it." The need in his voice surprised him, and from the look on Roxie's face, it caught her off guard, too.

She hooked her legs around him, her heels pushing against his butt until he was seated deeply inside her again. "With all my heart. I love you."

Cash gritted his teeth, struggling to hold back. Being with Roxie, connecting to her emotionally and physically...it hijacked his self-control. "I love you. And it's my duty to make you happy." He growled the words, pumping into her furiously now. He drove them both over the edge and when they fell back to earth, he discovered something precious.

"Home," he murmured. "You feel like home, Roxie."

Epilogue

Harley was on his best behavior, though he watched the swimming pool with obvious gusto. Cash stared until the dog eyed him guiltily and sat down next to the judge. Cash waited under a rustic arbor made of branches and twined with flowers, flanked by his solemn brothers. Well, all but Chase. Cash's twin grinned like a fool.

All the Tates were in attendance, some with plus-ones. His sisters-in-law sat together. More fences needed to be mended there. He'd promised Roxie he'd try, and she'd promised to help. His gaze fell on Kade Waite, and he recognized a kindred spirit. He resolved to look into that situation, too. The man who might be a Barron brother stood off to the side with Pippa Duncan. Interesting.

At that moment, Leo, looking like a fashion plate in his dove-gray tuxedo, emerged from the house. Big John appeared, Roxie on his arm. Deacon strummed a complicated melody on an acoustic guitar as Cash's bride glided toward him.

Their vows were simple. They promised to remain true to each other in good times and bad, in sickness and in health, through failures and triumphs. They vowed to respect, comfort and encourage, to dream, share and cherish, for as long as they lived. Then the judge pronounced them husband and wife. Cash branded Roxie with his kiss, one as deep and abiding as his love for this woman.

After dinner, Leo stood and pinged a champagne flute with his fork. "I need y'all's attention!" When he had it, he turned to Roxie. "Girlfriend, I am so happy you finally took my advice and snagged this fine, *fine* piece of man candy." He sniffled dramatically and dabbed at his eyes. "You make me so proud." He tossed back the champagne in his glass and sat.

Chase rose next, waiting while people quieted. "To my brother Cash and his beautiful bride. From this day forward, you will never walk alone. May your heart shelter the other always and may you always find your way home in each other's arms."

Lifting Roxie's left hand, Cash kissed her wedding ring. "You are my home, Roxanne Barron. You are my life, my heart, the very best of me. Now and always."

He brushed her tears away with his thumbs as he cupped her face and kissed her. They'd both searched all their lives for love and acceptance, and had found them in each other. She whispered against his lips, "You are my home and family. I love you."

Those were the words he needed. Together, they discovered the family they hadn't dared dream of. "Yes," he agreed. He was a man who understood his duty to family—and to the woman he loved.

* * * * *

If you loved this story,
pick up the other RED DIRT ROYALTY *books*
from Silver James!

COWGIRLS DON'T CRY
THE COWGIRL'S LITTLE SECRET
THE BOSS AND HIS COWGIRL
CONVENIENT COWGIRL BRIDE

Available now from Mills & Boon!

* * *

If you're on Twitter, tell us what you think of Mills & Boon! #mills&boon.

How did she walk away? Lydia wondered.

How did she go over and kiss that sulky mouth and say goodbye when really she wanted to climb back into bed?

But rather than reveal her thoughts she flicked that internal default switch which had been permanently set to 'polite'.

'Thank you so much for last night.'

'I haven't finished being your tour guide yet.'

He stretched out his arm and held out his hand but Lydia didn't go over. She did not want to let in hope, so she just stood there as Raul spoke.

'It would be remiss of me to let you go home without seeing Venice as it should be seen.'

'Venice?'

'I'm heading there today. Why don't you come with me? Fly home tomorrow instead.'

There was another night between now and then, and Lydia knew that even while he offered her an extension he made it clear there was a cut-off.

Time added on for good behaviour.

And Raul's version of 'good behaviour' was that there would

be no tears or drama as she walked away. Lydia knew that. If she were to accept his offer then she had to remember that.

'I'd like that.' The calm of her voice belied the trembling she felt inside. 'It sounds wonderful.'

'Only if you're sure?' Raul added.

'Of course.'

But how could she be sure of anything now she had set foot in Raul's world?

He made her dizzy.

Disorientated.

Not just her head, but every cell in her body seemed to be spinning as he hauled himself from the bed and unlike Lydia, with her sheet-covered dash to the bathroom, his body was hers to view.

And that blasted default switch was stuck, because Lydia did the right thing and averted her eyes.

Yet he didn't walk past. Instead Raul walked right over to her and stood in front of her.

She could feel the heat—not just from his naked body but her own—and it felt as if her dress might disintegrate.

He put his fingers on her chin, tilted her head so that she met his eyes, and it killed that he did not kiss her, nor drag her back to his bed. Instead he checked again. 'Are you sure?'

'Of course,' Lydia said, and tried to make light of it. 'I never say no to a free trip.'

It was a joke but it put her in an unflattering light. She was about to correct herself, to say that it hadn't come out as she had meant, but then she saw his slight smile and it spelt approval.

A gold-digger he could handle, Lydia realised.

Her emerging feelings for him—perhaps not.

At every turn her world changed, and she fought for a semblance of control. Fought to convince not just Raul but herself that she could handle this.